WHEN THE DEAD AWAKEN

WHEN THE DEAD AWAKEN

Steffen Jacobsen

Translated from the Danish by Charlotte Barslund

New York • London

Quercus

New York • London

© 2013 by Steffen Jacobsen
English translation © 2013 by Charlotte Barslund
First published in the United States by Quercus in 2015

ISBN 978-1-62365-868-7

Library of Congress Control Number: 2014954167

Distributed in the United States and Canada by
Hachette Book Group
1290 Avenue of the Americas
New York, NY 10104

Manufactured in the United States

10 9 8 7 6 5 4 3 2 1

www.quercus.com

With thanks to Thomas Harder for everything Italian.

CHAPTER 1

Port of Naples, September 1, 2010

Gaetano Costa had long since ceased to notice Naples's famous red lighthouse, which filled the cabin of his crane with white, red, and green light every fifteen seconds. His eyes were fixed on a monitor that showed the freezer container, which weighed eighteen tons, swinging under the crane's spreader, fifteen meters below his cabin and thirty meters above the quay. He adjusted the joysticks that were controlling the container's journey from the trailer truck on Vittorio Emanuele II Quay to the top layer of containers on Pancoast Lines's newest container ship, the three-hundred-meter long *Taixan*. Gaetano was proud of his hands and what they could accomplish. Some people had the stamina and the concentration to become the invisible link between the gigantic winch of the Terex crane, the flexible steel wires, the moving container, and the pitching ship's deck—whatever the weather or visibility—but others never mastered it.

Earlier that evening American engineers with broad smiles and thumbs-ups had said good-bye to an anxious Gaetano and his equally skeptical foreman. The job required the Italians to speak and understand a kind of pidgin English, and they had nodded, unconvinced, in response to the engineers' parting cry of "Don't worry, guys!"

Nevertheless, Costa had to admit that the crane now worked like a dream. It was as if the American engineers in their white overalls had integrated his spine into the crane's control systems.

It had been a good shift. A thin crescent moon sat high in the sky, the sea was black and calm, and the last container of the night hung safely below. He had the Chinese loading officer barking orders into one ear of his headset and John Denver singing in the other. When the white container with the green Maltese crosses on its sides had been delivered and secured, the ship would slip its moorings and reverse into the basin to make room for yet another of the illuminated container ships anchored on the dark roadstead of Naples like a never-ending chain of fairy lights.

Gaetano would climb down from the cabin, change, chat briefly with his replacement, and swallow two painkillers for the left-sided headache that the signature flashes of the lighthouse always induced before spending a couple of pleasant and uneventful hours at a late-night café drinking coffee, smoking cigarettes, reading *La Gazetta dello Sport,* and most likely indulging in an erotic fantasy featuring the almond-skinned waitress, Giuseppina. When the sun rose, he would cycle home to his bachelor pad in Via Colonnello Carlo Lahalle.

It was by no means the first freezer container with the distinctive green cross that Gaetano had loaded onto a Pancoast-owned ship. Always late at night. Always as the last item and always when Filippo Montesi from Autoritá Portuale di Napoli, the Neapolitan Port Authority, was the harbormaster on duty. The container had been delivered by an anonymous truck that had kept its engine running and had driven off the moment the crane had removed its load.

The screen by Gaetano Costa's right knee showed him the details of the container's bar code. The consignee was an anonymous warehouse in Macao, the sender a shipping company in Hanover: two destinations that deviated completely from the normal traffic. However, the fifty-five-year-old crane operator, whose body had molded itself to the shape of the cabin with the passage of time, had, like everyone else in the port, learned never to ask questions. The Port of Naples processed twenty million tons of freight every year, and the freezer container represented barely a single particle in that unimaginably extensive stream of goods.

In this mighty port, the Camorra had a thousand eyes and ears, and not one container moved without its knowledge.

The monitor by Gaetano's knee displayed the section of the quay between the crane tracks and the ship. Traffic usually was barred from this area during loading and unloading, but this night was an exception: a camera crew from the British television station Channel 4 had been granted access to shoot a popular series with a breathless globetrotting host.

It was the absence of a particular sound that made Gaetano mutter the word "no." The missing sound made the sweat break out under his orange overalls. The ratchet-locking pin in the cable drum above the cabin was no longer transmitting its solid clicks—the spreader was in free fall. The numbers on the drum's digital revolution counter spun faster than the eye could follow. Costa flicked open the safety cap on the emergency brake, and his palm hit the red button to release the secondary locking clamps that bit deep into the oiled cable to break the fall of the runaway container.

An ear-piercing metallic sound made Gaetano Costa look up. While he muttered "no" again and again, he bashed his hand until it bled on the emergency-brake button. Then he saw the fifteen-ton trolley keel over right above his head. Sparks flew from the undercarriage of the drum housing, and the colossal construction rocked menacingly.

The white container tumbled toward its doom, condemning Gaetano Costa to certain death at the hands of the Camorra in its wake.

The TV host on the quay heard the high-pitched squeal above her and watched in disbelief as the soundman was replaced by the shipping container on the square of tarmac he had been standing on a second ago.

The impact of the container caused her and the rest of the camera crew to jump twenty centimeters into the air, and she felt her hair stand on end. Everyone was momentarily deafened, and many experienced various degrees of deafness in the days that followed.

The producer landed first on his Italian loafers and shouted in a thick voice: "F-u-u-ck! Did you get that, Jack?"

Then he discovered a part of his tongue that he had bitten off, instinctively caught it in his hand, and fell silent.

A veteran of Beirut, Tikrit, the Foreign Correspondents' Club in Hong Kong, and Wilma's Bar, the Irish cameraman was the first to pull himself together. He held the camera steady and zoomed in on a twisted aluminum bar, a microphone, a cable, and an undamaged tape recorder that were the only visible remains of the soundman. Next he peered at the open doors of the smashed container from which white cocoons spilled out onto the tarmac through an ice-cold hoarfrost that reeked of diesel and then a wall of perforated and rotting black garbage bags from which human body parts in every stage of decomposition were sticking out. A skeletal hand ended up a few centimeters from his Converse sneaker. He held his breath as he let the camera light up every gruesome detail of the steel coffin.

Through the glass floor of the cabin, Gaetano Costa saw with a kind of gloomy joy how the elegantly uniformed Filippo Montesi tried to yank the camera from the cameraman, who, without straining himself and with the camera still securely resting on his shoulder, knocked the harbormaster to the ground.

Costa, who had seen a thing or two during his time in the port, frowned. Herding Chinese workers from the Camorra's sweatshops into a garage with rubber seals on the door and connecting a hose from the exhaust of a trailer truck to a pipe in the wall generally was regarded as an effective and humane way of putting down worn-out slave labor. After they had been gassed, every form of identification was removed from the deceased and the bodies were vacuum-packed in white plastic. The containers were eased overboard when the ship was directly above the three-kilometer-deep Agadir Canyon off the coast of North Africa. However, the containers didn't usually contain black garbage bags with body parts. This was a first.

The production assistant punched in the numbers of the Italian police, the ambulance service, the fire service, and Channel 4's news desk in Rome on her cell while the host frantically delved into her artistic persona for a suitable character who would appear both resourceful and glamorous.

The crane cabin was equipped with a small but powerful pair of binoculars. Costa put the strap around his neck, opened the door, and climbed out on the ladder to the crane's main tower. After two minutes of careful climbing, he reached the long loading outrigger above the cabin, edged his way past the trolley and the capsized cable drum, and found a suitable vantage point high above the loading deck of the *Taixan*. Through the windows of the ship's bridge he could see the Chinese officers frantically waving their arms. A small circle of condensation had formed on the storm glass in front of each open mouth. The loading officer was standing on a separate gangway above the deck at the same level as Gaetano. He had his back to the crane operator and was shouting into a walkie-talkie, but Costa had only John Denver's "Leaving on a Jet Plane" in his earpiece.

Costa saw the reflection of the emergency vehicles' flashing lights on the facades of every building in the streets that radiated from the hub of the port. The sky was no longer empty but covered with white clouds like shimmering fish scales. He looked east as the quay filled with ambulances, police cars, media vans with skyward-looking satellite dishes, and the Carabinieri's cordons. He saw Mars rise above the horizon in the east and studied the red planet until it was obscured by clouds; he felt the steel construction vibrate under all the official boots. Gaetano Costa aimed the binoculars at the farthest, darkest part of the quay.

He observed the dark blue Audi A8 that rolled onto the quay between the warehouses, its lights turned off. A small, straight-backed figure got out, and through the lenses of the binoculars the crane operator watched the silhouette, the man's signature ivory-headed walking stick tucked under his left arm. At this distance the man's eye sockets were pools of black ink.

Urs Savelli from the Camorra.

Gaetano Costa let the binoculars dangle from the strap and ignored the shouts from the crane tower behind him. He lit a cigarette, took a single deep drag, flicked it into the darkness, and with a curse closed his eyes and let himself fall onto the container fifty meters below him.

The host got her second shock of the evening when Costa hit the tarmac two meters away from her. Undaunted, she continued smiling at the camera through the mask of tiny bloodstains that covered her face.

CHAPTER 2

Assistant Public Prosecutor Sabrina D'Avalos parked her old Opel behind a row of containers sheltered from cameras and onlookers and walked across the yard to the newly erected white plastic tents where medical examiners were working on the contents of the container, making dental imprints if any teeth were left, fingerprinting if any fingers remained, determining cause of death, taking tissue samples, and doing DNA profiling.

The September sun was approaching its zenith and cast hardly any shadow. The port area was quiet, even the seagulls unusually contemplative. The *Taixan* still lay by the quay, invaded by police in dark blue uniforms and customs officers in black. The Chinese ship's officers were on the defensive, simultaneously subservient and furious.

Though she was only twenty-eight years old, Sabrina already had listened to the eulogies delivered for a female driver and a male bodyguard killed by a car bomb that bore all the hallmarks of the Terrasino family. Three years earlier her father had been murdered by the Camorra, the Cosa Nostra, or the 'Ndrangheta. He had been at the top of the death lists of all three crime syndicates; it was a political killing that remained unsolved.

From a lazy journalist's point of view, she was the ultimate cliché—young, pretty, and aristocratic—and people assumed that she would walk forever in the shadow of her famous father. General Baron Agostino D'Avalos had been the head of the Carabinieri's antiterror unit, the GIS—Gruppo di Intervento Speciale. She was a member of a brand-new unit, the NAC—Nucleo Anti Camorra—created by the public prosecutor in Naples and closely watched by the media. It was yet another instrument in the never-ending war on the Camorra. This specialist unit recruited members from the Carabinieri, the national police, and the public prosecutor's office and had unique extended judicial powers. NAC members were usually armed and had to complete a five-month course in forensic medicine, surveillance, defensive driving, close combat, and the use of weapons. Sabrina D'Avalos had been one of the first prosecutors to volunteer and had finished at the top of her class.

Sabrina, however, had no intention of becoming a stereotype and fiercely defended her right to be herself. She was unmarried and had no children. She belonged to a new generation of public prosecutors, often younger women, frequently educated in the United States as well as in Italy, incorruptible, and extraordinarily ambitious. She spent more nights in her office at the Palace of Justice than in her apartment in Via Andrea d'Isernia. In her spare time she read novels, watched black-and-white movies, went to Zumba classes, and took evening classes in Arabic. She also had befriended a traumatized eleven-year-old boy at an orphanage.

She called the boy Ismael, which was as good a name as any.

La baronessa was slim and slightly below medium height and walked with a very straight back. She had slanted, smoky eyes beneath a high forehead. Her mouth was sensuous but perhaps slightly too wide, her nose was narrow but possibly a little too long, and her face always reflected her mood.

To eliminate any doubt that she was modern and capable, Sabrina D'Avalos wore reflective Ray-Ban Aviator sunglasses and carried a BlackBerry on her belt. She often had a mug of Starbucks coffee in her hand, an iPod headset in her ears, and a nickel-plated Walther PPK—the James Bond model—with a mother-of-pearl handle in her shoulder holster. She wore her dark brown hair in a tight ponytail, and so everyone could see the deep scars in her forehead and above her right cheek caused by the car bomb. She used only mascara and followed Paloma Picasso's edict of wearing only black, white, or red but never wore red.

The car bomb hadn't been intended for her but for her boss, Federico Renda, the public prosecutor for the Republic of Naples and the founder of the NAC. Sabrina, however, had been in the second car of Renda's motorcade and had been injured by shell fragments and glass splinters.

As an assistant public prosecutor, she handled interesting cases but not the really juicy ones that could make a prosecutor's career overnight. She didn't deal with the Terrasino family, the Camorra clan that controlled Naples's sweatshops. She had been sent to the Vittorio Emanuele II Quay today because the container had hit the already overworked public prosecutor's office like an earthquake. All leave and vacation had been suspended, and additional staff had been brought in from Rome and Salerno. Sabrina D'Avalos's staffers were responsible for identifying victims with surnames from F to L.

She was from Lombardy in northern Italy and detested the dying Port of Naples. After three years there she still felt like she was living in exile. Her family had been soldiers or lawyers for as long as anyone could remember. Throughout her childhood her father, the general, had been posted as the Carabinieri's head of security at several of Italy's overseas embassies, so before she turned thirteen Sabrina had lived on every continent except Africa.

After a posting to Norfolk, Virginia, her father accepted the job as head of the Carabinieri's antiterror unit, the GIS, and the family was able to settle down at last. Sabrina D'Avalos had loved her new existence, life in the huge apartment on Via Salvatore Barzilai in Milan, and the view across the parks. She fought with her heavy-handed brothers as an equal and enjoyed summers spent at the family's villa in the mountains surrounding Lake Como. And she had the opportunity to get to know her father. The general's devotion to all his children was unconditional, but Sabrina was his favorite, and she could always be found right behind him. An old dog with his pup, as her mother would say.

Near the tents the air vibrated from the generators. Fans in the trucks ensured a low temperature and rapid air circulation inside the tents. The trucks had been provided by the United Nations Protection Force, UNPROFOR, and had last done service during the excavation of mass graves in Bosnia-Herzegovina.

Her father often had remarked that a story always found its author rather than vice versa, and now this story had found her. When Sabrina had entered the tents for the first time, she had felt ready, but she was no longer sure. She didn't think she would be able to contribute very much that the medical examiners hadn't already found out.

Outside the tents, staffers in blue scrubs were smoking and talking in several different languages. Twenty-five vacuum-packed Chinese bodies and the remains of another thirty-five people of European descent meant that medical examiners from other European countries, Canada, and the United States had been flown in. She nodded to a young civil servant from Salerno. The woman was sitting cross-legged on the tarmac inhaling a cigarette, ashen-faced, like most people who had done the rounds of the tents.

She walked through an air lock and into the women's changing room. The white plastic walls moved in sync with the breathing of the compressors. She folded her clothes, placed them in a fiberglass cupboard along with her shoulder holster, and locked it. Two women were huddled under the showers behind a frosted plastic wall. They spoke quietly in a language she didn't know.

The smallest coveralls were too big, but she had learned to wear thermal underwear underneath them. The temperature in the tents never exceeded 35°F, and her breath was clearly visible in the air. She tightened the strap on her breathing apparatus, tucked her hair under the hood, and entered the first tent.

The bodies had been removed from the plastic wrapping, the same stiff white material that Camorra waste-management firms used to

dispose of the toxic, nondegradable waste that suffocated Naples and its suburbs, and each sweatshop worker had been placed in a ribbed white plastic tray with a drain and a numbered tag tied to the right big toe. The Camorra had removed all fingerprints with acid, and no dental records existed. The idea of the Chinese as individuals had to be abandoned.

She continued down the rows of plastic tubs.

Human trafficking and slave labor in the sweatshops where these people were worked to their deaths were crimes against humanity, but it was a dead end from a career perspective. Many previous public prosecutors and police officers had faced this prospect, and Sabrina had no intention of joining their ranks.

She squeezed through a blue plastic air lock into the European section and turned on her breathing apparatus. Whiteboards were lined up along the tent wall. Body parts in every stage of decomposition were being assembled like jigsaws in the plastic trays. Many had been identified already, and Sabrina recognized most of the names. The trays contained a fraction of the Camorra's victims over the last thirty years. Conservative estimates put the figure of those killed since 1980 close to 3,660: teachers, journalists, mayors, priests, city counselors, North African human traffickers, business owners, and any Camorrista who had challenged the sovereignty of the Terrasino family. The fact that these bodies were lying here right now—that they had been found at all—was pure chance.

Three kilometers off the coast of Torre Picentina, one of Europe's biggest offshore wind farms was being built. Transporting the colossal turbine towers, generators, and blades had necessitated the construction of a bypass from Strada Statale 18 to Strada Provinziale 175, a project that meant the compulsory purchase of several small farms, some truck farms, and three old garbage dumps.

Sabrina imagined how the Camorra, in the nights preceding the arrival of the contractor's machines, had tracked down and dug up the evidence of their old sins from the garbage dumps, loaded them onto trucks, and piled them high inside the white containers.

*   *   *

The medical examiners had been working around the clock, and the number of question marks on the boards was decreasing. More and more fields had been filled in with names, social security numbers, and last known addresses.

She would have liked to take the day off: have a manicure and pedicure, wash her clothes, do some shopping, pick up Ismael and take him to the zoo. However, Dr. Raimondo Sapienza called her because he had discovered something unusual. The doctor from Rome supervised F-to-L identifications. Even though he was wearing the same blue scrubs as everyone else, the eminent pathologist was easy to spot. His enormous gray beard tried to escape from his mask on all sides. He waved Sabrina over to his office, which consisted of a door placed across two trestles; a plastic beaker containing a blue, a red, and a green dry-wipe marker pen; and a laptop. Confirmed identifications were green, doubtful were blue, and unknown were red. Gradually all the whiteboards had acquired a green glow.

"*Buongiorno*, Sabrina."

"I was hoping to take the day off, Raimondo," she said.

The eyes behind Dr. Sapienza's protective glasses expressed a kind of ironic empathy. He himself hadn't slept for three days.

"And I would never have called if it wasn't important, Sabrina. Or remarkable, at least. Number twenty-nine, thirty, and, yes, thirty-one."

"Remarkable?"

"Follow me."

He walked over to one of the tables, and her stomach churned.

Dr. Sapienza removed a thin sheet moistened with formaldehyde from one of the plastic trays and gestured for her to come closer. A child. A small human being the size of Ismael. A little bit of shoulder-length black hair stuck to the remains of the scalp.

"The only child in the container, Sabrina. A boy. He's twelve years old and has been in the garbage bag for around three years. Even so, the body is relatively well preserved, as you can see. This is partly due to the plastic bag and partly due to the weight of waste

on top of him, which will have forced the decomposition bacteria farther down."

Dr. Sapienza pointed to a light box displaying X-rays. Below a yellow Post-it note with the number 29 were two images of the boy's hands.

"Bone age?" Sabrina D'Avalos said.

"Yes. Bone formation in the carpus says twelve years. That matches the distribution of adult and baby teeth. A handsome little boy. Very handsome, in fact."

Dr. Sapienza replaced the sheet over the boy.

He took a step to the left. Number 30. Another sheet.

"A woman. We have spectroscoped her hair. Counted the rings, so to speak. And we've identified her via dental records from a dentist in Milan."

Sabrina D'Avalos nodded.

"She's thirty-five years old," he said.

The teeth in the tray were white as chalk, intact and even.

"Does she have a name?"

Dr. Sapienza pointed to the nearest board.

"Lucia Forlani, née Maletta. Born February 12, 1973, in Castellarano."

"Never heard of it," she said.

"It's a small mountain village in the north of Reggio Emilia. I went there once on a school trip," he said. "Napoleon stopped by in 1801." Dr. Sapienza pointed to something in the middle of the tray. "And that's number thirty-one, as it were."

A third, tiny skeleton lay protected by the woman's pelvic bones. The baby inside the woman had turned and was engaged with its head down and its back facing left. Ready and waiting for departure—for contractions that never came.

The sturdy gray cable strips with which the woman's wrists had been tied were indestructible. Dr. Sapienza had arranged her arms in front of her pelvis so that the bones of her hands were spread protectively across the remains of the fetus.

Sabrina's breathing apparatus hissed.

"An eight-month-old fetus," Dr. Sapienza said.

"Cause of death?"

"Unknown."

"Cover them up," Sabrina said.

"The woman was lying beside the boy. We've concluded that they're mother and son; the DNA profiles match up. There is no doubt."

Dr. Sapienza sat down in his office chair and started typing.

Out of the corner of one eye Sabrina noticed a burst of light. She turned around but saw nothing unusual. It could have been anything: a flashlight, a hiccup in the steady rhythm of the generators that powered the fluorescent lights. The blue figures moved methodically around the trays. Some were assembling cadavers as if they were shards of pottery from an archaeological excavation; others were photographing the bodies or taking tissue samples for microscopic or spectroscopic analyses. Others still were carrying trays of test tubes to the freezer where the samples would be stored until DNA tests could be carried out.

A man walked slowly past the whiteboards, taking notes. He had wedged his cell between his shoulder and his ear. Sabrina frowned. She thought the use of cell phones inside the tents was strictly prohibited. For the time being the Vittorio Emanuele II Quay existed in a state of emergency. No identifications could be leaked to the public until the next of kin had been informed.

"I thought you would want to see this," the forensic pathologist continued. "We've cross-referenced lists of missing persons from our Interior Ministry, the Red Cross, and Interpol in Lyon. Lucia Forlani is listed as missing. As is her son, Salvatore. They were last seen entering an elevator in Galleria Vittorio Emanuele II in Milan on September 5, 2007."

"Who was the last person to see her?"

"No idea."

"Education, relatives, addresses? What are you saying, Raimondo? What else have you got for me?" she demanded to know.

"Nothing! That's the problem."

He pointed at the screen over his shoulder. It displayed the Interior Ministry's authoritative and confidential list of missing persons, which was updated daily. The cursor blinked next to "For-lani, Lucia / Maletta, Lucia [35, Castellarano] & Forlani, Salvatore [12, Milan]." Their names were followed by the acronym MIPTP, an address in Milan, and the name of the case officer to whom all queries should be directed: Nestore Raspallo.

"Grazie," she said, and closed her eyes. The smell and the undulating tent walls overwhelmed her. The fifth of September 2007—three days before her father was killed.

It had become a habit to date everything from the death of her father. A rather unhealthy habit, according to her therapist. Sabrina had smiled without saying anything but had visualized the therapist in free fall from his office window to the pavement five floors below. The problem wasn't her father's death. It was the haunting, restless thirst for revenge that lived on.

MIPTP.

"What does that mean, Sabrina?" Dr. Sapienza said. "How the hell do you expect me to do my job when all information is classified?"

"I'll take care of it, Raimondo. Forget about it."

"Forget about it, forget about it—I'm paid not to forget, Sabrina, but to remember. All victims are entitled to someone who does that."

She blushed. "Of course they are, Dr. Sapienza," she said quietly. "MIPTP—Ministero Interno Protezione Testimoni e Pentiti—is a program for the protection of witnesses or their relatives. People who have helped the police solve organized crime. Do you understand?"

"So she's a witness?"

"Or she's related to a witness. Dr. Raimondo, few things in this country are hermetically sealed. The Vatican's antique porn collection perhaps, but even they aren't as impenetrable as witness protection programs. That's why we have the odd breakthrough every now and again, despite everything. You can't blame the program just because some remorseful Mafiosi, *i pentiti*, choose to compromise their new identities and resume their old sinful ways."

"A couple of bottles of vodka and I'll be prepared to over-look these intolerable restrictions," the giant said amicably. "But someone ought to know, Sabrina. Someone needs to know that they've been found."

Sabrina, who knew that Dr. Sapienza never touched alcohol, smiled and squeezed his shoulder.

"Of course. Someone will be told. I'll make sure of it. Personally. *Subito. Grazie.*" She walked up to the whiteboard, found a sponge, and erased the names. "I don't want to see those names here again, Raimondo," she said. "And call me the moment you know how they died."

She turned on her heel and headed for the exit.

Raimondo Sapienza looked after the straight-backed prosecutor with melancholic eyes and shrugged. He liked her and was saddened by the permanent twilight in which she seemed to exist.

The man with the cell turned and looked after her as well, but without much interest. A few minutes later he stepped out into the sunshine, lit a cigarette, and walked behind the nearest stack of containers, which the Carabinieri were using as part of their cordon. He stopped, unzipped his coveralls, and started to relieve himself. Making sure there were no curious onlookers nearby, he took the cell he had used to photograph the names of the victims, put it inside a polystyrene box, sealed it with tape, and threw it over the containers.

CHAPTER 3

Like everyone else, Sabrina D'Avalos to wait her turn in the queue
outside the office of Federico Renda, the public prosecutor of Naples.
Roughly every fifteen minutes, she moved one seat farther to the right
on the marble bench, and the next person in the queue behind her
moved from the wall to a seat on the far left of the bench. The tall
carved mahogany doors at the end of the archway were guarded by two
Carabinieri in combat uniform armed with machine guns. In Naples
the Palace of Justice was always a potential war zone. To her right was
a young civil servant she vaguely knew. The young man had loosened
his tie and was alternately typing furiously on a laptop balanced on his
knees and leafing through some papers. It was well known that Federico Renda gave short shrift to anyone who was ill prepared.

The young man eventually was swallowed up by the tall doors
and emerged ten minutes later, visibly downcast. Sabrina smiled at
him and got up, summoned by a curled index finger. The finger
belonged to one of the matrons in Renda's anteroom.

"Would you like to go straight in," said the woman in the flo-
ral dress.

It wasn't a request.

She walked through the dappled green light that filtered through
the inch-thick bulletproof glass in the windows. The walls were

lined with polished mahogany panels, the path to Renda's desk as long as a penitential walk. The thick Persian carpets silenced her footsteps, but Renda had heard her anyway. The public prosecutor's salt-and-pepper hair was combed straight back from his forehead, and his brown eyes were even darker than she remembered. As always, Renda was wearing a well-pressed dark suit with a vest, a white shirt, and a discreet tie. A pair of reading glasses was lying on his desk, and his hands rested on the arms of the wheelchair. The same bomb that had bestowed on Sabrina her scars and an occasional and irritating tinnitus had paralyzed the public prosecutor from the waist down.

Renda shied away from media attention, and gossip about his private life was unthinkable. Quite simply, the man had sacrificed too much and was regarded almost as a saint. Sabrina knew that he was unmarried and had no children. This ascetic way of life was something he shared with many other senior lawyers committed to a lifetime of fighting the Mafia.

Sabrina regarded Federico Renda as a good boss. He had no favorites and was equally blunt and impatient with everybody. He nodded in the direction of a low chair, and Sabrina sat down, crossed her legs, and folded her hands in her lap. Her shoulder holster bumped against her ribs, and she nudged it aside with her elbow.

"*Buongiorno, dottoressa.* How is it going?"

"We've nearly finished my area of investigation," she said. "We've identified a journalist and two young trade union members. There is a North African man in his thirties whose identity we haven't been able to discover."

She shifted in her chair.

"In addition, an unexpected discovery was made among the other body parts. Quite remarkable, in fact. I've just come from speaking to Dr. Sapienza."

She fell silent and was annoyed with herself: unexpected *and* remarkable. Great . . .

Federico Renda smiled graciously, though his eyes showed no desire to join in. He gestured for her to continue. Most visitors were aware that the public prosecutor would prefer it if they would manage to come somewhere close to speaking faster than he could think.

"A thirty-five-year-old woman and a twelve-year-old boy. Mother and son. The woman was eight months pregnant," Sabrina went on.

Renda leaned forward.

"Lucia and Salvatore Forlani. They've been missing for three years," she said. "The woman is from Castellarano, and the boy was born in Milan."

"Do you know the town?" he asked.

"No."

"Reggio Emilia in the Apennine Mountains," Renda informed her. "It has a well-preserved city wall and a convent school for the daughters of wealthy families. Napoleon camped near the town in . . ."

"1801," she said. "Yes, so everyone tells me."

The public prosecutor smiled faintly.

"The Forlani tragedy," he said, leaning back and hooking his thumbs into his vest. "You can be forgiven for not knowing the details, signorina. Circumstances forced us to play down the affair as far as the media was concerned. Defense of the Realm Act, for one thing. Whatever that means."

"I understand."

She looked directly behind Renda at the only photograph in the office: his obsession, L'Artista, the woman whose car bomb had put him in a wheelchair. The image was poor, the woman a blurred figure in an underground garage. The prosecutor had picked out the image from a closed-circuit television camera and had had it enlarged and mounted in an aluminum frame. A permanent reminder of the need for constant vigilance, Sabrina assumed. The woman had been caught midstride: dark clothes, sunglasses, a dark baseball cap pulled down over her eyes. The figure had stayed on the borderline between light and shade: the most difficult conditions for the CCTV cameras.

Sabrina had seen the legendary assassin out of the corner of her eye—but far too late. The woman was unrecognizable behind her sunglasses and crash helmet, dressed in the uniform of the Italian highway patrol, the Polizia Stradale, riding one of their Moto Guzzi California motorcycles.

Every day Sabrina had wondered if she had seen any hint of emotion in the woman's face.

The motorcycle had pulled up alongside Federico Renda's motorcade before the entrance road to the highway. Renda's driver had swerved to avoid a pothole, and that tiny maneuver had saved the public prosecutor's life, but the driver and a male bodyguard were killed instantly.

L'Artista was standing upright on the motorcycle's footrests. She raised her hand with the magnetic car bomb and held it over the roof of the car, but rather than attach itself right above the backseat where it undoubtedly would have killed Renda, the explosive charge had ended up on the side of the car.

To avoid the crash barrier, L'Artista had tilted the motorcycle over until sparks flew from the footrest screeching against the tarmac and escaped through a viaduct under the highway. It had been an awesome sight. The last thing Sabrina remembered before the eviscerating white explosion was the bright red brake lights of the Moto Guzzi.

She looked at the green windows.

"It was a tragedy not just for the family but also for all of Italy," she said. "Giulio Forlani and his business partner, Fabiano Batista, were eminent scientists with a powerful new invention. They were developing a device that would make it impossible to fake products made by the fashion industry. The technology could also have been used to protect passports, stock certificates, bonds, software distribution disks, and banknotes against forgery. Their company, Nanometric, had two employees, a German chemist by the name of Hanna Schmidt and a young computer expert, Paolo Iacovelli. Nanometric researched advanced nanotechnology and had worked out how to manipulate nanocrystals. The basic science was well known, but their methods of embedding crystals in a stable micro-environment were new. They had two investors: the EU through an ongoing research grant and the Italian fashion industry—the Camera Nazionale della Moda Italiana—through its director, Massimiliano Di Luca. The Camera obviously had a vested interest in the success of the technology—and the Camorra the opposite. Bootleg and fake branded products are their most important sources of income."

"I'm impressed," Federico Renda said quietly. "You've done your homework."

"Thank you."

Sabrina had spent two frantic hours researching various databases.

"Coffee?" the prosecutor asked her.

She muttered another thank you.

Renda filled two delicate bone china cups.

"I would like to have had access to the original case files. Officially the case is closed, but it ought to be reopened," she declared with greater conviction than she felt.

"Ought it indeed?"

"After today, yes. That's my opinion."

"For whose sake?" Renda asked.

"I've only had a couple of hours to familiarize myself with the story, dottore," she said. "But a couple of days before Nanometric could file the completed patent applications, on September 5, 2007, there was an attack on the company, and Batista, Hanna Schmidt, and Iacovelli were murdered."

"And Forlani?"

"Killed during a staged collision on a highway south of Milan," Sabrina said. "His wife and son disappeared the same morning from an elevator in Galleria Vittorio Emanuele II in Milan. The attack on the company and the related operations were brilliantly coordinated and executed. If you look at it as a technical achievement."

Renda's eyes were anything but unemotional.

"And now Lucia and Salvatore Forlani have been found," she said. "Perhaps it's the story that refuses to go away."

A pained expression crossed Renda's sleepless face. "Refuses to go away? Lucia Forlani was an orphan as far as I recall," he said.

"And her husband is dead. I can't see who would benefit from your efforts."

Sweat broke out between her shoulder blades.

The public prosecutor drained his cup and leaned back slowly. If he was in pain, he didn't show it.

"We're talking about an unsolved crime. A very serious crime," Sabrina said.

"I'm aware of it, dottoressa, but the case falls within the jurisdiction of the public prosecutor of Milan. Their best people investigated it and got nowhere."

Renda placed his hands flat on his desk, and Sabrina knew that her audience was at an end.

"It has been gathering dust in Milan for three years; that much is true," she said, making no effort to get up. "No progress whatsoever. The killers are from Naples. Everything else is a formality—in my opinion. Besides, the attacks on Nanometric and the murders of Batista, Schmidt, and Iacovelli were investigated by the Office for Organized Crime at Milan's Palace of Justice, the abduction of Lucia and Salvatore Forlani by Milan's central police force, while the car crash on the A7 was handled by local officers from the police station in Città Studi. No one ever tried to pull all the threads together."

She looked at her folded hands.

"I would really like to have a go," she declared.

"You said the killers were from Naples?"

"Urs Savelli and the woman up there." She pointed to the photo of L'Artista. "Hanna Schmidt was killed by a straight double-edged blade. The cut matches those on Savelli's other victims perfectly," she said. "His famous Basque walking stick. Furthermore, a witness reported seeing a young woman wearing a FedEx uniform enter the company's premises around ten o'clock in the morning. The witness, a retired army officer who lived nearby, had gone out for a walk with his old German shepherd. When he came back past the building ten minutes later, the same woman was just leaving in a FedEx car. He's certain. It was her."

"Or so you think. You're still a public prosecutor even though you're now a member of the NAC," Renda said. "We work only with evidence here—if you're familiar with that concept—not hunches."

"As far as I understand, the Camorra use L'Artista very sparingly and only for the most important assassinations, such as the attack on your own life," Sabrina persisted. "She reports directly to Don Francesco Terrasino, and no one else ever instructs her to carry out a hit. As far as I know, the Terrasino family or Savelli never employs any other female freelancers."

"But the link between Don Francesco and L'Artista has never been proved. I do so hate to repeat myself," the public prosecutor sighed.

"No, but we both know that it exists," Sabrina insisted.

She looked calmly at her boss. Renda looked back at her. Then he rubbed his neck and turned toward the windows. In any other man his expression would have been interpreted as indecision.

"Urs Savelli and L'Artista," Federico Renda said, slowly and clearly addressing the shadows.

A ringing began in Sabrina's left ear.

"I would like to review the case," she repeated. "I really would."

"I understand that," he said. "What do you know about Savelli?"

"He's Albanian. He's high up in the Terrasino family and responsible for liaising between the fashion houses in northern Italy and the bootleg factories in Naples and the Far East. The Terrasino family will never trust him completely because he is and always will be a *straniero*, an outsider, but he is good."

Sabrina began like the teacher's pet she always had been, but her words soon ebbed out.

"He is enigmatic . . . and . . . and . . ."

She looked at the public prosecutor, dreading his thin private smile, but Renda's face was devoid of expression.

"I don't know anything, do I?" she conceded.

"No, but I don't know very much more, and I've been looking for him for twenty years," Renda said. "All we have are rumors that have been repeated so often that they have become legends. I dislike mythmakers, Dottoressa D'Avalos, I prefer committed rationalists. Are you a rationalist?"

"I would certainly like to think so."

"Excellent. Savelli isn't, as you say, Italian, but Albanian. He comes from a small village in eastern Albania, Dunice, not far from Lake Ohrid. When he was very young, he made his living as a bear dancer. Hence his nickname Ursus—Urs—which means 'bear.' At least that's what many of his biographers are guessing. God knows what his family name was, but he took the name Savelli."

"Bear dancer?" she asked with incredulity.

"Yes. He owned a tame black bear. The boy and the bear walked from market to market to perform. It's a good story: the best of all the stories about Savelli's origins. Urs or Ursus played the flute, and the bear danced. A meager living at best. One day a gypsy stole his blankets, his money, and his food. A few days later Urs tracked down the thief in a forest and knocked him unconscious. When the man woke up, he found himself tied to the trunk of a tree with a noose of barbed wire around his neck. The gypsy had eaten Urs's food, sold his blankets, and spent his money in a traveling brothel. Urs made it clear to him that he had put him, Urs—and not least the bear—in an awkward situation. The bear had to be fed. Urs slit open the gypsy's abdomen with the man's own knife and let the bear help himself. Bears are like pigs, signorina; they'll eat anything."

Sabrina gulped. "And then?"

"I'm sure you can imagine that even the most backward country policeman could interpret that crime scene without too much difficulty. Urs was duly arrested in a nearby forest. The bear was shot, and the gypsy's hands and face found in its stomach, among other things. It's very hard to argue against that level of evidence. And I can't imagine that a single state-appointed defense counsel would even have tried. The boy was thrown into one of Enver Hoxha's notorious prisons. Most people with that kind of story would have disappeared without a trace."

"But not Savelli?"

"No. Legend has it that the boy was taken under the wing of the prison librarian, a kind of self-appointed Christian missionary who performed prohibited religious services, claimed to grant the absolution of the Church, and undertook baptisms and gave communion. He got access to Urs's body, and Urs in return got access to the protection of the congregation and the prison library. An excellent arrangement—if you're not of an overly sensitive nature. One day, however, a new prison governor arrived, an ideologically scrubbed-clean apparatchik who couldn't accept any other cosmology than the historical materialism right under his own nose. There wasn't a single country behind the Iron Curtain where religion was persecuted and suppressed as fiercely as it was in Albania, signorina. In order not to waste a bullet on a shot to the back of his head, the missionary was garroted in the prison yard, and Urs and other members of the congregation were thrown into solitary confinement. For two or maybe three years, Urs saw nothing but the hand that pushed a bowl of food through the shutter in the door to his cell; he heard nothing but the sound of his own voice, the slamming of the shutter, and the footsteps of the guards. But he was allowed to read and learned English, German, French, and Italian—and he taught himself to whisper to stay sane. He also developed a kind of sixth, seventh, perhaps even an eighth sense: no photos exist of Savelli. We don't have one, and neither does the FBI. From a long distance and with absolute certainty he can sense if anyone is aiming a camera lens or a telescopic sight at him, and he moves the instant a photo is about to be taken or the trigger pulled, so they say. He has numerous identities and secret residences around Europe."

"He got out? Did he escape?"

"Not at all. Hoxha died in 1985, and he was succeeded as president of Albania by the moderate Ramiz Alia. In 1989 Mother Teresa, who was herself Albanian, visited Tirana and met with Alia and Hoxha's widow. In 1990, the ban on religious institutions was lifted and anyone who had been imprisoned for reasons of faith or political affiliation was granted amnesty. Urs Savelli walked out of the prison gate in Pogradec in June 1990. Out into the sunshine and a glorious future."

"But he was in prison for murder," Sabrina objected.

"Technically the bear was the murderer," Renda said.

"Why are you telling me this?"

"For your own sake. Savelli is the most dangerous person you can imagine. Anything else?"

"No—yes, thank you. Are you telling me that I can—"

"Just a moment. Savelli stole a boat and went ashore in Corfu. Like the magician Prospero and his deformed slave Caliban in one and the same person."

"I beg your pardon?"

"*The Tempest*. Shakespeare's swan song," the public prosecutor said. "Following a mighty tempest the King of Naples is shipwrecked with his followers on Sycorax's island, almost an anagram of the old name for Corfu, Corcyra. Do you remember your Shakespeare?"

"No."

"Pity. After Corfu things get somewhat vague. Somehow Savelli reaches Brindisi. After Brindisi he takes control of his identity, his persona, and his name. Sources and informants dry up or are killed. Savelli understands that when people view him only through his legend, much of his work is already done. The myth is far more terrifying than the reality. It allows him to concentrate on the job in hand. He must have been spotted early on by one of the Camorra's talent scouts, probably here in the Port of Naples, and earned his advancement up the ranks very quickly." Federico Renda swallowed a mouthful of coffee and cleared his throat. "He was the ivy which had hid my princely trunk, And sucked my verdure out on't," he quoted.

Sabrina felt dizzy. The vast room, the dark panels, the green underwater light. The quotation. Her feelings were heightened by the fact that the usually very reserved man behind the desk was smiling broadly.

"Are you fond of Shakespeare, dottoressa?" he asked.

"Absolutely," she said, and thought that the public prosecutor was as lonely as a goldfish in a bowl.

"But there's a time for everything?"

"Definitely."

"I'm saying that you should devote your time to tracking down any living relatives that the victims may have," Renda said, leaning forward. "The container investigation has overloaded our resources, and I desperately need all the good people I can lay my hands on."

"I understand," she said.

Federico Renda held up his hand. He hadn't finished.

"I'm restating my opinion that there is no point to your current assignment. But perhaps the Forlani case needs a fresh pair of eyes, as you say. You might find family members or other relatives of Lucia Forlani who need to be told what happened to her and the boy."

"Boys. The fetus was male."

Renda nodded.

"The boys. You have a week. I'll make sure you're granted access to the files."

"But they're in Milan."

"Milan is remote in more ways than one," Renda conceded. "However, it's not the dark side of the moon. They will be brought to your apartment. Today if possible."

She had almost reached the door, but she turned around when he spoke again.

Federico Renda repeated his warning.

"The walking stick. Savelli's Basque stick. The makila. If you hear that stick—like a chisel against a gravestone—you must run as fast as you can without ever looking back. Will you promise me that?"

"Absolutely."

"*Arrivederci.*" He held up his index finger. "One week."

"Thank you."

The prosecutor was about to say something but changed his mind. Sabrina smiled politely. "Was there something else?" she asked.

Again he flashed her a smile that transformed his entire appearance.

"L'Artista. My brothers refer to her as my obsession. I'm perfectly aware of it, and if I'm boring you, please say so. She's probably Don

Francesco Terrasino's private executioner, as you said. They use her for complicated assassinations. For years I've been trying to find out how the two of them communicate. Don Francesco would never dream of confiding a word to a cell telephone, a landline, or an e-mail. So how does he do it? He's a simple man."

"Radio?"

Renda nodded. "A good suggestion. In our days radio is an over-looked means of communication. However, our best experts from the army and the navy have listened in on all frequencies around his residence for years. Nothing."

"A courier. A grandchild making the calls?"

"We've bugged the cells of all family members and employees. But if you have a flash of inspiration, please let me know."

"I'm sorry I can't come up with anything now."

"No, no, it's very frustrating," he said amicably.

She headed for the door, but Renda still hadn't finished with her. "Dottoressa D'Avalos."

She stopped.

"Please don't think that I have overlooked the obvious," he said.

"Oh . . . ?"

"MIPTP. If everyone is dead, who is being protected by the wit-ness protection program? And why?"

Her shirt stuck to her back under her jacket.

"Probably an administrative error made when entering Giulio Forlani's details into the system," he said almost to himself. "Such things happen frequently. Especially in Milan."

Renda was born in Naples and disliked people from northern Italy.

"I'm sorry. I keep forgetting that you're from Milan," he said.

Of course you do, she thought.

"I forgive you," she said.

"Thank you. Nor have I overlooked that it was your father who set up the witness protection program. Nor the fact that your father was killed just three days after the attack on Forlani and Nanometric. Pure coincidence, I'm sure—an unrelated incident. Do you under-stand? Please don't forget that you're employed in this department, dottoressa, to solve crimes, not to carry out personal vendettas, not even as a member of the NAC."

She nodded and looked at the floor.

"I look forward to hearing what you make of it," Federico Renda said.

"I hope you won't be disappointed, dottore."

The door handle felt damp under her hand.

She walked through the anteroom looking neither left nor right, but noticed that all the secretaries were staring at her, an assistant public prosecutor who had been granted almost half an hour of Federico Renda's time. This was unheard of, quite unprecedented, and the young woman wasn't even bleeding from her palms. They had heard the clattering of coffee cups. Berlusconi had been granted only twenty-five minutes and no refreshments.

In his shaded office Federico Renda studied the information that Sabrina D'Avalos had had access to—"Forlani, Lucia / Maletta, Lucia [35, Castellarano] & Forlani, Salvatore [12, Milan]"—from the MIPTP and the name of the case officer, Nestore Raspallo. He looked up a couple of things in his private files and leaned back. His screen listed the names of the senior officers who had been responsible for the Ministry of the Interior's witness protection program since 1990—both from the Central Committee and its "handlers"—trusted members of the Carabinieri's Raggruppamento Operative Speciale who were tasked with the practicalities of case processing and logistics: safe houses, new identities, personal papers, plastic surgery, physical protection, and so on. It was a short list, and one name stood out.

Renda had known the young assistant public prosecutor's father, General Baron Agostino D'Avalos, very well. An admirable, highly competent, and secretive man, head of the GIS and the longest serving head in the history of the Italian Special Forces. Perhaps these talents had been passed down? Perhaps not. However, in Italy the only ties that mattered were those of family, and the

murder of Dottoressa D'Avalos's father was still unsolved. That was
quite intolerable. Unforgivable. Again he compared the dates. The
chronological proximity between the murder of the general and
the annihilation of the Forlani family was purely coincidental.
Agostino D'Avalos's name had been at the top of the death lists of
the Camorra and the Cosa Nostra for years. Right above Renda's
own, incidentally. Anyone could have killed the general.

Urs Savelli was undoubtedly aware of the work being carried
out in the tents. And he knew Sabrina D'Avalos and her family, of
course. And he was presumably fully informed about the NAC. Perhaps, though it was rather unlikely, he might even find the young
assistant public prosecutor's efforts interesting. So much so that
he would leave his reptilian habitat and venture out into the sun.
Stranger things had happened in Renda's long career. It wouldn't
be the first time he would have had to sacrifice a pawn to take the
opponent's queen in this never-ending game of chess. He turned
his wheelchair around so that he could study the photograph
of L'Artista.

Renda decided that the young D'Avalos needed some inconspicuous assistance. From a more experienced, resourceful, and . . . more
objective person. Someone outside the public prosecutor's office.

CHAPTER 4

She found Ismael in the bathroom in the boys' wing of the orphanage. The skinny eleven-year-old sat on a stool in the middle of the floor with a towel over his shoulders. A young woman—a new supervisor—was shaving his head while she chatted on her cell, a cigarette dangling from the corner of her mouth. On the towel a dolphin was jumping up toward a faded beach ball. The woman smiled at Sabrina as she leaned against the wall, her arms folded across her chest. Ismael ignored her as usual. Below the partition of the cubicle farthest away she saw two feet, socks, shorts, and a pair of slim ankles, and she heard the pages of a magazine turning. There were no doors; the boys had long since smashed them to pieces by using them as surfboards on the stairs. There were white bars across the windows. They were intact, though they looked as if any well-nourished four-year-old could easily rip them out of the crumbling brickwork.

The coast guard had discovered Ismael at dawn in the surf on a beach near Amalfi next to an empty, battered life raft, the only survivor from a cargo of trafficked humans that had gone terribly wrong. He was probably from the Maghreb, and when he spoke, which was rare, he spoke Arabic. He fell outside any administrative category, the worst fate for an orphaned illegal immigrant. A bureaucratic loophole. The boy had languished at the orphanage for two years with no resolution in sight. Sabrina had decided to befriend this particular boy because the psychiatrists had diagnosed him as being in a worse state than any other child in the orphanage. The last black curls landed on Ismael's shoulders, and the woman put her hand on his neck and tried turning his head in Sabrina's direction. Sabrina knew it was futile. Ismael would look at her when he was ready. His head moved willingly, but his eyes stayed glued to the cracked floor tiles.

"Leave him alone," Sabrina said.

The woman glared at her. Two centimeters of ash fell from her cigarette onto the boy's scalp. He shook it off, got up, and handed her the towel.

"When will you be back?" she said.

"When we're back," Sabrina said.

"I need to record it in the log, signorina. You know that."

"Come, Ismael," Sabrina said, and left the bathroom without looking back. She heard the soft clip-clop of the boy's sandals behind her. They walked down a dark corridor that smelled of floor polish and glue, passing one dormitory after another. Everywhere children were sitting or lying. It was the silence of the orphanage that had first struck Sabrina. It was like a hospice. The endless waiting suffocated every emotion. It was as if the children were holding their breath.

The orphanage was in the Arenella district, and the zoo lay in the Posillipo quarter. They were stuck in a queue of traffic on Via John Fitzgerald Kennedy that moved at the speed of tectonic plates. Sabrina was sweating and chewing gum, her forearm dangling out the window. From time to time she would make a frustrated gesture or bang the car door when yet another idiot tried to push in where there was no room. She felt a strong urge to draw her gun and shoot the intruder's tires. Ismael's face was closed, and he sat glued to the side door, as far away from her as possible. The only thing moving was his jaw as he ground his teeth. Occasionally he would crack his knuckles. It was like sitting next to Pinocchio in need of oil. Was it because of her? Or because everything seemed pointless when you were an eleven-year-old African orphan?

Ismael slowly raked his hand across the millimeter-tall stubble on his scalp and sighed. He ground his teeth.

"I have to go away for a few days, Ismael," she said.

There was no reaction on the boy's face. He placed his hands between his knees and pressed them together.

Sabrina repeated the information in stumbling Arabic, and a scornful shadow flitted across Ismael's small features. She threw the Opel into first gear, pushing between a honking tourist bus and a three-wheeled scooter laden with yellow melons.

"I'll be back," she said to her hands on the steering wheel. "In a week. Maybe sooner."

Ismael always walked exactly two meters behind her. They moved like mime artists—when she stopped, he stopped. Sabrina was aware that they attracted a fair amount of attention. Right now they were eating ice cream. Ismael ate his cone with deep concentration so as not to waste a single crumb. She rested her elbows on the sturdy iron fence around the African savanna enclosure, bit into her cone, and tried to synchronize her jaw with the masticating dromedary right in front of them. The animal's girlish moist eyes watched her without blinking.

Ismael studied the dromedary, too. There was a special intensity in his eyes when they were near dromedaries, other camels, or ostriches. Sabrina imagined an oasis surrounded by soft, endlessly repeating sand dunes stretching all the way to the far horizon, salt caravans casting milelong shadows in the setting sun. Campfires, mint tea drunk from cups the size of thimbles, freshly baked flatbread, dogs poking around, and Arabic voices underneath the stars, and she wondered if Ismael had ever been to the desert.

The boy caught her eye, instantly switched off his interest in the dromedary, and took a bite of his ice cream.

They walked on.

* * *

The white enamel had flaked off the black iron bedstead in several places, as if the boy chewed the metal bars in his sleep. Because he often had nightmares, Ismael had been allocated one of the few single rooms at the orphanage.

As was his bedtime ritual, Ismael unlocked his locker with a key that hung around his neck on a piece of string, took the beaker with his toothbrush in it, and put it on the white bedside table next to his bed. Once she had gone, he would clean his teeth and lie down to sleep. She turned around while, like an army recruit, he folded his T-shirt and his underpants. He placed his clothes on the bottom shelf of his locker. The cessation of teeth grinding signaled that he had put on his pajamas and slid under the blankets. He turned to face the peeling wall while she found the book of fairy tales.

She would read for fifteen minutes while Ismael lay still. She had no idea if he understood a single word, but on the one occasion when she had forgotten to read aloud to him, he had taken the book and given it to her without looking at her. As always with Ismael, you never really knew who was doing what for whom.

But the supervisors and the overworked child psychiatrists had told her that Ismael became practically catatonic, unapproachable, and miserable whenever she was away.

She closed the book and took a deep breath. Ismael turned over in bed and looked at her expectantly from behind his long eyelashes. She blushed at this last and completely inappropriate point on the agenda. She pulled the shiny Walther PPK from her shoulder holster, emptied the magazine into her hand, checked the chamber for the bullet that was never there, and handed Ismael the gun. Sabrina had forgotten who or what initially had prompted this lunacy. With her hands she made a passable shadow bunny on the wall opposite. Ismael raised the gun with both hands and shot the bunny twice.

"Bang, bang," she said in a low, flat voice, speaking for both of them.

CHAPTER 5

The Opel was parked between the carcass of a BMW whose axles rested on the tarmac and a new gleaming chrome police motorcycle. It would end up like the BMW if it was left there overnight, but no one ever touched Sabrina's old Opel. She walked through the semidarkness of the archway and passed the old man, dark-skinned and gaunt, who always sat on one of the narrow steps in the stairwell. He recognized her footsteps and flashed her a toothless smile. The eyes of the old man were white from cataracts. She touched his long outstretched fingers, mumbled *salaam aleikum,* and received a *wa aleikum salaam* before she crossed the narrow courtyard. She shared this crumbling apartment block with illegal immigrants from North Africa: women and children. The men continued *al Nord,* to the factories and the lowest levels of the service industries in Milan or Turin. Her choice of accommodation in this small North African enclave had raised several eyebrows in her family and among her colleagues, but she liked the place: the smell of thyme from the pots in the courtyard, the nattering of old women, the large number of fatherless children, and the sleepy, khat-chewing young Somalis who played poker or Kalaha on a sheet of plywood on a cardboard box.

Even the screams from the makeshift dental clinic that occupied half the ground floor of the green and yellow back building where she lived fit in. The dentist, Dr. Khatib, was of the opinion that lido-caine should be reserved for major jaw surgery, which he was also happy to perform. His door was open, and Sabrina saw the fat den-tist stoop over a wriggling victim in the old-fashioned barber chair. Young Fakhry yawned as he pushed the pedal-powered dentist's drill. When he nodded off and the drill stopped in the depths of a molar, the patient's eyes were ready to pop out of their sockets, and Dr. Khatib's colorful curses would rain down over the boy.

She noticed something else: a motorcycle police officer in the smart uniform of the Polizia Stradale who looked like a young pea-cock. He was sitting on the second from bottom step in her stairwell with a red cardboard box and a gray sports bag between his boots.

"Dottoressa Sabrina D'Avalos?"

"Yes?"

He smiled broadly, got up, and saluted her while undressing her with his eyes.

She held out her identification card without a word, and he handed the items to her.

"Poor man," the officer said, gesturing toward Dr. Khatib's al fresco clinic.

"Yes, but he's cheap. Do I need to sign for these?"

"That won't be necessary. *Buonasera.*"

"'*Sera.*"

Four messages, ranging from the accusatory to the tormented, from her married lover were flashing on her answering machine. Roberto was an artist twenty years Sabrina's senior. The landscapes and the dispassionate portraits he painted might not be a true reflection of Roberto's character, but he compensated with other skills, and from time to time Sabrina would allow him to get her drunk on good red wine and take her to bed—always in his stu-dio, which was a mixture of workshop and gym. The artist was muscular and fit and regarded his body as a temple that had been subjected to the unfair erosion of time. He had never been to her home, which she had declared a Roberto-free zone. She deleted his messages and made a spur-of-the-moment decision never to see him again.

Roberto reminded her of her father, which was the root cause of the problem. She had feared that her father's chin would one day disappear, along with the exact color of his eyes, the tone of his voice, his laughter lines, the ironic gaze with which the general viewed the world, the trust and the understanding. She had dreaded waking up one morning to find that overnight her father's image had faded from her daily life. But it never happened. She remembered everything clearly.

Her hatred of his unknown killers hadn't diminished, either. Her therapist called it an amputated-father fixation fed by her choice of profession. It wasn't grief but phantom pains, he said. Find yourself a husband and have some children. Learn sign language or something else useful.

She told him about Roberto and heard the pieces fall into place behind the therapist's high forehead.

"It's obvious," he said. "You're not in love, Sabrina; you're trying to escape from reality."

"But I'm seeing someone . . ."

"Someone who doesn't pose a risk, Sabrina."

She had felt superficial. With the emotional depth of a Labrador.

"Maybe I just haven't met the right man yet," she argued.

"Perhaps—assuming that special someone exists. The whole concept is overrated. In my experience there is no Mr. Right until you choose to make him so. It takes compromise, hard work, and careful planning. You have to make an effort."

He made it sound like building a garage.

"Maybe love shouldn't have to be so hard," she said.

It was only later that she got angry. She despised this modern idea that everything was of equal value. Her family had been on this earth for 1,200 years. You just didn't kill its head and get away with it. It was unthinkable. It was equally impossible to explain this to the idiot across the desk. Even her brothers, who had chosen dull careers far removed from the law and the army, struggled to understand her.

* * *

She put the cardboard box and the sports bag on the dining table, opened the shutters, watered the pelargoniums in the window boxes, and scattered a handful of seeds on the bird table. Sometimes they would be eaten by the local sparrows, other times by the pigeons. She spent a moment looking at the red and deep blue sky above the black roofs, took a can of Coke from the fridge, and got down to work.

Many Cokes and nineteen Lucky Strikes later, Sabrina lay down on her bed and stared up at the ceiling.

At approximately 10 a.m. on September 5, 2007, Camorra killers had forced their way into Nanometric s.a. in Via Ippodromo in Milan, where they had shot the physicist Fabiano Batista, age sixty-three, in the head with a 9-mm pistol. Two burn marks from an electric stun gun were found on his neck. He had been paralyzed but conscious when he was executed, and it would appear that he had let his killers into the high-security building himself. The computer programmer, Paolo Iacovelli, age twenty-two, was shot twice through the heart while sitting on a chair in the kitchen. The ballistic report proved that the same pistol was used for both killings. The German chemist Hanna Schmidt, age twenty-eight, was killed by a single stab wound to her chest with a double-edged blade. The blade had severed the aorta, and death had followed a few seconds later.

The hard disk of the company's security cameras had been destroyed, as had the disks on all computers and servers. Two safes—one on the ground floor and one in Giulio Forlani's office on the first floor—had been opened with plastic explosives and emptied. The patent applications had been doused in gas and set on fire.

Giulio Forlani had been the victim of a staged traffic accident on the northbound A7 highway near the suburb of Assago at 9:45 a.m. The time had been verified by several eyewitnesses and a highway surveillance camera. Minutes before the crash Dr. Forlani had signed for a box of semiconductors at the General Electric dealer in Assago. The assassin had overtaken Giulio Forlani in a twenty-two-ton truck and had then braked hard in front of the Škoda Octavia, resulting in the violent collision. The wires between the brake pedal and the brake lights on the truck had been cut, and so Giulio Forlani hadn't realized it was braking. The assassin had proceeded to fire twice at close range at the badly injured physicist: once to his face and once to the right side of his chest. The assassin then had vaulted over the crash barriers that separated the northbound and southbound lanes and been picked up by a black BMW 320i. Both vehicles turned out to be stolen. Forlani was taken to the trauma center at the Ospedale Maggiore and pronounced dead at 6:15 p.m. after almost seven hours on the operating table. The head of the trauma team, Dr. Carlo Mazzaferro, had signed the death certificate himself.

Giulio Forlani's brother, Bruno Forlani, and his parents claimed the body, and Giulio was buried five days later in the family plot at Chiaravalle Cemetery south of Milan.

On the morning of September 5, Milan's most famous haute couture designer, Nanometric's main investor, and Giulio Forlani's good friend, Massimiliano Di Luca, had had a vague lunch appointment with Forlani at the restaurant Dal Pescatore. Forlani had never arrived, and Sabrina had read the testimony of Massimiliano Di Luca, which was detailed but not particularly helpful. The fashion designer had drunk a couple of martinis in the bar while he waited and studied the racing pages before giving up. His driver had then taken him from the restaurant to the San Siro racetrack, where he had spent the afternoon.

Sabrina inserted a CD from Galleria Vittorio Emanuele II into the computer and watched the grainy, blurred recordings from the two surveillance cameras in the shopping center on September 5, 2007, over and over again. She saw Lucia Forlani and her twelve-year-old son, Salvatore, step aside for a young couple with a stroller before entering an elevator on the ground floor. The doors had started to close when a man squeezed in at the last moment. She could see from behind that he was of medium height and was wearing a green oilskin jacket and dark pants. He had a cap on his head. Lucia Forlani had smiled at him, and he presumably had smiled back. Then he leaned forward and said something to her. Her smile disappeared. She staggered, and the man put his hand around her elbow to support her. Salvatore Forlani started to cry.

There could be no doubt about this: two cameras, one behind the till in a menswear shop on the other side of the shopping mall and one directly opposite the elevators, had recorded the incident. Sabrina played the recording at a slow speed, fast-forwarded it, and played it backward. She cut out sequences and viewed them in Photoshop, zooming in on the woman's face and what little she could see of the boy's.

If she had ever seen a smile of recognition, that was how Lucia Forlani had reacted when the man had entered the elevator.

She would have expected the trio to be picked up by the cameras that overlooked the café on the first floor, but they never arrived. In his report, the investigating officer had mentioned the possibility that cameras in the underground garage might have caught the boy, the woman, and the man. Those cameras, however, had been out of action by unfortunate chance or sabotage. Lucia Forlani, Salvatore, and the unknown man had vanished without a trace between three floors of one of the most frequented shopping centers in the world. An almost impossible achievement.

The officer had included a list of vehicles in the underground garage at the time of the abduction. Every owner had been interviewed with no result.

As the days and weeks passed, the tone of the reports grew increasingly despondent. The investigating officer had followed up even the most improbable theories, and Sabrina was impressed by his diligence. No one could find fault with the investigation.

Sabrina lit a couple of candles behind her bed and was holding a small strip of magic between her fingers. Thin, sharp, black, and bendy like celluloid. Half a centimeter wide and four centimeters long. The strip had fluttered down on her naked foot when she found Giulio Forlani's apparently empty wallet in a paper bag. On the paper bag was the name and address of a famous patisserie in Milan. She could still smell almond cake.

The magic ingredient was in the luminous green numbers and letters that could be read from any angle at which she viewed the strip:

WED 2010:09:08

That, as it happened, was today's day and date. The date was followed by a twelve-digit code. She had run a fingernail across the strip. The numbers and letters drifted apart but re-formed when she removed the pressure. It was extraordinary. She now started to understand the potential of the strip, not just for goods produced by the fashion industry but also for banknotes, DVDs, credit cards, passports, and driver's licenses. She imagined a yuppie on a rush-hour train in Rome or New York with a Prada bag and a date strip that displayed December 12, for example, at the height of summer. If the strip was sewn into or mounted on the relevant product, visible to anyone, with a date that changed at midnight like a clock, the combination would be unbeatable, and no fashion-conscious woman—or man—would ever risk exposing his or her expensive accessories as rip-offs.

She put the strip inside a copy of *Northanger Abbey* on her bedside table.

Forlani's wallet was covered in dried blood, and it had been emptied of photos, credit cards, driver's license, and banknotes, which undoubtedly had been handed over to his family. The wallet itself had been stored with his bloodstained clothes, shoes, and socks.

She poured the remaining contents of the gray sports bag out onto the floor; tiny fragments of glass from the Škoda's broken side windows sparkled like sugar crystals on Giulio Forlani's clothes. A dark blue anorak, socks stiff with congealed blood, a shirt that had once been blue, an enormous pair of moccasins, khaki pants cut from the cuffs to the belt loops, and black underpants. Sabrina picked up the shirt and poked her index finger through a sooty hole just the diameter of a fingertip high up on the right-hand side of the chest. A shot to the right lung, as the trauma doctor, Dr. Carlo Mazzaferro, had stated. This injury was in addition to multiple fractures, the gunshot wound to the head, internal bleeding, and two collapsed lungs.

Sabrina searched the pockets and cuffs without finding anything. Shards of glass from the Škoda pricked her fingertips. When she squeezed her fingers, tiny drops of blood appeared.

Federico Renda had requested the case files and Forlani's belongings from the various agencies in Milan that had divided up the investigation among them. It was as Sabrina had expected: no single coordinating officer or public prosecutor had previously looked at the case as a whole.

The forces of law and order in Italy were a battlefield for feuding intelligence services, departments, and police forces, each fiercely protective of its own privileges and mandates and engaged in a never-ending turf war. Her father had always advocated a centralized effort to fight organized crime like the FBI in America.

Perhaps that had been the real reason for his assassination.

She woke up at the sound of flapping wings and an excited cooing. She yawned, stretched, and discovered that she had fallen asleep fully dressed. Two pigeons were fighting over some seeds on the bird table. Sabrina took the last cigarette, lit it, scrunched up the pack, and threw it at the birds.

It was dawn, and the air was cool and clean. She finished smoking the cigarette, dropped the butt into a half-empty coffee cup, and pulled the comforter over her head.

that everyone hoped would last. The big conferences in the 1990s with the Cosa Nostra, the 'Ndrangheta, the Albanians, and the Ukrainians had put an end to costly and pointless strife. Urs Savelli had been a masterful negotiator for the Terrasino family, especially when it came to the Albanians.

Soon every decision in "the System" would be taken by well-dressed MBAs in air-conditioned meeting rooms. In another place and in a language other than Italian. Today most of the family's income came from legitimate waste-management firms, property companies, and farming that attracted generous grants from the European Union's Structural Funds. They had relocated practically all their bootleg factories to the Far East, just like legitimate businesses, to access the cheap, nonunionized, well-educated, and compliant labor in India, Taiwan, South Korea, Indonesia, and China. Countries only a mouse click away.

The age of the white containers was past. The wrecked container from the *Taixan* had been one of the last.

The nurse pushed Anna's wheelchair up to the open terrace doors. His wife could hear the birds and breathe in the scent of the flowers. He hoped that they would take her to a happy place.

She smiled when she saw him. She smiled at everyone.

Her eyes hadn't changed. They were still dark gray and bright even though they no longer reflected her soul. The Alzheimer's had eaten up Anna's mind. Like black snails devouring white mushrooms, he thought.

He kissed her cheek.

She smiled and moved her gaze to the pots of forsythia on the tiled terrace, but no transition was reflected in her eyes. Everything she saw these days had the same value.

The estate's staff knew that Don Francesco preferred silence and kept out of sight while the old man inspected his vines. He walked slowly while his brain calculated the position of the sun, the wind on his neck, and the humidity of the air: key factors. He opened the door to an ancient three-wheel scooter with a truck body, rolled up his

CHAPTER 6

Qualiano, Naples, the Estate of Francesco Terrasino

The nurse knocked politely on the door, but Don Francesco Terrasino already had heard her heels on the floor.

His fork hovered over the plate of ham and eggs, but he was no longer hungry. He was losing his appetite more with every passing day.

He opened the door to the gray-haired nurse.

"Can I see her now?" he asked.

"She has had a good sleep, signore," she said. "*La signora* has had a bath and eaten a little."

He followed her through a passage with a low ceiling to the living room and caught himself ducking under the door frame. When he and Anna had moved to the estate, the beam had been level with his forehead. Now he could pass under it with space above his head.

They passed a room that once had been the office of his closest adviser but now was used by his grandchildren when they came to stay. Don Francesco didn't mind. He had moved with the times. Today, his closest adviser was the senior partner in a major law firm in Rome and the family's accounts were handled by an international accountancy firm. The estate was no longer the headquarters of the Terrasino family. Feuding was over. They had entered a postwar era shirtsleeves, took a New York Giants baseball cap from the front seat, and put it on. He picked up a basket and walked over to the vegetable beds to select vegetables and fruit for today's dinner.

He weighed a bunch of Nebbiolo grapes in his hand but decided on another, picked a melon, and added eggplants, almonds, and nectarines to the basket.

He heard Savelli's footsteps on the gravel and turned around.

"Don."

"Urs. Welcome."

"How are you?"

"Well . . . very well, I think."

The old man offered him a bunch of grapes, but Savelli shook his head. He preferred his grapes at least five years old and in a bottle from an authorized Barolo producer.

"You should eat more fruit, Urs."

"I'll try," Urs Savelli said. "Your wife. How is *la signora*?"

The old man took off his cap and wiped his brow with the sleeve of his jacket.

"Her head is as empty as a drum. Perhaps she's happier than all of us."

Savelli nodded. "Perhaps."

They sat down on a bench shaded by the pergola. The two men couldn't have been more different: Don Francesco was thickset and weather-beaten, and Savelli was dark, lean, and sinister. Don Francesco had broad, skilled peasant hands, whereas Savelli's were slender and restless. Don Francesco Terrasino was always dressed in well-worn simple clothing, and Savelli preferred expensive black suits, shiny shoes, a crisp white shirt, and a dark tie. One spoke loudly and gesticulated eagerly, and the other whispered and let his eyes fill up the pauses.

The problem with these rare conversations was how to say the necessary without being specific. The bastards from the anti-Mafia unit, the ROS—Raggruppamento Operative Speciale—stuck to Don Francesco's lips like limpets wherever he went, with their blasted parabolic microphones, satellites, and drones, their lip readers and telephoto lenses, but within the walls of the estate, on his own land, it was still possible to speak openly.

Fortunately, the moves of the ROS were predictable. Their electronic gadgets would get them only so far. The art was to learn from the past. But the men and women in the ROS and the GIS were too young, too arrogant, and too lacking in imagination to understand that. The general, Baron Agostino D'Avalos, had been different. He had possessed the aristocrat's genuine respect for the peasant.

Savelli took out his cell and played the recordings from the white tents at the Vittorio Emanuele II Quay. The old man nodded.

"It's unfortunate," he said. "But does it matter? Everyone already knew."

"A random event," the Albanian said. "The container, I mean."

"It was an unfortunate coincidence. Most unfortunate," Don Francesco said.

Savelli nodded slightly and zoomed in on the last two names. Numbers 29 and 30.

"These two haven't been forgotten. Lucia and Salvatore Forlani. They've been identified. They were in the container."

The old man nodded. He had always had the strength to do what was necessary and to do it immediately. That ability had earned him a seat on the council; it had earned him the estate, status, and respect. Killing women and children would, however, always be a mortal sin.

He made the sign of the Cross, and his croaking voice broke.

"Is this really necessary, Urs. Now? It's been three years, hasn't it? Why do I have to think about them now?"

Savelli played the recording of Assistant Public Prosecutor Sabrina D'Avalos, unrecognizable in the blue suit, leaning over tray number 31, then easily recognizable, walking across the area between the containers on the quay. The pictures had been taken from one of the cranes at the port and from a considerable distance, but the quality was excellent. The assistant public prosecutor strode along, looking down at the tarmac. The sun bounced off her aviator sunglasses, and the camera had caught a glimpse of her nickel-plated pistol in its shoulder holster as she got into her car.

"Who is the woman?" Don Francesco asked.

"One of Federico Renda's young ones. She's in the NAC."

"Figlio di puttana," Don Francesco whispered quickly, as if the Albanian had spoken the name of the evil one.

He chewed a grape without tasting it, spit the seeds out into the palm of his hand, and flicked them on the ground behind the bench.

Savelli drew triangles in the gravel with the tip of his makila.

"She had a meeting with Renda two hours after she left the quay," he said. "We can only guess at the content of their conversation, of course, but I believe they talked about the woman and the boy. Incidentally, they're still in the Interior Ministry's witness protection program."

"Is she well connected?"

"She's the daughter of Baron D'Avalos, no less," Savelli said.

Don Francesco had to stand up. He walked over to a vine and tightened a wire loop to bring the stem closer to the post.

"How much does she know?" he asked.

"I'm not worried about her. She knows nothing, Don. There is nothing to know."

"Get someone to watch her, Urs. From a distance. You don't mess with a public prosecutor, you hear? Least of all her. That business with her father was bad enough. A sin. Like shooting the last elephant in the world," the capo said. "You destroyed everything in that office?"

"Of course."

"Good. Very, very good."

Don Francesco turned his faded green eyes on his captain.

"You don't kill a public prosecutor, Urs," he repeated.

Don Francesco constantly reiterated that the organization's new cause, its transformation, grew stronger with the passage of time. It was a simple message. They didn't need another martyr, a new Giovanni Falcone who would make the public rise up, turn over every sacred stone, test their frail alliances with emasculated and vain politicians in Rome, make young Vatican priests write thoughtless things on their blogs. Federico Renda was an isolated incident, and it had been purely a question of self-defense. Besides, he was from Naples and ought to have known better.

The Albanian didn't disagree with Don Francesco. The murder of General Agostino D'Avalos had been necessary, a means to an end. But the murder had caused a storm of protest and resulted in unprecedented political agreement to fight the Mafia. A tacit acceptance that retribution killings were carried out. This had meant new powers and resources for the ROS and the GIS. Leading figures in the Camorra, the 'Ndrangheta in Calabria, and the Corleone family in Sicily disappeared without a trace in the months that followed the general's death. Those killings continued until the leaders of the elite units managed to restore discipline.

"No idiots, Urs," the old man said.

Savelli straightened up and looked across the low yellow buildings to the white walls that enclosed the estate. As always the world—Naples—felt very far away. Here reigned the same timeless peace as in the mountains and the woods around his house in Orbara in the Basque countryside.

"I'll find a couple of men to follow her who aren't complete idiots."

Francesco Terrasino nodded. "I know it won't be easy," he said.

The Albanian smiled and stood up. He walked into the green shadows and disappeared.

It was so straightforward, Don Francesco thought. A masterstroke of simplicity. Savelli would open a trapdoor concealed under some empty feed sacks, climb down a ladder, and walk through the tunnel that stretched under the greenhouses, the outer wall, and the road outside. At the end of the tunnel, two hundred meters away, he would reach a door leading to the basement of an innocuous carpentry business. The carpenter was an old friend who sometimes would carry out work on the estate and who played cards with Don Francesco. There was a garage in the basement. Savelli would get into a van parked there and drive off.

CHAPTER 7

Sabrina packed quickly. Clothes, underwear, and toiletries were followed by her iPod, four identical cheap analog wristwatches, and an extra magazine for the Walther.

She sat for a long time holding her father's old short-barreled Colt .32 revolver before she put it in a side pocket of her sports bag. The holster was as soft as kid gloves and could be strapped around her ankle. This weapon was the only one of her father's personal possessions she had wanted after his death. The trigger of the revolver was as sensitive as a young woman's inner thigh—inasmuch as he could remember a young woman's inner thigh, her father used to say.

She swung the cylinder open and spun it. All the chambers were loaded except the last. The one that would lie under the hammer.

"Amazing. Very impressive."

Federico Renda was unaccustomed to uttering words of praise.

He found a magnifying glass in a desk drawer and subjected the black strip to fresh scrutiny.

Sabrina raised her hand to her mouth and yawned. Her eyelids kept closing in the quiet office.

"Three years," he said.

"The thing would appear to still work." She nodded.

"It's a miracle, Dottoressa D'Avalos, not a 'thing,'" the public prosecutor declared. "Where did you find it?"

"In a baker's bag."

"So you've received everything from Milan?"

"I think so. Thank you."

Renda twisted the small strip between his fingers.

"Perhaps it isn't totally indestructible, you know," she remarked.

"I'm sorry. Can I keep it?"

"I would rather you didn't."

"No . . . of course."

Reluctantly he pushed the strip across the desk; Sabrina picked it up between two nails and returned it to her purse.

"You're going to Milan?"

"Yes. I think I need to talk to the case officer from the witness protection program, Nestore Raspallo. If there is an error in the files, it should be corrected. Also, I would like to speak to Massimiliano Di Luca. Evidence suggests that Forlani and Di Luca were friends as well as business partners. They were photographed together on several occasions, including at Di Luca's home."

"Is he in Italy at the moment?"

"Yes."

"In his emporium in Via Alessandro Manzoni?"

"I presume so," she said. "He's launching his autumn collection shortly. I imagine he's being swept off his feet."

"Have you spoken to him? Made an appointment?"

"No."

Renda looked her up and down. He saw a scuffed light brown leather jacket, a gray T-shirt from the Naples zoo with a zebra on the chest, ripped jeans, and old sneakers.

"You'll be shot before you even get through the revolving door in that outfit."

"I've packed a change of clothes," she said. "Smart clothes."

"Even so, I'll call ahead," Renda said. "Is twelve noon tomorrow good for you?"

"You can do that?"

"I know someone who can," he assured her.

"Thank you. And another thing."

"Yes?"

"Did anyone take over the project? Did Camera Nazionale and Massimiliano Di Luca hire new scientists to carry on the work of Batista and Forlani?"

Renda nodded and made a note on a pad.

"That's a fair question, dottoressa," he said. "I'll look into it."

"Thank you. Dr. Raimondo Sapienza called me this morning . . . at a quarter past six. They have found lesions on the boy's throat that suggest he was garroted. His mother was shot in the chest, twice. The bullet holes were close, neat and professional. One of the slugs is well preserved. I would like . . ."

Renda leaned across the desk. Partly to ease his aching back, partly to study Sabrina more closely. He knew that she was intelligent and that she put in a lot of overtime at the Palace of Justice, that she was tenacious and apparently fearless—and that she was one of the first aristocratic staff members—but then, all his assistant public prosecutors were stubborn and uncompromising. It was a job requirement. Besides, his young staff's role models were practically unattainable: Giovanni Falcone, Paolo Borsellino, Chinnici, and Casson. The golden generation. Heroes and martyrs. But perhaps Sabrina D'Avalos really was something special. The GIS instructors who had been responsible for her advanced physical and military training seemed to think so. At the first confrontation with one of the GIS's barrel-chested close-combat instructors, the slender woman had managed to break the instructor's jaw and inflict severe bruising to his genitals. No one had ever seen anything like it. She had walked away without a scratch.

Sabrina D'Avalos's eyes studied the floor with their usual intensity.

"We ought to compare the 9-mm bullet from Lucia Forlani with the ones found in Paolo Iacovelli and Fabiano Batista," she said.

"I fail to see the connection," he said. "Lucia and Salvatore Forlani were abducted from Galleria Vittorio Emanuele II at the exact same time as the attack on Nanometric—and at the same time as the murders of Iacovelli and Professor Batista."

"There's no connection if one assumes that Lucia Forlani was killed on the day she was abducted," she conceded. "But it's just an assumption. No one knows for sure."

Renda looked at her.

"You're right, and I'm tired. It's an automatic subconscious assumption, as you say. I'll see to it."

"Thank you. I have another and final request, dottore. Something personal."

"A last request? That sounds serious."

"Just a wish, then, if you prefer."

Renda inflated his cheeks and let the air escape in a thin, controlled stream.

"What might that be?"

Sabrina told him.

When she had finished, she looked at him closely.

"If that's what you really want," he said.

"It is."

Renda nodded and looked into the distance.

"You want to start in Milan?"

"That was my plan."

"Perhaps you should consider stopping off in Castellarano. Form your own impressions," he said.

Sabrina raised an eyebrow. "Why on earth would I want to do that?"

"Why? It's almost on your way." He smiled. "It was where Lucia Forlani grew up. Where Giulio Forlani's family spent their summer holidays. His mother was born there. Perhaps they met each other in Castellarano. It's the start of everything. In this case, I mean."

"I thought you said there was no case."

Renda smiled again. He had spent his life in courtrooms, and no one, least of all a green assistant public prosecutor, would ever catch him in a contradiction.

"I was being kind, dottoressa."

CHAPTER 8

Castellarano, Reggio Emilia, Northern Italy

The small town rested on a slope under a pure blue sky with a river that wound through the low brown mountains like a green ribbon. The birthplace of Lucia Forlani. The city wall embraced the sand-colored houses. Sabrina had parked the Opel in the almost empty garage outside the tourist office. She walked under an archway and felt momentarily disoriented in the confusion of small streets behind the city wall.

It was outside the tourist season, and she wandered across piazzas where most of the cafés were boarded up. Chairs and tables were stacked, secured with long chains and padlocks; parasols were leaning against walls; the foliage of the plane trees had started to wither and drop. The leaves lay still on the cobblestones in this strangely airless town. She passed a small medieval castle with a hexagonal tower that she, with the help of a tourist brochure, identified as the Castle of Countess Mathilde. One of the Medicis. Everything was well cared for, in good condition, freshly painted and clean. There was no rubbish in the streets, no graffiti on the walls. It was hard to believe that Naples and this little town were in the same country. This place could have been in Switzerland.

She walked through a labyrinth of narrow streets where women with all the time in the world sat on doorsteps or white plastic chairs. They greeted her with a nod and a smile. Sabrina smiled and nodded until her jaw started to ache. Most shops were dark and deserted. Even the "For Sale" signs were faded and tattered. A few shops survived by selling regional culinary specialties and the usual rustic tourist junk.

The streets started to climb upward. The cobbles had been laid in wide, shallow steps, and she could see the sky open up ahead. She reached a park from which she could get an overview of the river and the mountains and a bit of a breeze.

Sabrina had the park to herself. She walked past a long washing trough carved out of granite. A jet of water spouted from the mouth of a crusader, and golden leaves whirled on the black surface of the water. She sat down on a marble bench and surveyed the soaring towers, walls, and battlements of Castellarano's famous convent school. Behind the convent lay a wide green common, the playing fields alive with tiny figures playing lacrosse or soccer or sprinting around the orange surface of the running track.

Lucia Forlani—or Lucia Maletta, as she then was—once had run around down there, Sabrina thought. She probably had strived for academic and sporting excellence. She knew that the convent school was one of the most desirable south of the Alps and that its students came mainly from Europe's wealthiest families, but 20 percent of each year's intake was made up of poor or orphaned girls who passed the entrance exam and were found deserving by a selection committee. The scholarship covered the cost of tuition, books, clothes, pocket money, board, and lodging. Lucia Forlani had been one of the lucky ones. Depending on how you looked at it.

Sabrina pressed the palms of her hands against the cold marble of the bench and raised her face toward the sun. She closed her eyes and let herself sink into the sunlight, listening to the distant sounds from the playing fields and the rustling of leaves across the cobblestones.

"Excuse me . . . ?"

The tall woman was watching her with a smile. She gestured toward the bench, and Sabrina moved up.

"Thank you."

The woman sat down. She placed her shopping bag between her feet and stretched out her arms toward the sun for a moment. She lifted her face and closed her eyes. The woman was slim and well built, probably in her early forties with gray in her curly dark brown hair. Her skin was smooth, golden, and healthy. She wore no jewelry. Her slate-gray dress was simple, and she had a thin woolen cardigan over her shoulders.

The woman found a brown paper bag in her shopping bag and pushed back the paper to reveal a bunch of blue grapes, which she offered to Sabrina.

She took a couple and ate them slowly.

"You're not from here, signora," the woman said.

"Signorina. No, I'm from Milan, but I work in Naples."

The other woman held out her hand.

"Antonia Moretti."

"Sabrina."

The woman smiled with a hint of pity. "Naples . . ."

Sabrina laughed. "I know what you're thinking, signora. I do. But even Naples has its good points. You just have to try harder to find them."

"I'm sorry. I didn't mean to . . ."

"Are you from Castellarano, signora?"

"I've lived here all my life. Or rather in an old grocer's shop just outside the town. It was my parents' shop. It's closed now. The traffic was diverted from the old road that went through the town to a big new ring road, and they built supermarkets along that road that are more convenient, it would seem."

She held out the bag again.

Sabrina took a few more grapes and stood up.

"Thank you, signora. Time for me to go."

"To Milan? You're going home?"

"Yes."

"Drive safely."

"Thanks for the grapes."

The woman smiled.

She had come straight from the undertaker's.

CHAPTER 9

The face under the hands of Antonia Moretti was a perfect oval, the features of the seventeen-year-old girl beautiful; nothing defining her character had developed under the smooth skin yet.

Above the white terry band following the girl's hairline, her black hair was matte and fragrant, and the silk under her neck was damp.

At the electric organ, Signorina Lombardi smiled and her down-at-the-heel shoes tapped out a simple rhythm from a dancing school long since sold. The organist had mastered the art of sleeping and sitting upright at the same time. Antonia pulled a sable-hair makeup brush from the bun at the nape of her neck, dipped it in the second square from the top on the palette, and traced the color from the bridge of the girl's nose over her cheekbones, from her chin over her cheeks and jawline, from her throat to her collarbone, from her finely plucked eyebrows to the hair band, and her face lit up; it almost came alive.

She hesitated. The reason was the multitude of holes in the girl's nostrils and earlobes. The corresponding studs, twisted silver rings, and beetle-black enameled pendants with yellow runes and symbols of rebellion lay untouched on the table. Her boyfriend, who had survived the crash, wanted the jewelry reinstated, and Antonia had wedged his proffered photo inside the coffin lid between the white silk and the oak, above the mirror that collected light from the lamp and showed her the far side of the girl's face.

Antonia looked at Enzo in the mirror. Her eccentric lodger sat in the back pew of the chapel of rest like a piece of driftwood. He usually accompanied her to Ugo Conti's firm of undertakers as if he didn't quite trust her to handle the emotions or didn't quite know what she did, whereas he was an expert on all matters relating to death. She didn't remember ever asking him, wishing for it, or giving permission. As usual, Enzo had enforced his will through deaf-eared brute stubbornness. Like certain children, he heard only what he wanted to hear.

Her lodger usually would daydream in his pew until Antonia had finished with the deceased. Then Enzo would leave the chapel by a side door before the mourners entered.

The boyfriend's photo showed the girl riding pillion on a yellow motorcycle, smiling triumphantly at the photographer. But the smile didn't reach the soft corners of her mouth, and the expression in her eyes didn't match the short tomato-red hair flattened and tousled by the black crash helmet on her lap.

Antonia restored collapsed nuances behind the cheekbones and under the jawline with powder, traced concealer to the corners of the eyes with the tip of her finger, and closed the girl's lips with a strip of Velcro. And froze at the sight of the parents' photo, which was next in line.

As in almost every one of these tragedies, the parents' suggestion was a posed photograph from the girl's Communion, taken in Matteo Rivolti's studio in Via San Michele, where the town's well-off citizens would go when their children were baptized, confirmed, or married.

Amalia Nesta wasn't smiling in this picture; the lower half of her face was obscured by the frilly collar of the white dress. Innocence embalmed.

She glanced up at the mirror. Enzo appeared to have fallen asleep.

* * *

The undertaker's wide back filled the space between the double doors that swung open with a squeak, which in turn woke up Signorina Lombardi. She raised her hands to strike a suitable elegiac chord, but Antonia shook her head.

"Antonia, Antonia . . . they're waiting. We're all waiting. Even poor Signorina Lombardi is waiting. Look at her, the poor woman. And the girl; she's not the Mona Lisa, is she? That's not what they're paying for. Not the Mona Lisa, Antonia. That's not what they're getting."

Up close, the undertaker looked as if he were carved out of African ebony. Ugo Conti was broader and darker than the men from the highlands around Castellarano.

He removed the big black glasses that matched a heavy, bluish lower face and dabbed his cheeks, eyes, and lips with a handkerchief. He looked only at Antonia—the firm's perfectionist prima donna—completely ignoring the meek Signorina Lombardi and the huge silent man in the back pew: Signora Moretti's strange pet.

"But she is, Ugo . . . That's exactly what she is," Antonia said.

"The father wants to murder the boy," Ugo said. "He blames him for everything. For the accident."

"I understand," Antonia said.

The undertaker stiffened.

"Antonia . . . pardon me, but you don't. You don't know what you're talking about. Now what are you doing?!"

The undertaker raised his hands as if he physically wanted to stop Antonia as she removed every trace of makeup from the dead girl's face with cleansing wipes. She took the boyfriend's and the parents' photos and handed them to Ugo. The jewelry followed suit. All of it.

Only one photo remained in the lid of the coffin.

"Silence, Ugo. Let me work in peace. *Per favore*. She's old enough to be herself now. She doesn't belong to everybody else."

In the mirror she received a nod of approval from Enzo. A faint smile in his beard. Perhaps she was imagining it. Enzo Canavaro was not a man who allowed himself to be easily read. It was as if most expressions had long since been washed from his lean, sinister face.

The girl's younger sister had slipped the bent photo into Antonia's hand when her parents' attention was momentarily distracted by the undertaker. The face of the dead girl in the photograph reflected the sun and the sea by the railings on a summer ferry. The angle showed the older sister looking up through the lens of a disposable camera. It had captured her smile and a glint in the eye that wasn't just a squint against the sun. The expression was genuine and natural.

Antonia's brushes instinctively found the right shades: the colors of a summer day; a smoky blue, like the water in the wake of the Adriatic ferry, was dabbed on the upper eyelid, and a blue eyeliner a shade lighter was applied to the edge of the lower lid.

Ugo Conti held his breath as he followed the last strokes that transformed the girl, that interpreted her far beyond her parents' or her boyfriend's restricted and irreconcilable expectations.

He clapped his hands together and breathed a sigh of relief. As he hastened toward the anteroom, he snapped his fingers at the right ear of Signorina Lombardi as if she were under hypnosis.

Enzo left.

The double doors opened to let in the mourners.

The girl's boyfriend limped to a chair on the left of the central aisle while the little family sat down to the right. The boyfriend was in pain; Antonia could see that. The muscles in his neck were tense, his lips bloodless. The little sister's face was soft and mournful, the father's was grave, and the mother was slowly strangled in the never-ending grip of grief.

Signorina Lombardi's crooked fingers worked their way through Ravel's *Pavane pour une Infante Défunte*, and Antonia, who had heard the piece far too many times before, felt the familiar tightening in her chest.

After her efforts, Signorina Lombardi's hands came to rest in the narrow lap of her dress. Very slowly Ugo Conti lifted his head and gestured for the family to come up to the podium. Close to the dead seventeen-year-old, it was impossible not to be deeply moved. Her face glowed against the silk. Deeply introspective and already in the next world. Recognizable but dragged there by force.

"My daughter," the mother said, at last pressing her face into her husband's shoulder. "She is sleeping. My daughter is sound asleep."

She kissed her hair and looked at Antonia.

The sister stood on tiptoe and placed a small bouquet of wild-flowers on the girl's chest.

"Good-bye, Amalia," she whispered.

The father's face darkened when he saw the injured boy, yet it was he who stepped aside and held out his hand.

The boyfriend got his minute by the coffin.

On the steps outside the chapel Ugo Conti watched the Nesta family drive past the white lion statue down by the road.

"You've done it again, Antonia! Forgive me for ever doubting you. It was just that the situation seemed so—well, so impossible. Deadlocked, I thought. The boy. The father. I don't know what to say. You brought them together!"

Antonia looked past him, across the small lawn, across the street and the row of houses on the other side.

Behind the houses, unseen, the river warbled.

"I forgive you," she muttered drily.

She made a point of looking at her watch, and Ugo remembered the envelopes in his inside pocket. Signorina Lombardi curtsied, sent Antonia a smile, took her walking stick, and walked away down the cobbled stones on the drive.

Antonia didn't stop to open Conti's envelope until she had rounded the corner. She counted the money and transferred the bills to her purse. She glanced sideways to Enzo, who was watching her silently with the loyal melancholy of a Saint Bernard. He took her bag, and together they walked down Via Fuori Ponti, above which the sky looked newly washed and where the sun cast shadows under the barred window openings. You could sharpen a knife on those shadows.

Enzo Canavaro never got lost in Castellarano's maze of small narrow streets, though he claimed never to have visited the town previously. He simply had turned up at her house one evening and asked to move in. Antonia and her fourteen-year-old son, Gianni, had heard a motorcycle pull up in the courtyard a few minutes earlier. She had converted her parents' old grocery into a kind of B and B, but weeks passed between visitors. He hadn't asked for a room for the night. He had asked if he could live there. Gianni had looked imploringly at his mother, but Antonia had ignored him.

The man had smiled shyly. He had stood precisely—and apparently by intuition—where the diagonals of the floorboards marked what once had been the layout of the shop. He had set down a bag stuffed to the brim beside one of his big black boots. His coat resembled a tent with sleeves, and his wild black beard reached down to its third button.

He smelled of the cold, deep ocean.

She had walked ahead of him up the squeaking staircase and opened the door to the three small interconnecting rooms. The man, who said his name was Enzo Canavaro, seemed delighted with them. He sent her a grateful smile when he closed the door behind him after paying her one month's rent in advance.

Crackling new euro banknotes that Antonia didn't bank for a long time.

Neither Gianni nor Antonia got much sleep that first night with Enzo in the house. The new lodger moved around above their heads for hours, and the next morning she found a long line of dust on her comforter. His hobbling footsteps were interspersed with deep groans, a strangled sobbing, and noises that sounded as if he were rearranging the furniture or indeed the walls. Gianni came into his mother's room, where he sat for a long time, rocking in a chair, pressing his hands against his ears.

"Mom, you have to get rid of him," he pleaded.

"Tomorrow," she promised.

The next morning a well-rested, neatly combed, and relaxed Enzo Canavaro, wearing a garish Australian T-shirt, had proudly shown her how he had aligned the double bed exactly along the east–west meridian. It was better for sleeping, he assured her. Lined up like the boats that sailed back and forth between the fishing grounds of Flemish Cap and Grand Banks.

He broke off suddenly as if he had said something inappropriate and stared down at the floor.

"Are you a sailor?" she asked, and the huge man nodded.

"I used to fish, but not anymore."

"My boy goes to school, Enzo," she said. "He needs his sleep. As do I. You have to be quiet at night or do your walking in the fields if you want to stay here. Otherwise you'll have to go."

He had held up his massive, chafed hands in total surrender.

He promised.

And he had kept his promise for almost two years now.

First the butcher and now the supermarket. She put a bottle of wine back on the shelf after debating whether to buy it.

The big man looked at her and her shopping bag when she came outside.

"No wine?"

"No, Enzo. No wine today. There is gnocchi with tomato sauce, water, and bread. I've got no money. There is no work for me. Italians no longer want to be beautiful. Neither the living nor the dead. Joanna, the hairdresser, says the same."

Enzo nodded gravely.

"I can pay more," he offered.

"You pay enough as it is. More than enough."

"Less?"

"No, no, no! Certainly not."

They walked down Via Don Reverberi and Via Chiaviche, narrow cobbled streets that once had been like a Middle Eastern casbah with dazzling textures of fabrics, brocades, leather of all colors, enamel, shoes, and bags. Where the sounds of looms and sewing machines on warm evenings—until the stars were high in the sky—once had poured from every doorway. In the narrow rooms you could see lines of women, their damp faces and shoulders hunched over endless rolls of fabric. You could hear their singing and complaining. The rivers of glittering fabric and tanned leather that once had run through Castellarano to Fendi, Valentino, Versace, and Armani in Milan had dried up in the little mountain town and resurfaced in bootleg factories in Asia.

As was their habit, they stopped at the bottom of the street leading to the small park. Antonia Moretti needed half an hour to herself when she had finished at the undertaker's.

"I'm going home," he said.

"Tell Gianni to do his homework and practice his cornet."

"Of course," he said.

He sent her a brief smile by way of good-bye and limped down the street. He moved like a man thirty years his senior. He once had told her there was more metal in him than in most cars.

She spotted a young woman on her favorite marble bench. The woman was pressing her palms against the seat and had turned her face to the sun. When she came closer, Antonia could see several deep scars on the woman's forehead and cheekbones. She didn't notice Antonia until she cleared her throat. Her eyes were hidden behind mirrored aviator sunglasses, but she smiled and moved politely.

Antonia sat down, exchanged a few words with the woman, and offered her some of the blue grapes.

The woman had a pleasant voice, quick and sure movements, and a calm expression. She also had a nickel-plated pistol in a shoulder holster, Antonia Moretti noted with some surprise.

The visitor rose after thanking her for the grapes and left the park. Antonia's eyes followed her. The woman skipped down the stone steps of Via Kennedy.

CHAPTER 10

The E35 to Milan

Sabrina had gone past Parma; the traffic flowed smoothly, there was no roadwork, and she had 1980s hits on her iPod. She sang along to Cock Robin's "Just Around The Corner," beating out the rhythm with her palms on the steering wheel, chewed gum, and thought about nothing much. It was one o'clock, and she had plenty of time to drop off her bags at her mother's before going on to the Palace of Justice in Corso di Porta Vittoria and seeing Nestore Raspallo at four o'clock. Raspallo's office address and position weren't listed in official databases or telephone directories. Perhaps Raspallo, like James Bond, was an inherited pseudonym. One of Federico Renda's secretaries had set up the meeting, and she had forbidden Sabrina to make any written notes of the details.

There were no troubling noises coming from her old car, but some were starting to come from her—sounds she initially chose to ignore. Her gaze started to wander from the side mirrors to the rearview mirror, and the scars on her forehead started to itch, something they hardly ever did. She dropped the iPod between the pedals and nearly hit the crash barrier when she bent down to retrieve it, listening to a fast, regular throbbing noise until she established that it was the pulse in her neck.

A large green Fiat van kept appearing in her mirrors.

When she reached a Shell gas station between Castione Marchesi and San Rocco, she was certain. She was being followed.

NAC members had to complete a course in defensive driving before being accepted into the new unit, and Sabrina, along with a handful of other young lawyers, police officers, and Carabinieri, had spent two weeks at a disused airport driving battered cars down runways, doing hand brake turns, and shooting through the windows of the car while driving at speed at disks that would pop up from concrete trenches along the runway. They also learned to interpret traffic patterns, especially patterns indicating that you might be being followed. The pursuers' standard formation was a square where the car was tailed by two vehicles, whether two-, three-, or four-wheeled. Two other vehicles, making up the top corners of the square, would be in front ready to anticipate and follow any spontaneous exits or sudden acceleration that the person in question—such as a desperate assistant public prosecutor—might consider executing. The trick was to ignore the square until a safe option to escape presented itself— or to feign ignorance and exploit the presence of the pursuers for your own purposes.

Sabrina pulled in at the gas station.

She parked the Opel in a queue of cars waiting for the car wash, where it would be watched by other drivers, and went into the shop to pay for a wash, which included a hosing down of the undercarriage—an excellent precaution if you suspected that it might be infected with electronic tracking devices—then went to the ladies' toilet with her shoulder bag. Inside a cubicle she unzipped the bag and strapped the holster with the Colt .32 around her ankle.

She carefully scanned her surroundings as she walked back to the car wash. The waiting or departing cars, trucks, motorcycles, and camper vans didn't stand out from those found at any other highway service station in Europe. No one was watching her, and she couldn't see the green van anywhere.

Sabrina stayed in the car while it was washed and used the privacy to search the inside with her flashlight between her teeth. Nothing. She closed her eyes, slumped back into the seat, shook the steering wheel, and screamed at the top of her voice.

CHAPTER 11

Milan

Staying with her mother in Via Salvatore Barzilai was now out of the question, so she drove around the center of Milan for an hour until she found a suitable hotel: a small *pensione* called Albergo Merlin in Via Durini whose facilities had been awarded a gloomy one star by the ministry of tourism. The street was cobbled, and the old-fashioned streetlights were set far apart. The place was within walking distance of the Palace of Justice and offered guest parking in the courtyard in front of the entrance, directly overlooked by the reception area.

A receptionist with a comb-over and a yellow nylon shirt open at the neck over a gray vest looked up at her without interest. He livened up a little when she explained that she wanted to book two double rooms for three nights, one overlooking the courtyard and the other the street, preferably no higher than the first floor, *per favore*. Sabrina told him that she didn't like heights.

"Are you expecting anyone, signora?"

He turned off his television under the counter and started looking for the keys.

"My husband and children will be arriving from Palermo tomorrow," she chirped happily. "Your hotel has special memories for us, signore. We're from Naples, and your hotel was where my husband and I stayed when we visited Milan for the first time. We were *very* young!"

She giggled bashfully.

The receptionist, who thought that *la signora* was still incredibly young, followed her gaze around the lobby as if seeing it for the first time. Then he smiled feebly.

"Aha . . . in that case, welcome back, signora."

"Thank you. Is breakfast included?"

The receptionist looked at her.

"No, sorry. I mean . . . we don't do breakfast."

"Never mind. I'll take them."

She smiled warmly.

The rooms were shabby but clean. A sheet of white chipboard with countless cigarette burns served as a kind of desk. She moved it away from the window and looked down. The Opel was sitting alone in the courtyard. Perfect.

The time was 3:10 p.m.

Before she entered the room facing Via Durini, she switched off the light in the corridor. The curtains were heavy and shut out the light when she closed them. She put a chair by the window, eased the curtain back, and looked up and down the narrow street. A hundred meters away, a large green van pulled up along the curb. In the windscreen was the reflected glare of the sun, so she couldn't see how many people were inside. She waited ten minutes, but no one got out of the van. She made a note of the registration number and got up.

One so far. There were bound to be more, and again her pulse started beating hard and fast in her temple.

She took a shower and then persuaded the receptionist to show her a way out through the grid of narrow courtyards behind the guesthouse. The GPS function on her BlackBerry had shown her that she should be able to reach the parallel street, Corso Europa, without having to walk through the archway to Via Durini—and the green van.

*   *   *

"Lucia and Salvatore Forlani have been found and identified?"

"Yes."

"Extraordinary. Are you quite sure?" asked Nestore Raspallo.

Sabrina didn't stop smiling.

"Absolutely."

The civil servant leaned back. "Delighted to hear it. Excellent news . . . I mean . . . all things considered."

She looked at the case officer. At his pale blue Oxford button-down shirt, the polka dot red-and-blue bow tie, and the well-fitting gray jacket. Under the table she could see a pair of elegant suede shoes. Raspallo didn't look a day over thirty. Far too young to carry the weight of so many lives on his tweed-clad shoulders.

Raspallo nodded pensively as he studied the empty desk in front of him. Eventually it began to dawn on him that his visitor from Naples was expecting more than thanks.

"Thank you for briefing me, dottoressa. I'll make sure the databases are updated."

He made to get up.

"My father created your job ten years ago, Signor Raspallo," she said without moving.

He sat down again, held up his hands, and started to examine the armrests.

"I'm aware of that. A great man. Much missed. But times have changed."

"Have they?"

"Yes. All procedures were reviewed when your father . . . was killed."

"Was murdered."

Raspallo nodded.

"When your father was murdered. I don't think you can blame anyone, signorina, if there were fears that before his death the general may have given away . . . revealed . . ."

"He was shot, Signor Raspallo. No one kept him prisoner in a basement for days, torturing him, pumping him full of scopolamine or some other truth serum. There was no sign of a struggle at the crime scene," she said. "None at all."

Raspallo smiled gently.

"I'm fully aware of the circumstances. In detail. We all are. But my job is purely to administer various bank accounts around the world. Bank accounts I don't even know the details of. Everything is encrypted, dottoressa." He paused. "Doubly encrypted," he added. "I don't know the location of the witnesses or their at-risk relatives, and likewise the ROS case officers have no idea where the money supporting the witnesses comes from."

Sabrina looked around the bare office. There wasn't a single sheet of paper or a ring binder to be seen. There was a laptop in front of Signor Raspallo—that was all.

"It's a highly successful program," the civil servant said.

"I understand. And Giulio Forlani?"

Raspallo watched her in silence.

He lowered his voice and folded his hands as if in prayer. It appeared that he was coming to a decision.

"Can I tell you something and be absolutely certain that you won't reveal your source? Ever. Not to anyone? It would cost me my career."

Sabrina nodded.

"As a mark of respect to your father. Please don't think that he has been forgotten. Definitely not. I myself had the honor of meeting him on several occasions when I started in the GIS."

"You were in the GIS?"

Sabrina had a hard time visualizing this well-dressed, sleek, clean-shaven young man as a member of the elite unit, wearing a ski mask and night-vision goggles, rappelling down vertical cliff sides, dangling from a parachute at night with foreign soil under his boots, or swimming long stretches underwater toward a secret rendezvous with only a compass for guidance. The man wore a bow tie, for heaven's sake!

Even she could hear the disbelief in her voice.

"I'm sorry," she said.

Raspallo shrugged his shoulders in a friendly gesture.

"Don't worry. Nanometric's research was funded by two independent sources . . . as you probably know."

"The EU and the Camera Nazionale della Moda Italiana." She nodded.

"That's only partly true," Raspallo said, and found an interesting spot on the desk that appeared to warrant closer scrutiny.

"Go on," she urged him.

The young man looked toward the door as if he expected armed men to kick it in and arrest him at any moment.

"Your father *was* the EU, signorina," he said slowly and clearly. "Giulio Forlani had applied to the European Union's Structural Funds for money and been turned down. The main reason was that Nanometric didn't have official business partners in other EU countries. Your father believed the work of Nanometric had enormous potential . . . and he believed in Giulio Forlani as an individual."

"They knew each other?" she gasped. "My father and Forlani? Are you sure?"

"Definitely. Somehow General D'Avalos managed to divert funding from an account in the Ministry of Defense to Nanometric. The company described the money as an EU grant. The paperwork was in order. This scheme operated successfully for years under the radar of the Public Accounts Office and the Ministry of Finance."

Raspallo smiled.

"Your father was a very secretive man, dottoressa. He used to say that he knew where all the bodies were buried. He still had the shovel somewhere. He said."

"My father must have trained you," she declared as her thoughts flew homeless through her brain. "Since you know so much."

Raspallo nodded. "It was a privilege."

"Thank you," she muttered.

"Your father was killed a few days after the Nanometric massacre," Raspallo said.

"It has crossed my mind that the two events might have been connected," she assured him. "But timing is all they have in common,

Signor Raspallo. As far as I know . . . But perhaps you know more than I do."

"I don't think so. As you say, it was purely a coincidence."

General Agostino D'Avalos was found in a motel near Val-malenco Laghetto in Alto Adige, close to the Swiss border. The general had rented one of the motel's remote cabins under a false name. He would appear to have arrived at the cabin alone in his own Range Rover. The car was parked outside the cabin and untouched. He was found fully dressed in the middle of the living-room floor, killed by two bullets from a 9-mm pistol. Every forensic test had proved negative. None of the motel's other guests had seen or heard anything. The time of death was put at 00:30, three days after the attack at Nanometric.

"Did my father enter Forlani into the MIPTP? But why, if he was already dead? People are asking questions. Including my boss, the public prosecutor, Federico Renda."

"I don't know. And I don't know if anyone does. All programs and procedures were reviewed afterward, as I've just told you. They put together a fast-track committee and followed its guidelines. The FBI assisted the committee. I myself only joined the program a year ago. I'm sorry. But I can understand why people are asking questions. Absolutely."

"Can you make an educated guess?"

"Sadly, no."

She rose.

"Please, could you check a van registration number for me?"

"Of course."

The green Fiat van that had followed her to the *pensione* in Via Durini turned out to belong to a builder in Portici, a small town south of Naples.

Raspallo didn't ask, and Sabrina didn't explain.

He stood up and shook her hand. He was taller and leaner than she had expected.

"Happy hunting," he said.

"Arrivederci."

*   *   *

From the window the case officer watched Sabrina D'Avalos walk down the broad steps of the Palace of Justice.

She might think she was ready to take on Urs Savelli, the Lord of the Camorra, but to Raspallo she seemed as helpless as a newborn kitten.

The petite figure stopped on the bottom step and looked up the facade, and he took a step back. She continued out between the barriers in front of the palace and disappeared.

He picked up the telephone and rang the rarely used direct line to Federico Renda. If Raspallo had ever seen a person on a mission, it was Sabrina D'Avalos.

He exchanged a few words with Renda, opened a cupboard, took the envelope that had been waiting for him, and rushed out.

CHAPTER 12

Castellarano

On Via Ludovico Ariosto, Antonia walked past the hedge to the municipal swimming pool and changing rooms behind which every fourteen-year-old girl in Castellarano kissed a boy for the first time. In Antonia's case it was Bruno, a demigod who visited the town every summer with his twin brother, Giulio, and their parents. Their mother was from Castellarano, their father American. It didn't bother her that Bruno marked the wall with a piece of chalk for each girl he kissed. She considered herself lucky. She had removed his politely attentive hands from her breasts and rewarded him for not persisting by opening her mouth against his so that her tongue bumped into his teeth and the lump of chewing gum behind them. Her knees and hips had trembled when his tongue found hers. The chlorine smell from the pool evoked memories of Bruno Forlani's twin, Giulio, in seclusion on a green towel near the edge of the pool. He had watched her as she came around the corner, and she had no trouble looking him in the eye. But he lowered his gaze when Bruno appeared.

The outside of the shop bore witness to centuries of groceries. As the years passed, painted advertisements for long-since-discontinued household articles remained, worn away. The words "Barzoni Pasta" were illustrated by a potbellied glutton under a tilted plate piled high with spaghetti, Bertolli olive oil was advertised by white fish sizzling to their doom on a black frying pan, and Olio Sasso was shown with torn white clouds and a windswept olive tree. The olive tree, the oldest image, would be the last wall painting to fade.

Even though the traffic today was led around the town on Strada Statale 486, the old road hadn't been completely forgotten. From Sassuolo to Torrente Dragone it wound its way through the heart of the town before running between her parents' shop and La Stazione restaurant. The memory of truck drivers turned out to be longer than that of the town's housewives, who had stopped coming to the shop, as La Stazione was still a popular place to eat.

The rooms were empty and quiet; from her son Gianni's room a guttural, breathless song could be heard.

The noise that Antonia identified as Balkan rap came from the old shortwave radio. Enzo had sourced antique radio valves for it from Rome and sanded and polished its mahogany cabinet until it shone like a japanned piano, all for Gianni's fifteenth birthday. On a good day the radio could pick up Montevideo and Moscow thanks to a five-meter-high aerial Enzo had mounted on the chimney, his boots dancing delicately on the loose roof tiles. A remarkable achievement from someone who could only turn his head slightly to the left. The bandwidth marker was tuned to some unholy place between Bratislava and Tirana, so she switched off the apparatus, picked up Gianni's gray school blazer from the floor, dusted it down, and hung it over a chair. The dark blue school pants had been tossed over an empty music stand, and the cornet case sat forgotten under the bed.

Antonia opened the kitchen window facing the courtyard and heard her son's and Enzo's voices drifting through the garage doors. From the window she had a view of the rest of the property: the cobblestone courtyard permanently overgrown with weeds, the boundary wall on top of which the family cat dozed in the sun, the garden with a few ancient apple trees, and the greenhouse with its broken ridge.

One summer Antonia and her husband, Tancredo, had fallen in love with the idea of growing their own vegetables. They had cultivated the high beds in the greenhouse with ridiculously small gardening tools and had sown eggplants, peas, zucchini, and tomatoes. They worked in the greenhouse while Tancredo grew thinner and paler until he was as transparent as the white painted windows. The vegetables thrived while her husband wasted away. A few months later he died from cancer.

What remained were brown stems, spiders, and the knowledge that they had had projects instead of each other. Tancredo had been in charge of matters of the heart, and Antonia of their other dreams.

She leaned out of the window and heard Enzo holding forth: "It's the little things, my friend. If you're to stay on top of the little things . . . pass me a twelve . . . then the big things won't control you."

Her son did not appear to disagree, and Enzo continued. "A flight mechanic, for example. Isn't he just as important as the pilot? Or even more important? Pilots are just glorified bus drivers, while a flight mechanic knows everything there is to know about every single bolt, gasket, pitot tube, every spring, every nut that keeps things in the right place and the plane in the air. He has no autopilot he can switch on, no control tower to ask for help. He has only his knowledge, his hands, his eyes, his manuals, and his experience to follow. Lives depend on him, Gianni."

Antonia sighed and walked down the kitchen steps. The courtyard lay in shadow, and she pulled her cardigan closer around her, balanced on the domed cobblestones, and skirted around the holes.

"Enzo! Gianni!"

Silence. Of the guilty kind. She could see only her son's lower legs, odd socks, and worn sneakers. The rest of him was hidden under Enzo's old Ferrari, which a year ago had been a complete wreck but had since been transformed by her lodger's miraculous hands. All she could see of Enzo Canavaro was his big boots. Chukka boots, the best in the world, obviously, made for him by a cobbler in Pakistan at the foot of the Karakoram's white peaks. All of Enzo's few possessions were special. From his diving watch to his metallic charcoal-gray, ultrapowerful motorcycle, a Honda CBR 1100XX Super Blackbird. With the exception of these few treasured objects her lodger would appear to be a man without needs.

"Out!" she shouted.

"The brake lines need soldering, Mom. I'm just about to—"

"I'm counting to three, Gianni! One, two . . ."

"Mom!"

The boy slid out on the mechanic board, a device Enzo had constructed from a sheet of plywood and an old skateboard. Her son was wearing an antique leather helmet and goggles and presented her with the deadpan face of a fifteen-year-old. His hair was black and thick and fell in long locks. The goggles held a reflection of Enzo Canavaro's Holy Grail: a perfect 1958 Ferrari 250T Testarossa. Even Antonia was awestruck at the sight of the ingenious monocoque bodywork every time she entered the garage—as neat and sterile as an operating theater. The twelve-cylinder aluminum engine hung suspended from chains above the empty engine compartment. Enzo had bought the car as a wreck from some friends in Castellarano, but the restoration was nearing completion.

The whole town was waiting for the engine to go in, for the Testarossa to erupt in a tiger roar of rebirth. But Enzo kept them waiting. The timing was never quite right according to some mystical calendar or planetary alignment known only to him.

Gianni's eyes were the exact the same shade of Black Sea blue as his mother's.

"Homework?" she snarled.

"Eh . . . yeah? What about it?"

"And practicing your cornet? You know you're playing tomorrow, don't you? Didn't Enzo remind you? I asked him to."

A groan of outrage. Gianni wouldn't dream of betraying Enzo.

"Off you go. Now!"

Sulking, the boy hung the helmet and goggles on the throttle of the Honda. He marched off without looking at her. She knew that

Enzo was hiding, waiting for her to leave the garage. But she stayed. Her toe tapped the concrete floor with impatience as her gaze wandered across the icons on the rear wall: Enzo Ferrari wearing big sunglasses with black crepe draped around the picture frame and the Ferrari Formula One drivers' line of succession from Juan Manuel Fangio to Michael Schumacher.

"Enzo? I'm waiting."

He emerged from under the car and stood up with a series of cracks from his back. He watched her with a kind of pious indifference in his boxer's face.

Enzo was wearing a spotless red Ferrari mechanic's coverall.

Antonia had seen him almost naked one morning when she passed the bathroom. He had worn only a towel around his waist. The door had been ajar, and she had stopped to close it when she noticed him. Enzo Canavaro's back was a battlefield of jagged scars and white patches from skin transplants. Some transplants had taken, but other sections of his back were nothing but gnarled red and white scar tissue.

He had seen her reflection in the mirror and turned around to close the door. But not before giving her a look she didn't think a human being was capable of.

Stripped of self-pity or embarrassment.

The look of a wild thing.

Enzo's chest and stomach had made the skin on his back look like that of a newborn, and she had cried the rest of the afternoon, hidden away in her bedroom.

"Gianni is my son, Enzo," she shouted. "Do you hear me? He's only fifteen years old. Too young to understand what it means to shoulder the heavy responsibility for other people's lives, don't you think?"

His brown eyes blinked. Enzo's gaze was focused on the cat on the wall. No one was ever too young for that, he would appear to think.

"Gianni isn't here to be your companion or apprentice," Antonia said. "He's my son. He has duties and homework and music practice. Do you understand? Tell me that you understand. That you're listening to me!"

Enzo cracked his knuckles and hung his head as much as a high priest of a Testarossa could. His enormous hands open in a display of feigned contrition, he hunched his shoulders, and his mouth started to open, but Antonia was not in a forgiving mood.

"Yes . . ." he began.

"Yes what?"

"Yes!"

She handed him an envelope.

"A letter for you." She looked at the address. "Enzo Johann Canavaro."

He took the envelope without saying anything and stuck it in the inside pocket of the flame-red coverall. Every month a letter in a plain envelope would arrive. Postmarked Milan. No sender, handwritten address. Antonia had no idea of the contents even though she had been tempted to steam open the letter several times.

But Enzo would have known immediately.

"Your blood-pressure medication," she asked. "Have you taken it? No, of course not. Your face looks like it's trying to escape. Have you had another nosebleed?"

"No."

Antonia folded her arms across her chest. The sun was setting behind the roof, and the garage light automatically came on in Enzo's five- by six-meter-square kingdom, for which he insisted on paying additional rent.

"Johann? Why Johann?"

Enzo smiled.

"Why do you think they call me 'the German'?"

"Because you're so . . . so . . . incredibly pedantic about everything?"

"Un-Italian, you mean?"

"No . . . Yes!"

She shook her head, as always in doubt about what was true, false, or irrelevant in Enzo's biographical information.

"I'm about to start dinner," she said.

"Did you get them?" he asked her in a different voice. "The papers?"

He stood in the shadow, and the light from the garage fell like a yellow cape around his shoulders. His figure grew denser and darker.

"Yes. I got them . . . It's the last time, Enzo. I'm not doing it again. Do you hear me?"

He ignored her protest.

"The girl . . . Amalia . . ."

"Amalia Nesta. Age seventeen. Motorcycle. The bridge by the gorge," she repeated, sounding tired. "She's dead, Enzo, stone dead."

The huge man nodded darkly. "Serramazzoni. It's the fifth time in three years."

"Then why do you need to know what happened? Tell me. It's not going to bring her back, Enzo."

"Bad luck or a preventable accident?" he asked. "Someone has to look into . . ."

Antonia knew that tomorrow Enzo would drive up to the bridge with his friends, all retired Ferrari mechanics. Like death's self-appointed actuaries they would take measurements, photograph the scene of the accident, study charts, and enter data into spreadsheets. Antonia thought their undertaking was offensive and morbid.

"We can't . . . control everything, Enzo."

"Yes! We have to. Don't say that! If I . . . if we just take enough care . . ."

He fell silent, but he had come close to gripping her forearm with his gigantic paw. He walked around her to get to the door to the stairs.

"Take your damn pills," she called out after him.

Enzo and the boy both ate in silence, barely taking their eyes off the plates, and Antonia said only as much as was necessary. Enzo got up as soon as he could, rinsed his plate under the tap, and put his plate, cutlery, and glass in the dishwasher. He looked at Antonia, took the case file, pressed it to his chest, and went off to his rooms. Enzo had fitted new and advanced locks on the doors; he had even offered to secure the whole shop with sophisticated electronic surveillance equipment, but Antonia had said no. There hadn't been a burglary in Castellarano for as long as anyone could remember, and she thought he was being ridiculous. She heard a window open and an electronic whirring from the garage: Enzo had burglarproofed his precious garage with a remote-controlled device.

Gianni made tea, and mother and son shared the last four cookies in the tin. He looked up at the ceiling, which resounded with Enzo's footsteps.

"Don't be mad at him, Mom," he said.

"I'm not. I'm mad at both of you."

"Okay . . ."

An hour later the boy opened the door to Apollonia and showed her into the kitchen. The blonde in the sharp designer glasses was the headmistress of the most exclusive girls' school south of Lausanne. Since 1733 the oldest and best families in Italy had sent their daughters to the convent school in Castellarano to lay the foundation for a successful marriage and a well-run household. And instill a favorable disposition toward sending their own daughters to the school when they themselves became mothers.

Her skirt was tight, and her jacket wrapped itself lovingly around her petite body. Only a gold crucifix with a single ruby red tear on the lapel of her dark gray jacket revealed Apollonia's rank within the Missionary Sisters of the Sacred Heart of Jesus. She was no older than Antonia.

Apollonia, too, was originally from Castellarano, the daughter of a pharmacist, and she had come back home: the little mountain town held an irresistible attraction for anyone who was born there.

She sat down on a kitchen chair, accepted a cup of tea, folded her trench coat in her lap, and came straight to the point.

"*The Mikado*, Antonia, is this year's performance for the old girls' day. But my girls look like Katy Perry, Lady Gaga, or Beyoncé. They don't look like anyone from the court of the emperor of Japan and certainly not like anything Gilbert and Sullivan would recognize. They need serious styling. A total makeover, in fact. All of them."

Antonia pointed to herself. "Me?"

"If you have the time. It's a major commitment," the headmistress warned her. "They rehearse every Monday, Wednesday, and Friday. The first night is in two weeks. If Signor Conti needs you for a death, we'll understand, of course."

"There's nothing I would rather do. It sounds exciting!"

"Competent students from the upper school will help you." Apollonia blew steam from the rim of the cup. "We have plenty of white Kabuki paint or whatever you call it."

"Thank you. I would love to do it."

CHAPTER 13

Milan

Teenagers were skateboarding in the park outside the Grand Hotel, moving at dizzying speed between hedges, rock gardens, steps, and railings with the total lack of fear only fourteen-year-olds possess. Sabrina D'Avalos continued along the little street south of the cathedral. Regardless of whether she walked in sun or shade, she had a sense of being under surveillance. A tightness in her chest.

How strange to feel both lonely and observed at the same time.

She had identified two of her tails on the Corso outside the Palace of Justice. It wasn't difficult once you knew how. People's social interaction, even in open squares and in crowds, remained so predictable that deviations stood out, especially if you were as paranoid as she was. A man in a pavement café who was dressed like a tourist in shorts, fanny pack, and sandals with a camera slung over his shoulder had tried too hard to ignore her when she walked past. But when she was fifty meters away, he looked after her and got up; she could see him reflected in the window of a computer shop. He already had left the exact money on the table. Another middle-aged man, dressed like your average businessman, emerged from a drugstore ten meters behind Sabrina and adapted his footsteps a little too neatly to match hers.

The two men also walked at the same speed, as if a cable connected them. Her neck started to feel sweaty. Both men moved smoothly and economically and appeared to be in good shape. They were presumably faster than she was, even over a short distance. The tourist's fanny pack and the businessman's folded-up newspaper also meant the likelihood of easily accessible weapons.

She walked fast and didn't look back.

In Corso di Porta Vittoria she reduced her speed and arranged her entrance into a department store to put a group of college students between her and her pursuers. In the glass of the revolving door she saw the two men accelerate before their path was blocked by the impenetrable group of youngsters.

The Coin store was busy. Sabrina made her way through the crowds in the perfume section, went around a pillar, and ran downstairs to the basement, where lavatories, lockers, and telephone booths were located. She took the elevator to the third floor: men's and boys' wear. She found a black hoodie at least three sizes too big and a pair of black jeans a size too small. She paid without trying on the clothes and dropped her shoulder bag into the shopping bag. In the sports section she bought a pair of large masculine sunglasses.

On the floor below, Sabrina found a quiet changing room. She loosened her ponytail and combed her hair forward so that it covered the scarred part of her face, put her leather jacket and blue jeans in the plastic bag, and put on the hoodie and the tight jeans. She pulled the hood over her head, looked in the mirror, and applied thick black mascara and black kohl. She was fairly pleased with the result. Assistant Public Prosecutor Sabrina D'Avalos had entered the cubicle, and an introverted, androgynous emo had emerged instead—or so she hoped. She sat down on the stool in the changing room and placed the four identical cheap wristwatches that she had brought with her from Naples on the floor. She twisted off the plastic straps and tossed them. She put two of the watches in separate scrunched-up cigarette packages, one in an empty candy bag, and the last in an empty tampon box.

She left the changing room and tried to slouch like a boy. A pursuer would be looking out as much for a person's pattern of movement as for that person's external features when trying to identify his target.

At a side exit she mingled with another small group of teenagers on their way out through the revolving door. She asked a girl for directions to the nearest Internet café. The girl answered her as she would any other Milanese teenager. Sabrina almost smiled but stopped herself. Emos don't smile.

She hung around the area outside the cathedral for a couple of hours. Ate pizza slices, drank cola, smoked cigarettes, and sat on a bench in the square for a long time, watching early evening tourists and pigeons. A young couple sat down on the bench next to her and parked a sleeping child in a stroller in front of them. Sabrina looked at them and did a double take. She recognized the woman from her law course . . . Sofia something or other . . . and the young man had sat in the row behind her in the lecture hall for several years. The woman glanced at Sabrina's hooded figure and carried on talking. Shortly afterward they got up and left.

The sense of being watched was lifting, and Sabrina was just congratulating herself when a man sat down next to her.

"Signor Raspallo," she said with a sigh.

"Call me Nestore," he said.

He leaned forward and studied his elegant suede shoes. She noted to her satisfaction that he had taken off the bow tie.

"Nestore . . . damn you."

"An excellent disguise," he said. "The emo."

"Not good enough, it would appear. I assume you're not here by chance."

"Not entirely. But I come here often. I never tire of the cathedral. Do you know what I love about it the most?"

"Tell me."

"That it was created by anonymous and forgotten masons. They toiled for years, producing some of the greatest art the world has ever seen. Not for themselves, not for any recognition in their life-time, but for something higher."

"Perhaps they weren't anonymous in their lifetime," she suggested.

Sabrina, too, looked at the miraculous cathedral, which she had always felt lacked something. A unifying thought, possibly. It had borrowed freely from every European style from Gothic to late Romantic, and yes, the result was unique, but you had to look carefully to spot the original concept. However, there was something deeply Italian and life-affirming about the architectural clash.

Raspallo placed an envelope between them.

"Here are a couple of things I think will interest you."

"What things?"

"You'll know when you see them. There's also a number at which you can reach me at any time."

"In case anything happens?"

"In case of anything."

"Is that official, Nestore?"

"Yes and no."

"Yes and no?"

"I think it depends on whether you succeed. If you do, it'll be official, obviously; if not, they don't want anyone to know they were involved."

"I see. So who are you?"

"A friend, I think."

A friend under orders, she thought.

He described the two Camorra tails Sabrina had managed to lose at the entrance to Coin. After a brief deliberation the two men had wandered back in the direction of Via Durini and her hotel.

He stood up and looked at her gravely.

"It means that you're of interest to the Camorra. They would appear not to be indifferent to the identity of the bodies in the container. Perhaps they still retain an interest in Lucia and Salvatore Forlani. Did you drive here directly from Naples?"

"Yes," she lied.

"Although it might look like it, the Camorra haven't promised not to liquidate public prosecutors, though it has been a long time since the last one," he said. "Watch yourself."

"Thank you, Nestore. But I think they're waiting to see where I go and who I visit."

"Possibly."

It was as if the young man wanted to add something. He looked at her with some doubts. Then he went inside the cathedral.

She hoped he might consider lighting a candle for her.

It had grown dark when she turned into Via Durini. In the distance she saw the neon sign of Albergo Merlin flash out the guesthouse's position to the rest of the world. She had long since selected her candidates: the green Fiat van, obviously, the other white van with reflective foil covering the rear window, a new beige Ford Mondeo whose owner had been leaning against the door studying a map for a remarkable length of time, and a minibus that appeared to be empty. Behind the dark windows of the minibus she thought she saw a tiny movement, but it wasn't repeated. She couldn't see either the tourist or the businessman.

She walked along the pavement to the beat of Katie Melua. She let one of the cigarette packets with the wristwatch slip from her hand just behind the rear wheel of the green van. Then she entered a kiosk and bought a packet of chewing gum and a magazine with a latex-clad Lady Gaga on the cover.

She unwrapped a piece of chewing gum near the white van and let the paper and the other cigarette packet fall down behind its left rear wheel. Sabrina repeated the procedure by the minibus and the Mondeo. The man in the driver's seat had swapped the map with *Il Golfo*, a Neapolitan newspaper, and Sabrina frowned at this display of poor professional standards. She turned left at the corner of Via Borgogna and walked up the road that ran parallel to Via Durini.

In a quiet corner in one of the courtyards connecting Corso Europa and the Albergo Merlin she quickly changed her clothing, pulled her hair back in a ponytail, and stuffed the shopping bags from Coin into her shoulder bag. She removed the makeup with a cleansing wipe, and the emo was no more.

The receptionist managed to muster a feeble smile when she appeared at the counter.

Sabrina beamed back at him.

She nodded to the back room, where she could see a flickering computer screen.

"Good evening, signore. I've a favor to ask you."

"Yes?"

"Tomorrow my husband and children arrive at Milan Linate. The airport, you know."

"I have heard of it," the man said.

"Of course you have. I'm sorry. But please, could I ask you to check on your computer if there are any delays in flight traffic tomorrow at 12:05? Meridiana flight 2306. It would be a great help."

She folded her hands demurely on the counter.

The receptionist sighed and got up.

"All right."

"Thank you so much, signore."

The man closed the folding door behind him, and Sabrina slipped silently behind the counter and swapped one of her room keys with one from a room on the third floor. Earlier she had noticed that room number 307, like practically all the rooms at Albergo Merlin, was vacant.

She resumed her original position in front of the counter.

"There would appear to be no delays, signora," the receptionist said when he returned.

"That's great. Are you married?"

He looked at her. He evidently was trying to remember.

"Yes."

She nodded as if the two of them had now bonded and requested her keys. The receptionist handed them to her without looking at them.

"Good night, signore."

"Night."

"Sleep well."

"I'll try, signora."

Chapter 14

Castellarano

The door to Enzo's rooms opened when Antonia had finished in the bathroom. She counted eight steps as he crossed the landing to the stairs and knew that the front door would slam shut nine seconds later. She opened her bedroom window to the song of a blackbird on the roof across the road. The evening sky was dark blue. She tightened the cord of her dressing gown, gathered her hair at the nape of her neck, and leaned forward, resting on her elbows on the windowsill. Opposite, at their usual table near the garden and bowling alley of La Stazione, three regulars reclined in wicker chairs, elegant and colorful as only middle-aged Italian men can be.

The men spotted Enzo the moment he stepped outside her front door. They called out greetings that could easily be heard across the road. One got up and waved him over, but tonight her strange lodger ignored his friends. At times, without warning, Enzo could become as distant as a sleepwalker. Stiff and dark, he would march down the road and disappear in the shadows.

A few minutes later a bottle-green English car, which Gianni had identified as a Bentley Brooklands, would drive past the restaurant in grandiose silence and vanish in the darkness behind Enzo

Canavaro. No one knew who owned it, but every now and then it would appear like a ghost on the road, usually on evenings when Enzo was at his most twitchy and unapproachable. Speculations about the strange car had spread across the town for the last two years, but no one had come up with a plausible explanation.

Enzo's unfathomable behavior angered Antonia. Any rejection of intimacy, of any opportunity for happiness and enjoyment of life, outraged her. She felt the same indignation every night as she watched old Signora Pantoni's rituals: the dinner, the cutlery laid out for breakfast the following morning, a glass of water before bedtime, fifteen minutes of reading before the lights were switched off behind the blinds.

A strange wait for death without offering any resistance.

Antonia stacked up the pillows against the headboard. A bowl of candy and a pile of almost new fashion magazines were within sinful reach.

Later, she registered Enzo's footsteps walking up the stairs.

The American edition of *Vogue* featured an article on the Milanese fashion designer Massimiliano Di Luca's rise and . . . fall? American insiders were united in expressing doubt whether the master could survive the departure of his young chief designer, who had left to set up his own house.

Antonia pushed her reading glasses up her nose and studied Massimiliano Di Luca, who was locked in an embrace with an ecstatic Madonna and Scarlett Johansson on a glittering Paris runway. Signature black suit, open-necked white shirt, a virile and handsome face, a ponytail. His gaze was aimed at something that was not clear to anyone but Massimiliano Di Luca. He had designed several collections that had all been original and unique, giving the public the impression that he had arrived on earth in a rescue capsule from a dying star. For three decades Di Luca had left even his severest critics euphoric and his rivals in despair. At the same time his furious energy had enabled him to serve as president and director of the powerful fashion industry body, the Camera Nazionale della Moda Italiana.

Antonia switched off her reading light, tossed some of the pillows on the floor, and fell asleep to the sound of Enzo moving around in his self-imposed solitude.

Milan

In her room Sabrina opened the envelope from Nestore Raspallo while she contemplated his motives. He undoubtedly had spoken to Federico Renda, who was of the opinion that she needed help—something that infuriated her. Renda's influence extended far beyond Naples, and his condescending remarks about the north were pure affectation. He often entertained top politicians and important businesspeople from northern Italy. The president had visited him several times, and Renda had a seat on countless national councils and committees.

The envelope contained a log of calls to and from her father's cell phone in the last five days of his life. The final call was to a GIS captain, a Primo Alba, three hours before her father was killed in the cabin in Alto Adige. The list had been printed out on perforated printer paper from a well-known telecommunications company. It took up three sheets and was dated that day.

She let her eyes skim over the dates, times, call duration, and names of subscribers. In a few instances the name of the subscriber had been replaced with a line of X's. There was a dramatic accumulation of calls to and from her father's cell after the attack on Nanometric on September 5, 2007: from the local polizia municipale in San Siro, the ambulance service, the Carabinieri, and the Polizia Stradale. A few hours later calls from the traffic police in Città Studi south of Milan had come in when the rescue crew started cutting Giulio Forlani free from his wrecked car. She traced the list with her finger: Palazzo di Giustizia, Ospedale Maggiore, and so on. Nothing jumped out at her. Sabrina frowned when she saw that no calls had been logged to or from the cell phone between 11:15 a.m. and 12:15 p.m. Half an hour before and after the time Lucia and Salvatore Forlani were abducted, her father had switched off his cell. In the eye of the storm.

At 12:15 p.m. the general had turned on his cell again. The first call was an outgoing one, and according to the telecommunications company the number belonged to Emp. Massimiliano Di Luca, s.a.

Her father *and* Massimiliano Di Luca?

On the one hand, it was only natural that her father would contact Di Luca about the disaster if they were financing Forlani's and Nanometric's research. On the other hand, it seemed strange that he would risk exposing his involvement with Nanometric instead of making use of a front man and a fictitious EU Commission office as he usually did. She had no recollection of him ever mentioning copyright protection, Nanometric, or Massimiliano Di Luca at home. The latter undoubtedly would have caught the attention of his fashion-conscious daughter, who would have pestered him for tickets to Di Luca's shows.

Sabrina got up, put the plug in the sink, turned on the cold tap, and immersed her face in the water. She could feel bubbles trickle from her nostrils and tickle her cheeks. She stayed there until she no longer could hold her breath, then dried her face and massaged her temples while she thought about her father, who appeared to be helplessly entangled in the Forlani tragedy.

Nestore Raspallo's business card was the color of ivory. It listed only his name and a cell phone number. The young man was apparently always available.

Questions without answers buzzed around her brain. For a long time she sat on the toilet seat with her head in her hands. On the back of her eyelids images from the endless day flickered by. The park at the top of the hill in Castellarano and the tall woman with the grapes, the green van in her rearview and side mirrors, the changing room in the department store. The dark, soaring cathedral, her father's face, which ambushed her and stayed with her like the final credit in an emptied movie theater.

She thought about young Nestore Raspallo with the light brown hair and the bow tie and became aware of a reluctant smile on her lips. She wondered briefly what it would be like to be in love.

Exhausting weightlessness? Euphoria and distraction? A foreboding of catastrophe?

She put the log in her shoulder bag and Raspallo's business card in her pocket.

The guesthouse was as quiet as the grave. Sabrina tiptoed up the stairs and stopped outside room 307. She switched on her flashlight, removed the solitary lightbulb in the corridor, and put it in a cupboard with a fire hose and a powder extinguisher. She let herself into the room, placed the bedside table and a lamp in front of the door, loaded the Walther, dragged the mattress and the bed linen from the bed to the farthest corner of the room, and put her pistol under the flat, hard pillow. She slipped under the cold, thin blankets and crossed her fingers that no traveling salesman would wake the receptionist in the middle of the night and specifically request this room.

She folded her hands, said her prayers, and fell asleep.

CHAPTER 15

Milan

Overnight the receptionist had been replaced by a shapeless middle-aged woman with thick glasses and pink lipstick drawn considerably outside the natural lip line. Her colorless hair was pressed against her scalp by a Hello Kitty hair band that Sabrina imagined might be more suitable for someone under the age of nine.

The woman watched her over her newspaper, an espresso by her elbow. Sabrina felt a pang of envy. She could have killed for a cup of coffee and a cigarette. Instead she launched into a long and imaginative explanation about why she—despite every intention to the contrary—would have to leave this fine establishment. A child. A sick child. Sabrina rummaged around her tired brain for a brief moment before she seized on . . . mumps.

"Haven't you had your child vaccinated, signora?"

There was disapproval in the oyster eyes.

"Of course I have. Our daughter has just been vaccinated. However, the weakened virus turned out to be not so weak after all. They have recalled the vaccine, but how does that help us? Our holiday. My little girl."

She was distraught.

The woman smiled. Or her upper lip curled, at any rate. Sabrina was mesmerized by tiny clumps of lipstick stuck to the black strands of hair on her upper lip. Like tiny unripe cherries, they swayed in the stream of air to and from the nostrils.

"Is your daughter often sick, signora?"

Her husband's family tended to be a little . . . delicate, Sabrina admitted. The woman behind the counter prepared Sabrina's bill while muttering something about mothers-in-law.

She drove the front of the car up onto the pavement and pretended to look for something in the glove compartment for so long that even the most hopeless tail in Via Durini would notice that she was leaving the guesthouse. She waited until a bus, a truck, and a couple of cars had driven past before she signaled right and pulled out. She turned left into Via Borgogna and onward to Corso Monforte. Even a Camorra driver from Naples should have no trouble following her. As she joined the slow-moving, dense morning traffic, Sabrina thought about the woman behind the reception counter, who she assumed was the wife of the receptionist. Or his sister. They shared the same browbeaten expression.

The time was 8:30 a.m. She had three and a half hours before her audience with Massimiliano Di Luca. She started challenging her tails, changing lanes and ducking and diving in between trucks and buses. A hundred meters before the next set of traffic lights, she slowed down. Green. Eighty meters. Sixty meters. Still green. A taxi in front of her was driving at the exact same speed. Sabrina knew that the cab driver would know to the nearest second when the lights would change. The taxi slowed down. Twenty meters: the lights changed to red. The taxi came to a halt, but she overtook it on the inside. A cast iron fence encircling a tree snatched her side mirror; Sabrina looked left at the ashen-faced taxi driver. His mouth was hanging open. Sabrina continued out in front of the avalanche of braking, hooting, and swerving cars coming down the Corso. She turned right down Via Conservatorio and stepped on the accelerator, rolling down the window and extending her middle finger to

the drivers behind her. They sounded their horns furiously. Halfway down Via Conservatorio she took a sharp left, hoping that the
multistory garage that had always been there had not been turned
into a supermarket or a cinema.

Twenty minutes later and once more dressed like a postapocalyp-
tic emo, Sabrina was strolling down the streets around the Albergo
Merlin. In the high, bright September light she felt that she was
painfully conspicuous, but no one seemed to give her a second
glance. In Via Durini she found the cigarette packets and the tampon box in the gutter. None of the suspicious vehicles were still in
the street, but the minibus was filling up with children and adults
from a nursery school. She left the candy wrapper with the watch
behind its rear wheel.

She found a quiet Internet café in a side street, bought herself an
hour online and a Coke from the zombie behind the counter, sat
down in the darkest corner, and, hidden by the computer screen,
opened the packages.

It was the oldest trick in the book but still good enough to be
included in the latest editions. The broken wristwatches showed her
the exact time the rear wheel had driven over them. She opened
a notebook and chewed her pen. She had left the guesthouse at
08:27:30 exactly. The Ford Mondeo had left Via Durini at 08:28, she
noticed. She underlined the car's registration number and wrote
a brief description of the driver. The white van had left the area
at 23:47 the previous night, and so she crossed out its registration
number. The green Fiat van had set off from Via Durini at 08:29.
She had no description of the driver or any passengers, only the
registration number she already had given Raspallo.

She drank the Coke and looked around. The Internet café was
practically deserted. A couple of sleepy teenagers were playing *Call
of Duty* with the deep concentration of a concert pianist.

The café's lavatory was in the basement. It was shared by every possible gender, and Sabrina touched nothing.

Raspallo answered after two rings.

"*Pronto?*"

"Sabrina D'Avalos. About yesterday . . . did you mean *everything*?"

"Yes."

"Do you have a pen?"

"Of course."

She gave him the registration number of the Mondeo and a description of the driver and repeated the registration number of the green Fiat van.

"Where are they?" he asked.

"In Via Conservatorio or in the streets around Via Durini. Possibly in the multistory garage in Via Conservatorio. Do you know it?"

"Yes. Is that where your car is?"

"At the moment, yes."

"Leave it there," he said.

"I love that car."

"It's just a car," he said.

"My first."

He laughed softly. If voices had colors, Nestore Raspallo's voice had the same light brown shade as his hair.

"You never forget your first one," he said.

"*Ciao,*" she said. "And thank you for the call log."

"Think about it," he said.

"I think of nothing else."

She found the large green Fiat van in front of a church on the corner of Via Cesare Battisti and Via Filippo Corridori, and she had good reason to be impressed with young Raspallo's efficiency a few minutes later.

A minibus with no identifying features stopped diagonally in front of the van; six people wearing ski masks, black bulletproof vests, and black combat uniforms jumped out and assumed their positions around the van. The only source of identification on the soldiers was the reflective CARABINIERI on their chests and backs. None of them spoke. Sabrina watched from the pavement opposite.

One of the black figures smashed the van's side window with a sledgehammer, stuck in an arm, opened the door, and climbed in. She couldn't see what he did next but assumed that he—or she—continued destroying an internal window and then, to distract the now trapped Camorristas, threw a stun grenade into the body of the van. There was a hollow boom, white smoke poured from every crack and the broken windows, and the van rocked on its shock absorbers.

The back doors were twisted off their hinges with crowbars, and three Carabinieri jumped inside. A few seconds later they reappeared with two dazed-looking men who were pushed against the hood of the van and had black hoods pulled over their heads and their hands tied behind their backs with white plastic ties.

The patrol cars from Milan's Polizia Municipale pulled up next to the minibus, and uniformed officers started dealing with the crowd of onlookers in the street. The prisoners were thrown inside the minibus; the black-clad soldiers got in and closed the doors, and the minibus drove off.

The whole incident took only a few minutes.

Her cell rang.

"Happy now?" Raspallo asked her.

"Please tell me they weren't just a couple of builders or windsurfers."

"Windsurfers? What are you talking about?"

"Nothing. Who were they?"

"Not your usual handymen, certainly. The back of the van was filled with guns, cameras, and electronic surveillance equipment . . ."

"Uh huh?"

"And an extensive dossier on you that someone is reading to me right now. Hold on."

Sabrina stared at the pavement until Raspallo returned.

"Several excellent pictures of you. Your address in Naples. Telephone numbers, e-mail addresses . . . and the IP address of your computer. They'll definitely have hacked it by now. Interesting area you live in," he commented.

"Yes, very."

"And you've befriended a boy in an orphanage in Via San Tommaso d'Aquino?"

"Ismael, yes."

She was beginning to wish she had simply shot the two men herself.

"I suggest you alter all your routines and any habits until this is over. And get yourself a new cell right now."

"How long can you hold them?"

"Given the guns and the bugging equipment? A long time. If it proves problematic to charge them, we'll have them convert to Islam."

"Did you find the Mondeo as well?"

"Of course."

"Are you in trouble?" she asked.

"Why?"

"Over this."

"I was only doing my civic duty by passing on an anonymous tip-off to an old friend in the Carabinieri," he said. "Two suspicious vehicles with armed men had been observed by alert citizens."

Nestore Raspallo sounded remarkably laid back.

"Good-bye, then. And thank you," she said.

"You're hoping this will wake up Urs Savelli, I presume," he said. "Lure him down from the mountains?"

"Yes, if that's where he is."

"That's your . . . plan?"

"That's a grand word for it. But I have to know what happened to my father."

"I understand."

For a long time she pressed her cell against her ear, waiting for comfort, advice, brilliant ideas, but nothing more was forthcoming. She looked at her phone and dropped it between the bars of a sewer grate.

If Sabrina had been in possession of superhuman powers, she might, by lifting her head and turning it slightly to the left, have recognized a face in a taxi parked by the curb a hundred meters away. The taxi driver who had sworn at her an hour earlier in Corso Monforte had watched the arrests from his car. Five minutes earlier the last of the four-man-strong surveillance unit from Naples had met with the same fate. The Ford Mondeo's driver had been stopped in a side street to Via Conservatorio, where he had been driving around hoping to find Assistant Public Prosecutor Sabrina D'Avalos again. He had had the presence of mind to hit the speed dial for the coordinating surveillance leader in the taxi and mutter a few words into the cell before his side window was smashed and he was dragged out by his hair.

The taxi driver then called Urs Savelli.

"Yes?"

"It all went belly up," the taxi driver said.

"Why?"

The driver lit a cigarette.

"I'm not sure," he said. "I think she must have been on to us for a long time. Since yesterday. She must have alerted them. It was the GIS. There's just me left now."

"One young woman against four armed men," the voice said. "The math simply doesn't add up, my friend."

The taxi driver closed his eyes. He would have preferred a string of curses and threats to Savelli's flat monotone whisper.

"I know, signore. What would you like me to do?"

"Did she drive directly from Naples to Milan?"

"She made a stop in a mountain town along the way. Castellarano."

"What did she do there?"

"Nothing, signore. Looked at the shops and buildings, that kind of thing. Sightseeing."

"Did she speak to anyone?"

"No."

"No one at all?"

"Well, to some woman in a park. They exchanged a few words. It didn't look like they knew each other."

"Do you have pictures of the woman?"

"Of course."

The taxi driver wished more than he had ever wished for anything that the pictures of the woman and the assistant public prosecutor in the park in Castellarano were good and clear.

"Do you think you're capable of staying put until I or other competent people turn up in Milan?"

"I think so. Thank you."

"Don't thank me yet."

CHAPTER 16

Lake Garda

The wind changed direction on the hour. Rather than rise along the lake toward its northern shore, it turned 180 degrees and started blowing toward the southern shore of Lake Garda. The water was choppy with white horses playing on the surface. Long waves with foaming crests rolled down the middle of the lake. Those white horses merged into larger groups as small waves started to form, following the wind.

An unbroken band of heavy clouds lay across the mountains, which only a moment ago had been unobstructed: the foehn wind had arrived, the sun had disappeared, and someone had switched on the colossal weather machine of the Alps.

From the old stone house outside the town of Saló, halfway along Lake Garda's western shore, he had an unhindered and fascinating view of the changing weather that played out in the valley of the lake every day.

The rain started battering the windows.

Urs Savelli put down the cell phone, looked at the thick anthropology book that lay open on the long table, and tried to concentrate on the rapid steps that characterized a Sorgin Dantza from the town of Lasarte-Oria. It was a monster of a Basque dance: fierce, forceful, and acrobatic. It demanded a certain level of concentration, and that had just been broken. Following a single young and inexperienced assistant public prosecutor wasn't a difficult task, one would have thought.

"No idiots," Don Francesco had said.

It was easier said than done.

Savelli sat on the table, dangling his legs over the edge. His heart was no longer in the dance. He was wearing the traditional white Basque dance costume with a red cummerbund. Under Generalissimo Franco a red cummerbund, proof that you had killed at least one member of the Guardia Civil, meant life imprisonment—if you were caught—or a bullet to the back of the head.

"Castellarano," he muttered to himself.

Lucia Forlani had been from Castellarano. And it was hardly a coincidence that the irritating assistant public prosecutor had stopped in the mountain town.

He had never been there himself but seemed to remember it featuring in Napoleon's campaign.

The house, like all of Savelli's secret homes, had been chosen with care. It was built at an elevation of eight hundred meters, and the meter-thick stone walls ensured a pleasant temperature in both summer and winter. His years of isolation meant Urs Savelli had poor tolerance of temperature extremes. The basement prison cell seemed to have installed a thermostat in his brain that switched off his thinking when the temperature rose above 70°F or fell to below 50°F.

He got up, went over to the windows, and traced the journey of a raindrop down the pane with his fingertip. He looked out across the lake, which was almost invisible now. His claustrophobia stirred, and he started a series of breathing exercises. Spending three years in a cell measuring 1.5 meters by 2.5 meters had instilled in Savelli an inextinguishable need to have an unbroken view to the horizon.

He didn't know how old he was. His best guess was that he had been in the cell from the age of seventeen until he was around twenty years old.

*   *   *

Urs Savelli's earliest memory was of waking up because he was cold. Snow covering an empty landscape outside windows he was barely tall enough to look out of, a naked room, and a kitchen with a table, a bench, and a stove, which had been cold to the touch. It must have gone out long ago. On the bench lay a skinny woman dressed in black. Old far beyond her years. He had tugged at her, tried to wake her up, but her arm was as stiff as the branch of a tree.

He remembered a green truck and a man in a large black coat with a long black beard and black boots who had opened the door to the kitchen a couple of days later. He had taken him by the hand and lifted him up into the body of the truck, then had given him some sacks to cover himself with and a piece of bread to eat.

Ten lean wild black dogs were already lying on the floor of the truck. When he woke up, he was warm. He could see through the tear in the tarpaulin that the truck was driving down an endless snow-covered road; the dogs had snuggled up to him and kept him warm with their bodies.

Later the boy learned that the man with the beard was called Hristo. He sold guard dogs to farmers. He was famous for his dogs all over western Albania, or so he claimed after the second of his daily bottles of vodka. He once had sold a dog to the boy's father, and since his father's disappearance he had stopped by occasionally to see the woman on the kitchen bench.

"What was my mother like?" the boy had asked once, and was rewarded with a clip around the ear that nearly knocked him unconscious.

"A good hooker," the man had said after giving it some thought. "Or rather . . . she wasn't any good, but she was the only one south of Ohrid!"

He howled with laughter at his own wit and lay down to sleep with the dogs.

One day, while drunk, he had gone outside to urinate and fallen through the ice on a bog. The boy and the dogs had watched from the shore as the man's face paled and his movements grew slower and less coordinated. He tried to wiggle out of his coat and pull off his boots while he stared at them, screaming. Eventually Hristo fell silent even though his mouth was still open. Eventually he was pulled under the ice by his waterlogged clothes. His fur cap continued to float on the surface of the water, and the boy fished it out with a long stick. It was a good cap.

At a market in Berat the boy traded the dogs for a dancing bear.

There was another reason. An old restlessness, which other people might call fear, rumbled inside Savelli. For a shipwrecked, orphaned *straniero*, he had been incredibly lucky. He had had a fantastic career with the Terrasino family. But with great luck came an equally great debt of karma. It was inevitable. Urs Savelli was extremely conscious of the cosmic balance sheet. He knew he would have to pay the bill one day. The art was postponing that day to extreme old age, when nothing really mattered.

Lucia and Salvatore Forlani. Yes, they were dead. He had been there when it happened. And he had seen Baron Agostino D'Avalos shot and killed in the Alpine cabin. The old man had looked into his eyes while his pupils dilated and the last breath left his chest. Even though the baron was dying, even though he knew he was beaten, Savelli had seen his own freshly dug grave in his fading green eyes. The old man's gaze had promised him that.

Then there was Giulio Forlani, the genius physicist with his copyright protection invention that would have ruined everything for them.

Savelli closed his eyes and rested his forehead against the cold windowpane. He grabbed the makila and swung it through the air. As always, a certain sense of reassurance flowed from the carved ivory bear on the handle, his totem.

Castellarano.

He rang a man in Naples and appeared to have caught him in the middle of lunch, because there was an infernal noise from a television, clattering cutlery, bickering children, and an outnumbered woman trying to control them.

"Cesare?"

"Yes."

Savelli didn't introduce himself. His voice sufficed. Cesare. Rarely had a name been more ill chosen. This soldier was anything but aristocratic. A fat psychopathic toad who dressed in shiny, colorful sports clothes, also painfully ill chosen. But Cesare did what he was told to, though his mental capacity would forever keep him in the family's lower echelons.

"Cesare?"

"*Si, signore.*"

"Either you strangle your reptilian children and shoot your wife or you find a quiet place. This instant. Do you hear?"

A door was slammed shut in the apartment in the Neapolitan suburb, and Savelli could hear himself think again. An irritating slurping noise continued.

"Cesare?"

"Yes."

"Right now you're picking semimasticated beef from your molars with your fingers, am I right?"

"Yes, signore."

"Do you think you could leave the animal alone and go back a few years with me? Do you think you could do that without overtaxing your brain powers?"

"I think so, signore."

"Good."

Savelli was a vegetarian.

"Three years ago I gave you an entirely manageable task. You were to stop a green Škoda Octavia on the A7 south of Milan and take out its driver."

"And I did, signore."

"So you did, my friend."

Savelli pressed his eyes shut.

"This man. Are you absolutely sure that he was dead when you left him? Think very carefully before you answer. This is very, very important."

"Yes."

"Yes, what?"

"I'm sure, signore."

The words rolled out slowly.

"Because you checked the pulse on his neck? You checked whether his pupils were reactive? That he had stopped breathing?"

"He was a mess, signore. Completely smashed up. There was blood everywhere. I shot him twice. Once in the head and once in the chest. He was stone dead."

"So there was no pulse?"

Cesare was silent.

"Was there a pulse, Cesare? Did his eyelid twitch? Was he breathing?" Savelli insisted.

"I'm sure, signore. Quite sure. I didn't check those things you mention. I know if a man is dead or not from looking at him. There was no point."

Savelli sighed.

"Of course not, Cesare. Go back to your family. Don't give it another thought."

Cesare stuttered something, but Savelli ended the call and stretched out on the rough floor boards.

Figlio di puttana!

Savelli massaged his eyes and pondered his next move. He could ask Don Francesco for L'Artista. If she was given the job, the nosy little assistant public prosecutor Sabrina D'Avalos would be dead and gone within twenty-four hours. No power on earth could prevent it. But L'Artista was for very special occasions. A last resort. Don Francesco guarded her jealously.

The young woman who had helped them gain entry to Nanometric was an enigma: a fly constantly irritating Urs Savelli's flank. She was the only person in the world he was scared of. Among the few facts he was allowed to know was that she had a daughter who was around six, that she was married to a disabled painter, and that she lived with her family at a former cider press near Brescia. When Don Francesco had told him about her over a glass of apricot liqueur, he had warned him under no circumstances to ever try to identify her.

"She's for the finer things, Urs. Delicate, difficult things. Things that can't be solved with a baseball bat, a *lupara,* or plastique; do you understand? And only for special occasions. She's an athlete. Athletes must rest in order to give their best. I know you don't like the idea of working with someone you don't know well, Urs, but in her case you must make an exception."

The captain had adopted a solemn expression and assured him that he understood—of course he did—while he thought (1) about how much time the old man had left, (2) that these days no one ever used *lupare,* crudely sawed-off shotguns, as they had in the old man's violent youth for close-up wet work but machine pistols or automatic carbines, (3) that it was a long time since anyone had referred to plastic explosives as "plastique," (4) that his status in the council was promising when the devil finally decided to come for the old man, and (5) that he wouldn't dream of working with, let alone trust, someone like L'Artista without knowing everything about her.

But an order was an order, and the old man was still as dangerous as a cobra.

Urs had hired a private detective in Milan to investigate her. The middle-aged retired policeman had been told to follow the young dark-haired woman late one night as she left a hauling company in Via Riccardo Pitteri in an eastern suburb of Milan. The hauling company transported eco bales for the Camorra; shrink-wrapped unprocessed waste from the city with more than a million inhabitants was moved from one illegal rubbish dump to another in Italy while attracting generous state and local authority subsidies. An eternal lucrative circle. The hauler had decided to hold back income from the Milan city council, money the Camorra believed it was entitled to. An example had to be made, and Don Francesco had assigned the task to L'Artista.

Savelli had told the private detective to ignore the police scanners and any emergency vehicles that might turn up and concentrate solely on the woman.

When the gunfire from the Quonset hut that served as the hauler's office died down and columns of flames from the torched trucks colored the sky, the detective saw a figure leave the hauling company by scaling a high wire fence and jumping on a motorcycle.

The detective threw his half-eaten sandwich out the window, counted to twenty, and started his anonymous Volvo.

The woman adhered to every traffic regulation and speed limit on her ride to the center of Milan, and the detective made sure that there were at least three vehicles between him and her motorcycle.

He watched from a professional distance as the woman drove down the ramp into a multistory garage in Via Melzo. He assumed that she would shortly reappear behind the wheel of a car or on another motorcycle. He knew the garage well, and the only way in or out was this one underground ramp.

He was wrong.

The detective heard a click from his Volvo's back door, and the cool night air that flowed into the car made the hairs on his forearms stand up.

Three days later Urs Savelli had been woken by a frantic knocking on the door to his secret apartment in Rome. He had arrived after midnight and was bleary-eyed when he opened the door to a stream of complaints from a distraught concierge. The woman was wringing her handkerchief in front of her red face. It could not go on. He, Signor Mela, would have to do something . . . immediately . . . *subito!* . . . There had—handkerchief pressed against the face—been . . . complaints . . . many . . . he couldn't expect that decent people . . . the other residents in the block . . . would be able to tolerate—the handkerchief again—she would alert the authorities at this instant . . . if he didn't immediately . . .

Savelli eventually managed to extract a relatively coherent explanation from her. The mailbox. The residents all had mailboxes in the lobby. He followed her downstairs, breathed in once in front of the square gray mailboxes, and ordered her back up the stairwell, citing a possible risk of infection. He unlocked his mailbox, paled, and locked it again.

He decided to deal with the problem himself. He had veterinary training and considerable experience in handling decomposing organic material, he told the concierge. In his apartment on the fifth floor Savelli found plastic gloves, tinfoil, garbage bags, and duct tape; he ran downstairs, ensuring that the concierge remained out of sight, and with difficulty eased the head of the private detective out of the mailbox. He wrapped the head in foil and put it in a plastic bag, which he sealed with tape. Then he scooped a handful of wriggling, homeless maggots into another bag, dried the inside of the mailbox with copious amounts of kitchen towel, and washed it down with ammonia and water.

As he drove away from the secret apartment with the head of the private detective in his trunk, he thought about the small apple wedged between the detective's teeth.

Savelli's responsibility had been the containment and neutralizing of Forlani and Batista's new and dangerous invention. He had suggested a political solution to the council: that influential members of the Camorra should encourage politicians in Rome—a braying herd, as Don Francesco, ever the peasant, had called them— to suppress the technology in the usual manner: by appointing a government committee and producing an endless stream of white papers, considerations, and provisional circulars until the Camorra had found a final solution.

But in vain. The council opted for a conservative—that is, violent—solution.

Celebrities such as Giulio Forlani and Massimiliano Di Luca would be the death of him, Savelli feared. Impossible to eliminate without a public outcry from a world where people lived their lives through celebrities rather than living their own lives. The container catastrophe on the Vittorio Emanuele II Quay had caused outrage. The council usually preferred to do business without attracting attention, lurking in the shadows of centuries; Savelli agreed with them. But there were certain things—coincidences, one-in-a-million chances, twists of fate bordering on the miraculous—that no human being could predict. Incidents that defied every attempt at careful planning. Like now with this blasted, defective American container crane, the English camera crew, Assistant Public Prosecutor D'Avalos's tail in Milan—and Cesare.

Savelli undressed and took a cold shower. He called his driver in the gatekeeper's house down by the road and told him to get the car ready.

"Where to, signore?"

"Milan. I have an appointment with a doctor."

CHAPTER 17

Milan

Massimiliano Di Luca was shorter and looked older and thinner than Sabrina had expected. In fact he proved to be something of a disappointment as a fashion icon. It took a couple of seconds before she recognized his luminous blue eyes and tanned face and the long gray hair that reached his shoulders in a ponytail. He called out orders to the slaves down on the floor below in English, Italian, German, and French. The fashion king met her on a white gangway under a glass ceiling, suspended several meters above the floor in a building that once had been northern Italy's biggest cotton mill. The colossal looms, which could have been removed only by tearing down the walls, had been sandblasted and spray painted in a range of neutral colors so that they now looked like prehistoric monsters, their wild outlines sharp against the matte black floor.

The designer smiled at the slim goddess who had escorted Sabrina from Di Luca's flagship store on Via Alessandro Manzoni through long corridors, design studios, workshops, and halls where seamstresses and designers worked frantically at tables overflowing with fabrics, leather, and brocades. The girl was mixed race and like all the other store assistants and secretaries at least a head and a half taller than Sabrina.

If Di Luca felt any surprise at Sabrina's peculiar emo outfit, he didn't show it.

Sabrina knew she would remember the events leading up to their meeting in painful detail. The security guard at the door with his mouth hanging open. Outraged whispered conversations erupting between the beautiful women of all ages who moved around the store with lazy familiarity. The dreadful moment when she passed a mirrored wall and realized that she had forgotten to change for the appointment, when she remembered the elegant suit and the smart high-heeled shoes at the bottom of her shoulder bag. Her mascara and her heavily kohl-rimmed eyes staring out from under the hoodie, making her look like a raccoon with dangerous intentions. Federico Renda would have shuddered. And then sacked her on the spot.

Nevertheless, she had summoned up a beaming smile when she addressed one of the store assistants with her highly unlikely claim to have an appointment with the designer. The girl had quickly—as if Sabrina were radioactive—passed her on to a secretary from farther inside the emporium.

This secretary had carried out a hushed conversation on her headset before welcoming her with a nervous smile.

The next mortifying incident occurred when a security guard insisted on scanning her with a hand-held metal detector. The detector howled when it picked out the Walther and the Colt. Sabrina waved her government identification card with her arm outstretched, a centimeter from the guard's nose, and intimidated him with her best lion-taming gaze.

Di Luca held out his hand, and they introduced themselves. He then rested his forearms on the railing of the gangway. The entire end wall had been replaced by an ingenious system of glass, aluminum, and rainbow-colored slats that could be turned on their own axes by dozens of small electric motors under computer control. The system permitted varying levels of daylight onto the monumental runway: the launch pad for Di Luca's collections.

And the hall was vast; it could easily accommodate the audience, journalists, photographers, and celebrities, as well as bars and tables piled high with goodie bags, canapés, and champagne.

On the runway a director was bossing around a group of whippet-thin models in miraculous dresses, shoes, and hats big enough to block out the sun.

The designer pointed.

"What do you think, signorina?"

"They're amazing," said Sabrina, and meant it.

"And this?"

He pointed to a gigantic aquarium on wheels in which other models dressed in gauzy mermaid dresses floated around gracefully. Another director was in charge of those girls; photographers and assistants on ladders and walkways were lighting, photographing, and shouting out words of encouragement.

"A bucketful of piranhas and an electric eel would work wonders." Sabrina smiled and could have bitten off her tongue. "Liven it up a bit, I mean," she mumbled.

Di Luca looked astonished. Then he threw back his head and laughed out loud, and Sabrina could see a small fortune revealed in his dental work.

She smiled back. The fashion god was wearing a pair of worn light brown cords and a washed-out polo shirt and had stuck his tanned feet into a pair of down-at-the-heel deck shoes. Each hand was rough and calloused between the thumb and index finger.

"Do you sail?" she asked.

He held up his hands and looked at them.

"As often as I—"

He was interrupted as a row of women in full Rio costume, sequined dreams, white teeth, and ostrich feathers sambaed into the hall. Behind the women came virile, athletic men, their torsos naked, who accompanied them on flutes, drums, and marimbas. It was impossible not to move your hips to the rhythm of the music.

"My autumn collection. *Carnevale.* A caravan of sensuality moving through the streets for the Milan Fashion Week at Rho Fiera.

Snapshots of Rio, New Orleans, and Venice, my hometown. Plenty of pomp and circumstance . . . to disguise a total lack of originality, of course." He smiled bitterly. "My chief designer took that with him when he left. The press is right."

"I don't think, maestro, that anyone believes that you can't still create wonderful—"

"When you create, you're nothing but a worm. If you want to dress women, all you have to do is look at Dior's drawings and you want to kill yourself. If you want to write, all you have to do is read ten pages of Elsa Morante or Hemingway and you want to stick your head in the nearest gas oven. It's a doomed enterprise."

"Not when you succeed," she said.

"You never fully succeed; not if you're really passionate about something."

She wondered if Massimiliano Di Luca was in a relationship. Most people believed that *il maestro* was gay, but the paparazzi had never succeeded in identifying a lover. Di Luca loathed physical intimacy. Colleagues, models, photographers, stylists, and journalists were made aware that a kiss on the cheek or an attempt at a hug meant a one-way ticket to the outer fringes of the galaxy as far as the Milan fashion world was concerned. Massimiliano Di Luca was a direct descendant of the doges of Venice and regarded others as inferior. But the main cause of his isolation was anxiety about the purity of his voice. He regarded himself as a randomly chosen medium for a divine talent. Like Mozart. The least he could do was to let the voice ring clear in a cathedral rather than in an attic room filled with lovers, children, pets, or spouses. "If you hear everybody else, you'll hear yourself last" was one of his mottoes. Perhaps that was why he sailed. Di Luca was said to have had a difficult childhood in the family tailor's shop in Rome, but he had said that a happy childhood was anathema to creativity and that he had always been and always would be the black sheep of the family.

"We've found Lucia and Salvatore Forlani, signore."

He didn't look at her. He looked at the multicolored daylight that fell through the slats and across the black floor. It reached his face the same moment as the information, and Sabrina noticed hundreds of fine lines and wrinkles and tiny white stubble that covered his chin and cheeks. Her words switched off the electricity in his blue eyes.

"They're dead, aren't they?"

"They are," she said.

"Where?"

"Do you have somewhere we can speak in private, signore?"

The women kept dancing, and the instruments sounded without rhythm, echoing, out of tune. The models in the aquarium looked as if they were drowning.

Di Luca looked at his hands gripping the white steel railing.

"Are you hungry?" he asked.

"No."

"Me neither. But I know a quiet place, signorina. *Per favore*," he said.

Quiet, like a prayer.

"Of course."

CHAPTER 18

He led her through narrow corridors and up and down stairs until they emerged under the open sky in a sunny courtyard. A dozing driver in a bottle-green Bentley jerked upright at the sound of Massimiliano Di Luca's knuckles on the roof. The man extricated himself from the driver's seat, got out, and smiled at Sabrina. He had a handsome broad, tanned face. He opened the doors for the designer and his strange-looking guest.

"Dal Pescatore, Alberto."

"As you wish."

The engine must have been running already because the car moved off immediately. The creamy leather seat continued to swallow up Sabrina until she began to worry that she would end up in the trunk. She had heard about the restaurant with Italy's only female chef to have three stars in the Michelin Guide, the formidable Signora Santini. Together with elBulli, Dal Pescatore was every gourmet's Holy Grail.

"You were waiting for Giulio Forlani in the bar of Dal Pescatore that day, signore? On the fifth of September 2007."

"Yes. We used to meet there every Tuesday."

"What was he like?" she asked.

"Funny and serious, only more so than other people. Shy and brilliant. A gentle giant with enormous hands. Perhaps we should talk about Giulio Forlani once we've eaten." Yet he added: "Giulio wasn't autistic . . . as such . . . Asperger's? Definitely. You don't get his mathematical skills without giving up something in return. He didn't have the gift of imagination, for instance. His world was absolutely concrete. It was what he could see and measure. He wouldn't know what an association was if it bit him on the ass. If his life became unbearable, he couldn't compensate like the rest of us. It was demanding, not least for the people around him. I've never met a more vulnerable person."

"Vulnerable?"

"Yes. What do you know about fashion, signorina?" Di Luca asked.

Sabrina looked herself up and down.

"Nothing, clearly."

"Do you think it's an art?" he asked.

"Definitely."

Massimiliano Di Luca nodded with satisfaction.

They passed the Giardini Pubblici on their way down the stately Corso Venezia.

"You're from Venice, signore?"

"The Di Lucas are mentioned in the *Golden Book* as one of the ten families that founded Venice," the master said proudly. "In the year 965."

Sabrina smiled, impressed. She omitted telling him that the D'Avalos family was listed in church records in Bergamo in Lombardy from the eighth century.

"Was there ever a happier and more carefree decade than the 1950s, signorina?" Di Luca asked. "After the war the Marshall Plan was like a saline drip into the veins of our poor country. Everyone got fridges, optimism, Vespas, and televisions, and the tourists flocked to the Eternal City. Fellini and Rossellini made Italy chic. There was no fashion industry fifty years ago. The textile factories made uniforms, the rich had their tailors—my father was one of them—and the poor made their own clothes. Now it's one of the biggest commercial operations in the world. It started with the Fontana sisters who dressed Audrey Hepburn in *Roman Holiday*. It continued with

Ava Gardner and that crazy Swede . . . Ekberg." His face cracked into a dreamy smile. "Such modest beginnings. And yet so formidable. Roberto Capucci, Simonetta Fabiani, Fernanda Gattinoni. An amazing generation."

"Designers discovered the New Woman who worked outside the home," Sabrina said, "who wanted to look elegant and feminine when she went to work at the factory or at the office and who now earned her own money."

He nodded enthusiastically.

"She was the best invention of the war! But not just the woman at the factory or the office—there are also those we today would call international trendsetters. Icons. Stars! Jackie Kennedy was a Democrat, so she wore the same clothes—almost—as the masses. Her body preferred Fontana, she said. Elizabeth Taylor was another like her."

He nodded to himself.

"But we were also a bunch of pathetic, narcissistic children. We played sun kings, we pranced around in our perfumed ivory towers, we let our power and our self-importance go to our heads. Armani, Gucci, Fendi, Prada, Ferragamo, Versace, Di Luca; we created, idolized, and celebrated each other and left the rest to the Camorra. They made our holy works in terrible factories in Naples, imported fabrics and leather into the country, exported clothes, shoes, and bags out of it. Factories where we would never set foot for fear of being contaminated by reality. We whined about the explosion of bootleg copies, but still we delivered the sketches for next year's collections to the Camorra and the Chinese in plenty of time for them to produce our products in even more appalling factories in India, Korea, and China. Same quality, same season. Made in Italy. The fashion industry in Italy lost forty thousand jobs last year. And they won't come back. Last year Italians spent €6.3 billion on bootleg goods. But of course, you already know that."

Sabrina nodded.

"I don't feel sorry for the fashion industry, Signor Di Luca. You failed to act because everyone could tell a cheap fake from the real thing. Besides, the Camorra handled recruitment and disciplined your workforce, they murdered trade union leaders and local politicians and mayors, they circumvented all environmental regulations for you, thus helping you keep down production costs in Di Luca's factories. Way down."

The designer narrowed his eyes. As if she had been a little out of focus before.

"That's the popular version, but there is a simpler one, signorina: mortal fear. Rubens Daniele was the most principled of all of us, and he refused the Camorra its pound of flesh. He was with me for several years, and he took my best model, Mona, from me and married her. Mona was my model for ten years. I thought about her when I designed. Lagerfeld has Daria Werbowy and Raquel Zimmermann, Valentino has Karolina Kurkova, and Oscar de la Renta has Jacquetta Wheeler. They're essential."

He looked down.

"Mona disappeared exactly like Lucia Forlani, and Rubens subsequently committed suicide. Something like that makes an impression. Inevitably. That day I promised myself to drive the Camorra out of La Camera. I pinned my hopes on Nanometric for that reason."

He looked at Sabrina.

"The killings also sent another message. There were no repercussions. No one was ever charged."

"You're right," he continued. "At the start we didn't think bootleg copies were a problem. Anyone could see the quality of the fake products was poor, and the people who bought them were teenagers, glamour models, Filipino maids, trainee hairdressers, or office juniors. Not a clientele we would ever want to serve. Today no one can tell the difference. The same seamstresses, shoemakers, leather workers who make official Armani products during the day work for the Chinese at night. Why? Because they're the best in the world. You've heard the astronomical figures, signorina, and they're correct. Members of the Camera Nazionale della Moda Italiana employ 700,000 people in 7,000 businesses in this country with an annual turnover of €54 billion. But the bootleg industry is snapping at our heels, and their turnover has risen by 1,700 percent since 1993. The Camorra is close to slaughtering the golden calf. Us, that is."

Di Luca chewed the inside of his cheek.

"And who can really blame a young woman for paying €300 for a fake Gucci bag in a garage rather than the official €1,300 in the flagship store down on Via dei Condotti if there is essentially no difference?"

"It just seems insane and shortsighted," Sabrina said, and blushed. She was herself the owner of a Prada bag and an Alberta Ferretti dress with a rather dubious provenance.

"You think that because you're simultaneously underestimating and overestimating the Camorra, signorina. The Cosa Nostra doesn't try to keep addicts alive so they'll continue buying heroin. Customer service isn't a concept they're particularly worried about. When our industry has died, they'll start selling coffins, bridges, roads, wind turbines, CO_2 quotas, or drinking water. It makes no difference. It's merely a question of restructuring."

CHAPTER 19

The Bentley pulled up outside Dal Pescatore, and Massimiliano Di Luca walked across the restaurant's shaded courtyard like a watch about to stop. Before they had left the car Sabrina had told him where Lucia and Salvatore Forlani had been found and how they had died.

Conversations between the other restaurant guests died in their wake. Of course everyone recognized Massimiliano Di Luca, but his hooded companion with the sunglasses was delightfully enigmatic. An unknown daughter? A charity case? A new wunderkind to replace his recently departed chief designer? This month's flavor of *puttane*? Boy or girl?

The fashion king's private dining room was bare like a monastic cell, furnished purely with the essentials. The only object in the room that had no useful purpose, strictly speaking, was a Swiss cuckoo clock in the corner, the home of an ancient wooden cuckoo that carried out its duties with breathtaking inaccuracy.

The table was set for one person only.

Massimiliano Di Luca stopped just inside the door, which closed silently behind them, and looked at the table.

"Did you know that I kept having the table set for Giulio for many months? I kept thinking that he would come back one day."

He gestured to the empty chair.

"Though there is no need to point this out, I'm not very tall, but Giulio was a giant. The furniture represents a compromise. My feet dangled an inch above the floor, and Giulio's knees scraped the tabletop. That's the nature of compromise. A state that satisfies no one but which leaves everyone with the consoling certainty that everybody else has also been screwed."

They sat down, and Sabrina watched Di Luca's hands, which were busy polishing the already shiny cutlery with the napkin. He arranged the implements with precise accuracy in front of him and held up his right hand the very second the eggplant-colored, silk-wrapped menu was placed there by the chef herself, the legendary Nadia Santini.

"I brought a guest, signora. She'll be joining me."

Sabrina smiled politely at the chef.

"And no, she isn't a Romanian street orphan I picked up on the way but an assistant public prosecutor from Naples, Ph.D. law graduate, et cetera," Di Luca said.

"With distinction," Sabrina added.

"With distinction," he said.

Signora Santini smiled warmly: "Of course, dottoressa."

"One menu will suffice."

Di Luca looked at Sabrina.

"Will you permit me to order for you?"

"Yes, please."

The designer concentrated and marked the menu with his Mont Blanc pen before passing it to Sabrina.

"Do you approve?"

"It looks delicious. I'm looking forward to it," she said.

The designer had marked the chosen dishes with tiny stars.

"I really thought we had reached a crossroads with Nanometric's invention," he began. "That when it was finally fully developed, it would mean an end to bootleg products."

"Which would solve the Di Luca Paradox."

"Exactly."

In a famous interview with *The Economist*, the designer had explained his doctrine, later known as the Di Luca Paradox: the distance from the mediocre to the best was always shorter than the distance from the best to the mediocre. If you are used to wearing Di Luca, it is difficult to go back to off-the-peg clothes. If you have lived with a sea view, it is hard to settle for a backyard. The paradox is that in order to appreciate the best, you need to have experienced mediocrity. People privileged from birth valued nothing at all.

"Nanometric's concept was beautiful," he said. "Giulio always said that he knew he was on the right track when the equations started to become beautiful."

"And did they?"

"Yes, but it took him and Batista years. They didn't make real progress until two international breakthroughs. The first happened at the University of Manchester, where Andre Geim and Konstantin Novoselov invented graphene and later graphane, a man-made substance one atom thick and stronger than steel. The next breakthrough took place at the Massachusetts Institute of Technology, where Professor Mai Luán and her team began to train nanocrystals to behave predictably. Giulio Forlani had studied at MIT and knew Mai Luán. The two ideas were ideally matched, but it was Giulio and Batista who were able to make them work together."

He drank from his water glass, and Sabrina copied him. Her fingertips left moist, dewy marks on the side of the glass.

"In our industry, as in many others, we've tried everything to protect our products against forgery: complicated engravings, watermarks, copper threads, seals, holograms, and so on. Without much success. Nanometric's invention was, quite simply, the answer."

Sabrina nodded.

Insalata di fagiolini gialli patate e tartufo was slipped in on the service plates, and cold Pinot Grigio poured into their glasses. They toasted each other, and Massimiliano Di Luca took the napkin from the table and tucked it into the neck of his shirt. The master ate three microscopic mouthfuls, which he chewed at the front of his mouth. He pushed the plate away and looked at Sabrina, who also was eating like an ailing monk. "We're like two ten-year-olds at a high-class brothel," he said. "A total waste. And anyway, the beans are too salty. I've said so before."

"Are you feeling unwell, maestro?"

He looked up and smiled.

"A little, signorina."

"The nanocrystals. How do they work?"

"They must be triggered by a ray of light. Like a clock being wound. It's photo-induced conversion of nanoprisms, to be precise. The technology behind it is simultaneously very complicated and very simple. The crystals or the prisms have been extracted—'chipped'—by silicium, silver, and glass. They're invisible as single strands but can be arranged in vast crystal grids by charging the ions on their surface. They merge and become visible to the human eye."

Sabrina opened her purse and pushed the magic strip across the table. Massimiliano Di Luca stared at it. Carefully he picked it up, and his eyes grew moist.

"May I ask how you got this?"

"Of course, but I can't tell you."

He nodded and examined the black film. He emptied his wine-glass, and a noiseless waiter refilled it immediately.

"Leave us, please," Di Luca said.

Sabrina sipped her wine. It was starting to take effect. She pushed the wineglass away and picked up her water glass instead. Her fingers were dry now.

"Batista and Giulio were able to make the grid or the strings form numbers and letters," Di Luca said slowly. "They could make them change color and shape with the precision of an atomic clock."

"Every night at midnight," she said.

"At midnight or at noon, depending on how you calibrated the crystals."

"But surely the changing of the numbers and dates must depend on time zones, datelines, magnetic fields?"

"I'm not a physicist, dottoressa. Far from it. I'm just trying to repeat Giulio Forlani's version of the holy text. How that man suffered whenever he had to explain the details to me! Well, the crystals are activated by a specially encoded lamp whose light is within a very few angstroms of a particular light in the electromagnetic spectrum," Di Luca continued. "We imagined that authorized dealers would be issued with their own personalized lamps to trigger the process. In the form of a subscription. When the customer had selected their product, the shop assistant would activate the crystals for the actual geographical location and the day's actual wavelength. If you bought your Gucci bag in Rome airport precisely at twelve midnight on your way to Moscow, for example, the date would obviously not change exactly at midnight the following day but be staggered with the two eastern time zones between Rome and Moscow, that is to say at two o'clock in the morning. Do you follow?"

She nodded.

"The lamp terminals in the shops would be linked up to a central computer that would change wavelength and amplitude daily. When the system was up and running, it would network like ATMs."

"But computers can be hacked, optical fiber cables can be tapped," Sabrina objected.

Di Luca shook his head.

"Every terminal would be unique," he said. "It would refer to three satellites in the U.S. Air Force's GPS system. And the satellites would get their encrypted radio signal from the aforementioned computer, which would be unconnected to the rest of the world."

Sabrina hiccupped and dabbed her lips with her napkin.

"Pardon me. Please continue, maestro."

"As the position of the lamp is fixed, the satellites would react if it was moved from its position—in case of theft, for example. If it was activated at unauthorized times of the day or night, it would shut down and remain inactive until it was found or reactivated. The name of the manufacturer and the serial number would obviously form a part of the labeling, and the strip would be mounted where it's visible to all."

The waiters replaced their barely touched starters with risotto al Barolo e Castelmagno. Their glasses were filled with Giuseppe Mascarello e Figlio Barolo 1993.

They didn't do justice to this dish either.

Di Luca tasted it, turned the plate around, and looked at the food with a kind of tortured yearning. Like a dog looking at an unattainable squeaky toy.

"Excessive use of Barolo," the Venetian declared. "Wouldn't you agree?"

"I think it tastes wonderful, maestro," Sabrina said politely. "Would you excuse me, please?"

She rose, and Di Luca got to his feet.

"Down the hall to the left."

"Thank you. May I?"

"Of course."

He handed her the date strip, which she returned to her purse.

CHAPTER 20

Sabrina marched to the ladies' bathroom and began to panic, realizing that there were no available cubicles. She had gone to the sinks to throw up when a young fake-tanned, platinum-blond trophy emerged from a cubicle at the far end. The woman watched her nervously and took a step to the side as Sabrina passed her.

Sabrina fell to her knees and sacrificed Signora Santini's masterfully composed dishes to the toilet bowl. She lay there for a long time with cold beads of sweat on her forehead. If death had a taste, it was the taste of gall, she thought. "Oh God, oh God," she mumbled into the bowl as the sight of her own vomit made her throw up again.

She pushed up limply, flushed the toilet, and slumped down on its seat. Dark clouds closed around her head. She knew that she would never be able to crack the case or even produce any useful leads. She would never find out who killed her father.

Everything was too big. Too complicated and utterly impossible. Unmanageable, enormous. The satellites . . . the fashion king who was waiting for her, encoded lamps and billions of euros, a building full of dead scientists, cars full of smashed-up geniuses, dead young mothers and dead boys, and dead baby boys ready to be born, thrown into black garbage can liners like rubbish.

Sabrina pummeled her face, giving herself a couple of echoing slaps to come to. She felt dispersed. Like a random, loosely connected cloud—of nanoparticles, for example, that were about to flee their fixed positions in her body, dissolve, and mix with the molecules of the toilet bowl, the door, the toilet paper holder, the bolt . . . *"Stop!"* she shouted, probably out loud. Agitated muttering ricocheted off the tiled walls and hard floors. Sabrina heard how the other women in this most defenseless of situations panicked to finish their business, how they struggled with toilet paper, clothing, zippers, and obstinate doors to get out and away.

She understood them. A sudden outburst of madness in a lavatory would have made her react in exactly the same way.

"I'm sorry," she cried out in a half-strangled voice, which only led to further suppressed upheaval. Milan was a European metropolis, the restaurant was a place of pilgrimage, and there were expressions of outrage in several languages. A child started to cry. Without looking to either side, Sabrina left the cubicle, washed her hands and face at the sink, and rinsed out her mouth.

She retrieved her best imitation of a natural smile and returned to her world-famous host.

Massimiliano Di Luca smiled politely. Sabrina knew she was as white as a sheet. She sat down, hid a last hiccup behind her napkin, and looked desperately at the next dish that had been served in her absence.

Trancio di rombo ai funghi porcini con puré di patate. Wither Hills Marlborough Pinot Noir gleamed in the glasses, 2003. Miserably, she swallowed a mouthful of mushrooms.

Di Luca found the mashed potatoes too hot and the mushrooms stale. He attributed this to perversity on behalf of the chef since this, too, was something to which he had previously drawn her attention.

"I'm actually not very hungry," he admitted when the waiters had left the room. "Strange, really. I belong to a generation that elevated gluttony to an art form. Later, we called it self-expression and handed the bill to our children."

"Who was going to operate the system?"

"The Swiss, of course," Di Luca said. "If you were to place the strip under a microscope right now, you would be able to see a line of small numbers and letters and a twelve-digit code under the crystals: Swiss Electrotechnical Committee ISO 9001:2000."

"Why the Swiss?" she asked.

"There's no avoiding them. Their forte is to place their broad backsides—in the form of their venerable institutions—on every serious international certification. That committee was set up in 1889 when the rest of Europe barely knew what electricity was. Today it employs 210 people in Fehraltorf and Lausanne. It describes itself as a nonprofit organization, which must be a unique example of Swiss humor. You know the story about the hair and a silver thread, don't you?"

"No."

"No? Right, in order to demonstrate their microtechnology superiority back in the sixties, General Electric sent a human hair lined with a silver thread to Switzerland. A few weeks later the hair came back from Bern. The Swiss had hollowed out the silver thread and fed through it an even thinner copper thread. When scientists in California pulled it out under an electron microscope, the copper thread formed itself into the word 'Swissmade.'" The fashion designer smiled indulgently. "It was one of Giulio's favorite stories. I imagine you have to be a nerd to appreciate it fully."

"I can see that, signore," Sabrina said.

Massimiliano Di Luca smoothed the napkin on the table.

"The date in the crystals changes. As regular as clockwork. As far as I understood Giulio—and he always found me unbelievably dense—the physical properties of the crystals are transformed to the rhythm of the heartbeat of the earth's magnetism. The rest was, according to Giulio and Batista, a relatively simple question of chopping the transformation into twenty-four-hour segments so the strips would show the exact date throughout the next millennium. The Camorra would never be able to copy it. The technology is too advanced, and once in place, any attempt at selling fake products would reduce their profit margins to zero."

"Some people might regard the timing as suspicious," Sabrina interjected casually.

"I beg your pardon."

She smiled.

"They point out that the attack on Nanometric was carried out a few days before the patent applications were about to be submitted."

Massimiliano Di Luca dabbed his lips.

"And who might they be, signorina?"

"The public prosecutor in Naples."

"What's the real reason for your visit? I thought you had come to tell me that Lucia and Salvatore had been found."

"It's my understanding that you had a personal connection to the Forlani family. That your relationship wasn't purely professional."

He smiled.

"Of course. I was very fond of the family."

She leaned back and played with her wineglass.

"I thought it only proper to tell you in person," she said.

"And I'm grateful. Are you making progress? Do you think someone betrayed Nanometric?"

"My superiors are convinced that the case is closed and should remain so," she said lightly. "It was thoroughly investigated here in Milan but finally shelved as unsolved."

She opened her mouth to utter more noncommittal words, and again she felt the blood drain from her face to her chest or wherever it is blood flows to. She could have sworn she had seen the top of a cell phone in his shirt pocket when she went to the bathroom. It was in a different pocket now.

She despaired at herself.

Massimiliano Di Luca was undoubtedly one of the world's most celebrated men. His cell must be close to meltdown most hours of the day. However, it had been completely silent all the time she had been with him.

"Dottoressa?"

"I'm sorry?"

Di Luca smiled.

"I asked if you would agree with your superiors' assessment of the case. Dead or alive?"

"Dead or alive?"

"A figure of speech. The case, I mean."

"Yes. Of course. After all, everyone is dead, aren't they?"

"So what are you doing now?"

"Heading home. Incidentally, did anyone carry on the work of Nanometric?"

Before Massimiliano Di Luca had time to reply, the waiters returned, this time supervised by Signora Santini in person. Rumors and complaints from the ladies' lavatory had undoubtedly reached her ears.

Torta di pesche all'Amaretto. Château d'Yquem in new glasses, 1990.

They ate their dessert in silence. This time—and not without a certain amount of irritation—Di Luca found the dish to be perfection.

"I never harbored any hope that others would carry on," he said at last. "It would surely mean a one-way ticket to the hereafter. I can't risk exposing any more innocent people to what happened to Nanometric and Giulio's family."

"What about the Americans? Professor Luán, for example."

"They're welcome to it. The Camorra can easily buy plane tickets to the United States."

The cuckoo jumped out of its Swiss chalet and called three times even though the time was 1:30 p.m.

Sabrina took a deep breath and looked at the Venetian with all the concentration she could muster. She was about to make a big leap.

"You knew my father, Signor Di Luca," she declared.

"Did I? I know many remarkable people, signorina."

"General Agostino D'Avalos. He certainly knew you. He called you on the fifth of September 2007 at 12:15. Around the time Lucia and Salvatore Forlani disappeared from Galleria Vittorio Emanuele II. He was Nanometric's other investor. I assume that the two of you joined forces."

Di Luca was impossible to rattle.

"Absolutely. A wonderful man. Your father, did you say? My condolences."

"Thank you. So you knew him?"

"Of course. Very well, or as well as anyone ever did. He was by virtue of necessity a private man, dottoressa. He rang me on the fifth to brief me on Giulio's accident and the attack on Nanometric, but he said nothing about Lucia and Salva. Three days later I was told that he had been found dead in a motel near Switzerland."

"Did you work closely together?"

"Totally. It was a partnership."

From the backseat of an Audi parked two hundred meters from the restaurant Urs Savelli told the driver to start the engine, let it idle, and turn up the car's air-conditioning. He took the white earphones out of his ears, wrapped the cord around his fingers, and put them in his pocket.

The bug he had hidden long ago in the Swiss cuckoo clock had transmitted Di Luca and Sabrina D'Avalos's predictable exchange to Savelli's earphones. Over the years the microphone had picked up every conversation between Di Luca and his prominent guests in the private dining room, including his weekly meetings with Giulio Forlani.

People were very much creatures of habit, he thought. He himself slept in a different place every night.

The designer's bottle-green Bentley pulled up in front of the restaurant. The designer and the straight-backed assistant public prosecutor were waved off by Signora Santini herself.

"Massimiliano . . ." Savelli mumbled, and shook his head.

He leaned back in the leather seat and loosened his tie.

"*Andiamo,*" he said to the driver.

CHAPTER 21

None of the confessionals was vacant, so Sabrina was reduced to sitting on one of the rear pews in the cathedral. She tried to let herself dissolve in its gray vaulted light.

Her nausea came and went.

The Bentley had dropped her off near La Scala opera house, and people on the pavement had looked at the emo with undisguised bemusement when the elegant car eased away from the curb. Mortified, she had pulled the hood over her head and hurried on.

She left the cathedral with a group of Russian tourists.

The sky was clouded, and a drop of rain hit her hood. She crossed the cathedral square and took shelter in an archway. The rain started washing the tourists off the square. She had bought a new cell phone and a pay-as-you-go SIM card in a supermarket and memorized the phone numbers she would need. She called the orphanage. It was answered by one of the supervisors she knew well.

"How is he?" she asked.

"Quiet. Except at night. The usual nightmares. They've put him back on medication."

She knew that Ismael didn't care. He swallowed every pill they put in front of him.

"Can I speak to him?"

"Hold on."

She heard a clattering sound as the handset was placed on the metal shelf next to the pay phone on the wall of the boys' wing.

The handset was picked up, and Sabrina told herself she could hear breathing. She started to cry—but silently. An audible sob would make Ismael drop the phone instantly. She knew that from previous episodes when she had allowed her feelings to get the better of her.

"Ismael? It's Sabrina. Are you all right?"

There was no sound from the other end.

Something welled up inside her chest, and she pressed the handset against her sleeve.

Then she heard the slow, measured grinding of Ismael's teeth.

The boy waited.

"I'm in Milan," she said. "I'm looking at the cathedral, Ismael. I've sent you a postcard. With dragons and monks and gargoyles and more monks and griffins. Griffins are half lion and half eagle. You wouldn't believe how many saints there are here."

She knew that her postcard would be stuck to the wall above Ismael's bed with all the others she had sent.

"I'll be home soon," she said with tears streaming down her face.

His breathing changed pace.

"I'm fine," she said with all the conviction and composure she could muster.

The air moved more slowly across the sensitive microphone in the orphanage.

"We'll go to the zoo as soon as I get back," she promised, as if they had already penciled it in and the rest was just a question of fitting the trip into their busy schedules.

"Ismael?"

She was aware that a stray sob was on its way, and she banged her head against the wall. *Porca puttana!*

Ismael quietly cleared his throat, and Sabrina smiled. A warm feeling began to spread through her body.

"Thank you, Ismael," she said. "Thank you."

Another irritated grunt before the handset bounced off the wall on the third floor of the orphanage in Naples. The boy was gone.

*   *   *

She took refuge under the awning of the nearest pavement café and ordered a Vecchia Romagna brandy and an espresso. Then she smiled brightly to a man braving the rain with hunched shoulders and an open umbrella. The man stopped in the middle of a puddle and returned her smile.

Sabrina acknowledged him and thought about Nestore Raspallo. She had started to regard him as the genie of the lamp. All she had to do was rub a cell phone and he appeared, ready to fulfill her every wish.

"Raspallo."

"Sabrina."

"How are you?"

"Have our 'handymen' started talking?" she asked.

"It's a little too soon. Perhaps they will once we've gathered more evidence, linked them to some unsolved crimes, lowered their expectations a little. If they still won't talk, then we'll waterboard them. They're with the ROS now, not the Boy Scouts. Where are you?"

"Nowhere," she said.

"What's it like there?"

She looked around. The square was deserted.

"Empty and wet."

"Your boss, Federico Renda, would like a word with you," he said.

"Thank you."

"Where are you going?"

"I thought I might pay a visit to the hospital."

"Dr. Carlo Mazzaferro? Giulio Forlani's doctor?"

He kept catching her off her guard. It was a kind of amicable sparring match, like the hundreds of battles she had waged with her brothers, but Nestore Raspallo hit home. Just as her brothers had. They usually pretended to be ninjas while Sabrina was . . . the job.

She made no reply.

"I've been reliably informed he has left Milan for an extended break in the mountains," Raspallo told her.

"Have you now? Where has he gone?"

"I don't know, but don't forget you're not the only one who can join the dots, Sabrina. They're not morons."

"You've been waiting for me," she said with sudden, disturbing insight.

She imagined his gray eyes. Right now they were probably pressed shut with irritation.

"I don't know what you're talking about. But there may be people out there who have been waiting for someone like you. The murder of our former boss, your father, has not been forgotten. An unsolved murder of a man like the general changes the way the Camorra looks at the world, in an unacceptable way. They think they have become inviolable. Talking about people waiting for you, don't forget to call your boss."

She hung up and lit a cigarette.

The rain was falling more heavily, and she raced across Corso Vercelli and took shelter under a doorway next to a Vietnamese restaurant.

Before her departure Federico Renda had given her his private number and she had felt suitably honored. She didn't know if he was answering his cell from his office or his home.

"How is your investigation going, Dottoressa D'Avalos?"

"Quite well, I think."

"I'm delighted to hear that, and I know you're in good hands with young Raspallo."

"I'm not sure that I'm in anyone's hands, signore."

Small talk had never been Federico Renda's strong point.

"No, but nevertheless I am sure that you are. By the way, the bullets are a match. The gun that was used to kill Fabiano Batista and Paolo Iacovelli in Nanometric was also the gun that killed Lucia Forlani, wherever she was, and . . . General D'Avalos. Your father."

Sabrina rested her forehead against the cold bricks and felt black exhaustion rise up within her.

"L'Artista," she said. "It was her. She killed them all. My father—"

"That's correct. That would be my guess, too."

"I've been thinking . . . or dreaming, about your problem, dottore," she said.

"Which one?"

"How Don Francesco Terrasino and L'Artista contact each other. You'll no doubt have thought about this already, but you described Don Terrasino as a medieval peasant."

"Because he is," the public prosecutor said. "Decidedly basic technology. He uses only natural fertilizer on his estate, and everything is picked or harvested by hand. There isn't a telephone in the house or a computer, barely a fridge. The only high-tech equipment is his cameras and alarm systems."

"I've got a bird table outside my window," she said. "Pigeons come there. The most basic technology I can come up with is homing pigeons." She smiled. "Ridiculous, I know. But they usually get there, and if you want to be sure, you just send several with the same message. The Cosa Nostra in Sicily uses homing pigeons."

"The thought had crossed my mind," he admitted. "But the ROS has had the estate under surveillance for years. There is nothing to suggest a pigeon loft."

"Have they been inside?"

"That's impossible. The estate is hermetically sealed."

"It was just an idea," she said.

"You mentioned something the other day that I have given thought to," Renda said magnanimously. "You can imagine all sorts of things, of course, but what if messages were passed to a man who kept pigeons? I'm going to start looking for such a man. Did you manage to speak to the eminent Venetian?"

"We had lunch together."

"And?"

"I told him that Lucia and Salvatore Forlani had been found. He seemed shocked and sad. Appropriately so, I thought."

"What did you make of him?"

"Very charming," she said.

"That's not what I meant."

"He seemed genuine, I thought. Sincere."

"I see. What are you doing next?" Renda asked.

"Looking for a place to sleep. I'm tired."

"Pleasant dreams," he said.

"Thank you."

She had never felt more awake.

She looked at the cell, dropped it through a grid in the gutter, and peeled the cellophane off the next one.

CHAPTER 22

Qualiano, Naples

Renda wasn't in his office or at home when he spoke to Sabrina D'Avalos but in an ordinary Quonset hut that served as a cell lunchroom for the road maintenance department of Qualiano. Two sturdy maintenance workers had carried Renda's wheelchair inside the hut and closed the door behind him while his official car left. This was not an area where a customized Mercedes GL blended in naturally with the urban landscape. This was Qualiano, a fairly bleak Neapolitan suburb dominated by small businesses, truck farms, small farms, and very few residential properties.

The Quonset hut was on Via Nicola Fele, one hundred meters from the tall white wall that surrounded Don Francesco Terrasino's estate. The Mafia boss's house was hidden behind a construction supplier, a supplier of swimming-pool cleaning systems, and a row of trees.

Renda looked around the inside of the Quonset hut.

"Nice."

The man with light brown hair whom Sabrina D'Avalos knew as Nestore Raspallo and whom Federico Renda knew under his real name, Captain Primo Alba, looked at the walls, which were decorated with *Playboy* centerfolds, and grinned.

"Definitely," he said. "Quite inspirational."

He sat on a wooden bench with a laptop on his knees. Next to him was a visibly uncomfortable and sweating city engineer called Franco. Just Franco.

"So tell me the story, Franco," Renda asked him.

The man unzipped his orange coverall and revealed a muscle shirt and a chunky gold chain whose links bounced off his hairy chest.

"There's not a lot to be said, signore," the engineer replied. He unfolded a large-scale map on the coffee-stained Formica table, and Federico Renda wheeled himself over.

The man pointed at the map with the tip of his pencil.

"This is our most important tool," he said. "This map shows us every fixed underground installation in the area. That is, cables, drains, fiber-optic cables, water pipes, archaeological sites such as aqueducts, burial places, deconsecrated cemeteries—insofar as we know of them—sewers, and so on."

Renda nodded.

"Where are we?"

The tip of the pencil landed in the middle of Via Nicola Fele, where it left a small dent. The engineer ripped off a sheet of kitchen towel and mopped the sweat off his forehead and neck.

"The construction supplier called us yesterday. They had noticed that the tarmac at the end of their access road was sinking slightly and seemed unstable. They use heavy trucks when they receive goods and deliver building materials. The outlet opened three months ago, and before that the road was used only for domestic traffic."

"I understand."

"Thank you."

The tip of the pencil hovered over the entrance to the construction supplier.

"Yesterday my staff came to inspect the damage—that tarmac has sunk. Not by much, by three centimeters at the most, I would say. The strange thing was that the unstable area was regular and reached across the road to the opposite curb."

"How wide is the indentation?" Renda asked.

"It's around two meters wide and eight meters long."

"And what's under the tarmac?"

The engineer looked at the public prosecutor, pressed a clenched fist against his abdomen, and suppressed a burp.

"Nothing. According to the map. Apart from a narrow sewage pipe that runs close to the curb and under the pavement," he said. "It was a mystery, Signor Procuratore—until we got the first underground photos, and then I thought it was best to inform you straight away. Especially since . . ."

The engineer gestured vaguely to the north. In the direction of Don Francesco Terrasino's estate.

"You did the right thing, Signor Franco," the public prosecutor said warmly. "We're very grateful. Aren't we, Primo?"

"Definitely," the young man said without looking up.

The pencil traced the rectangle in the road, and indeed there were no explanatory symbols on the map.

"This morning my people dug up a section of the tarmac and discovered that the gravel foundation under the tarmac was seeping away at the deepest point of the fault. It can only go one way, Signor Procuratore. And that's down. I sent for a flexible camera. There is a tunnel under the road. An unauthorized shaft of some kind. At first we thought it was an old unmarked sewer or the remains of a Roman aqueduct. We've seen that sort of thing before."

"Mining?"

"Never."

"We have visual contact," Captain Primo Alba said.

The engineer sighed while Federico Renda lifted his head like a hunting dog on the scent.

A van from the National Highway Agency was parked behind the Quonset hut. Renda and Primo Alba had made sure that the van's logos and name had been obscured with plastic foil. A gray plastic pipe ran from the back of the van and into the ground where Franco's men had removed the tarmac. From inside the van technicians had maneuvered an armored, flexible fiber-optic camera and a light source into the underground void. The technicians were transmitting the images to the computer on Alba's lap.

"We normally use the equipment to look inside blocked sewer pipes and drains," Franco explained. "It works just like those cameras doctors use to look in your stomach ... or ... up your backside. I myself have—"

A glance from Renda silenced the engineer.

The camera panned across a steel beam, a pole, a thick white perforated concertina tube hanging from an iron bracket in the tunnel's concrete roof, and a thick black cable with sockets and light-bulbs. Both ends of the tunnel faded into total darkness far beyond the range of the built-in light source.

"It's unlikely to be a Roman aqueduct, Signor Franco," the public prosecutor said, pointing to the cables and the ventilation tube on the computer screen. "Unless we've seriously underestimated the technological capabilities of our ancestors."

Franco nodded.

"Unlikely," he said sadly.

"Is it possible that such a tunnel, a fine, straight, beautifully constructed, well-ventilated, and presumably well-lit tunnel, exists in the middle of your city without anyone knowing about it?" Renda asked as he leaned back in his wheelchair.

"I wouldn't have believed it if anyone had told me," the engineer said. "Until today."

"Let's take a look at the floor," Primo Alba said, and Franco gave a quick order into the walkie-talkie.

The camera discovered a small cone-shaped pile of gravel on the floor, close to the wall, where the stabilizing gravel under the tarmac of Via Nicola Fele had found a crack in the tunnel's concrete roof.

"Laser," Alba requested.

The laser range finder built into the apparatus measured a distance of 103 meters to the south, straight to an end wall well within Don Terrasino's property and 105 meters in the opposite direction.

The engineer and the public prosecutor hunched over the map again. With a compass, Franco read the map's scale and measured out 105 meters to the north from their position.

Renda pointed to a small cluster of buildings.

"What have we got there?" he asked.

"A carpentry business," Franco said. "It's always been there. The carpenter is old; his name is Signor Marchese. He does a bit of work for the council every now and then. He lives there with his wife."

"And he would appear to have a second source of income," Primo Alba interjected.

"So it would seem," Franco admitted.

"Thank you," Renda said.

He turned to the engineer.

"Patch up the hole in the tarmac, Signor Franco. Tell the manager of the construction supplier to carry on as usual. Make something up. Say that the ground has stabilized. And get your people and your vehicles out of here. Now."

Franco rose, relieved at the prospect of leaving the Quonset hut.

"Signor Franco?"

The engineer turned around.

"Yes?"

Franco looked at the handsome, smiling young man on the bench. There was something about Alba's chilling smile that sent shivers down his spine. Then he looked into Federico Renda's grave brown eyes.

"I don't wish to threaten you with death and disaster if anything at all about this leaks out," the public prosecutor said. "About the tunnel, I mean. But . . . No, I've changed my mind. I'll make you wish that you had remained forever a hopeful glint in your mother's eyes."

Renda folded his hands on his lap.

"You're an intelligent man, Signor Franco. You can easily imagine what I'll do to you if the Camorra hears about this. Make sure your men understand it too. *Capisce?*"

"Of course."

The engineer turned around again and took one step. He had put his hand on the door handle when Renda's voice stopped him in his tracks once more.

The public prosecutor smiled.

"This Marchese. The carpenter. Do you know him?"

The engineer shrugged slightly.

"A bit."

"You wouldn't happen to know if he's interested in pigeons by any chance?"

For the first time Franco smiled, genuinely surprised.

"He talks about nothing else, Signor Procuratore."

"Thank you."

"Can I go now?"

"Of course. I'm sorry."

"Bloody hell," Primo Alba said.

"It's absolutely insane." Renda looked at the map on the table. "There is a grain store and a smaller silo behind the carpentry business. Get some people up there. Tell them they may have to be there for a long time. The moment Signor Marchese takes a pigeon from the loft, they must stop him."

"And the tunnel?"

"A stroke of luck," Renda said. "Get someone down there tonight. Remove the spilled gravel and mend the hole in the ceiling. Rig up microphones, sensors, and cameras. And look after Signorina D'Avalos for me. We owe it to her father. How is she?"

"Under pressure but still functioning—even though she's an amateur."

"Arm's length," Renda said. "And only you. Savelli can smell a trap ten kilometers away. He must come to her of his own free will."

"And when he finds her?"

Renda shrugged his shoulders.

"We'll think of something. Nearer the time. Nothing else will happen in the meantime. Perhaps nothing else will ever happen."

"No, perhaps not," the young man said.

Neither of them believed that for a second.

"So it was her," Renda said in deep thought.

"Who?" Alba asked.

"L'Artista. Damn it. She killed General D'Avalos, Lucia and Salvatore Forlani, Fabiano Batista, and Paolo Iacovelli."

A thin layer of moisture covered Renda's forehead.

"So Sabrina D'Avalos was right all along about that," Alba said pointedly. "And about the pigeons."

He looked at the public prosecutor.

"Don Terrasino, the tunnel, L'Artista. What more do you want?"

"Savelli. Savelli would be good."

He turned to face the young man.

"I know that we agreed on your services for only forty-eight hours, but would you be prepared to extend that?"

"Of course."

CHAPTER 23

Milan

Dr. Carlo Mazzaferro was a worrier, but he couldn't have done any-thing about it even if he had wanted to. It was like having freckles or an underslung jaw. Just a fact of life. To him, anxiety was a com-fort blanket. Any carefree, happy times that fate granted him only caused him stress. When he became conscious of feeling untrou-bled, he would instantly seek out a reason to worry. Whenever people talked of happiness, he felt like a blind man to whom a sunset is being described. Of course there were varying degrees of anxiety. He had learned to navigate it. His life was a never-ending series of hurdles that had to be cleared. No hurdle could be too high or too low, and it was his task to jump one after the other. Always looking for what would happen next.

Carlo Mazzaferro knew he was destined to travel through life with chronically wet feet, but at least he wasn't in water up to his neck. If his clinical career and research were flourishing, he fret-ted about the absence of love in his life even though he had been married for nineteen years and had two sons whom he definitely loved at that particular distance from which he viewed the people in his life. If he took a mistress, as he currently had, he agonized that he might be ill. Right now he enjoyed the benefit of the young woman sitting on the train seat next to him, plus good health, and he recently had been appointed professor at the Ospedale Niguarda. It was difficult, very difficult indeed, to maintain his pessimism, and it made him twitchy and anxious. He was convinced that the gods soon would notice their neglect and return to punish such hubris. With a vengeance.

Laura was lovely. She was twenty-five years old and a former Ph.D. student of his. She was beautiful and intelligent. She came from a respectable family of lawyers but had an unconventional, refreshingly artistic mind-set as well as several tattoos that only a few people had ever seen.

She rested her head on his shoulder, and Professor Carlo Mazzaferro looked at her dark fragrant hair and at the raindrops lashing the window of the train. The suburbs of Milan seemed to him gloomy, rain-swept, and bleak. He caught sight of his own smiling reflection and tried to add it to his memories.

They were on their way to his vacation house at Lake Como. They would have the place to themselves for a couple of days before he would have to put Laura on the train back to Milan—before his wife and sons arrived.

They had boarded the train at Milan's Porta Garibaldi station. They had the first-class compartment to themselves. Laura kissed him and found a couple of apples in her shoulder bag. She offered him one, but he shook his head. He leaned forward and looked out the window. No one on the platform seemed to want to travel north. The few passengers who got off the train made a dash through the rain for the shelter of the canopy. He let himself fall back into the seat when the train pulled out of the station. He did not want to see anyone he knew.

Laura kissed him again. She tasted of apple as she pried open his mouth with her pink tongue.

The door to the compartment was opened, and the noise from the corridor burst the bubble that surrounds all lovers. Laura pulled away and smiled. The stranger returned her smile, checked his seat number and reservation, and sat down opposite her. He placed a black briefcase between his boots, wedged a long walking stick into the corner, and started reading his newspaper. The man was eminently forgettable. The black coat was expensive but nothing out of the ordinary. The creases of his pants were sharp, and his shirt was white as snow.

The stranger disappeared behind his newspaper, and Laura rested her head on Mazzaferro's shoulder. She yawned, closed her eyes, and dozed off while Mazzaferro played *Tetris* on his cell. The professor looked up when he heard voices outside the compartment. Two businessmen had stopped in the corridor. Their broad backs in raincoats blocked the door. He heard a window open, and both men took out cigarettes, leaned against the wall in the rattling train, and carried on with their conversation. The new arrival looked dry even though he was not carrying an umbrella. It would seem that he had boarded the train at Porta Garibaldi but hadn't found his seat until now. Given that the train was only half full at best, this surprised Mazzaferro, but he brushed it aside. Perhaps the man had enjoyed a cup of coffee and a grappa in the dining car.

Mazzaferro looked up from his cell and discovered that the man opposite was studying him over the top of his newspaper. His gaze shifted to Laura's peaceful face, her high forehead with the tiny scar above her left eyebrow, her dark curly hair, and her smile like that of a sleeping child. Laura had tiny freckles everywhere, and her hair had a deep chestnut glow. All her hair. Her skin was milky white, and she never tanned properly, she had told him. Mazzaferro loved the exquisite white skin across her breasts and stomach. It was even whiter against the stripe of her auburn pubic hair. Laura had lips redder than any other woman's, and right now they were slightly parted. Carlo Mazzaferro saw her eyelids twitch.

"She's dreaming," the man opposite said softly. "That's good."

Mazzaferro was about to straighten up but sank back into the seat in order not to wake Laura. The man's remark was inappropriate. Too intimate. It might have been acceptable to comment on a sleeping child, but not on another man's woman. He glared at the man without replying and hoped that by doing so he had signaled his indignation.

The man's face disappeared behind the newspaper once more. A ticket collector spoke to the men outside before opening the door to the compartment, and the stranger folded his newspaper and took out his ticket from the inside pocket of his coat. The man's movements were precise and economical. Mazzaferro rummaged around in his leather jacket behind Laura's head and fished out their tickets. The ticket collector looked at them, smiled politely, and wished everyone a pleasant journey. He closed the door behind him and squeezed past the businessmen in the corridor.

The rain pelted the window of the train, and the man opposite him checked his watch.

The train entered the first of many viaducts that took the line through the low northern hills. The carriage swayed and rattled through a set of points, the compartment darkened, and Mazzaferro felt Laura's head roll onto his shoulder. She twitched like a dreaming puppy, her body tensing briefly. She sighed, and he wondered if she was having a nightmare. He had never spent an entire night with her. He stroked her face and smiled at the warm wetness on the back of his hand. Women. Tears of joy. Or perhaps she had dribbled a little in her sleep like a baby. He heard the newspaper rustle opposite him. The squeal from wheels echoed against the brickwork of the viaduct, and once more they found themselves in the suburbs. Across the roofs Mazzaferro caught a glimpse of a purple sunset sky between black clouds and dark, naked facades. He looked at his hand. His palm was dark in the yellow light, and a long tongue, black like his palm, colored the front of Laura's white shirt. It reached the belt of her jeans and seeped from a small, still breathing cut to the base of her long white neck. Carlo Mazzaferro leaned forward. Laura's arms hung limply down her sides; her hands lay open in her lap as if she were offering him everything in the whole wide world, looking directly at him. Her fine eyelids with the delicate veins trembled.

The man opposite lowered his newspaper and smiled at him.

"She's still alive, Dr. Mazzaferro," he said in a conversational tone of voice. "Just about. If I were you, I would say my good-byes now."

The long walking stick lay across his knees.

"What—"

Carlo Mazzaferro moved to get up. His mouth opened, but no words came out. He looked at the two men outside. How strange that they hadn't noticed anything. Their backs still blocked the door to the corridor.

Mazzaferro never saw the movement, but the pain exploded under his right shoulder joint. He stared at the long steel blade that had grown out of the stick in the stranger's hand. The blade must have damaged the nerve beneath his collarbone before penetrating the dark blue upholstery of the seat. A burning sensation ran through his arm right down to his fingertips. The blade disappeared into the stick, and Laura's head lolled toward the window. Carlo Mazzaferro looked at the sleeve of his jacket, at Laura's head, and started to cry.

The stranger smiled. A crooked but apologetic smile sparkled in his eyes. They even expressed compassion, solicitude. His hands, which Mazzaferro now noticed were gloved, rested quietly on his walking stick.

"I regret that we have to meet like this, Dr. Mazzaferro. I'm sorry—*Professore* Mazzaferro. Congratulations."

The professor's eyes flitted from his own bloody armpit to Laura's half-closed eyes.

"I don't think she felt anything, Professore. Apart from surprise, of course. My blade penetrated the lower part of your girlfriend's throat and severed the spinal cord between the sixth and seventh vertebrae. She was paralyzed instantly. Not a bad way to go, in my opinion."

The pain gripped Mazzaferro's arm like a vise. He gasped loudly and looked from the man's face toward the two deaf and blind men in the corridor. The emergency brake was a red handle just above his right arm.

The stranger followed the direction of Mazzaferro's eyes.

"They're my people outside, Doctor. I'm sorry. You see, there really is no sudden salvation or miraculous escape."

Mazzaferro tried to breathe as slowly as possible so as not to disturb the severed muscles in his armpit.

"You're looking at my walking stick," the man said. "It's a makila. In the olden days Basque men of a certain standing would carry a stick like this. To protect themselves against robbers, bears, and wolves in the mountains. Are you listening to me?"

The professor nodded.

"The Basques are an interesting people," the man said. "Their language is one of the oldest in the world, and the Basques themselves are genetically different from all other European races. Take the unique distribution of their blood types, for one thing. No one really knows where they came from. From the ruins of Carthage? The last survivors of the massacres by that butcher Scipio Aemilianus?"

Mazzaferro looked as if he might lose consciousness at any moment, and the man hurried up.

"What I want to tell you is that there are many types of death. For years I have administered death in every imaginable way, and so I really do know what I'm talking about, Doctor. As indeed do you—on the other side of the table, as it were. So . . . did you fake the death certificate of Giulio Forlani on the fifth of September 2007? I need a quick answer, Professore."

Saliva bubbled helpfully on the surgeon's lips, but he was incapable of saying a word. He removed his left hand from the cut under his shoulder and made a helpless gesture with it.

The stranger sighed. "We'll do this another way. Did you treat Giulio Forlani after the traffic accident on the A7?"

Mazzaferro nodded. His wet hair flopped into his eyes.

"Did he survive?"

Mazzaferro's mouth was moving, but no words came out.

Eventually he nodded furiously.

"Thank you. My compliments. It was an outstanding achievement. General Agostino D'Avalos asked you to certify him dead?"

Mazzaferro nodded sickly.

"Do you know where he is now?"

The doctor shook his head.

"You're going to kill me," he whispered.

"I promise I'm not going to kill you, Professor Mazzaferro. You have my word. So do you know where he is?"

"No, but I know you're going to kill me."

The man shook his head and stood up. He balanced like a dancer against the jerky movements of the train.

"Arrivederci, Professore."

He opened the door and left. The two men outside came into the compartment.

The train entered another viaduct, and if anyone had been standing by a window in one of the bleak high-rise buildings and looked over at the Como Express, that person might have wondered at two sudden flashes lighting up one of the compartments.

The sturdier of the businessmen looked at the doctor on the narrow floor between the seats. He shot him through the head once more, put the pistol in his briefcase, looked at the girl, and thought what a pity it was. She really was lovely.

The man closed the curtains, left the compartment, shut the door behind him, and wedged it closed.

The three men got off the train at the next station, dashed through the rain, and reached the curb at the same time as the dark blue Audi.

The bigger man got into the passenger seat while the smaller squeezed into the corner in the back next to Savelli.

The Audi set off. Urs Savelli leaned back, closed his eyes, and surrendered to his private meditations.

Giulio Forlani was alive. *Vaffanculo!*

He made a mental note to give Cesare, the truck driver, an extended lesson on how to identify unmistakable signs of death in people he assumed were dead. He would use one of Cesare's children for demonstration purposes.

"Back to Milan, signore?" the driver asked.

"What? Yes, let's go back."

CHAPTER 24

The raindrops tasted of kohl and mascara. Sabrina knew she must look like a wet tragic clown.

She was in an alleyway between a patisserie and an ironmonger's. The garbage cans smelled of cinnamon, chocolate, and vanilla, and her stomach churned. She had been standing in the rain for half an hour opposite her mother's apartment block, freezing but vigilant. There were only a few people in the street: a girl with a guitar on her back, a man walking a small dog, and a couple of boys engrossed in a conversation intelligible only to other thirteen-year-olds. There were no people in the parked cars as far as she could see, no suspicious vans with blacked-out windows, no taxis waiting for customers who never came, none of the motorcycles or ordinary sedans that usually kept returning to Via Salvatore Barzilai like spurned lovers.

Sabrina extricated herself from the shadows and crossed the street to the block next to her mother's; pressed the buzzer for the dermatologist on the third floor, who always automatically opened the door on evenings when he had consultations; and entered. The aged elevator in the center of the stairwell came clanking down to the ground floor as if it suffered from rheumatism. She opened the gated door, pulled it closed, and pressed number 5. The elevator seemed to summon up the courage before starting its ascent. Sabrina tilted back her head and looked up through the mesh in the ceiling of the elevator. As always, she imagined that she was traveling in a spacecraft: the roofs over the elevator shafts were covered with large glass domes. In the summer they glowed opal blue, like the sea under a rock, and she experienced a feeling of weightlessness if she kept staring at the dome as she traveled up. On cloudless September nights, the domes became observatories filled with stars, planets, and the navigation lights of passing airplanes.

Tonight they were blacked out by the darkness and the rain.

She exited the elevator and walked up the stairs to the top floor. Two cleaning carts were parked on the landing. Next to the carts a ladder had been bolted to the wall; a hatch at the top provided access to the attic.

The elevator started traveling down. She pressed herself against the wall and held her breath. The elevator continued its endless journey down, and its old, dry gears screamed out in protest. At each floor the elevator produced a trembling, almost human sigh. Sabrina could hear no voices coming from below, no hard steps across the marble floors. Whoever had called the elevator had to be alone and very quiet.

Her hands were damp on the rungs of the ladder, and she couldn't feel her knees. Still, she pulled herself up by her hands and swore softly when the handle of her pistol clanked against the metal bars. The hinges of the hatch groaned loudly with each degree they moved. She heard the elevator start its ascent. Sabrina wriggled through the hatch and onto the dusty attic floor and closed the hatch behind her, resting it on a trembling finger so that she could see the top of the staircase through the crack. She eased the Walther out of the shoulder holster and aimed it at the spot at the top of the stairs where the person's head would appear.

The elevator stopped at one of the middle floors. She heard a front door open and cheerful everyday voices echoing and winding their way up the spirals of the stairwell.

She was on the verge of tears and gasped for air. Breathing again required an act of will.

*   *   *

She knew every square centimeter of the dusty attic corridors. The attic had provided the scenery and setting when Sabrina and her brothers played their deadly serious games. It was crammed full of dark nooks and crannies, and she relived the fears of her childhood as she tiptoed through the darkness, convinced that at any moment a black-clad ninja would kick her legs out from under her or throw her to the floor. She had left at least half a pint of blood, some skin, and a couple of teeth up there.

Earlier that day Sabrina had checked into the five-star Grand Hotel Duomo in Via San Raffaele. She believed it was the last place anyone would think to look for an emo. The concierge already had prepared a smile of rejection when a soaked Sabrina reached the mahogany counter with a queue of much more desirable operago-ers behind her. However, his smile warmed by several degrees when she handed him her MasterCard wrapped in a €100 note.

The man's last line of defense was to offer her the bridal suite, "the only room available tonight, signorina, I'm afraid." The emo with the dead stare silently stuck out her hand for the key.

Sabrina emptied the minibar of potato chips, salted almonds, two Cokes, and a gin and tonic in a matter of minutes. She found the suite's bedroom and instantly fell asleep on the white heart-shaped bed.

And woke up at eight o'clock.

It took her several long moments to remember where she was. She found the remote control, sat up against the headboard, and pressed "on" without being able to see a television. There was an expensive humming sound before some panels slid aside to reveal a large flat-screen television mounted on the wall above a sideboard.

She channel hopped until something caught her attention. The towering platinum-blond—and frightened—beauty who had relin-quished her cubicle to her in the ladies' lavatory at Dal Pescatore appeared on one of those forgettable talk shows with a fairground set design, this time wearing a green cocktail dress sprinkled with sequins and with a neckline that went all the way down to her belly button, leaving absolutely nothing to the imagination. She was eagerly sparring with her silver-haired, somewhat shorter male cohost in the discipline of excitable nonsense.

She flicked to a local news channel. Emergency lights, blankets of rain drifting past streetlights and flashing cameras. Behind the female reporter, Sabrina could see rail tracks, overhead cables, ambulances, police cars, cordons, and railway buildings of a station she failed to identify. She was about to change channels again when the reporter's breathless words made her sit up.

"The bodies of fifty-seven-year-old surgeon Professor Carlo Mazzaferro and a twenty-five-year-old doctor, Laura Rizzo, were found in a locked first-class compartment on the Como Express. Preliminary investigations suggest that the two Milanese doctors were traveling north on a private visit when they were killed by unknown assailants for reasons yet to be determined." The reporter's face was suitably sober as the nature of the gloomy feature demanded, but her voice lingered seductively over the words "twenty-five-year-old" and "private."

Sabrina pressed the Off button, and the picture disappeared.

She tossed the remote control aside, got up from the bed, and started pacing the room in ever decreasing circles until she stopped and bent over with her hands on her knees, the bedroom still spinning behind her eyelids.

Back in her mother's apartment, a fresh shiver almost made her knees buckle. She rubbed her palms together, blew on them, and walked down the passage.

Something rubbed against her legs, and she bent down to scratch the old, half-blind tomcat, Ziggy, behind the ear. The cat pressed its head against her hand and followed her into the kitchen with a meow.

That afternoon she had ordered her mother out of the apartment and up to the family's vacation home by Lake Como. Her mother had asked few questions; forty years of marriage to the general had instilled a set of reliable automatic reflexes in her that Sabrina shamelessly activated.

"One suitcase and you're leaving now, Mom, do you hear? Take a taxi to the station and don't speak to anyone. I'll explain later. A couple of days. I need a couple of days."

The call had lasted less than a minute, and Sabrina had promised to feed the cat.

She wondered if her mother had caught the same train as Dr. Carlo Mazzaferro and his young friend, Laura Rizzo.

She turned on the lights in the rooms facing the courtyard and sat by the kitchen table for a long time. She traced patterns on the checked oilcloth with her spoon and ate slowly. She had heated up a tin of minestrone, found some bread and a bottle of Chianti, and was dozing her way through the joyless meal. Her eyelids were as heavy as lead.

When she had finished her meal, she emptied a can of cat food into a bowl, found a can of tuna in a kitchen cupboard, and served up it up to Ziggy for dessert. The cat blinked, surprised at this royal treatment, and its purring grew deeper and stronger. She looked at it with envy while it ate—and kept putting off what she had to do next.

Finally, she went down the corridor and into her father's old study. The room would forever smell of his tobacco. His pipes were still sitting in a stand on the desk. She closed the door to the passage and took down a photograph from the wall. She had glanced at it a hundred times without ever really looking at it. As far as she knew, it had always been there, but the recollection had hit her like a kick in the stomach that afternoon when, after speaking to Federico Renda, she had passed a hunting shop in Via Case Rotte and noticed a selection of oilskin jackets in the window.

The color photograph had been taken sometime in the 1980s during one of her father's frequent hunting trips. A black Labrador was lying on the ground gazing adoringly at the photographer, who she assumed was one of her father's hunting friends. Its jaws were wrapped around a beautiful dead drake, giving the dog an idiotic circus-clown grin. Her father was standing with a pipe in his mouth, smiling at something one of the other men in the picture had said. His eyes were crinkled with laughter.

Wellington boots, broken shotgun on the elbow, oilskin jacket, and a checked flat cap: the man who had entered the elevator in Galleria Vittorio Emanuele II in Milan with Lucia and Salvatore Forlani three years ago was her own father.

She was certain of it.

It took her five minutes to find her father's old tweed cap in a wardrobe in the corridor. She photographed it from several angles with her cell before putting it back.

She found the key to the gun cabinet under the pipe stand and remembered that her father's expired passports were kept on the top shelf in the gun cabinet with ammunition for the shotgun and the hunting rifles. She stuck his most recent passport in her anorak pocket and was about to close the door when she spotted his old oilskin jacket. On impulse she checked the pockets. There was a half-empty pouch of pipe tobacco in a side pocket. She opened it and inhaled the scent. The general always used to put a small piece of apple in with his tobacco to keep it fresh.

As Sabrina put the tobacco back, she felt a piece of paper under her fingertips: an ordinary pari-mutuel ticket from the San Siro racetrack. The lucky owner had won €12 on a horse by the name of Bucefalo in the sixth race, the odds-on favorite, on September 5, 2007, at 16:05. On the back in black ink someone had written the words:

CDS janus seeks friendship with MINERVA****

She had never known her father to have been interested in horse racing. Sabrina yawned and scratched her cheek; she was about to put the ticket back in the jacket pocket when her heart skipped a beat.

She had seen those tiny five-pointed stars before. Today. A few hours ago.

Massimiliano Di Luca had marked the dishes on the menu with tiny stars.

And Bucefalo had crossed the finish line two hours before Giulio Forlani had been pronounced dead by Dr. Carlo Mazzaferro, the next person on her short list of leads.

She shook her head in despair at her own slow-wittedness. Of course: "CDS Janus seeks friendship with Minerva****." A personal ad in the newspaper *Corriere della Sera*. What could be a more classic or simpler method if you wanted to contact someone? A man presumed dead, for example. If you couldn't access the print version, you could always find it online.

Little by little she was able to breathe again. Nose, airways, lungs. Exhale air out of her nose. And inhale it back in. It was easy once you knew how.

Her old bedroom would remain unchanged for as long as she needed it; her mother had promised her that. Sabrina navigated her way through the darkness, found the box of matches on the shelf below her private altar, and lit the tea light under her holy icon: the framed cover of David Bowie's *Heroes* album.

As always, the master's white healing hands and prophetic eyes instilled a certain amount of serenity in her. She sat on her bed for a long time with the hunting photograph in one hand and the pari-mutuel ticket in the other without thinking of anything in particular.

Much later she got up, put the photograph back on the wall in her father's study, and whispered good-bye to the cat.

CHAPTER 25

He checked his watch: 2:51 a.m. The hour when the defenses of the human body were at their weakest and vigilance at its lowest.

He crossed Via San Raffaele and headed for the hotel entrance.

In his highly polished shoes, well-fitting suit, white shirt, neutral tie, and respectable black coat he looked like just another guest returning to his room, and the night porter's eyebrows didn't even twitch. He walked through the lobby and called the elevator. Earlier that evening he had called the hotel and asked to be put through to Signorina D'Avalos in room 608.

The receptionist had automatically corrected him and said room 712—the bridal suite—which made him smile before he hung up.

He stood without moving for several minutes in the empty hotel corridor outside the bridal suite.

Then he knocked and waited.

Nothing.

He knocked slightly harder with the same result and frowned. He looked at the door handle and the lock. Grand Hotel Duomo had retained the old hotel keys with brass tags rather than replacing them with electronic key cards, presumably to emphasize the elegance of the establishment. He took a step back and made sure he would be undisturbed. In his inside coat pocket he found a small leather case containing slim steel instruments.

It took him thirty seconds to pick the lock.

He could see her in the bed. Sabrina D'Avalos was lying on her back on a ridiculous heart-shaped double bed, the comforter reaching halfway up her chest, her arms resting peacefully on top. Carefully he took one noiseless step and then another. Whispered her name. Hesitated. There was no movement in the bed. Raindrops rolled in golden trails down the windowpane. Her eye sockets were black pools, and he could see the sharp bow-shaped shadow under her upper lip. It looked as if she were smiling in quiet ecstasy, though he could see no reason for her to smile. He could say something, of course, but he was scared that she might scream. He took a few more steps and looked down at her face. The black hair was spread across the pillow . . . and . . . he blinked in alarm . . . he noticed the thin white cables leading to her earphones.

And then he saw the whites of her eyes.

The assistant public prosecutor stared right up at him but didn't move a muscle. His right hand had almost reached her chin.

When his hand got there, Sabrina D'Avalos was gone. She had rolled out from under the comforter, fluid and forceful, and she was now somewhere diagonally behind him. He was about to straighten up when her knee hit the side of his chest with a dry crack. The air left his lungs, and everything went black behind his eyelids. He had time to roll with the kick and felt the air pressure from her clenched fist as it passed over his scalp.

Why didn't she scream?

He opened his eyes and was about to say his name when he received a blow to his temple. The assistant public prosecutor appeared to favor strike combinations. He grunted furiously and warded off a kick to his stomach. Sabrina D'Avalos was a flickering liquid silhouette in the dark. He tried a circular kick to the top of the form. If it had hit home as he had hoped, the assistant public prosecutor would have been unconscious before she hit the floor, but it hit nothing, and he knew even before he had finished the movement that (1) she had ducked under his foot and (2) he had fatally exposed himself.

He didn't know which came first: that thought or the indescribable pain when Sabrina D'Avalos's fist precisely and with full force landed in his solar plexus.

His old close-combat instructors would have hung their heads in shame.

It took an act of will not to roar out loud. He resisted the natural reflex to clutch his stomach with both hands and hobble to a distant place where he could mourn his wounded vanity. His superhuman composure seemed to surprise Sabrina D'Avalos because she remained standing with her arms dangling along her sides to assess the impact of her blow.

Instead he landed a lucky punch on her forehead. Triumphantly he saw her stagger, and he took a step forward to end her resistance with a decisive blow to her throat or chin. But she ducked under his arm and continued toward a chair by the wall. On the back of the chair he could see a black leather holster. Sabrina D'Avalos was heading for her weapon with terrible speed.

He reached her just in time by flinging himself through the bedroom and across the bed. He grabbed the neckline of her T-shirt with one hand and closed the other around a warm bare breast. Together they fell to the floor, and he heard Sabrina D'Avalos whisper in his ear.

He froze at the sound.

It was hard to believe that a human being could make such a noise. He hesitated even though it might prove fatal. It was too much . . . too uncivilized . . . bestial. She was a young lady from a good family. One of the oldest and finest in Italy. One of her ancestors had been La Gioconda, the Mona Lisa model, for God's sake! He landed on top of her and knew that her knee was aiming for his groin, an unbearable prospect, or heading toward his stomach, which didn't bear thinking of either. The pain brought tears to his eyes. Her probing fingernails were scurrying across his head and face like lobsters feeding off the seabed, undoubtedly with the aim of digging out his eyes when they found them, and his nose and throat were filled with a disturbing smell of sweat and woman.

He quieted her down with a quick, sharp head butt and heard her teeth slam shut with a bang.

It brought him a brief respite, and he tried to get to his feet, to get away.

Her warm breast again. No matter where he put his hands, they enclosed a soft warm breast.

Sabrina's attacker wasn't a particularly repressed man, but there was something forbidden, something crude about groping a woman's breasts even if you hated her, even if she was your opponent, and even if she was trying her level best to cripple you.

So he lay down on top of her with all his weight so that his wet cheek touched hers.

For several long seconds the only sound was their rasping breathing.

"Stop," he whispered. "Stop it! It's me . . . Nestore!"

Slowly Sabrina D'Avalos turned her face to his, and her lips and tongue tasted salty. She kissed him hungrily, then softly all over his face, then hungrily again. And again his hand found a breast, and his other hand found a stripe of soft hair and all the heat and moisture between her legs that he could wish for.

They made love without saying a word. When her cheeks grew wet with tears and he paused and asked her if she wanted him to stop, she said no, no, for God's sake, don't.

At last she let him roll onto his back. He looked up at the ceiling at the pale gray fan pattern from the window and the strange shadows cast by the curtain pelmet.

"All you had to do was call," she said later.

"I did."

"I threw away my cell," she said. "You told me to, remember? I bought a new one."

"Perhaps it wouldn't kill you to use a phone more than once," he said, sounding tired.

"You could have knocked."

"I did. I guess you were listening to Jawbreaker or some other emo band."

"David Bowie. I've stopped being an emo, Nestore."

"Somehow I'm strangely pleased to hear that," he said.

"How did you get in?" she asked—or the assistant public prosecutor in her did.

"My upbringing wasn't privileged, Sabrina. But I learned some useful skills in the slums of Turin. I stole my first car when I was twelve."

"Could you reach the pedals?"

He laughed.

"Yes, but I couldn't see out of the windshield at the same time. I hit a lamppost after thirty meters."

"I knew it was you, Nestore."

"Really?"

He got up on one elbow and watched her grave battered face.

"I could smell you from the moment you entered," she said.

"I smell?"

She found one of his hands and kissed his fingertips one by one. "Only of good things."

He lay down on his back again but let her keep his hand.

"Then what the hell was all this for, woman?" he exclaimed, gesturing at the ceiling. "Fighting like lunatics?"

"I didn't want you to think I was easy," she replied.

CHAPTER 26

Bliss, doubt, and champagne bubbles in the blood and . . . yes, churning suspicion.

"I don't think I'll ever be able to breathe again," he said, gently massaging his sore stomach.

"It's just a sign of affection, Nestore. How did you find me?"

"You're a woman. You use your MasterCard at least once an hour."

"It's as simple as that?"

"It's what I do, Sabrina. I work with banks and bank accounts. I told you."

Gingerly he turned to face her.

"Giulio Forlani's doctor, Carlo Mazzaferro, was killed on the Como Express," he said. "Someone shot him. A twenty-five-year-old woman sitting next to him was killed with a blade through her neck. Urs Savelli would appear to have arrived in Milan, and I presume he's here to talk to you."

"I saw it on the news."

She pulled the comforter down off the bed and covered them with it.

"What could Mazzaferro tell Savelli?" he asked.

"That Giulio Forlani is alive," she suggested. "That Dr. Mazzaferro faked his death certificate at my father's request. That Forlani was spirited out of the country once he was well enough to travel. Something like that. It has to be. He must be alive."

She sat up with her back to the bed, pulled up her knees, and hugged them.

"Do you know where Forlani is?" she said.

"I've got no idea."

And you wouldn't dream of telling me if you did, she thought. Could you be in love with a man you didn't trust? she asked herself, and dismissed the question instantly. Of course you could. Perhaps it was the rule rather than the exception.

"Because you're just an ordinary civil servant working for the public prosecutor?"

"I'm sorry, but that's all I am," he said.

"But you have contacts everywhere. In the GIS, for example."

"A few old friends, Sabrina."

"So you say. By the way, it was my father," she said.

"Your father?"

"Who entered the elevator with Lucia and Salvatore Forlani. In Galleria Vittorio Emanuele II three years ago."

"Are you sure?"

He looked at her.

"Yes."

"How can you be sure? Did he leave a message . . . a letter . . . ?"

"The thought would never have crossed his mind," she said.

She pointed to her shoulder bag in the corner: "I have a DVD with a recording from a surveillance camera. It shows a man entering the elevator with a woman and a boy. You see only his back, but I know it was him. I recognized his clothes from a photo in my mother's apartment."

Nestore dragged himself over to her and kissed her shoulder.

"Where did you learn to fight like that?" he asked. "I used to think I was quite good."

Her eyes widened.

"I could tell you, but then I would have to kill you afterward," she said.

"A forgotten temple in Tibet? A secret brotherhood?"

"You could say that. I grew up with three brothers," she said. "They liked to pretend to be ninjas. And I was the target. I call it the Little Miss Girl Dragon versus the Three Brothers from Hell technique."

He laughed even though it hurt.

"Is it true that you're an aristocrat?"

"Yes. We have a coat of arms and have been blessed with the appropriate mix of industrious generations interspersed with degenerate wastrels and syphilitic charlatans. Accumulators and squanderers. Just your ordinary family. Why do you ask? If you're hoping for castles, horse-drawn carriages, and a life of leisure, you can forget about it right now. I have €1,500 in my bank account, and my apartment is rented."

"I'm very disappointed," he said.

"What did my father do with Lucia and Salvatore Forlani?" she said.

"Took them to the mountains. To the motel," Nestore Raspallo replied.

"Is that something you think or something you know?"

"He must have," he said.

"They found no trace of them," she said.

"They found no trace of anything, Sabrina." He winced as he changed position. "Christ, it's what the Mafia does. As far as I know, they've made almost four thousand people disappear in the last four decades. They're not short on experience."

"Have you heard of an assassin called L'Artista?"

"Yes; she has a remarkably high degree of success. Incidentally, your father was the most resourceful man I've ever met," Nestore said. "He always knew what to do; he had a plan within a plan within a plan."

"But still he didn't save them."

She started to cry.

"But he tried. And perhaps he saved Giulio Forlani," he said.

She closed her eyes.

"I want you to go now," she said.

"I don't think I can move," he said. "And it's raining. I'll get wet and catch pneumonia, and then you'll be sorry. I think I had better stay here. Recover. Look after you."

"You couldn't look after a stuffed panda. Good-bye, Nestore."

She started to push him away.

"What are you going to do?" he asked as he hobbled across the floor. "Did you manage to speak to Massimiliano Di Luca?"

She looked at him.

"You're having me followed," she said with the same feeling of betrayal she had felt when she sat in her mother's apartment with the hunting photograph.

He was putting on his pants, and she could not see his face.

"Not at all," he said, and she knew that he was lying. "It just seemed logical to me."

"I spoke to Signor Di Luca earlier today. Yesterday, rather," she said. "So your logic cannot be faulted."

"And?"

"Nothing. He and my father cofinanced Nanometric, and they appear to have known each other well. Very well. He wasn't what I expected. I found him very likable and straightforward. He reacted with what I think was genuine grief when I told him that the bodies of Lucia and Salvatore Forlani had been identified in Naples."

"People like him are never straightforward," Nestore Raspallo said, pulling on his socks.

"Probably not. What about you, Nestore? Are you straightforward?"

He made no reply but started looking for his shoe.

"How much do you and Federico Renda speak, for example? About me?" she asked. "Do you have a master plan depending on whether I survive the next twenty-four hours, or do you make it up as you go along? And do you have a substitute on the bench who can be brought into play when Savelli kills me?"

"What do you call people who think they're the victim of a global conspiracy, Sabrina?"

"Realists?"

"Have you seen my other shoe?" he asked.

There was a burning sensation behind her eyelids. She pressed her eyes shut.

She pointed to a corner.

"Behind you. Do you want me to help you get dressed?"

"Savelli is in town," he said. "That's the only thing you should be thinking about right now. I know you believe that you have a plan of some sort, but Savelli has upset it by killing Mazzaferro. You need friends, not enemies. So what are you going to do?"

She noticed that his consonants became curt and militaristic when he was angry, which further strengthened her suspicion that Nestore Raspallo—if that was even his real name—wouldn't know what a pension plan or an off-site conference was if it hit him on the head.

"I'll work something out," she said.

He sighed and took a step toward her on the bed, but she waved him away.

"Not now and not ever."

"What do you mean?"

"Nothing," she said, and knew that he would think she was petulant and childish. "You asked me what I'm going to do, and the answer is: nothing. I've already done something. And since I appear to be the only person interested in solving this case, I don't plan to consult anyone before I take action. Not you and not Federico Renda."

He stuck his hands in his trouser pockets and straightened up. Sabrina couldn't believe she had ever thought of him as a boy promoted beyond his ability and experience. He had the body of a gladiator and many strange scars—in odd places. He was actually rather battered. Given his age.

He smiled indulgently, which drove away her tears and infuriated her instead.

"We're employees, Sabrina. You and I. This is our job; it's not a state-sponsored personal witch hunt or a grandiose search to clear your family name or restore the reputation of dead people. Solving crimes and bringing hell down on the heads of the guilty is what we do. And you're being a little unfair. I think I've responded rather well to your requests for help."

"Please, would you just go now?" she said.

"Perhaps Forlani doesn't want to be found. Assuming he's still alive. Have you thought about that?"

"Go."

He held up his hand, but she didn't know whether it was in anger or affection.

When he reached the door, she said, "I placed an ad in the personal column of *Corriere della Sera*."

"Really? I never had you down as the type."

His voice was neutral as she clenched her fists under the comforter.

"*Figlio di puttana*," she yelled, but he already had closed the door and taken everything with him.

In the elevator, GIS Captain Primo Alba thought that he had never previously held a woman who fit in his arms like a key in a lock. That he had never been able before to lie close to a woman with whom he had made love. That he had never before been speechless for half an hour after making love to that woman.

And he thought that Sabrina D'Avalos had been as light and soft as a feather. That is, when she wasn't as hard as a pawnbroker's heart.

CHAPTER 27

Castellarano

The face at the hatch had been white as dough and framed by a starched black and white veil, and it had been vehemently dismissive, as if the mere sight of Gianni outside the door had been intolerable to behold. No male had been inside the convent school walls for two hundred years unless repair work, new building constructions, or parties for alumni required it, and the sister on duty had no intention of letting one in now.

The nun's lips remained tight in the face of the fifteen-year-old's plea; her gaze remained downcast as if she hadn't heard a single word he said. She hadn't even looked him in the eye, something for which Gianni was grateful. Everyone knew that nuns and priests could see inside your mind and read your sinful thoughts. This was God's reward for their sacrifice. Her lips were narrow and red, as if she had just downed a chalice filled with the blood of a newborn.

The steel shutter slid back in place over the door's peephole with a well-oiled click.

Gianni had sprinted across the fields and gabbled more quickly to the nun than he had ever spoken to anyone. Now he stood bent over, resting his hands on his knees with a galloping heartbeat, a stitch, and a feeling of emptiness within him. Again he considered banging his fists on the door or pulling the bell chain, which disappeared into the obscenely widened mouth of a bronze creature above him. He tried his mother's cell again.

Nothing.

Gianni took a few steps back and looked at the distant parapets and crenellations that cut small rectangles out of the sky. For a moment he thought he could hear distant piano music and . . . singing?

He had found Enzo lying unconscious on the kitchen floor with a broken water glass by his side. On the kitchen table was a pencil and today's newspaper, open on the crossword and personal ads page.

He had never imagined that Enzo's body could take up so much space. His eyes had been half open, but the huge man had stared right through him.

Gianni knew it was bound to happen one day: his mother's exasperated reproaches, the untouched pills, the constant headaches, the nosebleeds whenever Enzo's blood pressure caused a blood vessel to burst.

He had squatted down beside him, placed a hand on Enzo's shirt, and realized that his chest was moving. Gianni's brain had locked into basic first aid: free the airways, put the body into recovery position, call the emergency services—the things any son of a policeman would know.

When the ambulance crew banged on the door, Enzo opened one eye and was smiling at Gianni—or whoever he thought he was. The smile turned into a tragic distorted grimace, and Gianni started to cry.

He leaned his forehead against the oak door and closed his eyes. His mother must be told about Enzo. Immediately. The ambulance crew had fired questions at him that left him gaping like a fish. Who was Enzo's next of kin? Was he, Gianni, related to the unconscious man? Who was he, and who was the man? Allergies? Medication? Medical history? Had anything like this ever happened before? Did he know anything at all? He had escaped the stream of unanswerable questions by ducking under an outstretched arm, running down the old wooden steps that were missing the third step from the bottom, and sprinting across the yard and over fields to the tall walls of the convent.

He walked out into the sunshine and took another look at the parapet high, high above him. With his fingertips trailing the wall, he ran toward the eastern corner of the convent, where he was shaded by the vegetation. His fingers closed around a dry, fraying trunk of ivy, and he was three meters above the ground before he realized he had started climbing.

Gianni's sneakers had no trouble finding cracks between the old stones where the mortar had crumbled away. The thick branches offered excellent holds for his sweaty hands. The branches bounced and gave way, and the boy noticed from the shower of dried twigs and withered but previously undisturbed leaves that his body weight tore loose handfuls of the tiny invasive roots with which the plant had clung to the stones for centuries from the crumbling brickwork right in front of his face. He stared at the ground between his shoes, gulped, and decided to focus on the distant sky instead while he prayed that the nun's triumphant face wouldn't appear between the crenellations—a second before she tipped a vat of boiling oil over him.

Finally he could put his hands on the parapet and swing his legs over the stone wall. He was standing on a deserted watchman's gallery under an empty sky.

He scurried down the nearest steps, scanned the cloisters for the nun, who must have been swallowed up by the refectory or chapel, and ran toward the main building.

From an open window he could hear girls' voices accompanied by a honky-tonk piano.

It was like running through an underwater dream, a dream that was simultaneously wonderful and terrifying.

The vaults faded out of sight in the eternal twilight high above his head; founding fathers and saints glowered with disapproval at him from every pilaster, niche, and column. Gianni ignored them. While his sneakers brought him forward silently and quickly, his eyes were feasting. They were presented with one delightful tableau after another: everywhere he saw young, supernaturally beautiful girls. Some of them were dressed in silk kimonos with artful Japanese wigs on top of their white-painted faces, and many of them were dressed only in their underwear—most of them, in fact. They rummaged through boxes and suitcases for costumes or props or sat in front of dressing tables, bathed in a golden light from mirrors and lamps. Others were absorbed in scripts or sheet music, or they were on the stage at the far end of the hall. There was more naked flesh on display in the colossal room than he had ever thought possible. The unfamiliar smells and voices lingered between the columns. Subconsciously Gianni straightened his back, pushed up his chest—and was tackled mercilessly from behind by two well-coordinated lacrosse players from one of the senior classes.

He didn't mind at all.

Even though there was blood on the tiles right under his face from a split lower lip, he discovered, as his hands were competently twisted up behind his shoulder blades, that by turning his head to the right, he could study a smooth armpit and follow its outline to a finely curved breast in a white lace bra cup, and that by turning his head to the left, he could observe a thigh, the hollow of a knee, and a shin that continued into a narrow foot with red toenails.

He could happily have stayed there forever. The girls' skin was burning hot against his. He had their breathing in his ears and their scent in his nose: Gianni pressed his groin hard against the cold floor so that no one would notice his reaction to the ambush.

"Gianni? *Gianni?*"

His mother's voice.

The boy groaned.

"What are you doing here? How did you get in?" And addressing the girls: "Let him go! He's my son. I'm sorry."

The three singing geishas on stage broke off "Three Little Maids," and a little later Signorina Lombardi at the piano also noticed the upheaval and lifted her hands from the keyboard.

Gianni sensed the growing silence in the room, snapped out of his reverie, and rolled over on his back. He got up and rubbed his sore elbows. The two girls who had floored him were looking straight at him. Their underwear was bright white. Their arms hung along their sides, their hands still tense.

His mother had red spots on her cheeks. She had gathered up her hair in a schoolmistress bun at the back of her head, pinned up with two makeup brushes, with small squares of color tests high up her forearms.

Antonia folded her arms brusquely across her chest. He could see she was sorely tempted to slap him across the face.

His hands found each other in front of his shorts.

"Enzo has collapsed in the kitchen, and you didn't answer your cell," he said in a calm voice. "He has been taken to the hospital. He was unconscious, Mom."

Antonia looked at him as if she had never seen him before.

"Enzo?"

The boy's attention was magnetically drawn to the two Amazons, especially the taller of the girls, with the beauty spot above her left breast and the cold stare.

She had to be at least seventeen.

"What?"

"Unconscious. Almost dead," he said.

"Did he say anything?"

"No."

The girl's toes were perfectly straight. And the multicolored afternoon light that poured through the stained glass lit up fine, almost invisible golden down on her shins before bouncing off the varnish on her toenails.

"Nothing?"

"He looked at me, I think," Gianni said.

"That idiot!"

"Mom . . ."

She bit her lower lip in shame, but then she gave way to her indignation.

"I warned him, didn't I? Over and over and over! About his blood pressure."

She raised her hands to the Gothic vaults as if looking for a sign of agreement from the Almighty.

Apollonia, the headmistress, appeared out of nowhere as if emerging from a trapdoor in the floor. She nudged aside the two athletes and told the girls to put on some clothes—"At once, thank you!"—and then Antonia informed her of the reason for her son's presence.

The boy looked at the downy girl and thought that it might not be her fault she seemed so aloof. Perhaps the cold stare wasn't a reflection of her personality. Perhaps it was just how very clear eyes, gray like the sea, looked. Gianni was ready to forgive her.

"You should go," Apollonia said.

Antonia made a gesture that included all of the nave, the numerous tables, the girls, and the stage.

"Your friend Enzo is more important," the headmistress said. "I hope he's all right."

She handed Antonia her car keys.

"The blue BMW in the garage."

"Thank you. Thank you so much."

"Does he have any family?"

"No. Yes." Antonia blushed. "I don't know. I don't think so. I've never heard of anyone." She turned to Gianni. "Have you?"

"No," he said.

"Never?"

"No."

Apollonia herded them down the corridor.

"Come on, off you go."

"I'll deal with it," Antonia said. "Come on, Gianni. Now! And stop staring at the girl. She's eighteen."

CHAPTER 28

The nurse was sympathetic, as one would expect, but also matter-of-fact: the MRI scan of Enzo Canavaro's brain showed no abnormalities, but they believed that Signor Canavaro had suffered a minor stroke from a blood clot in one of the brain's smaller arteries that had yet to show up on the scan. They would repeat the scan tomorrow. The blood clot was probably the result of hardening of the arteries, which again was caused by Signor Canavaro's sky-high blood pressure and possibly a genetic predisposition. Did Signora Moretti follow? Her lodger was currently being kept in a kind of artificial coma on a respirator. He was not sedated, so he could wake up. He might experience paralysis and confusion, possibly speech difficulties. Prognosis? His future? The nurse's gaze became evasive. Her hands lifted with a shrug of the shoulders. Impossible to predict, signora. We can only hope for the best, can't we? On admission the patient's blood pressure had been terribly high, the nurse repeated. Was Antonia imagining things or was the nurse blaming her? It really was quite irresponsible, the nurse added. Antonia stuttered as she tried to explain Enzo's rejection of any reality check regarding his health . . . She had, and God was her witness . . . tried, she really had . . . but he was careless with his medication to the point of suicidal. The nurse nodded and turned to the bed, which the large bearded man filled from headboard to foot. Family? Did he have any? Not as far as Antonia knew.

The nurse found this most peculiar. She couldn't imagine anyone without a family.

"Paralyzed . . . ?" Antonia started counting the floor tiles. Then he would be better off dead. Enzo was as active as a sheepdog right from dawn to his late-evening walk. Sometimes he would even wander around all night when insomnia kept him awake. He encountered the world through his hands. Such a situation would be intolerable. As if she had read her mind, the nurse carefully explained to Antonia that obviously they had gotten the blood pressure under control at once and that they had started him on medication to break down the presumed blood clot; thrombolytic therapy, as the treatment was called, would—if all went well—restore the blood supply to the affected section of the brain. A new MRI scan would provide more information.

As would the patient's own responses, of course. When he woke up. Antonia looked at her. Was it really possible? It was. Both in theory and in practice, signora. Thrombolytic therapy had revolutionized neurology in the last five to ten years. Doctors now got patients through strokes mostly without permanent physical side effects. Obviously not every time. Far from it. But often.

While the nurse was busy at the neighboring bed, Antonia slipped her hand into the bedside table drawer and helped herself to Enzo's keys.

A young ghost was staring back at her from the wall. Antonia had automatically straightened the crooked frame before she looked at the picture. The frame wasn't dusty, and the wall behind it had not faded. It showed a grainy color photograph. It could have been cut from one of the old racing magazines piled up under Enzo Canavaro's desk, tied and bound with twine. As if they would escape if given their freedom.

The young god looked at her from the seat of a Formula One car. The visor of his helmet was up, and the visible part of his face was framed by the helmet's padding and the white fire-retardant cloth of the face mask. It might be a standard publicity shot, but Antonia didn't think so. None of the PR staff who fluttered around Formula One teams would have allowed this photo to be used to promote their driver. His gaze was far too bored, introverted, and unsmiling. The glamour coefficient was absolutely zero.

She had to sit down. She had known him once, and she had recognized him by his eyes. She had been looking at those same eyes every day for the last two years.

And she had kissed the man in the racing car. When he was a boy of only sixteen. It was a complete mystery to her until she remembered that Bruno Forlani, the man in the racing car, had a twin brother, Giulio—who she now realized was calling himself Enzo Canavaro.

So of course they had the same eyes, but now Enzo looked nothing like his twin.

The picture fell to the floor, and the glass shattered. But she kept looking at it.

Below the photo of Bruno Forlani there was a short article about a crash at Zolder in October 1993. The article was very brief and focused mainly on the coincidence that the far more famous Formula One driver Gilles Villeneuve had come off the circuit and been killed on the same stretch, Terlamenbocht, exactly ten years before the twenty-three-year-old Italian hope nearly lost his life at the same spot. The article was from Castellarano's local newspaper, *Mercurio Reggio Emilia*, which had long since gone to newspaper heaven, but its source was probably one of the international news agencies, such as AP or Reuters.

The smallest of Enzo's three rooms was a shrine to Bruno, a disturbing project. Everywhere there were photos from Bruno Forlani's short but spectacular career as a go-kart champion, a successful year in Formula Three, and finally the gateway to heaven: his year as a Formula One test driver for Ferrari in the 1992–93 season. Everything was categorized, laid out, and displayed as if it were a tribute to a saint.

In between the photographs of the brother, she found one of a married couple she vaguely recognized as the boys' parents taken during one of the family's annual visits to their mother's hometown. She saw the Castellarano background, which she knew like the back of her hand.

And she saw that everything had been displayed in a careful pattern centered on a single photograph of an attractive young woman and a smiling boy who had the same coloring and facial features as his uncle, Bruno Forlani, but with Enzo's dark, pondering eyes.

She hadn't been inside these rooms for two years and hadn't known what to expect. Certainly not this. She remembered the wooden crates from the freight company in Genoa that were delivered to the grocery shop every now and then. Remembered Enzo's anticipation and secrecy when he spotted them in the garage.

The walls seemed to close in on her. Antonia remembered that she hadn't eaten breakfast. She leaned forward with her hands on her knees and forced herself to take deep slow breaths.

She closed her eyes to Enzo's impossible, hopeless, and detailed reconstruction of a past and a future that could never be his. The woman and the boy. His wife and their son, undoubtedly. His twin brother, Bruno. Their happy parents. Enzo had approached the reconstruction in the only way he knew. The way he went about everything: dedicated, careful, detailed—and frustratingly unresolved . . . like the engine forever hovering over the empty engine compartment of the Testarossa.

As if that was enough. As if that could ward off a new tragedy.

And as if someone else might hold the key, interpret Enzo's photo collage, utter the secret password, and the wall would open like a door. As if a past come back to life was ready and waiting on the other side.

The three rooms were interconnected. Antonia walked back to the middle room: Enzo's bedroom. Once it had been her parents'. Now the double bed was standing in the middle of the floor, neatly made with a lace bedspread covering the blankets and the pillows and aligned on an east–west axis. On the wall behind the headboard there was a crucifix and a wedding photograph. The same woman again. Heartbreakingly beautiful. On the steps in front of the church in Castellarano. Under the wedding photo was a picture that made her shudder: a wild gray and black sea, the tilted deck of a fishing boat, spray cascading over orange oilskin-clad fishermen hauling swordfish on board. The fish glittered red and green, and the men grinned broadly under their caps and hoods.

To the left in the picture, turning half away and serious as always, stood Giulio Forlani, whom she knew as Enzo Canavaro. Antonia remembered how his hands had still been swollen and chafed the first night she saw him and that he still had the smell of the deep sea on him. From the trawler's radio mast, between lanterns, aerials, and radar domes, a torn Stars and Stripes was flapping in the storm.

With a pen someone had written on the lower edge of the photograph: "Flemish Cap, St. John's, Newfoundland, April 14, 2009, bloody, bloody hell!"

She sat down carefully on the edge of the bed and massaged her temples. From the garage she could faintly hear Gianni's cornet like a bittern's mournful call. The boy had refused to take part in this disloyal expedition to Enzo's past, and she understood why.

Antonia would not have believed it possible that any human being could move so quietly, least of all a man almost two meters tall whose weight was on the respectable side of one hundred kilos, but she didn't hear him enter. Enzo Canavaro walked straight past her, opened a wardrobe, and started putting things into his old salt-water-stained sea bag.

Antonia blinked.

Then she blinked again. She was sure that if she blinked hard enough he would be gone, preferably back in the hospital bed.

"Enzo . . . ? Enzo! What in God's name . . . ?"

He glanced at her while he stuffed a sleeping bag into the sea bag but said nothing. His movements were miraculously steady and measured, and his eyes and face devoid of expression.

"I am . . . I'm sorry, Enzo." She made a helpless gesture toward the open door and the bundle of keys hanging from the lock. "I know that . . . What are you doing? Where are you going?"

She began to cry.

"You can't just leave," she sobbed.

A leather jacket and a white silk scarf that Enzo wore only when he rode his motorcycle. Leather gloves.

Antonia rose and placed her hand on his arm.

He stood still and looked at her hand until she removed it.

Antonia leaned back and folded her arms across her chest. She tried anger instead.

"So who are you? Enzo Canavaro? Giulio Forlani? Bruno Forlani's brother? All of them?"

Jeans, underwear, and shirts. A small laptop on his desk. Her eyes widened when he casually stuffed a couple of thick bundles of banknotes into the inside pocket of his leather jacket. There were many more neat stacks like them on the top shelf of the wardrobe. She gulped.

"You can keep the rest, Antonia," he said. "Spend it on yourself and Gianni as you see fit. He's a good boy, and I've been glad to know him. He's bright. He deserves a good education. There's enough for both of you. More than enough."

"Enzo . . . I don't understand what's going on. Do you think you could stop for one minute and . . ."

He straightened up and finally looked at her.

His mouth opened, and she could see that he was searching for the words but had to give up.

She was crying openly now.

"Is that what Gianni was? A substitute for your own boy?" she asked.

She pointed to the photograph of the woman and the boy on the wall.

"No! . . . No!"

She held out her hand.

"I'm sorry, Enzo."

"Giulio."

He placed his hands on her shoulders, and she sank down on the bed. He sat next to her and took her hand.

"You've been great, Antonia. You're the best person I . . . the very best. Really. You're very . . . fine."

With the tip of her finger Antonia stroked the gnarled, scarred bumps that made up his knuckles. She could see nothing of her hand, which had disappeared into his enormous warm paw.

"Yeah, right," she muttered.

"I mean it."

"What happened to your face? Where did it go?"

"What do you mean?"

"Your brother, Giulio! When you were sixteen you were the spitting image of your brother, and now you look like a train wreck."

"I know that you have a million questions, Antonia. Of course you do. But I can't say anything right now; do you understand?"

"More than a million, Giulio."

She pointed at the seasickness-inducing scene on the wall.

"Your ship?"

He nodded.

"Not mine but Fred Wilson's, the skipper of the *Roseanne* from Gloucester in Massachusetts. Or perhaps it doesn't belong to him but some consortium. It's complicated."

"Why Massachusetts?"

"My father is from Boston."

She hid her face as tears dripped quietly down from her fingers onto the floorboards, leaving perfectly round circles.

"Where are you going?" she said.

"My wife and my son have been found," he said. "They went missing three years ago."

She looked at him.

"What do you mean, missing?"

"The Camorra took them."

"The Camorra? Why? Are they alive?"

"No."

There was a hint of a terrible smile.

"No," he said again.

She pointed to the central photo on the wall. "Is this your wife?"

"Yes, that's Lucia."

"Was she from here?"

"Yes. She went to the convent school and later worked as a law-yer in Milan."

"Did you meet her here . . . during one of your summer holidays?"

"Yes and no. I saw her here but didn't give her a second glance. Later I recognized her in Milan at a concert."

"Who was she with?"

He blushed.

"You ask a lot of questions, Antonia."

"Who was she with?"

"Eros Ramazzotti."

"Why did the Camorra take them, Giulio? Why did they take your wife and son?"

"Not now! I was an idiot. I was working for . . . various industries. I had started a business with a friend. We thought we could take the bread from the mouths of the Camorra and that they would just roll over. I was an idiot, Antonia. The police said they would take care of us, that nothing would happen, that we were safe."

He buried his face in his hands and his shoulders tensed up, but he didn't let go of her hand.

"I kissed your brother once," she said.

He said nothing.

"By the swimming pool," she said.

"Behind the changing rooms." Giulio Forlani nodded. "You wore a yellow dress."

"What?"

"I saw you. And Bruno, of course."

"Do you really remember that?"

"Bruno was always the lucky one," he said.

"Will you be coming back?" she asked. "Gianni would like . . . I don't know what . . . I would also like . . ."

"I'll speak to Gianni. Perhaps, if I'm lucky, I'll come back."

"Would you like that?"

"Very much."

"What happened? This morning."

He touched his neck and looked out of the window.

"Nothing. It was nothing. I was just startled by something I saw."

"The nurse said you had a stroke."

"It was nothing, Antonia, really. I'm okay."

"Don't forget to take your pills," she said, and dried her eyes angrily with a corner of her cardigan.

"I've packed them. And I won't forget to take them. Thank you. *Arrivederci.*"

"Take care of yourself," she mumbled.

She heard him on the stairs and took a pillow and pressed it against her face.

Antonia continued to sit on Giulio Forlani's neatly made bed; she stayed there while she heard him speak to her son through an open window and when the motorcycle started up. The engine howled between the garage walls as if in purgatory. It clattered across the cobblestones in the courtyard and onto the road before the sound faded away. She remained on the bed, staring at the floor, and again the sound of Gianni's cornet rose up from the garage. Each note was more tense and melancholy than its predecessor.

Later she went downstairs to the kitchen, swept up the shards of the broken water glass, and put them in the garbage can. She sat down at the kitchen table and glanced at that day's *Corriere della Sera,* at the crossword and the dense columns of personal ads. The crossword was half completed in Enzo's—Giulio's—neat handwriting.

Antonia let her eyes glide down the columns with their cryptic and coded personal ads. Halfway through the third column she wondered why the same phrase appeared twice with a couple of other ads in between:

Janus seeks friendship with Minerva

In the first one "Minerva" was followed by the word "Milan" and "****," but only two stars followed "Minerva" in the second. A cell telephone number was listed in the first, but there was nothing in the second. Giulio Forlani had circled the ads with a fine pencil.

Antonia put down the newspaper and looked at the ceiling. It was quiet upstairs. Far too quiet.

CHAPTER 29

Milan

Sabrina woke up in the bathtub at five o'clock in the morning and found it impossible to get back to sleep. Not because the bathtub was uncomfortable but because she was afraid. It was like staring down a black drain where everything whirled around before being washed away. She had been woken up by her own inchoate shouting: strange words that lingered between the tiled walls long after she had opened her eyes and closed her mouth. Sabrina had placed both the Walther and the Colt within comfortable reach on the bathroom's bidet and arranged comforters, pillows, and blankets in the tub after Nestore Raspallo had left. He hadn't just left; he had walked out on her.

This enigmatic young man was unlikely to be the only one capable of tracing the use of a MasterCard in Milan.

Sabrina decided to chase him out of her consciousness with an imaginary baseball bat every time he pushed his way in, something he was doing with alarming frequency.

The Camorra didn't murder public prosecutors or high-level police officers. It was an inviolable rule. Every clan and every individual Camorrista looked down on the Cosa Nostra, especially the Corleone family, for the murders of the investigative judges Giovanni Falcone and Paolo Borsellino. The killings were counterproductive, they attracted publicity, they damaged vital links to politicians who, of course, had to profess loyalty to the forces of law and order after each high-profile assassination, and they washed away the financial and political lubricant that oiled the wheels—political alliances that ensured the Camorra new lucrative contracts for road building, public sector construction projects, and waste management.

The Camorra preferred to destroy the reputation of a public prosecutor; they ruined his career by making him the subject of scandal, by getting him pilloried in the press, making him look suspicious, ridiculous, accusing him of fraud, incompetence, nepotism, or abuse of power, and getting him transferred to some bureaucratic gulag where he would be harmless and disillusioned. The methods were many and subtle. The attack on Federico Renda had been an exception and a weighty decision, which had undoubtedly given the System plenty to think about and created internal hostilities and long, heated discussions. The attack was sanctioned only because it was regarded as a financial necessity. Renda had grown too mighty, too effective and successful.

But even the Camorra drew a line. On one side of that line, you were faceless, a respectable agent of law and order like thousands of others, an understandably anonymous and tolerated public servant who was simply doing her job. On the other side, you had earned a name for yourself, a face; you became someone who failed to respect the status and dignity of the old clans, an unforgivable threat. A person many Camorristi talked about. Someone a young, hotheaded Camorrista might be tempted to go after. Sabrina knew she was well on the way to getting a name and a face, and she hardly dared think the thought through to its conclusion. Her brothers, her mother . . . even Ismael . . . could be targeted by the Camorra. They could make her turn right or left or force her to disappear into the witness protection program—sell flowers in Stockholm or hire out surfboards on Lesbos for the rest of her life.

She climbed out of the tub, carried the bed linen back to the bed, returned to the bathroom, and took a long hot shower while she suppressed the new warm sensation in her groin and inspected her injuries in the mirror. She had an interesting discoloration and bump on her forehead where Nestore had hit her. Her lower jaw hurt when she rocked it from side to side. She brushed her teeth with some difficulty. She tried to cover the worst damage to her face with a little foundation but despaired at the result.

She got dressed, lay down on the bed, and switched on the television. The murders of Dr. Carlo Mazzaferro and Laura Rizzo were breaking news on every channel. Photographers sent to an exclusive property in the Porta Romana district had found a tall, slim woman dressed in black, silk scarf around her head, and wearing sunglasses getting into a Mercedes with tinted windows. On the other side of the car two teenage boys were making their way through the throng of journalists and photographers. Mazzaferro's wife and sons. They looked exactly like grieving relatives in news broadcasts always did, as if the bereaved had been told how to dress and behave by the media.

Sabrina switched off the television.

An hour later she got off the bed, put on her anorak and boots, armed herself, and threw her rucksack over her shoulder.

In the lobby she found that day's *Corriere della Sera* and entered the quiet dining hall with its high ceiling, where she attracted the inevitable polite attention from the other, very differently dressed guests. Sabrina didn't care. After she had turned up as an emo in Emporio di Massimiliano Di Luca, nothing would ever be as embarrassing again.

People instinctively avoided her at the colossal buffet, and she forced herself to pile her plate high with scrambled eggs, bacon, bread, cheese, butter, and jam.

She drank juice and coffee, munching her breakfast mechanically without tasting it as she flicked through the newspaper. She found the ad halfway down the third column and was about to turn the page when she spotted an almost identical ad a little farther down. Only two stars after the word "Minerva." No telephone number. No "Milan" or other geographical location. Sabrina checked her new cell. There had been no calls while she showered.

In the absence of any better interpretations, she had assumed that the number of stars after "Minerva" referred to the four weeks in a month. Today was the eleventh of September; the front page of the newspaper was divided between the ninth anniversary of the attack on the World Trade Center, the murders on the Como Express, and a suicide bomb in a market in Baghdad, so perhaps she should have limited her entry to two stars. But then again the number of stars—which she was sure wasn't coincidental—could mean so many things.

She folded the newspaper, glanced around the dining hall without noticing anything unusual, and stroked the newspaper absentmindedly with a finger.

A hotel side exit took her to Via Agnello; she pulled her hood up and walked slowly around the back of the building and into Galleria Vittorio Emanuele II. There were few people in the shopping arcades so early in the day, which suited her fine. Identifying potential tails when the streets were practically empty was much easier. At one point her heart skipped a beat when out of the corner of her eye she saw a figure who could have been Nestore Raspallo. The acute joy ambushed and shocked her, and she cursed herself, yet she could not help turning around to look for him while forbidden joy bubbled up inside her despite her self-reproach. But the figure was gone.

She ended up in front of an exclusive menswear shop. The shop assistants were getting ready to open. Behind the counter she spotted one of the two surveillance cameras that had been the mute eyewitnesses to the disappearance of Lucia and Salvatore Forlani—accompanied by her beloved father. She turned around and examined the elevators opposite. There were four, with stainless steel doors and two sets of illuminated buttons.

She went over to them.

One of the elevators opened with a ping and startled her.

A Filipino cleaner looked at her in surprise. She wheeled her cart out of the elevator, and Sabrina looked inside. No power on earth could make her enter that elevator. She smiled to the woman and began a short conversation, which despite some language problems resulted in the cleaner photographing Sabrina with her own cell next to the elevators with many smiles and gestures.

Sabrina thanked her and offered the small woman a €10 note for her troubles, but she refused to accept it.

The zombie behind the counter of the Internet café recognized her and nodded when the door closed behind her. Sabrina could have sworn that the two boys from the other day hadn't moved an inch from *Call of Duty: Modern Warfare* in her absence.

He handed her a frosted can of Coke from the fridge without asking, and she sat down in front of a vacant computer and transferred the photograph taken in the Galleria to the PC via her cell's mini-USB cable. Sabrina knew that she was exactly 167 centimeters tall. Her boots made it 168.5 centimeters. She had been standing close to the elevator door when the cleaner had taken the picture, and with the help of a simple drawing program she could calculate the height of the elevator door accurately.

According to her father's passport, he had been 175 centimeters tall in his stocking feet. She cut and pasted the old recording from the surveillance cameras into the photo-editing program and froze the sequence at the moment when her father passed the elevator door and confronted Lucia and Salvatore Forlani. She moved the grid over the image. The man in the oilskin jacket was exactly 176.5 centimeters tall. Her father obviously would have been wearing shoes or boots. She sighed and drained the Coke. Her father's flat cap matched the one in the pictures exactly. Everything added up. Her own father had been the last person to see Lucia and Salvatore Forlani alive. Apart from L'Artista, of course.

The streets were already filled with cars, trucks, scooters, motorcycles, and pedestrians, the deafening noise of traffic and voices; Sabrina felt overwhelmed, invaded, breathless. She knew that even the cathedral, her usual place of refuge, would be packed with tourists, gesticulating guides, nuns on pilgrimage, and groups of schoolchildren. Without further ado she continued across the cathedral square, hailed a cab, and asked to be taken to Milan's Lambrate Station. She went into the ladies' lavatory and left immediately. She was hoping to wrong-foot anyone who might be watching her, but no one at the busy commuter station staggered, turned around, changed direction, or behaved suspiciously.

She drank some more coffee, bought a one-way ticket, and found a vacant seat on the 11:25 a.m. regional service to Bergamo, forty kilometers northeast of Milan; it had been the D'Avalos family's ancestral home for the last 1,200 years and was a town she knew inside out.

The fashion house had taken a deep breath—and was holding it: in twenty-six days, four hours, and twenty-two minutes the carnival procession would dance through the streets of Milan, unveiling Di Luca's summer collection. Everyone expected it to be the triumph it always was. Front and center pages in every exclusive fashion magazine would be cleared by those editors and photographers who had been lucky enough to be invited, and the designs would make every rival designer contemplate suicide or a career change. A gigantic digital clock suspended in the old factory hall showed the countdown to a hundredth of a second. The mood was tense and heightened but not feverish. The fever would set in three or four days before the procession. Assistants, stylists, and seamstresses would dart around with their pincushions, beauty boxes, tape, and scissors and tear around the city in taxis or riding pillion on messengers' scooters, their cells glued to their ears, clutching bottles of Evian water and labeled bags with G-strings, bras, dresses, shoes, and stockings for each model's change. Some models would change up to eight times behind the runway, redo their hairstyle and makeup, and replace every item of clothing, shoes, bags, accessories, and jewelry.

Of course everyone loved the hysteria, the rows, the occasional fistfights between the prima donnas—male and female—the tweaking, the improvisations, the disasters, and the last-minute rescues—as long as the collection was a success. In the days that followed the show and the parties afterward people would lie coma-tose in their own homes, in the beds of total strangers, in hotels, or in apartments commandeered at short notice before they would be summoned back to work and the models would move on to new assignments like flocks of exotic migrating birds.

But now, when the staffers needed their maestro more than ever, their great helmsman, Massimiliano Di Luca, was strangely absent-minded, irritable, and distracted, and the stress spread like ripples in the water.

"Yellow? Chintz, organza, or organdy, maestro?"

The head seamstress, Signora Zeffirelli, watched him as she waited, and the nervous junior designers held their breath, adjusted their large spectacles, and exchanged looks. For some reason all the men in the emporium this autumn wore their hair short and sported large glasses even if they had perfect vision and dressed in cheap T-shirts but expensive Seven Jeans. Di Luca assumed they were all hoping to be mistaken for Marc Jacobs. Balancing on tow-ering heels and motionless in the middle of the enormous work-table in the central dressmaker's workshop, the tall model watched the Venetian like everyone else. She held up a hand to stifle a yawn. She was wearing what everyone expected would be the collection's pièce de résistance, a formidable rebuttal of every rumor of the mas-ter's waning sense of style and creative powers, his bravura number: the wedding dress. A dream of silk, organza, and organdy, layer upon layer of light, clearly defined, more architecture than haute couture, a masterpiece in terms of both artistry and engineering. The thirty-something petticoats had been made weightless and kept their shape through a system of unique vertical organza pockets while the silk bodice wrapped itself lovingly and asymmetrically around the model's torso. A lattice of black velvet ribbons embroi-dered with brilliants and pearls wound its way through the bodice and the crackling white petals that covered the petticoats. The dress was adorned with 1,250 brilliants and 1,400 small pearls.

Massimiliano Di Luca walked slowly around the table, and the seamstresses and junior designers stepped aside. He nodded to an engineer from Aero Sekur, one of the world's leading parachute manufacturers. The man returned his smile. His daughter was one of Di Luca's assistants, and it was she—an experienced parachute jumper—who had drawn Di Luca's attention to the new types of parachutes with air-filled pockets whose fabric had a rigidity that kept a parachute open even under varying wind conditions.

Dior. Di Luca had returned to Christian Dior, for whom he harbored colossal respect, as he always did when he was in a crisis, felt exhausted, lost for idea, and drained of inspiration. The brilliant Frenchman had been active for only ten short years, but in Di Luca's opinion he had never been surpassed. He had borrowed the principal idea behind the layered petticoats from a Dior wedding dress and had made the construction even lighter by using the new parachute technology.

He completed his journey without generating a single constructive thought. His eyes kept returning to the open copy of today's *Corriere della Sera* on the table. His cell had rung three times from three different numbers, all unknown, which in itself was a form of identification: Giulio Forlani.

Slowly he ran his hand across his face. The stubble rasped against his palm. Approximately twenty pairs of eyes followed his hand. He folded his arms across his chest and pinched the bridge of his nose hard with his thumb and index finger.

He looked at Signora Zeffirelli, whose mouth opened slightly. She leaned forward, afraid to miss a single syllable. He seemed to wave her away with his fingers and instead turned his gaze to Kevin, a new talent from Liverpool and the only one of those present in whom Di Luca saw any kind of potential. He was also the only one not wearing glasses. Kevin looked at him without expression. As far as Di Luca knew, the young man was happily married and heterosexual—the only complaint he had about him. Everything was so much easier when everyone had the same sexual orientation.

Personally, he had never really understood the appeal of the fashion industry. Young starstruck people flocked to the houses in Milan and Paris like lemmings to a cliff edge, bringing with them their portfolios and dreams. Now more than ever, it would seem. He was besieged. But then again, we live in a narcissistic age, he thought to himself, which in turn was probably what made it so hard for young people today to love one another or devote themselves to anything. It required a soul—or a personality at least—to lose oneself in something bigger. These days they all were conceived in fertility clinics, designed to certain specifications, and their unimaginative provenance gave them the mistaken belief that they were somehow unique, interesting, or especially precious.

He shook his head.

Looked again at the open newspaper in the corner.

He beckoned the Englishman closer.

"What would you have been doing now, Kevin? If you hadn't ended up here, I mean."

"Designing cars."

The young man smiled.

"And you, maestro?"

Behind them the room exploded in shock.

"You'll probably find this hard to believe, Kevin, but once upon a time I was quite a talented basketball player."

The boy looked the short fashion designer up and down.

"I can see that, maestro," he said with a wide grin.

On the table the model swayed. She looked as if she had fallen asleep, or perhaps her blood sugar was low.

"I'm taking the rest of the day off, Signora Zeffirelli," Di Luca said casually.

Everyone stood rigid as a pillar of salt.

Signora Zeffirelli started to cry.

"The collection, maestro?"

"There's plenty of time," he said, which everyone knew was a lie.

"Yes, maestro."

"I'll be back tomorrow. Kevin, you finish the wedding dress and the samba costumes. You know what to do."

"Of course, boss."

"Good. The rest of you do what Kevin tells you. No questions, no fighting, no backstabbing. Show some restraint and be professional—even though it's not in your nature."

Di Luca handed a handkerchief to Signora Zeffirelli so that she could dry her tears, turned on his heel, and disappeared.

But not without taking the newspaper with him.

CHAPTER 30

Bergamo

For Sabrina, Bergamo was where everything started.

She left the railway station and headed toward Città Alta—the upper, older town—with its impregnable city wall and the towers of the Basilica di Santa Maria Maggiore, the church where she and every other child in the D'Avalos family had been baptized.

The sand- and ocher-colored housefronts were stacked on top of one another from the foot of the mountain to the old city behind the Venetian wall and, almost defying gravity, farther up to the bell tower of Palazzo della Ragione. The evening sun stood at right angles to Bergamo's pale walls, and Sabrina knew that Città Alta lit up the west-facing Lombardy plain like a mirage.

She walked through Città Basso—Bergamo's lower town—along Viale Vittorio Emanuele II. Everything was named after that man, she thought, from the container quay in Naples to the galleria in Milan. Together with Giuseppe Garibaldi he was the architect behind the united Italy and the country's first king. As far as Sabrina recalled, his primary stroke of genius had been to appoint Count Camillo di Cavour as prime minister and leave the running of the country to him. After which he could spend his time tending to his monumental beard and sitting for portraits and equestrian statues.

In Via Porta Di Punta she bought a ticket to the hundred-year-old orange funicular that rode up the mountain and through the city wall to Piazza Mercato delle Scarpe. An elevation of only fifty-eight meters but a journey through six centuries.

She thought Di Luca would have felt at home on the checkerboard that was Piazza Vecchia. This square was Venice without the canals, flooding, exorbitant prices, Russian and Chinese nouveaux riches, and gondolas. Crisp, light Venetian-style buildings surrounded the square; it was architecture better suited to exquisite patisserie, she had always thought.

Sabrina walked across to the Contarini Fountain, tossed a coin in the water, and made a wish as always. She never would have believed that she would be making today's wish or that it would be the most pressing of all her desires.

She walked through Città Alta's narrow streets as darkness fell over the city and the spotlights under the monumental buildings were turned on. Too restless to sit, too restless to eat or drink. Instead she sought out the old buildings, statues, streets, steps, and views that had made up her private world from her earliest childhood, when her family visited the town. When she was a student, she often would catch the afternoon train to Bergamo when Milan became unbearably noisy, crowded, alien, and hot. Sabrina experienced a strange feeling of invincibility when she found everything in its rightful place.

The family's old house in Via Solata was now a spa and beauty salon. An overconfident great-grandfather had placed the deeds to the house on black rather than red in accordance with an infallible mathematical system of his own invention at the roulette wheel in Monte Carlo. His bones now rested in the small, picturesque cemetery behind the casino in the company of other incurable and ruined gamblers who had put a bullet through their brains on the casino's terrace—but the house remained lost, and his bitter descendants had torn his photos out of the family albums and exiled him from their history. The D'Avalos family still fasted each year on December 13, the day when her great-grandfather's fatal error of judgment had forever and shamefully driven the family from Bergamo.

Sabrina looked at the front of the house and on impulse went inside. The place did exactly what she had hoped it would: switched off her brain for an hour and a half as she discovered that she also had a body. A body that was waxed, exfoliated, massaged, moisturized, awakened, and spoiled rotten.

Glowing, she left the sanctuary and went back to Piazza Vecchia. It might have been because the streets sloped downward or it might have been the skillful massage therapists and beauticians, but later she couldn't remember touching the cobblestones as she floated across the square. She found a vacant room in a B and B in Via Salvecchio. The woman who checked her in was also running a small bar crammed with impatient and thirsty students. Bearing in mind the words of He Who Must Not Even Be Thought About, she paid cash, and the woman was too busy to ask for ID.

She got her key, walked up the stairs, threw her knapsack on the bed, and went out again immediately.

She found a quiet corner in a restaurant near the hotel and was halfway through a portion of linguini and a welcome glass of Brunello when her cell rang. She accidentally bit the inside of her cheek.

"*Pronto?*"

"Janus?"

A man.

"Er . . . yes. Yes. Minerva?"

An almost inaudible sigh. Sabrina could hear traffic noise in the background.

"I'm Minerva. Who are you?"

"I'm Assistant Public Prosecutor Sabrina D'Avalos from the public prosecutor's office in Naples, signore." The words nearly tumbled over each other. "I have—"

"You're in Milan?" he interrupted her.

"Bergamo, signore."

"Why Bergamo?"

Sabrina looked around.

"I'm from here, but I can easily get to Milan if you prefer. I would really like to talk to you," she said with a mouth as dry as the Gobi desert. "It's important."

"To whom?"

"To everyone," she said.

"Are you alone?" the man asked.

His voice revealed no emotion. The tone was exactly what she would have expected it to be in a man who had lost everything.

"Of course."

"If I discover that you're not alone, if I discover that you're not who you say you are, if I discover that you have endangered my very being, I'll kill you. Stay in Bergamo."

"Signore . . ."

The man hung up.

"*Porca puttana,*" she whispered, and jumped when the waiter asked if there was something wrong with her linguini.

"No, no, absolutely not," she said, flustered. "It's delicious."

The waiter smiled and gestured to her cell. "Bad news, signorina?"

"I don't know yet."

She emptied her wineglass and ordered another one but pushed her plate away. She interlaced her fingers in front of her face and watched her reflection in the restaurant window for a long time.

On the way home she bought a bottle of Vecchia Romagna brandy and spent the rest of the evening lying on the bed in the B and B staring at the ceiling while the level in the bottle, for some inexplicable reason, kept dropping.

The man had said "very being" and not, for example, "my life." Was he with someone? Did someone depend on him?

When Sabrina finally—and staggering slightly—got up to brush her teeth, Giulio Forlani was a lonely, glowing mark on the E64. He was approaching Erbusco at 225 kilometers an hour. Not because he was in a hurry but because he craved speed. The motorcycle wound its way through the slow evening traffic of weaving truck convoys, vans, passenger cars, and random police patrols. A couple of ambitious officers from Polizia Stradale had tried to catch him just outside of Brescia. They gave up at the exit to Biasca when the motorcycle effortlessly outran them. Giulio barely noticed the sirens. He just switched off the motorcycle's lights and opened the throttle another half inch. The flashing lights disappeared behind a ridge.

Everything tumbled out of the darkness.

The woman in Bergamo.

His brother Bruno.

When Bruno had been an apprentice with Ferrari in Maranello, the brothers had bought the effects of a deceased young motorcycle enthusiast, which included two incredibly fast MV Agusta F4-Tamburinis. When everyone else had gone home, when the lights in the halls in the workshops and office buildings were switched off and the security guards had been bribed, the brothers would race each other on Fiorano, Ferrari's private test circuit. Highly illegal and verging on the aerodynamically impossible.

As they had to duel in the dark, where the outline of the circuit was assumed rather than seen, they had built up a set of alternative acoustic reflexes. They navigated purely by the echo of tires and engines from the barriers, the spectator stands, and the pits.

They were like motorized bats, and so they nicknamed each other *pipistrello uno* or *due*, depending on the order in which they finished each day. Giulio was usually *pipistrello uno*. Bruno claimed his brother could see in the dark.

When they weren't driving blindly around Fiorano, they would take part—along with other young motorcycle fanatics, men and women—in the *tour la Tangenziale*, a suicidal race along Milan's ring road during the afternoon rush-hour traffic. The race was inspired by the equally insane *tour du Périphérique* around the outer ring road circling Paris.

He continued west around Bergamo down the A4, left the autostrada at Dalmine, and found a small country lane outside of Fosca. The motorcycle rattled down the dirt track. Giulio stopped at the foot of a lonely hill between rustling maize fields, placed a stone under the motorcycle's kickstand, stretched his aching limbs, and unhooked the sea bag from the luggage carrier. He found a relatively level patch of grass under a handful of cypresses, removed a couple of stones, and spread out his groundsheet and sleeping bag. He sat down with his hands on his knees and looked toward Bergamo, which lay like an illuminated island on the horizon.

It was almost two years since he had been more than a few kilometers outside Castellarano.

The woman on the telephone had sounded unbelievably, almost offensively young.

He had read the ads in *Corriere della Sera* sitting at Antonia Moretti's kitchen table. He had always known there was a possibility that the ad would appear one day, but he was far from prepared. He had read them and then . . . nothing.

Darkness. Exactly like the day in the Škoda on the A7. But without the flashing mouth of the pistol.

The next thing he saw were the perforated ceiling panels above the hospital bed.

Again he thought about Bruno. Bruno was an innocent memory from a life before he met Fabiano Batista and heard his brilliant idea for a copyright protection device that would make history.

Giulio looked toward the distant town and thought about the day they nearly got killed in the mountains over Castellarano. His father, Bruno, and he. Suddenly and without warning, a wet southerly wind, atypical for the season, had risen from the floodplain and brought with it impenetrable white clouds. What should have been an ordinary stroll before lunch became a confused nightmare. The moist clouds had drenched their all too light summer clothing, and they had begun shivering from the cold. The twin brothers had been thirteen. He had been trudging along behind Bruno, who was a blurred silhouette only one meter in front of him. And Bruno was following on the heels of their father.

Upward. Keep going upward because it was too dangerous to go down, their father had said. Ultimately it was harder to fall up a mountain than fall down one.

When they finally broke through the clouds and arrived at the ridge, Giulio could suddenly see his hand, his arm, and one of his legs slice through the abrupt transition between clouds and blinding white sunlight. And even though they were still shivering, even though they were still scared and exhausted, they were in the sun, and from the stony ridge they could look down on the white clouds that filled up the valleys and they could see the other ridges, peaks, and mountaintops that lay like sleeping whales in the white sea.

Once more Giulio found himself in a white nothingness, and he didn't know whether to go up, go down, or stay where he was. His stomach lurched, and he thought back to the last day he had been Giulio Forlani.

Time miraculously stood still.

The red truck that overtook him on the inside and pulled out in the fast lane. Flickering images of Batista, Hanna, Massimiliano . . . Lucia and Salvatore, the taste of iron and catastrophe when the red wall that was the rear of the truck stopped dead in front of him. The sound of metal tearing and glass shattering; he remembered the steering wheel turning into a triangle in his hands before being wrested from his grip . . . and then . . . nothing, a gray darkness. Perhaps he remembered the fire from the muzzle of the pistol that lit up his consciousness like a photographic flash, or perhaps he was rationalizing it later when the old man told him that the driver had gotten out of the truck, walked over to the crushed Škoda, and fired the pistol twice.

The pain came much later.

The old man, the general, had sounded impressed that he remembered as much as that.

CHAPTER 31

It wasn't going the way she had planned it at all.

It hadn't started out well, and it was getting worse.

Forlani seemed completely uninterested. Empty. Vacant. Like a closed-down theater.

They were standing at the top of the bell tower of the Basilica di Santa Maria Maggiore, and for the moment they had the viewing platform to themselves. Above them was the verdigris green dome of the basilica—Bergamo's famous landmark—and above that hung a low, gray sky.

The man who used to be Giulio Forlani leaned against the stone balustrade and stared out at Città Basso and the plain. Next to him was a coin-operated telescope through which Sabrina had followed him going through some of the maneuvers that finally brought them together.

He had called shortly after ten in the morning, had woken her from a dreamless sleep and introduced her to a monumental hangover and a mouth that—as her father would have put it—tasted like the inside of a wrestler's jockstrap. In a flat voice Giulio Forlani had ordered her to go to the funicular and catch the 10:25 a.m. departure down to Città Basso, twelve (twelve!) insane minutes later. He had asked her to get some tape (which she stole from the reception desk) and stick her identification card under the funicular's northern bench (which way was north?), after which she was to make herself invisible.

Or else . . .

She was getting fed up with threats. Real as well as imaginary.

She reached the funicular three seconds before departure with the taste of blood in her mouth and on trembling, aching legs. The cabin was full to the brim, and it had required extensive fidgeting with her shoelaces with her head down between her knees to Scotch tape the identification card furtively to the underside of the bench.

Afterward she did exactly as she had been told: she made herself invisible in a café where she alleviated the hangover with coffee, cigarettes, and a beer.

But Minerva was a difficult man to please. He had also demanded that she—now traveling in the ascending funicular—stick a note with her log-on details, passwords, and access code to the public prosecutor's intranet under the bench. No doubt so that he could log on to her private drive in Naples from a laptop with a wireless Internet connection. He also had asked her which year she had graduated from law school in Milan. No doubt to check if the photograph in the university's yearbook matched the reality.

She had borrowed a notepad from the waiter in the café and again played along without asking questions.

From the station at Piazza Mercato delle Scarpe she had raced across town and had sprinted up the bell tower's seemingly endless internal spiral staircase to the viewing platform. She had pushed a child away from the telescope, stared down its outraged parents, pushed a €2 coin into the slot, and aimed the telescope at the funicular.

In vain.

No one who in any way met Giulio Forlani's known physical criteria—197 centimeters tall and weighing roughly 108 kilos—had entered or left the funicular station. But she had spotted a boy walking purposefully across the piazza and disappearing behind the corner only to return a minute later, this time visibly more relaxed and smiling as if he had just earned a very generous hourly rate for running a small errand.

"Her cell rang.

"You are who you say you are, so I've decided to meet you," the voice said.

"Where?"

A few seconds of pensive silence.

"At the top of the basilica's bell tower, signorina. What I'm saying is you can stay where you are."

"All right," she said feebly, and let go of the telescope.

The place was well chosen. From the viewing platform there were only two ways out: down the spiral staircase to the nave and over the balustrade to the narrow road thirty meters below. She wouldn't have had a chance: the man was enormous. His hands looked as if they could strangle an ox. He looked more like a leather-clad foreman at a marble quarry in Carrara than a potential Nobel Prize–winning physicist, and somehow it seemed to confirm that he was uniquely gifted.

In her mind she had rehearsed over and over how she would tell Giulio Forlani that his wife and child had been found.

She had practiced her speech in front of various mirrors.

But the very first thing Giulio said was: "You've found my wife and my son, signorina. Thank you. I can imagine where and how."

Her mouth was already open to deliver the paralyzing message and then express all the sympathy she was capable of. She would even have offered him a warm handshake or a brief embrace.

Instead she closed her mouth and muttered a feeble, "You're welcome."

An anticlimax at the top of her own church, she thought.

"The Camorra isn't what you think it is, Signor Forlani," she then began.

"Giulio. Giulio is fine."

"Okay . . . It's not what you think it is, Giulio. Not at all."

"And what do I think it is?" he asked.

"A faceless mass. It calls itself the System. It's deliberate, to make people think that it's invulnerable so that they feel beaten before they start. But there are names, Giulio. Faces and bodies. This System is made up of individuals."

"Then give me a name."

"Urs Savelli is one," she said. "He was behind the attack on your firm. He ordered the murders of Batista and Paolo Iacovelli, and he killed Hanna Schmidt."

He merely nodded, and she realized that he already knew that.

"How did you find me?" he asked.

"By chance. I found a pari-mutuel ticket from San Siro the day . . . the day . . ."

"I was killed?"

"Exactly. From the day you were killed, Giulio. It was in the pocket of a man's jacket, and there was writing on the back of it: 'CDS Janus seeks friendship with Minerva.' I discovered it was written by your friend Massimiliano Di Luca. Who is probably the man behind the almost identical ad in yesterday's *Corriere*."

"Let's hope so," he muttered.

"Have you spoken to him?"

"Of course."

Of course, she thought.

"It was Max . . . Massimiliano who suggested I meet with you. Listen to what you have to say."

He looked at her blankly.

"You made a good impression on Max."

"Thank you. And you trust him?" she asked.

"Of course."

"Why?"

He flung out his hands.

"Why? Because he's Max! He has known where I was all along."

"What?!"

"I've met with him several times since I came back to Italy," Giulio said. "He keeps me up to date, sends me things from . . . our home in Milan. My personal effects. The two stars in the ad was a code we had agreed on. Two stars meant that Lucia and Salvatore had been found."

"And four stars?"

"That I had been discovered. That I had to disappear immediately."

Christ! She leaned against the balustrade and buried her face in her hands.

"What did you think I was living on?" he asked. "Max sent me money every month. He helped me. He would call me Johann in his letters if he wanted us to meet." He looked at her. "I'm sorry that I can't offer you something as tragic and sensational as being betrayed by a good friend. My apologies, signorina."

She held up a feeble hand near his face.

"Stop," she said.

"But if anything happens to him," Giulio Forlani continued. "If anything happens to Max because you went to see him, then I'm going to—"

"Kill me?"

The eyes in the dark, lean, and ruined face studied her in depth.

"No. Because Max is already dying. But he should be allowed to die in his own way."

"What are you saying?" she said, alarmed.

"He has liver cancer. I assume you had lunch together."

"Yes, at Dal Pescatore."

Giulio Forlani smiled.

"Just so. He told me you threw up. A sinful waste," he said. "Well, did he eat anything?"

"Practically nothing."

"Then he really is dying," Giulio Forlani declared laconically. "Max loves his food."

He closed his eyes tightly and opened them again. But she didn't look at his face. It was impossible to look at his face.

Sabrina had spent hours studying every available photograph of the physicist. Photographs that were completely different, distractingly different from the bearded and scarred boxer's face that now belonged to Giulio Forlani.

"What happened to your face?"

Forlani's eyes were distant, almost lifeless creatures.

"A plastic surgeon and a man in a truck," he said. "I don't know who was more effective. Someone helped me afterward."

"General Agostino D'Avalos?"

"Yes."

"He was my father," she said.

There was a glimpse of interest before the eyes returned to the view of the endless Lombardy plain.

"My condolences, signorina. He . . . General D'Avalos . . . got me out of Milan. I was flown to a hospital in the United States. Bethesda Naval Hospital in Maryland." Forlani rubbed his forehead with one of the shovels. "I had more surgery. And then some more. Before they sent me on to . . ." He snapped his fingers, and it sounded like a saloon rifle in the quiet air. "A center for war veterans in Fort Worth in Texas. They did a good job."

"Were you able to sleep?" she asked.

"No."

"Did you talk to someone?"

"Yes . . . yes. I got the whole package. Post-traumatic stress disorder. What they called grief in the old days. Several other diagnoses with long names. In that respect it was a good place. Everyone had lost someone or something of themselves, arms or legs, and there were a lot of priests, psychologists, psychiatrists . . ."

She glanced at him and saw the pain she had been looking for.

"I started sleeping a little when I was on the boat. And when I came back here," he said. "I sleep well at the place I live now. Mostly."

Sabrina lit a cigarette but struggled to keep her lighter steady.

"How long is it since you came back?"

"Almost two years."

"And before you came back?"

"I fished. When I studied at MIT in Boston, I used to earn money in the summer vacations by fishing from Gloucester. I got a job on a boat with a skipper I knew from the old days. A man who knows how to keep his mouth shut. At the start it was hard because I can only turn my head to one side and my hearing in my left ear is poor. I didn't have all my strength back then. But I was mostly on the bridge manning the echo sounder. The sea was good. I made some friends."

"Why did you come back to Italy?"

Giulio Forlani shrugged and looked at the enormous chronometer on his left wrist.

"It felt right, signorina," he said calmly, as if she would never be able to understand.

She narrowed her eyes: "In Milan, did they know—in the witness protection program—that you had come back?"

He made no reply.

"You see," she said, "it seems strange to me that they would have agreed for you to leave your relatively safe life in the United States to return to Italy."

He looked down.

"They didn't know," he said.

"You're insane, Giulio."

"I'm in an insane situation, signorina."

Sabrina took a hard drag on her cigarette. She was going to sound like the clerk in a lost property office, but she didn't know how else to put it. "You can obviously have your wife and son's bodies released whenever you want. I presume that you would like to bring them . . . I mean bury them in the cemetery in Chiaravalle."

"Where I was buried?"

"Yes."

"Thank you," he said.

"Who is in your coffin?" she asked.

"I don't know. Your father said he would find someone."

"My father was dead when you were buried," she said.

"Then it was his assistant. Some Carabinieri captain. The same man who put me on a military plane to the United States. He sat on the floor next to my stretcher the whole way to Maryland reading aloud to me."

"From what?"

"*The English Patient.*"

He smiled. But slowly. As if his face had forgotten how to.

"Did he have a name?" she asked suspiciously.

"I don't know. I suppose so. I can't remember. Primo . . . something."

"Gray eyes and light brown hair? . . . Handsome?"

"That sounds like him." Giulio Forlani nodded.

"That asshole," she burst out.

"I rather liked him."

"He wasn't called Nestore Raspallo?"

"No."

So this Primo-Something-Nestore-Raspallo had known everything all along. He already knew!

Giulio Forlani suddenly extended his arms and pulled them back hard and vertically with a series of dramatic cracks from his neck and shoulder joints. Like a wet cormorant drying its wings on a rock.

Sabrina dropped the cigarette from her mouth and stepped back until there was only the balustrade between her and certain death.

"I'm sorry. It's just . . . I don't know what it is. It comes and goes." He smiled bashfully. "I think they might have stitched together a couple of wrong nerves by accident."

"Don't mind me."

"Are we here because of my wife and son or because of your father?" he asked. "Because you want to get famous by wiping out the Camorra single-handedly?"

Sabrina had expected the question—to some extent—because she was asking herself the same question or variations on it roughly every five minutes, and she had an indignant protest ready at the tip of her tongue. But Forlani's small, patient smile made the protest die on her lips.

"I think that I—at some point—hoped that if you were alive and if I was ready, then we could help each other," she said. "But I see now that I'm not ready. And you're alive . . . but you're not ready, either."

He watched her pensively.

"I agree," he said. "I just want to be left in peace, and I appreciate your honesty. I really do. If we had had this conversation a couple of years ago, then I would . . ." His hands spread out. "Everything! All of it! I would have done whatever it took to get this Urs Savelli. But no more. I no longer believe that killing him will make any difference. If it's not him, it'll be someone else or then someone else again . . . I simply want to be left in peace, Sabrina. The psychiatrists in the United States called it the five steps of grieving. Steps. They were right, I think. I actually believe I have a kind of life now."

It was the first time he had spoken her name.

She nodded.

"It might be a bit late for that, Giulio. For both of us. Though I think I understand you. The doctor who treated you at the Ospedale Maggiore—"

"Mazzaferro," he said.

"Precisely. Dr. Carlo Mazzaferro. He signed your death certificate, and he was murdered two nights ago on the train on his way to Como. Together with a twenty-five-year-old woman, incidentally. Of course I don't know exactly what happened, Giulio, but I presume that Mazzaferro told his killers that he forged your death certificate. I presume that was what they wanted to know. You really shouldn't have come back."

"You're a dangerous acquaintance, Assistant Prosecutor," he said.

"I never got to talk to Dr. Mazzaferro," she said.

"Don't you feel responsible?" he said.

"I'm responsible for so many things. What are you referring to?"

"Awakening the dead, Sabrina," he said mildly. "But to what kind of life? I hope you've given that a little thought. Or maybe you haven't."

"Of course I have, Giulio. Of course," she said.

That was correct. Forced resurrection was not a topic you could discuss with very many people. Right now she couldn't think of anyone who had useful experience in this area except Jesus Christ.

"I mean . . . all sorts of strange things could happen," Giulio Forlani said. He started to breathe faster, and his hands trembled as if a mild epileptic seizure was imminent. "They already are. All around you."

"Do your parents and your brother know that you're alive?" she asked.

"No."

He scrutinized her.

"They don't, do they?" he asked her.

His large hands gripped the green railing around the viewing platform as if to tear it out of the brickwork.

"Do they?" he repeated.

"Of course not, Giulio."

"Of course, of course," he mimicked her angrily. "But the Camorra knows that I'm alive?"

"Yes. I would think so."

"But that's terrible," he said in desperation. "Now I'll have to start all over again. How can they know that I'm alive? Apart from Mazzaferro, I mean. Something or someone must have alerted them?"

"Initially? Pure chance. Your wife and son appeared on every list of missing persons under the heading MIPTP, the Interior Ministry's witness protection program. That obviously shouldn't have happened. It attracted the attention of the Carabinieri and the forensic scientists. Sooner or later someone would have looked into it. It just happened to be me."

"What did they look like?" he asked into the great void around them.

Sabrina woke up the cut to her inside cheek by gnawing at it. This was impossible. There was no right thing to do or correct thing to say. She couldn't even reach out to him. She couldn't offer Giulio Forlani anything that wasn't pathetic, bogus, hollow, banal, far too inadequate. It was not enough.

He turned his face to her, waiting.

"I think all three looked good, Giulio," she said.

He nodded.

"They were fine," she said.

"Thank you."

They looked at each other. Then he swallowed something.

"An administrative error? Is that really all it takes?"

"Just a coincidence," Sabrina said.

"I don't believe in coincidences," he said. "And I don't believe in you."

"Perhaps you should start now. Believing in someone, I mean."

"Perhaps you shouldn't believe in them, either," he said. "Do you really think it was by pure chance that you got this assignment? An assignment in which your own father is deeply involved?"

"Yes, I think so."

His face took on a wild expression.

"I didn't want to be found, Sabrina!" he shouted. "I don't want to be a part of your CV, do you understand? One of your success stories. I was all right where I was! There are . . ."

"People who depend on you?" She completed his sentence.

"Yes."

He gave her an almost pitying look as if she were a dense student who had long since reached the limit of her ability.

"Have you considered that it's the same for me?" she said, thinking of Ismael.

She was starting to get angry.

And she liked it.

"I haven't followed you all the way here, Giulio, and exposed myself to all sorts of danger to annoy you," she said. "Only to discover that it was my own father who hid you. That it was my own father who spirited your wife and son out of Milan and got himself killed in the process. He was another one who was just doing his job—as well as he could in the circumstances. And he left behind a wife and four children. It was pure chance. It happens. Do you understand? Your wife and son fell out of a container, but they weren't the only ones. They were in a container with sixty other people who also had wives and fathers and children . . . and who will never know a damn thing about what happened to their loved ones."

His forehead knitted under his black dense hair.

His eyes were no longer quite as lifeless.

"What did you say?"

Again his fingertips twitched. It mesmerized her. It was as if his hands had a life of their own.

"Have you been listening to a word I said?"

It was Sabrina's turn to throw up her hands. A middle-aged German couple were struggling to reach the last stretch of the spiral staircase, sweating, out of breath as they chatted. The couple took one look at Sabrina and the giant in the black leather clothes and turned around on the spot.

"Are you deaf? I said that in the container there were—"

"Your father?"

"Yes. My father."

"With Lucia and Salvatore?"

She stared at him. Perhaps he had suffered brain damage after all.

"He took them to a motel in Alto Adige," she said. "Where he was shot in the back, your wife was shot, and . . . and . . ."

"What? What did they do to Salvatore, Sabrina? What?! I know you want to tell me. So tell me! What did they do to my son?"

"They . . . garroted him with a piece of wire."

He moved incredibly smoothly and quickly for a man of his size, despite all the scars, the metal brackets, and the titanium nails and screws in his bones.

Sabrina found herself lifted half a meter up by the neck of her anorak. Giulio Forlani pushed her back over the railings. She felt gravity pull her down as the balustrade dug into her lower back. Giulio Forlani's enormous hands were strangling her—very slowly. He was distant as he pushed her over the railings. It was as if the man's face were carved in stone. Locked and inaccessible. His eyes were blank.

Patterns like glitter balls in a nightclub started blossoming behind her eyelids, and her consciousness grew sooty and black around the edges like burning paper.

Sabrina hit him as hard as she could, her palms connecting with Giulio Forlani's ears. Executed correctly, the blow ought to have

burst his eardrums. Or at least given him something to think about for a couple of minutes. Giulio Forlani let go of her, put his hands over his ears, and staggered back three paces with a grim expression on his face.

Sabrina landed on her feet and had the barrel of the Walther pressed hard against one of his melancholy eye sockets in less than a second. She released the safety catch and cocked the gun.

Her index finger was white on the trigger, and Giulio Forlani's free eye pondered her trigger finger in surprise.

"Your son was garroted, Giulio," she whispered. "Plain and simple, and then both he and his mother, your wife, Lucia, were put in black garbage bags and tossed into a hole in a dump outside of Naples, do you hear? That must mean something to you! Do you just want me to pull the trigger and put you out of your misery right now? Or are you ready to start listening to me?"

He took a step back and rubbed his eye.

Sabrina cupped a hand behind her ear. The pistol was still aimed at his face.

"What did you say? I can't hear you," she said.

The huge man nodded.

"It does mean something, Sabrina, and I will start listening to you," he said as calmly as if they were discussing some arcane aspects of nanotechnology.

The physicist seemed to have been fitted with some sort of on–off switch.

"Thank you."

"It was Paolo Iacovelli who betrayed us," he said in a loud and clear voice.

It seemed she had damaged his eardrums after all because a thin trickle of blood was running from one of his ears and under the collar of his jacket.

He pressed a finger against his right ear and studied the blood-stained fingertip mournfully.

"It'll get better soon," she assured him. "The computer whiz kid? But he was just a boy."

"What? Yes, he was. And he would have been a very rich and evil boy if they hadn't killed him as well. It was he who made me drive to the General Electric importer in Assago so they would know exactly where I was. Stupid boy! Max found a hacker, a guy who called himself Columbus. He discovered that large amounts of money had been deposited in Paolo Iacovelli's name in various bank accounts in Liechtenstein and the Channel Islands before the attack. He was able to trace the money back to various companies controlled by the Camorra. By then the transactions had already been reversed, of course."

Sabrina returned the pistol to the holster and began to breathe more normally.

What was wrong with the men in her life? Forlani was the second man she had almost had to kill in the last forty-eight hours. And they were supposed to be on her side. What would happen once she got to Savelli or L'Artista?

It was like sitting in a cage with a huge Bengal tiger that might start to lick its lips in anticipation of its next meal at any moment. Perhaps the tiger was your friend. Perhaps you had misunderstood everything . . . such as thinking that it might be love.

"Can I have a cigarette?" he asked.

"What? Yes, of course," she said. Still feeling nauseous from the adrenaline.

She lit it for him.

Forlani smoked like someone trying his first cigarette, smiled apologetically, and coughed.

"I've never smoked before," he explained. "But suddenly I really wanted a cigarette."

"That's all right," she said. "I have that effect on people."

CHAPTER 32

Castellarano

"Signor Savelli?"

"Mmm?"

Urs Savelli's driver had opened a wardrobe in one of Enzo Canavaro's three small rooms and was showing the captain the bundles of euro notes on the top shelf.

"Leave them," the Albanian said.

The young man nodded and switched on his metal detector.

Savelli watched him with quiet satisfaction. One of the few things he respected was people with real skills, and Claudio possessed a quiver full of talents: he was an excellent driver; he was pleasant, polite, and reserved in company; he was a first-class picklock and electronics expert; and he could perform miracles with a computer.

Claudio had been duly impressed at Enzo Canavaro's locks and alarm systems but far from deterred.

He started moving the metal detector across the floorboards methodically while Urs Savelli continued to sit on Enzo Canavaro's bed. He studied the photographic collage on the walls: Enzo Canavaro's, or Giulio Forlani's, past life. The twin brother, Bruno, his parents, his wife, his son. The wedding. The town.

The Albanian felt uneasy without his makila, which he had left in the stolen red and white Telecom Italia engineering van that currently was parked in Antonia Moretti's yard, out of sight from the road. He felt ridiculous in the telecommunications company's white and red uniform.

It had proved surprisingly easy to identify the woman from the park who had shared blue grapes with Sabrina D'Avalos. And they had been phenomenally lucky: the woman had led them directly to the resurrected Giulio Forlani.

A freelance reporter had been the key to locating him. Don Francesco Terrasino's firm of lawyers in Rome had used her before. The firm's senior partner, Don Francesco's closest ally, told her a story about possible heirs to a minor fortune from an eccentric old woman who had just died in Rome. The family had been clients of the firm for generations. A distant great-grandchild possibly living in Castellarano in Reggio Emilia. Nothing sensational, signora, but still a respectable amount. They had a couple of photographs belonging to the deceased to go by. Could she help? Discreetly. Very discreetly. An unexpected inheritance always brought out the worst in people, didn't she agree? It should be a straightforward job.

Early that morning Urs Savelli had received an e-mail from the woman with a brief report attached. A few inquiries around Castellarano was all it had taken. Signora Antonia Moretti, age forty-three, a widow, living in the old grocery shop opposite La Stazione restaurant. She worked as a beautician, mostly for the undertaker Ugo Conti, and ran a small B and B with one permanent lodger, an invalid who called himself Enzo Canavaro. He had been living there for two years. Perhaps they were a couple; who knew? If they were, it would be a blessing for them, people said. They both had suffered misfortunes. The widow had a son, Gianni, age fifteen. A boy like all other teenage boys.

Later that morning Savelli and Claudio had parked the stolen telecommunications van under shady trees on a side road with a full view of the grocery shop. They had watched as the boy cycled to school and the tall woman laden with boxes and bags got into a dark blue BMW, which she drove in the direction of the convent school.

Her son's school and the convent were both being watched by other members of Savelli's small but carefully selected unit. The best of the Terrasino clan.

The metal detector buzzed when Claudio reached a small kilim rug in the next room. The young man moved the rug and knelt down.

Savelli rose and watched while Claudio removed a couple of shortened and skillfully camouflaged floorboards with a small crowbar. Where the boards had been was a hatch with a combination lock.

Claudio placed a revolving magnetic device on top of the combination lock, hooked it up to the shop's own power supply and a computer, entered a few commands into the computer, and then began reading a book about safecracking. Opening the box would take time. The electronic code breaker could spin through combinations with ten thousand permutations a minute. Even so, in theory it could take up to eleven hours before the correct combination of four digits was identified and the box opened.

Savelli went downstairs and into Antonia Moretti's clean but plain bedroom. He opened her wardrobe and noted that the widow's basic wardrobe consisted of two pairs of jeans, a couple of dresses, and a number of cheap T-shirts and shirts. The television was an old black-and-white apparatus. Above the widow's bed there was a photograph of the sublime Ferrari Testarossa in the garage. A dark-haired boy was behind the wheel. Moretti, smiling and beautiful, was sitting next to the boy, and on the rear wing sat an unrecognizable bearded, dark-haired giant. One massive hand rested on the boy's shoulder, the other on the widow's. The man looked straight into the camera with an anxious smile and narrowed dark eyes.

Evidence of real devotion there, he noted.

He turned around at the sound of Claudio's footsteps.

"All done?" he asked.

"The safe is open, signore."

"That was quick."

"We were lucky, signore."

Anyone working with Claudio should regard himself as lucky, Savelli thought.

The recessed fireproof box was empty apart from a stack of identical gray envelopes. Urs Savelli sat down on the bed with a pile of them on his lap and opened the first one.

It would appear that someone wanted Enzo Canavaro, also known as Giulio Forlani, to be provided for. Well provided for. The contents of the envelopes explained the banknotes in the wardrobe—and the Ferrari in the garage. Since August 1, 2008, an unknown benefactor had transferred €30,000 every month to Credit Suisse in Rome. The contents of the envelopes were always the same: a bank statement. Apart from the Ferrari, this new version of Giulio Forlani would appear to be remarkably frugal, and the car presumably had been a wreck when he bought it.

He estimated that Forlani's wardrobe contained about €50,000 and was in no doubt that the cash was a getaway fund in case the Camorra was about to close in on him.

He passed a bank statement to Claudio, who entered the details into his laptop.

"Let's go," the Albanian said.

The young man nodded, put the envelopes back in the box, closed the lid, and set the combination lock to the default position. Using an ultraviolet lamp and specialist goggles, he checked that Giulio Forlani hadn't used saliva to stick a hair or some other telltale sign on the fold of the lid, replaced the floorboards, and put back the rug.

Urs Savelli drove the Audi to Naples while Claudio sat in the back, hunched over his computer, muttering when something failed to go the way he had hoped but never giving in; there were no problems as far as Claudio was concerned, only challenges of varying degrees of difficulty.

They were outside Barberino di Mugello on the E35 when the young man cleared his throat.

"Signore?"

"Yes."

"The Credit Suisse benefactor. I have a name."

Savelli looked at the young man in the rearview mirror.

"The benefactor," Claudio repeated patiently. "It's Emporia Massimiliano Di Luca s.a., Milano–Rome–London . . ."

"Are you sure?"

The question baffled Claudio, and Savelli elaborated: "Have you hacked into Credit Suisse, Claudio?" He looked at his watch. "In one and a half hours? That's . . . that's . . ."

The young man laughed.

"No one can hack into a Swiss bank, signore. Certainly no one I've heard of. An American bank might be possible. There was this Russian, Levin, who stole ten million dollars from Citibank, but he had someone on the inside. But a Swiss one, no. The Americans or the Israelis might be able to; I don't know. Possibly. But it would require enormous resources." Claudio looked dreamily at the flat landscape outside. "Possibly the brains who put the Stuxnet worm inside the Iranian uranium enrichment plant could . . ."

Savelli wondered how much longer he could expect to keep Claudio. Sooner or later he would be headhunted by some intelligence agency. It was bound to happen.

"So what did you do?" Savelli interrupted him. "And pretend you're explaining this to your mother."

"I can't, signore," Claudio said apologetically. "It's very difficult to explain. It either happens or it doesn't. But if you know that someone has an account with a specific bank, you might be lucky enough to find a ghost trail on a server that person has used from their personal computer when logging on to the bank. If they don't, you're out of luck. I simply found a temporary Internet file on a server that collects data transfers from Castellarano. The file contained Signor Canavaro's passwords and access codes."

"Excellent."

"Thank you, signore."

Savelli shook his head in despair.

"Max, Max, Massimiliano Di Luca . . ." he muttered.

Cold shivers ran up Savelli's spine, and he shuddered. He looked out across the landscape along the autostrada. Far away on the other side of this deserted no-man's-land of truck farms, gas stations, workshops, supermarkets, garages, abandoned farms, fallow fields, and forgotten half-dreamed and half-finished building sites, cumulous clouds were stacking up. They were white where they met the blue vaulted sky and gray and dark blue where they touched the horizon.

He was in a dangerous mood and he knew it. The most dangerous of all. A state where something deep inside him had decided that he wanted to—ought to—fail.

Behind him Claudio was still absorbed by the computer. Claudio undoubtedly had grandiose dreams of being hired by Shin Bet or the NSA. To have the chance to use all his skills. And who could blame him? Urs Savelli thought. Ultimately was there anything more fulfilling for a human being than to discover his true vocation?

CHAPTER 33

Ticino, Milan

"You can open your eyes now," Giulio Forlani said.

"Pardon?"

"We've arrived," he said.

"What?"

He pulled the motorcycle onto its kickstand and turned off the engine.

Carefully and for the first time in an hour Sabrina opened her eyes and looked around. Forlani had been a gentleman and offered her his crash helmet while he made do with only sunglasses during the entire terrible ride.

The helmet was far too big and kept slipping over her eyes.

At one point she had been foolish enough to push it up, lean forward, and look at the instrument panel in front of Giulio. The speedometer showed 230 kilometers an hour; at that speed the six-lane Milan–Brescia autostrada was the width of a rail track and the other traffic looked stationary. It had been like sitting on a motorcycle falling from an airplane.

*   *   *

Fearing the worst, she looked down between her legs. She would be mortified if she had wet herself. She was numb from the waist down from the cold.

"If you want to dismount, you'll have to let go of that strap," Forlani said.

"What? Yes, sorry."

She had to pry her frozen fingers from the passenger seat strap.

He helped her unbuckle the helmet and supported her when she reached the ground.

"Thank you."

Again Forlani did the same big, wide, and involuntary flapping with his arms he had done at the top of the basilica. She ducked to avoid a gloved fist that would have sent her flying across the yard. Forlani was standing with his back to her, looking at the house.

She had no recollection of agreeing to this insane ride. They had walked down the endless steps inside the basilica's bell tower. Her hangover had returned with full murderous vengeance and her brain had almost turned to mush when they reached the bottom and looked out across the nearly deserted and drowsy Piazza Vecchia.

"What now?" he had asked, and she didn't have a clue.

His eyes had started flickering as if there were a loose connection in his brain—just as they had before he started strangling her—and she quickly muttered something about Federico Renda, police protection, Naples, going somewhere he could gather his thoughts, when he suggested Massimiliano Di Luca's property by the Ticino River, fifty kilometers west of Milan. Hardly anyone knew the master spent his summers there.

Sabrina looked back down the winding dirt track that disappeared behind the low coniferous forest. Behind a cluster of birch trees she could see the shallow gravel bed of the Ticino. Apart from birds and insects it was completely quiet here. A forgotten place.

The house was one of those old Tuscan farmhouses she loved so much: a house that blended into the landscape as effortlessly as if it had been left behind by a melting glacier. An old building with a boulder foundation and a sloping roof of fat red tiles that looked like an upside-down pâté.

In an open barn she spotted Di Luca's bottle-green Bentley, and in the doorway to the house the small Venetian was standing with his hands buried deeply in the pockets of his light brown cords.

He embraced Forlani somewhere around his waist, and Sabrina got a quick handshake, a nod, and a blank look.

Massimiliano Di Luca led them through low rooms that, although cozy and comfortably furnished, were surprisingly ordinary. Sabrina didn't know whether to be disappointed. It was a nice place, no doubt about it, homely even, but she had been expecting something extraordinary from the world-famous designer. Not necessarily a branch of Versailles but certainly something more glamorous than worn stone floors, brown corduroy sofas, simple black-and-white photographs on raw stone walls, and a long kitchen table covered by a red oilskin cloth—exactly like her mother's apartment. The only concession to glamour was a black-and-white poster that covered the whole of the end wall: a mature but instantly recognizable Claudia Schiffer wearing only a cat and a Di Luca handbag. "To Max, all my love, Claudia," she had written in the corner.

Sabrina stopped in front of the wall.

"Is that Helmut Newton?" she asked.

"Mario Testino."

"Yes, of course."

She sat down on the kitchen bench and looked around. The light flooded in through the small recessed windows. The best light of the day, she thought. When it was low, long, golden, and endless. With considerable effort Giulio Forlani edged his way in beside her.

Sabrina studied one of the photographs on the wall, which showed Di Luca in the cockpit of a large sailboat. The boat was on the verge of keeling over, its sails filled with wind. The Venetian had one hand on the tiller, and man and boat seemed perfectly balanced.

"Do you sail, signorina?"

"No."

"It's in Portofino," he told her.

"What's her name?"

"Mona."

Di Luca's missing muse and favorite model, she recalled.

She smiled politely.

"I see."

"Coffee?" Di Luca offered.

"Yes, please."

She had expected that the designer would now ring a silver bell to summon Filipino waiters in starched white mess jackets and cease this ridiculous illusion that he was a simple Lombardy peasant, but Di Luca got up, switched on an espresso machine, and started looking for cups.

"Are you disappointed, Dottoressa D'Avalos?"

"Not at all," she lied.

"I'm not Versace. I never have been," he said. "But I had a big house in Milan once, crammed with French Baroque furniture, butlers and maids, everything gilded, ridiculous statues, tapestries, Persian rugs, and a private cinema. I felt like Randolph Hearst or Gloria Swanson. Buried alive. I want to leave my door open, signorina. Speaking metaphorically, of course. I wouldn't want to be overrun by the rabble."

"No, of course not."

Forlani hadn't moved. He appeared to be absorbed in prayer.

"Now that you've found Giulio, dottoressa, what are you going to do with him?" Massimiliano Di Luca asked. "Save him from the Camorra again?"

Forlani was as quiet as a conductor before the first downbeat. The psychopath foaming at the mouth who had been on the verge of throwing her from the bell tower of the Basilica di Santa Maria only a few hours ago seemed never to have existed. Only this virtuous, peacefully meditating man who would never dream of hurting a fly.

"If that's what it takes," she said.

"Sugar, milk?"

"Both, please," she said. "I presume that you've heard about Dr. Carlo Mazzaferro, maestro? The doctor who declared Forl— . . . declared Giulio dead."

"Of course. Poor man . . . and poor girl," the Venetian muttered.

She was tempted to say that it wasn't she who had put Urs Savelli on to Mazzaferro, that she hadn't planted the idea that Giulio Forlani might not be dead in the brain of the Camorra, but decided against it. She knew from court proceedings that protesting was as good as admitting your guilt.

She turned her head and met Giulio Forlani's scrutinizing stare.

"There doesn't seem to be a way back," she said. "They know that you're alive, and they know that you would be capable of re-creating your frankly wonderful invention."

Forlani and Di Luca exchanged quick glances.

She looked at the giant more closely.

"Because you would, wouldn't you?"

She opened her jacket, found her purse, and placed the small date strip on the oilcloth next to an enormous scarred hand.

Forlani looked at it without touching it.

"Wouldn't you?" she repeated.

"Yes."

"As far as I've been told, no one has continued Nanometric's work," she said. "So your . . . crystals are still the best bet for the copyright protection that everyone so desperately needs."

"I expect that I could re-create it," Giulio Forlani said after another sideways glance at the designer. "With the right facilities. We patented several of the key processes. The patents are valid for a few more years before other companies can use them."

He smiled at her but looked at the strip.

"I'm sorry, Sabrina. It feels so very far away. Do you understand?"

"Of course."

"Can't I just go back to where I came from?"

"Where is that?" she asked.

He smiled.

"The south."

She felt a desperate urge for a cigarette and asked if she could smoke. Massimiliano Di Luca rose and produced a silver ashtray. She lit a cigarette and without thinking pushed the packet across the oilcloth to Forlani, who also took one.

"The Camorra will always see you as a clear threat," she said.

His face disappeared momentarily behind his hands. Somewhere behind them he nodded.

"I know, I know . . ."

The smoke seeped slowly out of his nostrils as his face reappeared.

She got up and went over to one of the small windows. She folded her arms across her chest and looked out into the yard. The driver, Alberto, was busy oiling a teak bench. He was tanned and muscular, wearing a pair of faded jeans and a khaki T-shirt. On the far side of the yard the meadow sloped down toward the river. Sabrina was transported back to the summers of her childhood by Lake Como, where she had learned to shoot with a bow and arrow, ride, swim, build a decent kite, and keep it away from the kite-eating trees opposite the house.

This investigation had changed her; she knew that. Changed her—or had she found herself?

"Dottoressa . . . ?"

Massimiliano Di Luca had walked up close to her without her noticing him.

She picked up the concern in his voice.

"I'm fine."

"Perhaps we're all a little tired," he said, and gestured her back to the table.

She looked over her shoulder toward the distant trees, raised her hand, and waved good-bye.

Chapter 34

Qualiano, Naples

Afterward, there was a moment of awestruck silence before young voices filled the earpieces. The girl with the tattoos mumbled into her throat microphone that it had been like seeing Kurt Cobain walk again, and one of the boys said it was like seeing Michael Jackson.

He indulged them. How many times in their hopefully long careers would they come into close contact with a myth, a ghost, who up until now had been made of the same substance as dreams—and paranoid delusions? However, after thirty seconds of excited chattering on the strictly guarded radio channel, Primo Alba told them to shut up.

Urs Savelli, complete with his trademark Basque walking stick, had just passed under the well-hidden cameras that GIS experts had installed in the roof of the tunnel the previous night.

The brim of his hat hid half of Savelli's face, and he had moved swiftly and purposefully. Shortly before he appeared, an unmarked van had driven down the ramp under Signor Marchese's small workshop next to his house, and the old man had closed the garage doors after it himself.

It was exactly as the city engineer, Signor Franco, had told them: the old man loved his pigeons. From the corn silo behind

the carpenter's house members of Primo Alba's young team had
admired Signor Marchese tirelessly tending to his beautiful pigeons,
both white and speckled, that lived in large wire cages in the yard
behind his workshop. He chatted to them as if they were his beloved
grandchildren, constantly replacing their water, food, and bedding,
then took them out, stroked their feathers, and trimmed their claws
with a pair of small nail clippers.

Primo Alba slowly turned onto his back. Absentmindedly he
watched a busy spider fashion a new web between two laths in
the silo's ancient roof construction. Dried-up pigeon droppings
crunched under his leather jacket. If he had wanted to, he could
have reached out and touched the young man who was operating
the telescopes and cameras pointing at Signor Marchese's courtyard.

They had lifted a couple of roof tiles to accommodate the telescope, the camera lenses, and the CO2-powered rifle that if and
when the need arose would fire a dart containing a needle and a
glass ampoule containing enough fentanyl to knock out an elephant
into Signor Marchese's unprotected neck.

With his left hand Primo Alba would be able to reach the young
woman, one of the first in the history of the GIS to achieve full
active field status. The girl was a goth and the European tae kwon do
champion at her weight. She should really be sleeping now but was
probably too agitated at the sight of Urs Savelli to nod off. Just like
Primo, she was lying quietly looking up at the roof.

Primo Alba entertained himself by visualizing a bare-knuckle
fight between the young female GIS soldier and Assistant Public
Prosecutor Sabrina D'Avalos.

He had no doubts about the hypothetical outcome.

The Little Miss Girl Dragon versus The Three Brothers from Hell
technique. Few things could match that, he thought.

He sent an encrypted text message to Federico Renda's cell
informing him of Savelli's arrival. He assumed that Renda was
nearby in his customized Mercedes.

They had reviewed their options: (1) They could arrest Savelli
and undoubtedly have him put away for a long list of murders, but

they would lose L'Artista, the fabled female assassin who was at the top of Federico Renda's personal wanted list—after all, it was she who had put him in a wheelchair. However, the public prosecutor was a rational man and would at all times set aside private motives in pursuit of the greater good. (2) They could let Savelli carry on, let him drip his poison into the ear of Don Francesco and subsequently hope that their sinister plans would involve activating L'Artista with a homing pigeon—if that really was what Signor Marchese's pigeons were used for—and then what? Wait for the assassin to execute yet another innocent victim—perhaps Sabrina D'Avalos herself—before they intervened?

Everyone had been allowed to voice his or her opinion. Captain Primo Alba was a democratic leader. Within reason. The girl with the tattoos had suggested positioning a group of falconers around Signor Marchese's house and pigeon cages to catch and intercept the lethal message with their hawks and falcons. Primo Alba had asked if she knew of any. And what was the overall success rate of a goshawk? Unless it was 100 percent, they were back at square one. The lad had suggested using one of the military's unmanned drones to follow the pigeon, but a call to a specialist in the air force had put an end to that idea: no matter how advanced drones were these days, they were unable to follow a specific bird through an airspace of possibly several hundred kilometers populated with other birds of the same size and with the same infrared signatures. Pigeons are social animals, the man had told them. It would probably join up with other pigeons and roost at night with them.

The tranquilizer had been Primo Alba's suggestion: knock out the old man before he had time to dispatch the pigeon, find Terrasino's code, and break it as quickly as possible. Then send another pigeon fitted with an electronic tracker device and follow it to L'Artista's hideout.

And that was the plan.

The cell vibrated his hand.

Renda.

Wait, was his order. Wait and see.

He whispered the command into his throat microphone.

The young woman sighed and closed her eyes.

Don Francesco and Urs Savelli were sitting on their usual bench shaded by the pergola. Savelli leaned back and looked at the vines while he let Don Francesco digest the news. Good as well as bad.

"This Cesare," Don Francesco said. "He couldn't tell the difference between a dead man and a living one? He crushed Forlani's car and then he shot him?"

He made an impatient gesture with his liver-spotted hand. He had never been in any doubt whether a man was dead or alive.

"I don't suppose a man's responsibility exceeds his ability, don."

"Are you making excuses for him?"

"No, I don't think I am. I'm . . ."

The capo looked closely at Savelli.

"What's wrong, Urs? Have you made up your mind to fail?"

"You're very perceptive, don."

The old man shrugged his shoulders.

"It's what we do. We know about people."

"I'll speak to Cesare," Savelli promised. "At length."

"You do that. But Massimiliano Di Luca is a problem."

"He is famous," the Albanian said.

The capo nodded.

"A genius, they say. At dressmaking."

"If he dies, the media will—"

"Without a doubt. But he can do a lot of damage to us, Urs. The Venetian and this Giulio Forlani. Again."

"We can't kill him, but equally we can't let him continue."

The old man looked toward the veranda. He could just make out the outline of Anna, his wife, in the deep shadows. She hadn't spoken an intelligible word for three years.

Urs Savelli followed his gaze.

"Not dead and yet not fully alive," Don Francesco pondered.

He turned to the Albanian.

"Somewhere in between, Urs."

Savelli looked into the other man's eyes. The old man never ceased to amaze him.

"Datura?" he suggested.

"Why not?"

"L'Artista?"

"Of course. He'll be forgotten, Urs."

"And Forlani?"

"They're friends, aren't they?"

"Yes."

"Where one is you may find the other."

It was harder than Primo Alba had thought. The hardest thing he had ever done in his GIS career. Just watching Urs Savelli, the artist of death, was intolerable, to see him stroll back through the tunnel, stopping briefly in Signor Marchese's house—possibly to deliver a vital message or possibly not—and drive away from the carpenter's house, unchallenged.

Every instinct in Primo Alba begged and pleaded with him to hit the send button on the radio and give the order to the young man who was pretending to fix his perfectly functioning motorcycle by the curb in Via Nicola Fele opposite the carpenter's house, to the young couple out for a walk with an empty pram a little farther down the road, to the man who was busy loading floor tiles into his van in the garage outside the construction supplier. All were members of the GIS, all were excellent marksmen, and all longed to blast Urs Savelli out of his expensive Paul Smith socks. Once and for all.

The girl, who was now manning the telescope and the CO_2 rifle didn't move. Primo Alba could hear her steady breathing.

"Wait," he said. "Do nothing."

The sun was about to set when he sensed a further heightening of the girl's concentration. Primo Alba crawled on his hands and knees across the treacherous planks and put his eye to the telescope.

The carpenter had opened the door to the courtyard with the pigeon lofts. It was dark enough for the light from the kitchen to cast an elongated rectangle across the flagstones. Signor Marchese was carrying a small wooden cage in his hands. The girl took a deep breath and pressed the rear sight to her eye. Slowly she exhaled till her lungs were half full and then held her breath. The breathing of the long-distance sniper. Primo Alba placed his hand on her thigh and bent his fingers to signal to her silently. Marchese's head and shoulders disappeared behind the middle of the three pigeon lofts. Primo Alba counted the seconds. The carpenter's head appeared. The girl took another precise breath. She was as still as a statue.

Everyone had expected the pigeon to be thrown up into the air like a child tossing a handful of seawater into the sun.

Just before that point the girl would fire the tranquilizer dart.

But Signor Marchese never raised his arms in the expected sacrificial gesture. He merely closed an invisible hatch in the pigeon loft, turned around, and went back into the kitchen with the cage.

Primo's earpiece crackled from everyone's voice.

"Was there something in the cage?" he said, not directing the question at anyone in particular.

"Don't know," muttered the girl on her exhale.

"Giovanni?"

"I didn't see," said the boy who had wedged himself in next to Prima Alba.

"*Vaffanculo!*" the girl muttered.

"Now!" said a new voice in the earpiece.

"What?!"

The young biker outside the carpenter's house reported in an agitated voice that Marchese had just launched a bright white homing pigeon from his front garden. The bird had soared in a tight spiral before setting its compass to north-northeast. Like an arrow. It was gone. And hadn't any of the geniuses in the corn silo noticed the low-hanging high-voltage cables that went across the industrial area just south of Marchese's house? Of course he wouldn't send his pigeons that way!

Primo Alba removed his hand from the girl's leg and leaned against a crumbling beam.

And put his hand right into a pile of fresh pigeon crap.

Porca puttana!

"Perhaps it was nothing," the boy said out into the darkness.

"I agree," the girl said quietly. "Probably just a bird for another nerd from their little brotherhood of pigeon fanciers. A breeder, something like that."

It was hard not to love them.

The public prosecutor, His Excellency Federico Renda, wasn't quite so gracious, but neither did he waste time pointing a finger. What was done was done, and in every field operation, no matter how well planned, there was always an unexpected, infuriating element of randomness.

Had Captain Alba heard from Sabrina D'Avalos? Where she was, for example?

Primo Alba had called her last known cell telephone number at least ten times and sent her a series of inquisitorial text messages without results. Total silence.

Go home, Federico Renda advised him. Get some rest. Regroup. If something unusual happened in the next few days, something that could possibly be the work of L'Artista, they would bring in the carpenter.

A sack over his head and a truck battery were sure to produce some much wanted answers.

Chapter 35

Ticino, Milan

"Who are the people looking for Giulio?" Massimiliano Di Luca asked that same evening over the rabbit ragout that Alberto had prepared.

Alberto joined them for dinner and turned out to be a pleasant and witty man. Sabrina noticed that the Venetian never gave him a direct order.

She glanced at Alberto.

"I don't believe we have secrets from Alberto," Giulio Forlani muttered.

"Certainly not," the designer said.

"The Terrasino clan. The aristocracy of the Camorra," she said. "The biggest, oldest, best-organized, and wealthiest family. They have interests in container ports, landfill sites, and waste management, every new building and public construction project in and around Naples . . . and the piracy industry. They still have a handful of sweatshops in Naples where illegal immigrants from Eastern Europe and China work, but most of their bootleg products are now manufactured in Macao, Mumbai, and Shanghai. They make sure that the designs and the know-how reach the Far East, and the Chinese take care of the rest."

Massimiliano Di Luca nodded. "That part we already know, dottoressa, but who exactly are they?"

"Urs Savelli," she began. "An Albanian. He's a senior Camorrista responsible for the family's bootleg industry. He organized the attack on Nanometric, and he personally killed the chemist Hanna Schmidt and, more recently, Doctor Mazzaferro's girlfriend. We have no photographs of him. No description. We know he carries a walking stick, and that's it. No one knows where he comes from, how old he is, or what his real name is. Perhaps even he doesn't know. As a criminal he's a complete success: a killer with no identity."

"Go on."

"Then there is L'Artista. The sharp end of the Camorra. A younger woman. She is Francesco Terrasino's black angel of death. She is used for executions and has an almost 100 percent success rate. She was the one who put my boss, Federico Renda, in a wheelchair."

"A young woman?"

"Yes."

"Do you know what she looks like? Christ, how are we even supposed to know what we're looking out for?"

"You won't ever see her," Sabrina assured him. "She's a specialist assassin for difficult, famous, or inaccessible people. She travels. She will kill all over the world for Don Terrasino. She's well educated and innovative. She killed Paolo Iacovelli and Fabiano Batista." Sabrina looked down at the table. "She killed Lucia and Salvatore Forlani. And my father."

"Are you sure it's a woman?" Di Luca asked. "Maybe I'm old-fashioned, but I really can't—"

"We have a single nighttime recording from a surveillance camera in a multistory garage in Milan. She's walking across one of the levels. Later you see her getting into the back of a Volvo belonging to a private detective. A former police inspector. He was good at his job. His body was later found in the trunk of his car, but he was buried without his head."

Sabrina looked at the designer.

"I'll make sure you get protection, maestro."

"Me? I think you should spend your resources on my friend Giulio."

"I'll take good care of him, too," she said gravely.

"I don't feel at risk, dottoressa. As far as everyone—including the Camorra—is concerned, I was merely one of Nanometric's backers. Nothing more. Besides . . ."

"Yes?"

Massimiliano Di Luca looked at Giulio and Alberto, who both shook their heads.

"Yes!" The Venetian looked at Sabrina. "I'm dying. I wouldn't mind leaving with a heroic monologue . . . for an audience of three . . . That's not asking too much, is it? But the point I'm trying to make is that there isn't very much to protect anymore, signorina. You're looking at the sad remains of what was once Massimiliano Di Luca."

"As you wish. But I think you underestimate your own importance. If Savelli knows that Giulio is alive and on the run, he'll expect him to call on old friends. And he'll undoubtedly know of this house."

"If the Camorra starts killing designers, who will make the things they rip off? Besides, Giulio could be anywhere in the world. Absolutely no one knows that he and I have been in contact in the last few years."

"I'm not sure that the Camorra thinks like that," Sabrina said. "But tell me what happened on the fifth of September 2007. Did you meet my father?"

She found the pari-mutuel ticket in her pocket and put it on the table.

Di Luca turned it over in his hand.

"Bucefalo. A fine animal. Everyone knew he was, obviously, so the odds were low. Your father found me at San Siro. I had been waiting for Giulio in Dal Pescatore. Our lunch date was a bit vague because I knew he was busy with the patent applications, but I hoped that he would have time to stop by. Drink a toast. It was a big day for the Camera Nazionale. A very big day."

He looked at Giulio Forlani across the kitchen table. In a presumably extremely rare attack of affection they clasped each other's hands. Then Di Luca's hand returned to the stem of his wineglass. He hadn't touched a drop and had eaten practically nothing. He rested his chin in his hand, blinked wearily, and looked at Sabrina.

"I don't know . . . I heard strange music on the radio in the bar as though a radio channel from the twenties had suddenly sprung to life, and I had this terrible premonition. And I just knew . . . I just knew something dreadful was about to happen."

"And my father?"

"Your father was unique in every way, dottoressa. He told me about Giulio. Together we went to the Ospedale Maggiore, but Giulio was in the theater. Afterward he drove me to my studio. He often spoke about you, signorina. More about you than about your brothers. 'The family's last warrior,' he said. I can see that he was right."

"Thank you. And the code? *Corriere della Sera*?"

"Oh, yes. That was my idea. Your father was obviously busy organizing everything. Hiding Lucia and the boy, taking care of Giulio, getting a handle on what had really happened at Nanometric. He had already arranged to have Giulio flown to the United States if . . ."

"I survived." Giulio Forlani completed his sentence.

"Exactly. If you survived. I thought about how we could all keep in contact when everything had . . ." The designer blushed slightly. "It's a bit *Boys' Own*, I admit. But it was a good method."

"And it worked," Forlani said, looking at Sabrina.

"So the Camorra will carry on?" Alberto wanted to know. "Until they find Dr. Forlani again?"

"Or until he dies again," she said, instantly wishing the ground would open up and swallow her. "I'm sorry. I'm so sorry!"

She cast her eyes down at the table and went red.

But Giulio Forlani and Massimiliano Di Luca were both laughing.

"Now that might be an idea," Di Luca said.

"I know an undertaker," Giulio Forlani said.

Sabrina looked at him.

"Who?"

"Forget it," he said.

"No. What did you mean, Giulio?"

"Nothing. Like I said, forget I ever mentioned it."

CHAPTER 36

Ticino, Milan

The house was more than quiet. There was a deep humming silence like the noon hour by Lake Como, when the cicadas fell silent and the wind calmed down.

When the rest of her family was asleep, Sabrina would lie awake in her bed—not so very different from the one she had been shown to by Alberto—and gaze at the columns of sunlight between the shutters. Stare as far into the light as she dared, because she knew that deep inside a white light there was a black core that one should never look at for a long time.

She had thought more about her childhood in these last few days than she had for many years.

The glow of her cigarette had almost reached her fingers when she remembered her cell. She had heard it ring from the guest bedroom upstairs while they ate. Only the blasted Primo–Nestore had that number, and she had no wish to talk or listen to him. It would mean new thoughts, new impossible choices, new disasters, new dead doctors and mistresses in first-class train compartments—and yearning—if she answered that phone.

She stubbed out the cigarette and sat up. Found another one in the almost empty packet and wished she had something to drink. Perhaps she could sneak down to the kitchen and steal a bottle.

There wasn't a sound to be heard.

Of course . . . of course she had convinced herself two dozen times, at least, that she could hear crunching earth and pebbles against tires, cars stopping just behind the trees, car doors being closed by armed, dangerous, and silent men. Footsteps on the grass, on the cobblestones in the yard—a window routinely eased off its hinges. A catch scraping against the woodwork. And numerous times she had told herself she had seen headlights reflected in the sky, between the trees.

Sabrina knew it was all in her mind. Of course it was.

She smoked the cigarette greedily and weighed the Walther in her hand. Its safe, reassuring weight offered her no comfort this time. She let the cigarette dangle from the corner of her mouth, narrowed her left eye against the smoke, and pulled the Colt from the ankle holster. She pointed its barrel at the narrow stripe of moonlight between the shutters, aimed at a star above the distant conifers, and thought about Ismael.

"Bang, bang," she muttered, and imagined shooting down the star.

What she needed was peace and quiet, some answers . . . and then three months in a mental health clinic.

Her cell buzzed with a new text message, and she put down the weapons.

She looked at the display, read the messages from Primo, who continued to sign himself "NR" as if they were still keeping up his ridiculous fiction, and then read the message again. And again.

She got up from the bed, tiptoed on bare feet through the room and out into the passage, saw the flickering light under Forlani's door, and knocked.

"Yes?"

"It's me, Sabrina."

"Go away."

She looked at her feet, which were ghostly white in the moonlight.

"May I come in?"

"No."

She tried the handle. The door was locked, as her own door ought to have been.

At school she had been a fairly competent diver from the high board. Her coach had described her as fearless, and Sabrina wondered if he might have meant that deep down she was utterly reckless. Now she was breathing the same way she had during preparations for the ten-meter platform.

"Castellarano, Giulio. It wouldn't happen to be Castellarano, would it? Where you've been hiding for the last couple of years, I mean. It wouldn't be there, would it?" she whispered.

A simple no would have been enough to make her go back to her room, lie down, and go to sleep.

But the door was torn open, and the towering figure, partially dissolved in the darkness, stretched out one of his industrial-size scoops and dragged her into his room.

Déjà-vu.

For the second time in this never-ending day her feet left the ground as Giulio Forlani lifted her by the scruff of the neck. This time he executed the feat with one hand. The other was still resting on the door handle.

Sabrina let her head slump backward so that she could still breathe and waited for him to tire, to get it out of his system. Soon he would once again become the harmless, well-mannered scientist he had been all afternoon.

Or perhaps he was calm and safe to be around only when Massimiliano Di Luca or someone else he knew was present.

She dangled with the blood roaring and the sound of the ultra-calm deep breathing of Giulio Forlani in her ears.

"Are you done yet?" she squawked.

The faint glow from the candle behind the potential Nobel Prize winner was starting to fade.

"Yes," he mumbled eventually. "Sorry."

He released her, and she tumbled forward on weak legs and bumped her head on the door frame.

"I would hate to be present during a domestic dispute in the For-lani home," she said, rubbing her scalp.

"What . . . ? No. No."

In the candlelight Giulio Forlani's face was more asymmetrical, scarred, and furrowed than ever. Like congealed lava that one day might melt again and assume a happier expression.

"Not Lucia . . ." he said, sounding far away. "Never. Besides, I was . . . Everything was different."

He looked at her.

"I'm not a violent man, Sabrina."

She touched her neck gingerly.

"Of course you're not, Giulio," she said.

His expression became doubtful and searching. Then he nod-ded gravely, and she remembered how Massimiliano Di Luca had described his friend: for him the world is concrete. It's what he can see and measure.

She assumed that hints, irony, and sarcasm were wasted on the physicist.

"What did you just say?" he asked.

"May I sit down?"

He nodded in the direction of the bed.

"What did you say?" he asked her again.

"Castellarano," she whispered.

She glanced up, saw the look on his face, and buried her face in her hands.

"Oh, God! I'm sorry!"

Giulio Forlani shook her the way a terrier shakes a rat.

"Speak!"

"There were some men, some Camorristi who followed me from Naples. I . . . I'm so sorry."

He let her go and rested his forehead against the wall. His hands hung—for the moment—idly by his sides.

"Go on."

"I drove past Castellarano on my way to Milan." She started to cry. "I don't know why . . . Your wife, Lucia, she went to school there . . . It was just a whim. My boss thought Castellarano was where it all started."

"Did you speak to anyone?" he asked the wall.

"No."

"Yes!"

"A woman I happened to meet in a park. You can see the river from there. It was only a moment. We shared some grapes."

"Blue grapes," Forlani said.

Sabrina hiccupped, and the tears kept flowing in a way that she knew would not stop.

"How do you know they were blue?"

Giulio Forlani didn't appear to hear her.

"What did she look like?" he asked.

"She was a tall, attractive woman, I thought. She had a slightly strange smell about her. I recognized it, but I can't remember where from."

"Formaldehyde," he said. "She works for an undertaker."

She wiped her eyes with her sleeve.

"She always wears that gray dress when she goes to the undertaker's," Giulio Forlani said. "When she comes home, she washes it and hangs it on the clothesline to dry so it can be aired in the sunshine. She says it's the only thing that makes the smell go away."

"Who is she?"

"Antonia Moretti."

"Who is she, Giulio?"

"She is . . . damnit, Sabrina, the widow with whom I've been staying for two years. She's my landlady."

There was a dangerous glint in his deep eye sockets.

"So they followed you and they photographed you with Antonia, and now they've found her," he declared.

"We don't know that for sure, Giulio." She got up and started pacing up and down. "We don't know that for sure . . ."

"You're beautiful but useless, Sabrina," he said. "You really are."

Giulio Forlani started rummaging around in his biker jacket for his cell.

"Antonia has called me several times today, only I didn't hear a damn thing because you blasted my eardrums!"

"You tried to strangle me!"

"I wish I'd succeeded," he said.

He pressed the keys like a madman, but the call went straight to Antonia's voice mail. He tried Gianni's cell next and finally heard the boy's sleepy voice on the handset.

"Gianni? It's Giulio. Enzo, I mean."

The boy seemed to have been sound asleep, and as far as Sabrina could make out, he sounded completely normal. Giulio Forlani straightened up, and his movements became a little less tense.

"Wake your mom up, Gianni. It's important. It's extremely important. Do what I say now, okay?"

He listened for a moment and scowled at Sabrina.

"An unknown woman has been asking about Antonia in Castellarano," he hissed. "And someone was at the house. Gianni said his mom could smell that someone had been there."

"I'm sorry," was all she said. "So sorry."

Shortly afterward Antonia Moretti was on the phone. She seemed to be a woman who used many and strong words because the giant held the phone a couple of inches away from his ear.

A few times he managed to interject a simple "But," "Sorry," or "Antonia, please listen to me, it's—."

And in Sabrina's opinion it was nowhere near productive enough. She pressed the speed dial for Captain Primo Alba.

"Sabrina?"

He sounded as if he had had at least eight hours of sleep in a good bed.

"Yes. I got your message," she said. "Thank you."

"How did you get—"

"Shut up . . . Primo or whatever you call yourself these days, listen to me."

"Of course."

"You're definitely not the public prosecutor's office boy. I'm sure of that now."

"No."

"Good. I need a helicopter. Not in a moment but right now. Do you understand?"

"A helicopter? Let me check if I've got one lying around."

She wanted to scream, but Forlani was staring attentively at her. The agitated female voice could still be heard from his own cell.

"Now, Primo Alba. I want you to pick up two people in Castellarano in Reggio Emilia—Antonia and Gianni Moretti—and take them to a safe place."

"I'll probably need a good reason to mobilize the air force," he argued. His voice was intolerably calm, intolerably languid, and intolerably professional. "Why, Sabrina?"

"I'm with Giulio Forlani. He has lived with Antonia Moretti in Castellarano for the last two years. The Camorra knows it. The Camorra has identified her, and they have been to her house."

"Address?"

She sat down, placed her hand over the microphone, and looked at Forlani.

"The address, Giulio?"

"Via Santa Caterina. The last house before the fields. It's opposite a restaurant called La Stazione."

Sabrina repeated the information.

"Any weapons in the house?" he asked.

Hand over the microphone.

"An old shotgun over the fireplace," Forlani said.

"A basement?"

It would have been so much easier to pass the cell to Forlani, but she knew that the physicist would inevitably become unresponsive at the sound of a new and unfamiliar voice.

"There is a basement," Sabrina told Primo Alba.

"Good," he replied. "I imagine they're watching the house in the hope that Forlani will return. If he does, all they have to do is kill him and everyone can go home: job done. What we need to do is perform a single low flight over the house. Soldiers will rappel onto the house and secure it. It'll be frightening for Signora Moretti and her son, but they'll just have to deal with that. Tell them to take the shotgun and go to the basement. Don't turn on any lights. And they mustn't come out until the head of the operation calls out a code word. Any suggestions?"

She asked Giulio Forlani if he had any ideas.

"Einstein," he said.

"Walther," she decided.

"Good," Prima Alba said. "The code word is Walther. I'll call you back."

He hung up, and Sabrina looked at the cell in her hand. It weighed a ton.

She nodded to Forlani, who interrupted her and repeated the instructions.

It took some time.

Finally he was able sit down and lean against the wall.

"Are they really that important to you, Giulio?" she asked.

"Yes, but I didn't know till now."

CHAPTER 37

Ticino, Milan

Sabrina was pacing up and down the floor. She checked her watch every minute while Forlani, brooding and immobile, perched on the edge of the bed. Every now and then, in a tacit choreography, they would swap places.

"She sounds . . . assertive, your landlady," she said at one point.

"Antonia? Most certainly. Merciless. On the surface, at least."

"Do you still not believe in coincidences, Giulio?"

"What you mean?"

"That it happened to be Antonia Moretti I met when I spent just five minutes in Castellarano."

"I don't believe in coincidences, Sabrina. They're a manifestation of a system, a logic, we have yet to understand," he said solemnly.

Sabrina sighed.

"I've got a text message from the man I was speaking to just now. I was followed from Naples by some Camorristi from the Terrasino family. I didn't discover them until after Castellarano. I managed to get some of them arrested but not all of them, it seems. One of them has now admitted to following me to Castellarano. I'm sorry. I don't know how they could have found your landlady so quickly."

He waved away her apology.

"You were trying to find me to tell me about Lucia and Salva," he said calmly. "It's your job. You were just doing your job. I should be apologizing to you."

She looked at her watch: 2:34 a.m.

She flicked the last cigarette butt out of the window and went downstairs and through the old rooms with the low ceilings. She found a wooden box on a coffee table, sniffed it, and stole a generous handful of Turkish cigarettes. Her luck must be changing, she told herself when she also found an unopened bottle of Napoleon brandy in the larder. She took two glasses and returned to Giulio Forlani's monastic cell.

She held up her spoils in triumph and was rewarded with a small smile.

She poured, and they clinked glasses without saying anything.

The cigarettes were perfumed and could be smoked only at a time like this, for want of anything better.

At the point where the bottle was three-quarters empty and they had both lit fresh cigarettes and Sabrina sensed more than actually saw dawn at the horizon of the eastern sky, Giulio Forlani suddenly leaned forward and started to laugh.

Sabrina was speechless. A couple of times she had seen the hint of a smile in the man's face and taken it to be the upper limit of his ability to express joy. Was he hysterical? Psychotic? She couldn't blame him. Personally, she had been on the verge of a nervous breakdown for days. Yet Forlani's laughter sounded completely authentic, though also strangely forced. He tried to drink but hiccupped instead, and the glass clanged against his teeth; he had to put it down again as he convulsed in laughter. Highly inappropriate when the lives of his landlady and her son were hanging by a thread. Sabrina could feel her face starting to mimic him. Forlani's laughter was infectious. She bent double in a fit of giggles and had to stuff her arm into her mouth not to wake up the whole house.

They couldn't stop laughing.

It was both incredibly liberating and terribly surreal.

Every time they looked at each other, they would laugh even harder. Sabrina was close to wetting herself and held up her hand.

"Stop it! Stop it at once, Giulio."

The physicist gasped for breath . . . and was overpowered by a new fit. A few seconds later Sabrina had to follow suit.

"Now stop it!" she shouted in desperation with tears rolling down her cheeks.

She pulled out the Walther and pointed the pistol at his head.

"I mean it! I'll shoot you!"

He looked at her, then at the pistol, and howled with laughter.

Merriment rolled over them in huge waves that eventually subsided and left them like washed-up survivors from a shipwreck on a nameless beach.

They lay on the bed with their feet dangling toward the floor and cognac glasses in their hands. At last she turned to face him. Small laughter hiccups like aftershocks rippled through them from time to time.

"What was all that about?"

"What?"

"What were we laughing at, Giulio? I need to know," she said.

He looked up at the ceiling.

"The invention. I don't think it ever worked."

"What? What the hell are you talking about?"

She wiped the final tears of laughter from her cheeks.

"The invention. It . . . well, I don't know how else to put it. It just didn't work."

"Why not?"

She went through her jacket pockets, found her purse, and held up the date strip. Today the digits were yellow like tiger eyes. And they showed the correct date.

"Looks all right to me," she said.

He glanced at the strip without interest. Then he looked sadly back at the ceiling.

He stood up and found his biker jacket and wallet. He rummaged around one of its many compartments and then tipped a small heap of identical black strips into her hands.

They were nearly all blank. On some of them she could still make out a single number or letter.

"Jesus, Mary . . ." she muttered in shock.

"Your strip works because it hasn't traveled. It hasn't crossed datelines. They can't travel, Sabrina. And they had to be able to. Max had sent these strips to me in Massachusetts. Only one small test remained outstanding before we could file the patent applications. I had sent a few dozen strips around the world with a freight company. They returned to Nanometric two days after the attack. It would appear they can't tolerate traveling through timelines. The earth's magnetic background radiation, the radioactivity of the atmosphere . . . something, I don't know what, killed them. They weren't strong enough."

He emptied his glass, and Sabrina lit another cigarette. She would have to make a second trip downstairs soon.

"Good grief," she said, and closed her eyes as the implication of the words started to sink in. "But this is terrible, Giulio. It's absolutely awful."

"Yes. It is. Everyone has died for nothing."

"Do you think that's funny?" she asked him.

Giulio Forlani looked at her with the most brooding expression he had yet worn.

"No. No, Sabrina, it's not funny. It's tragic. What's funny is that the Camorra is chasing me for no reason. The invention doesn't work, though they would never believe me if I told them. Now that is funny, don't you think?"

"No, Giulio. I think that part is damn tragic, too."

Forlani's cell rang. He got up and started pacing back and forth again. He mustered a feeble smile, and Sabrina offered up silent and heartfelt thanks to Captain Primo Alba. Forlani's smile widened, and finally he thanked him profusely and switched off his cell.

He sat down and grabbed Sabrina's hand. And broke every bone in it. Or at least that was how it felt.

"Thank you, Sabrina."

"Are they okay?"

He nodded with a big new smile. The giant was happy, and Sabrina was given back the remains of her hand.

She herself received a laconic text message signed "Primo Alba," filled with words such as "airborne" and "NATO Aviano Air Base" and "ETA 04:15."

"Now what?" Forlani said.

"More cigarettes and a toast to a successful mission?" she suggested.

"The bottle is empty."

"You're right, Giulio." Her voice was starting to slur. "So it is. But it wasn't alone in its little larder. It had good friends and neighbors. I'm an investigator, Giulio. I see things that other people don't, do you understand? . . . I've got this special ability . . ."

Her voice was now more than slurred; it was thick.

"Perhaps I should make the trip downstairs," Giulio Forlani offered chivalrously.

"Do you know something, Giulio? I think that's a super idea . . . super."

When the physicist returned with a bottle of Calvados and a carton of Camels, he found the young assistant public prosecutor sleeping peacefully in his bed. He put a blanket over her without her even stirring and tiptoed to her room. He left the Calvados and the cigarettes on the bedside table, where they would be the first thing she saw when she woke up. The surprising baronessa would appreciate it.

CHAPTER 38

Ticino, Milan

She groaned softly when Giulio Forlani shook her until she woke up, and she lashed out at his hand without hitting it. She didn't open her eyes but pressed them together hard.

"Wharra you doin'?"

"Max is waiting for us. Breakfast is ready."

Once again his voice was as solemn as the Pope's midnight prayer. The intoxication of the night and its bizarre abandoned merriment had been forgotten.

"I'm not hungry."

The bed keeled over when he sat down on the edge.

She opened one eye and pulled a face.

"Oh, God."

Giulio Forlani was in need of a bath, she thought, and wondered what she herself smelled like.

"We stink," she said.

"Do we?"

"I think I'm going to be sick," she groaned.

He got up quickly and moved over to the window.

"I don't think Max would approve, Sabrina. By the way, he's leaving soon. He says he has a collection to finish."

"And?"

He fidgeted.

"Nothing."

Sabrina managed to get up onto one elbow and shielded her eyes with her other hand.

She retched, then belched. She swung her feet down on the floor and rested her head in her hands and her elbows on her knees. If she sat exactly like this for a very long time, Giulio Forlani and the rest of the world might just have disappeared when she opened her eyes again.

"Come on," he said.

"I can't! Give me a minute, would you? Just one minute, for pity's sake."

The physicist made a small impatient click with his tongue as if she were a horse refusing to move.

"Do you want me to carry you downstairs?"

"Leave me alone," she moaned.

Sabrina sat down at the kitchen table, where she could avoid the morning light pouring in through the small windows. She grabbed a cup of espresso and downed it without breathing.

Alberto sent her a sympathetic smile.

Massimiliano Di Luca said nothing. She watched him over the rim of her cup, and she saw it now: the man was wasting away. The disease was melting the flesh off his bones. A little bit every day. What once had been the whites of his eyes was now yellow, and what had been a fine tremor in his fingertips yesterday was today a shiver.

Alberto poured her another cup.

She shook her head when he offered her the breadbasket.

"Just coffee, please," she mumbled.

Massimiliano Di Luca looked from one to the other.

"If I didn't know any better, I would think that the two of you had . . . but you haven't, have you? So . . . what did happen if you haven't fucked each other's brains out?"

Sabrina glared at the designer in disbelief. Giulio Forlani placed a hand on her arm. The physicist was munching a large slice of bread.

"Ignore him, Sabrina. The man is an incurable provocateur. Exhausting and unstoppable. I imagine you enjoyed pulling the wings and legs off flies when you were a boy, Max."

The Venetian's eyes widened with indignation.

"Me? Never? Certainly not flies."

"Cut it out, Max."

Forlani looked at Sabrina.

"Any suggestions?"

"I'm happy to shoot him if you help me bury him," she said.

He smiled, and Di Luca laughed.

"I would be delighted, but what I meant was, do you have any ideas as to what our next move should be? If we need to make one. Today, I mean."

Her hangover defied description.

"Perhaps it would be good if we could stay here for a day," she said feebly. "Gather strength. Think things through."

They had tacitly agreed not to tell the others anything about last night's rescue operation in Castellarano.

"Can we stay here, Max?" Giulio Forlani asked.

"Of course, but I need to warn you that Alberto has locked away all cigarettes, wine, and spirits in the cellar and that he has swallowed the key."

Sabrina stared at the table.

"When will you be back?"

"If we leave now, I imagine we'll be back around five," Di Luca said.

Alberto nodded.

"I can shop for a good branzino al basilica if you fancy sea bass," he said helpfully.

"Lovely," she said with a queasy smile.

＊　＊　＊

They went outside to say good-bye. Massimiliano Di Luca smiled and waved through the rear window of the Bentley. Alberto smiled to them in the side mirror.

The car disappeared behind a bend and reappeared. Then it disappeared completely between the conifers.

Sabrina shielded her eyes with her hand.

"Does he have someone?" she asked. "I mean, I've read at least two hundred articles about him, and no one has ever identified a woman, a man, a nice dog . . . nothing."

Forlani smiled.

"You're right; everyone has rifled through his private life," he said.

"So . . . does he have someone?"

"Of course he does, Sabrina. Max is a charming man. They just haven't been looking in the right place."

Slowly she shook her head.

"The driver. Alberto. Of course . . . invisible and right under everyone's nose."

"No comment."

Nor was one necessary.

CHAPTER 39

Outside Brescia

"It's only a game. Nothing will happen to Mommy. I'm like Hector; I've got nine lives. At least."

The young woman stood in front of the mirror in the nursery while her daughter, Abrielle, who was still wearing pajamas, watched her from the bed. It was early morning, and the sky was dark. The six-year-old nodded gravely and stroked the cat curled up on the bedspread.

The woman had been busy all night. She had been woken up at midnight by the small alarm bell over the pigeon loft; she had removed the metal cylinder attached to the leg of the pigeon, read the short encoded message, and started her research.

It was almost indecently little time to prepare the assassination. Her employer obviously knew this and had doubled her usual fee. For the first part of the job. The second part was regarded as routine.

She put on elbow and knee pads, pulled the hip guards over her head, and slammed the palm of her hand against her chest shield.

"We're Spartans!"

Abrielle laughed out loud and startled Hector, the cat.

"Spartans!" her daughter echoed.

The woman pulled a pair of tracksuit bottoms over her armor and tied the laces of her running shoes. A loose-fitting sweatshirt and an oversized anorak came next so that no one would know that she wore padding under her clothes.

She stood by the bed and gave her daughter a look they both understood, and Abrielle let go of the cat and jumped down onto the floor. The cat licked its back and leaped up onto the windowsill and out onto the roof. Its usual route would take it across the ridge of the old cider house, down a trellis, and into her husband's studio.

The mother stretched out on the floor and did breathing exercises while the daughter got dressed.

"I'm ready, Mommy!"

"Great. Gloves?"

Abrielle waved her hands in front of her mother's face. On the inside she wore latex gloves, and on the outside beautifully embroidered cotton gloves. A dark brown velvet dress, white stockings, and shiny shoes. As if she were on her way to a dancing lesson or her first day at a new school.

"Let's go and say good-bye to Daddy," her mother said.

As always when they were alone, they spoke Romanian.

Mother and daughter stopped on the marble tiles outside the studio. Bach's *Goldberg Variations* floated out through the open windows like crystals. They had chosen the extension as her husband's studio because it was cool and the ceiling was high, the windows faced north, and there was an acidic smell from the apple presses and cider vats that had lived there for centuries—and because the door was level with the flagstones, which eliminated the need for a ramp for his wheelchair.

Her husband was sitting in front of the easel with the brush handle between his teeth. The young woman ran her hands through his long thick hair, and quick as lightning he swung around the light aluminum wheelchair and smiled. His upper body was still agile and strong. He lifted Abrielle up onto his lap and balanced on the rear wheels of the chair. The wheelchair pivoted on one wheel, and Abrielle squealed with delight.

Her mother clapped her hands and threw a glance at the circus poster above the work desk: the trapeze trio the Blind Eagles. Her husband permanently suspended in the air at the apex of his triple somersault and her brother-in-law, who would catch him, hanging by his knees with long outstretched hands that had just delivered her to the bottomless dark under the circus dome. She herself was a tiny, curved, and glittering figure on an endless journey toward the recently vacated trapeze four meters away. The trio had been blindfolded during the entire act, and nothing had ever gone wrong until the day a truck with a sleeping driver behind the wheel had crushed their van and everything else—their bodies, their costumes, their equipment, and their future. Her brother-in-law had been killed instantly, her husband had broken his spine, but she and her beloved had retained their foothold on life. Through discreet channels in the global community of circus artistes she had learned about the unusual requirement in southern Italy for performers with certain talents, jobs that demanded particular physical as well as mental abilities, and she had been thoroughly tested. She had carried out fiendishly difficult missions bordering on the suicidal in Indonesia and Singapore and had built up a fine reputation as a freelance assassin.

The Camorra expected that as was usual when Massimiliano Di Luca left his house in the country, the Bentley would drive east from Ticino, taking the scenic route through the villages of Cuggiono and Mesero before taking the Turin–Milan highway. The route allowed the maestro to rest his eyes on the fields and low forest before joining the dense highway traffic.

L'Artista had chosen the usually deserted road between Cuggiono and Mesero as her point of attack.

Outside Mesero

Massimiliano Di Luca wasn't being entirely fair when he claimed that Alberto didn't know any other gears of the Bentley but the first. The large bottle-green car was in fact going at a respectable speed down Via Annoni when it happened.

If the maestro in the back of the car had looked up from his brandy glass and enameled pillbox, he would have noticed a fresh southern wind that skimmed the wheat fields; he certainly would have noticed the straight-backed little girl at the side of the road, walking as delicately as a bird, bouncing a blue ball in front of her, because Massimiliano had an unfailing eye for agility, coordination, and elegance; he would have nodded his approval of the dark brown velvet dress with the old-fashioned lace collar, the white stockings, and the gloves, and he would have thought that in today's cultural wasteland some mothers still knew how to dress their children properly—though the mother's own outfit left a lot to be desired: the usual baggy, boring, synthetic leisure clothes.

The mother and her daughter were the only people on the road.

Perhaps he might have had time to put his hand on Alberto's shoulder when the blue ball left the girl's hand and bounced out into the path of the car less than ten meters from the Bentley's massive chrome radiator grille. Perhaps he might have had time to shout a warning when the girl ran after the ball, and perhaps he might have smiled with relief when the mother yanked her back—only to call out again when the woman stumbled out onto the tarmac and the Bentley hit her.

Instead, Massimiliano Di Luca was brutally roused from his unusually dark thoughts. The enameled box's contents, small white pills, spilled across the seats and blankets in the car, and he looked up bewildered as Alberto swore and slammed on the brakes.

Even though the British car weighed almost three tons and the woman sixty kilos at most, the impact of the collision was felt with shocking clarity. The young dark-haired woman tumbled like a rag doll over the long hood, crashed into the windscreen with a tragic crunch, and disappeared out of sight on Alberto's side.

Before Massimiliano slid across the seat and opened the door on the road side, he glanced at the pavement and saw the face of the little girl. She had the darkest eyes and the palest skin, and her wide-open mouth was the blackest he had ever seen.

Chapter 40

The woman registered the consequences of the collision without any particular emotion. Her calculations had been a little off. The speed of the Bentley had been more like sixty kilometers per hour rather than her prediction of fifty. She hadn't managed to turn her left leg as she rolled over the hood, though the subsequent forward roll over the tarmac was executed to a satisfactory extent. She knew that a ligament on the inside of her left knee had been torn or sprained despite the knee guard, and her right wrist had started to swell.

When she heard the driver's footsteps, she groaned, studied the tarmac two centimeters below her nose, and bit through the tiny bladder of pig's blood she had concealed in her mouth. There surely could be no other substance in the world that so magnetically attracted immediate attention as blood on the face of a young woman.

Especially if you had caused it to be there.

Alberto carefully turned the woman over onto her back and breathed a sigh of relief when her pupils contracted. Massimiliano Di Luca mumbled a mixture of curses at Alberto's bowed neck and apologies to the woman's bloodstained face. Shifting from foot to foot, he was busy pulling out a business card and handkerchiefs from the pockets of his jacket, and neither of the men noticed the girl on the roadside quickly cutting away a square of the ball's plastic skin with a Swiss Army knife. Pressing her nose and mouth against her velvet sleeve and holding the ball in her outstretched hand, she pumped the ball with her fingers and watched the clouds of dust disperse inside the Bentley. She aimed the hole in the ball at the front seats and pressed again. Then she put the ball in a double plastic bag exactly as her mother had instructed, removed her gloves and put them in the bag as well, closed the bag, and tied a knot.

"Mommy!"

Alberto lifted up the girl, who buried her face in his shoulder. The woman staggered to her feet. She swayed, took a step to test her leg's ability to support her, and even attempted a smile.

"You must excuse my driver, signora," Di Luca mumbled. "He's as blind as a bat. He's—"

"It's nothing, signore. It was my own fault. The ball. My daughter. Foolish. Idiotic, in fact."

The woman had tears in her eyes, and she wiped the blood from her face with one of the maestro's handkerchiefs.

"Your face."

"I think I'll survive, signore. *Grazie.*"

She limped to the side of the road, and Alberto put down the little girl. A couple of passing cars slowed down at the scene, but Alberto waved them on.

"Mommy's fine, darling."

Massimiliano Di Luca followed her, wringing his hands while Alberto hung his head.

"We need to contact the police, signora. I insist. They'll need to make a report—my insurance company will obviously—otherwise I will personally—"

"No, no! It really was nothing, signore. It was entirely my own fault. Please don't blame your driver."

Massimiliano Di Luca cut short his flow of words as if an insect had flown into his mouth and began studying the woman more closely. There was something—the accent, it was obvious now.

He shook his head at his own stupidity. The woman and her daughter were clearly Eastern European; like so many others, they might be in the country illegally, and her reluctance to involve the police now became obvious.

While the woman continued consoling her daughter, Massimiliano Di Luca whispered his assumption to Alberto, and the driver nodded.

"Perhaps some small recompense would be in order, maestro?"

"You're suggesting . . . ?"

Alberto nodded.

Massimiliano Di Luca fished out a rarely used wallet from his inside pocket and opened it. Good! It was filled with banknotes. He handed all of them to the woman, who shook her head.

"There's no need, signore. It really was nothing."

She stuttered with embarrassment.

In the course of the next minute Di Luca and the woman performed a sincere exchange of offers and rejections with the girl and Alberto as their silent audience. At last the immigrant capitulated and put the banknotes into the pocket of her anorak with two fingers. She took her daughter's hand and limped back the way they had come. The woman had firmly declined their offer of a lift with a kind of fraught bashfulness, which further confirmed Di Luca's suspicions that the woman and girl were illegal immigrants, desperate to get away.

Mother and daughter found their sensible Citroën Berlingo on a forest track a few hundred meters from the road.

L'Artista muttered a few words into a walkie-talkie, and they got in the car.

She removed the last of the blood from her face with a wet wipe, pulled down her tracksuit bottoms, and inspected the already swollen and discolored knee. Then she flexed and bent the fingers of her right hand. They all worked. In the back her daughter put on her seat belt and started playing on her Game Boy. Her mother opened a cold box in the passenger footwell, found an ice pack, and strapped it to the inside of her knee.

"Do you want an ice cream?" she asked the girl.

"Yes, please."

"You did very well, sweetheart."

The girl nodded, totally wrapped up in her game.

"Here you go," her mother said.

She handed her daughter an ice cream cone and opened a can of Coke for herself.

"What are we doing now, Mommy?" the girl asked without looking up.

"You're not doing anything, darling. You're going home to Daddy. I've got to go out and do something."

"Were they bad people?"

"Make sure you don't get ice cream on the seat, sweetheart."

Massimiliano Di Luca and Alberto Moravia drove off together without exchanging a single word. Massimiliano leaned back in his seat, frowned, and held up his hands. He rubbed his palms together and studied the tiny dots of blood on the tips of his fingers. The blood kept flowing even though he pressed his fingertips together. He looked down at the pale leather seat and wondered about the fine layer of dust.

His fingers started to convulse involuntarily. His arms flopped into his lap, the nerves unresponsive.

With great difficulty he managed to lift his head and found Alberto's eyes in the rearview mirror. His driver was sitting in exactly the same position as he was; his hands had let go of the steering wheel and were resting on his thighs, and his eyes were unresponsive like his own. The Bentley drifted to a halt on the verge, and the engine stalled. Di Luca and Alberto both slumped forward at the same time and threw up.

Di Luca's eyelids were as heavy as the sins of the world, and the sweat poured over his eyes. He couldn't utter a single word. If he had been capable of speech, if Alberto hadn't been in as bad a state as he was, he would have asked him to find the old Colt .45 in the glove compartment and shoot him through the heart.

A tow truck pulled up in front of the Bentley, and two men wearing overalls climbed down from the driver's cab. They set about maneuvering the truck's towing brackets underneath the front wheels of the Bentley.

One of the men smiled at Massimiliano Di Luca, who was now lying in a fetal position in the back, incapable of movement but fully conscious.

The two men pushed their shoulders against the rear of the Bentley and rolled it onto the tow bars. They secured the front wheels with chains, lifted up the front of the car, got back into the driver's cab, and drove off, towing the Bentley.

The whole sequence of events took only a few minutes.

CHAPTER 41

Outskirts of Milan

The irony of the situation had temporarily stumped Urs Savelli. He was a fan of Massimiliano Di Luca, and over the years rip-offs of the designer's creations had earned the Camorra more money than all the other Milan fashion houses' products put together.

That it would all come to an end in a derelict warehouse offended Savelli's sense of decorum.

He sat motionless on an office chair in the warehouse on Via Carlo Montanari in one of Milan's outer industrial areas; the building had been abandoned by its owners and no longer had any purpose. The few unbroken windows had been painted white, the doors had been removed, and the openings had been boarded up.

A rat scurried across the floor along the edge of a sunbeam, and he noticed a couple of pictures of girls torn from a tire-company calendar fluttering through the shadows. One of them flew past the chair, and he stepped on it with the tip of his boot. The blonde had a curly 1980s hairstyle and eye makeup to match. Apart from the makeup, the girl was naked: kneeling, inviting . . . but with a pneumatic tool strategically placed in front of her crotch. He lifted his foot, and the girl whirled on. He looked up. The old plywood ceiling was close to giving up the ghost, and the wooden walls, roasted by the sun, were dry and fraying.

It was a good place. Several of the sheds around the warehouse had burned down, and Savelli had big plans for this final building—and for Assistant Public Prosecutor Sabrina D'Avalos. She was a young witch, and witches should be burned.

The tow truck's crew kept a respectful distance from Savelli. The only one moving was the doctor Urs Savelli had insisted should be present during the abduction. The doctor was tending to the two stretchers where the fashion designer and his driver were lying. Massimiliano Di Luca's and Alberto's eyes were open and staring at Savelli's face. They lay curled up in the characteristic fighter's position in which the stronger flexor muscles of the joints dominate the stretching muscles. Their fists were clenched, and their knuckles bloodless. He knew that they were awake and listening even though they couldn't move.

The doctor was wearing a white nylon hazard suit with a hood and a breathing apparatus. He adjusted the electrodes on the fashion designer's bare chest and tore off a strip of paper from a printer. He studied the electrocardiogram as he walked toward the captain.

He stopped two meters in front of Urs Savelli's chair. Less than two meters was inadvisable: he might be contaminated with glass dust.

"I'm not entirely happy, signore," the doctor said.

"No?"

"No." The doctor shook his head. "The oxygen levels in the blood of both patients are normal. They're awake but paralyzed, obviously. However, Signor Di Luca has cardiac arrhythmia. It ought to be treated."

"Cardiac arrhythmia?"

"The atria of the heart are beating too fast compared to the ventricles. The heart's neural transfer is irregular, thus reducing the pumping ability of the heart. Signor Di Luca is likely to develop blood clots." The doctor looked gravely at the Camorra captain. "Normally one would try to re-create the heart's rhythm with digitalis medication or with an electric shock and then try to prevent clot formation by administering a blood thinner."

"Can you do that?"

The doctor straightened up. His eyes behind the reflective visor continued to study the electrocardiogram. The furrow of concern refused to be smoothed.

"Of course . . ."

"But?"

"I'm not entirely clear what level of treatment you wish me to administer."

Urs Savelli studied the leaden tip of the makila placed exactly halfway between his boots.

"You must do your duty and treat Signor Di Luca in accordance with the best specialist practice. I certainly want him to live for as long as possible and in the best possible condition, Doctor."

The doctor quickly started to open various bags.

The Albanian rested his chin on the bear head of his cane and followed the doctor's preparations.

He had observed L'Artista's attack at a distance and had been impressed. Remarkable couple, mother and daughter. Extraordinary.

His contact with the Chinese triads, Mr. Chun, had provided him with the glass dust that L'Artista's daughter had scattered across the seats of the Bentley.

The microscopic shards of glass were impregnated with heparin, which blocked the blood's ability to coagulate, and tetrodotoxin, an extract from the fins, skin, and intestines of the puffer fish and the second most poisonous substance known to science, after endo-toxin from the poison dart frog.

The formula originated from West African and Creole-Haitian voodoo: in order to ensure obedience in his servants, the voodoo priest, the *houngan*, would spread ground glass grains impregnated with puffer fish poison on the doorstep of suitable candidates. When the victim trod on the splinters with his or her bare feet, the inevi-table transformation from human being to slave, to zombie, would begin. Urs Savelli found the correct ethnographical description,

Lave Tet—brainwashing—most apt: the victim's personality, will, and memory were wiped as thoroughly as a computer's crashed hard drive.

The murder of Gianni Versace and the furor that had ensued were still painfully clear in Savelli's memory, but it would be nothing compared to the death of Massimiliano Di Luca. *Il maestro* would be given a state funeral, and there would be a national outcry for a police investigation to find and punish the guilty. Every stone normally regarded as untouchable would be turned. Old friends in the Senate in Rome would lose their confidence in him and turn away. This was much better. Don Francesco had been right.

Savelli rose, walked over to the stretchers, and stared into the eyes of Massimiliano Di Luca. At a safe distance.

"Can you hear me? If you can, please blink once."

Massimiliano Di Luca's eyelids closed and opened. His knuckles were no longer white, his hands were starting to relax, but his fingernails had left bleeding half-moons in the palms of his hands; the tetrodotoxin was almost washed from his spine, and in a few minutes Di Luca and his driver Alberto would regain control of their limbs.

"I intend to take everything from you, signore . . . including your mind. Everything but your life. I don't need you dead; I need you forgotten."

Di Luca's eyes remained half shut. His gaze no longer took in Savelli but was focused on something far away. Far away in the fifty-eight-year-old man's happiest memories.

Then he looked at Savelli and smiled.

His mouth formed words, and Urs Savelli leaned forward until the doctor's warning stopped him.

"Keep your distance, signore!"

Savelli ignored the doctor.

"What did you say?"

"It never worked . . ." Massimiliano Di Luca whispered.

"What?"

Di Luca's chest heaved, and on the exhaling breath he repeated: "Forlani's invention. It never worked."

Savelli's fists clenched behind his back.

He didn't believe the Venetian, obviously. It was a final desperate attempt to save Forlani. Admirable, really. Noble.

He nodded to the doctor, who was removing a cylindrical metal container from a foam-padded aluminum suitcase. Once again ambitious assassins could do well to study the ancients. They could start with Homer. The pharmaceutical explanation for the orgiastic Dionysus festivals of ancient times was not only the consumption of copious amounts of raw fermented grape juice but also the inhalation of smoke from the embers of thorn-apple twigs, *Datura stramonium*. The priestesses of Delphi—the Oracle—knew all about this potent and treacherous nightshade plant. Its psychosis-inducing effect was due to its high levels of various hallucinogenic alkaloids. Such as ergot. Every part of the plant was rich in these alkaloids, but the line between undesired death and desired ecstasy was paper thin.

An old Greek living on the island of Samos still knew the art of collecting the smoke from the twigs in large glass balloons, distilling the toxin in water-cooled copper pipes, and extracting the alkaloids in alcohol.

The doctor hooked up the pressure flask and placed a rubber mask over Di Luca's mouth and nose.

Then he checked the monitors that tracked heart rhythm and oxygen saturation.

Di Luca's irises rolled behind his eyelids.

"He's out," the doctor said.

"Are you sure?"

The doctor nodded.

"Quite sure. The datura is mixed with LSD and scopolamine. So—" The doctor shrugged his shoulders. "—bon voyage."

Urs Savelli looked at the unconscious fashion designer.

"Terror?"

"I beg your pardon?"

Savelli smiled.

"What's it like in there? Fear? Terror?"

The doctor looked uncertain. Fine drops sparkled on the upper lip of the Camorrista even though the air in the hall was cool.

"I imagine it's like having untreated schizophrenia," the doctor said slowly. "Terror, possibly. Certainly. The subconscious in free fall."

The doctor was keen to please Savelli.

"And they can't be brought back?"

The young man smiled.

"No, no," he said. "Datura administered in these doses over the next couple of hours will cause lesions to several brain centers. No, they'll stay as they are."

Savelli nodded and turned on his heel.

"We have work to do," he said.

CHAPTER 42

Milan—Ospedale Maggiore, Niguarda Ca' Granda

Even though they were separated by only a few meters, they could have been on different continents. The unconscious fashion designer had dispatched Sabrina and Giulio Forlani to the farthest recesses of his mind.

The afternoon sun went down while doctors, nurses, lab technicians, and Carabinieri officers went in and out of the isolation ward through the air lock, everyone protected by breathing apparatus, gloves, suits, and hoods. The doctors were dumbfounded, the nurses were efficient, the phlebotomists drew a little more blood from Di Luca's thin arms, and the officers whispered comments to Sabrina that she didn't hear.

It had been a call from Primo Alba that woke her up in the house in Ticino. That voice always meant disaster. After an anonymous tip-off to the Carabinieri in Greco Milanese, the designer's Bentley had been found in an underground garage in Porta Volta.

A careless Carabiniere had opened the driver's door, and Alberto had fallen out onto the concrete floor. The officer had begun to examine the driver but started convulsing a few seconds later; he had become nonresponsive, and his hands had started to bleed.

From that moment on Alberto and Massimiliano Di Luca were treated as if they were carrying a deadly virus.

Sabrina got up and went over to the window. Sweat poured down her back under the nylon coverall, and her hair was soaking wet. Enterprising journalists who had been listening to the police on a scanner had started gathering in front of the hospital's entrances. For the time being they were kept at a distance by the police, dogs, and cordons, but Sabrina knew that the vast hospital had hundreds of ways in and was impossible to secure totally. Sooner or later some journalist would find a white coat, a stethoscope, and his scoop. Massimiliano Di Luca's name had been mentioned on the police radio during the initial call, which had sent the media into a frenzy.

The hospital's large elliptical courtyard with its strict geometrical pathways and shrubs lay strangely peaceful and golden, deserted and unused.

After his initial contact, Primo Alba no longer was taking her calls, and Federico Renda was not available either, his secretary informed her. At least not to Sabrina D'Avalos.

She had been overtaken by events, and she could feel the fresh imprint of the pariah mark on her forehead. This was what Primo Alba had warned her about outside the cathedral. If she succeeded, everything would be official and hunky-dory; there would be toasts and champagne, applause and medals. If she was not, no one had ever heard of her and everyone would distance himself from her. She would be a rogue agent, an unreliable assistant public prosecutor who had put her private motives above her duty.

She would be famous, notorious . . . and forgotten. Perhaps her name might be whispered occasionally in the canteen of the Palace of Justice or in one of the cafés around Via delle Repubbliche Marinare by some careless junior assistant prosecutor who would quickly be silenced by an older colleague. Sabrina D'Avalos? Hush! For God's sake, never mention her name within the hearing range of Federico Renda if you value your career.

The next and final step would be relegation to the Vehicle Registration Agency, but she was too tired to care. She turned around and looked at Giulio Forlani, who hadn't said one word to her in the last three hours in the hospital ward; his rare glances in her direction had spoken volumes.

Sabrina sighed and tried to take stock of the situation: (1) She had found a genius who was presumed dead—who didn't want to be found—and an invention that didn't work; (2) she had caused the deaths of Professor Carlo Mazzaferro and his companion, Laura Rizzo; (3) given time, she would have ensured that the widow Antonia Moretti and her fifteen-year-old son, Gianni, met the same fate; and (4) she had turned the world-famous fashion designer Massimiliano Di Luca and his innocent driver into vegetables.

It was truly impressive. She was a human Bermuda Triangle.

The deep groan from the rubber edges of the air lock made her turn around: a man with an aristocratic face and half-moon reading glasses on a long patrician nose, tall and thin, had arrived.

He introduced himself as Professor Something or Other but did not shake hands.

Giulio Forlani rose to his feet. He positioned himself next to Sabrina.

"You are Signor Di Luca's next of kin?" the professor asked.

Sabrina nodded. As they waited for the doctor to deliver his news, they felt fairly composed.

Di Luca looked just the way he had at breakfast, Sabrina thought. It was possible that he looked even better. The color of his face was natural, and he was sleeping calmly. The monitors above his bed all showed normal green curves and numbers.

The professor cleared his throat.

"We're . . . dumbfounded. When I say 'we,' I mean the staff here at Niguarda. We don't understand what has happened to Signor Di Luca." He smiled faintly. "Normally we don't mind appearing all-knowing . . . far from it. But the truth is that we're totally at a loss. Almost."

"Almost?" Sabrina said with a glimmer of hope snatched from the darkness.

"Insofar as there are many causes of a coma which we can eliminate fairly easily: Signor Di Luca didn't suffer a stroke, his brain hasn't been subjected to trauma or violence, the MR scan of his brain was completely normal."

The professor's voice ebbed.

"Drugs?" Sabrina asked. "Toxins?"

"We haven't had any definitive results back yet," he said, then added quickly, "That doesn't mean that Signor Di Luca's mind hasn't been contaminated with some exotic substance. In fact, I believe it has. But we have yet to identify what it is."

"Did you notice his fingertips?" she asked. "I understand that a type of glass dust was found in the car."

"Yes, fascinating, isn't it? The fingertips were the entry point for what has now put him out of the running. Whatever it is."

Sabrina and Giulio Forlani looked at him.

"Fascinating?" Forlani muttered, and Sabrina had a vision of the aristocratic professor dangling, half choked, from the physicist's grip.

The professor held up his long hands.

"We'll have to wait and see, dottoressa."

Behind them Massimiliano Di Luca smiled and said in a loud and clear voice, "Corfu, Negroponte, Chania, Adrianopolis, Cyprus."

Then he fell silent.

The professor leaned over the patient.

"He's unconscious," he said. "What did the words mean, signorina?"

"He's a descendant of one of the doges of Venice, professore," Giulio Forlani explained. "In the fifteenth and sixteenth centuries their colonies included Corfu, Cyprus, and Chania on Crete. He's proud of his family."

He looked at Sabrina.

"He sounded happy when he said it, didn't he?"

"Definitely," she agreed.

While the professor, visibly excited, carried out his neurological examinations—pulling up eyelids, shining light at pupils, testing reflexes and muscle strength—Giulio Forlani stood there like an abandoned child on a train platform. Sabrina again picked up a yellow padded envelope that had been handed to her by one of the first Carabinieri officers on the scene. The envelope had been found on the passenger seat of the Bentley next to the unfortunate driver, and someone had written her name in capital letters on it with an ordinary ballpoint pen.

The officer had assured her that the cell telephone found inside the envelope was completely harmless: there was no trace of the strange glass dust on the surface of the cell, nor did it contain an explosive charge. It was a completely ordinary prepaid cell telephone of a well-known brand. The battery was fully charged, and there were no stored numbers in its memory. Nor were there any fingerprints on it.

"How is his driver, Alberto?" she asked the professor.

"The same. Except he hasn't said anything at all."

With a feeling of unreality, Sabrina heard Massimiliano Di Luca sing "Mad Dogs and Englishmen." With his eyes closed and still unconscious. She wouldn't have been surprised if Noël Coward, sporting a cigarette in an elegant holder and wearing a dinner jacket, had entered the ward and started to mix martinis.

"I don't think I can stay any longer," Giulio Forlani said.

"I agree. Let's go," Sabrina said.

The professor didn't hear them. He was making a telephone call requesting microphones and tape recorders, trembling like a radio astronomer who has just received a clear Morse code message from Saturn.

Silently they walked along numerous long hospital corridors and down cool stairwells until they reached the large courtyard. They found a bench, took a seat, and watched some patients who were shuffling around. Most of them were alone; a few were with family or friends.

"Now what?" Forlani asked.

Sabrina kept turning over the envelope with the cell. Then she put it down on the bench and had a look around.

The hospital's main entrance on Via Carlo Moreschi would be besieged by the press, so Sabrina decided their best bet would be one of the side exits to Piazza dell'Ospedale Maggiore.

"I've got to get you to Naples," she said. "I should have done that a long time ago."

"You could always call the police," he suggested.

"I've tried that. They're not taking my calls," she said.

She checked the cell again: no messages.

The tall, dark figure slumped a little more.

Or maybe they could just stay on this bench, she thought.

"I think we need to find a hotel room," she said, and got up.

The Camorra picked them up five minutes later.

CHAPTER 43

Milan—Ospedale Maggiore, Niguarda Ca' Granda

The abduction was so professionally executed that their attackers could have carried it out in their sleep; it was essentially utterly predictable, she thought while it happened. Because she totally deserved it; as a result of exhaustion or inexperience, she had forgotten the first rule of her profession, which her poor father, who probably was spinning in his grave, had drilled into her: "Never allow yourself to be reduced to a pawn in your opponent's game, Sabrina. If you do that, you will lose everything: your advantage, your freedom, and possibly your life."

That was exactly what she had allowed to happen by fixating on the damned cell that had been left for her. She had walked right into the trap, had convinced herself that the next move would come from the cell. She had grown lazy and dropped her guard while she waited for instructions, as if she would magically be preserved from evil until the cell rang. Which, of course, it never did.

They had walked past the lowest hospital buildings, which were in the east, passed a small rotunda to the left, continued past the emergency room and the ambulance stations, and were taking a quiet little shortcut with trees and bushes on one side and the garage on the other. Sabrina congratulated herself on avoiding the throng of photographers, broadcasting vans, and journalists in front of the main entrance. In the garage there was a hospital transport van, a kind of converted minibus, and a young ambulance driver was busy lowering the steel lift at the rear. Another ambulance driver was waiting with a young woman in a wheelchair.

He smiled to Sabrina and Giulio Forlani, who were level with the open side doors of the minibus, when the woman in the wheelchair looked up.

She was beautiful, dark-haired, with an ambulance blanket over her legs. Sabrina remembered her eyes from somewhere but couldn't place them. The next few seconds were protracted, elongated, and shimmering like a desert road because it wasn't the woman's eyes or features that Sabrina recognized—it was her character: her eyes were attentive, wide open, unblinking, and ready. They were the stuff of nightmares. They were the eyes she had been searching for in her subconscious for the last eighteen months, the ones she had seen in that long second before the white flash from the bomb over Federico Renda's car when L'Artista struck. The brake lights of the police motorcycle, the face behind the visor of the helmet. Her memory had been wrong: she recalled the eyes as black, dead, devoid of expression—and not at all like this woman's dark brown eyes, beautiful . . . animated.

The realization made her reach out for Giulio Forlani with her left arm while her right hand went for the Walther in her shoulder holster. As usual the physicist sensed nothing, lost in a world of his own.

Long arms from the inside of the minibus reached out for her, and she left the earth and was lifted into the darkness.

"Giulio . . ."

A paralyzing white pain exploded in the back of her head as one of her abductors struck her with a rubber blackjack. The sound of the blow had a surreal clarity: she heard teeth gnash together, heard her skin and scalp give and the bones of her skull groan. All strength and coordination left her body; she landed on the floor of the vehicle and looked out at Giulio Forlani's face, which turned to the doorway in slow motion, his mouth beginning to open, when the young woman, in a long, fluid motion, flung aside the blanket and leaped to her feet, holding an electric stun gun. The lunge for the physicist's neck was uniquely graceful and effectively executed. There was a brief blue spark from somewhere under his left ear, and the huge man collapsed—slowly, surprised, and with a strangely mournful expression—in midstep.

That was all she saw.

A blackout-fabric hood was pulled over her head, she was kicked into a corner of the minibus, and her hands were tied in front of her body with a cable tie that dug deep into the skin and cut off the blood supply to her hands. She felt the Walther being removed from the shoulder holster.

No one spoke a word.

The blood trickled from the back of her head under the hood, down inside the collar of her anorak, and spread with a not entirely unpleasant warmth to her shoulders.

There was heavy breathing from the fake ambulance men, and Sabrina felt the warmth and the weight of Forlani's body when they dragged him into the vehicle. The side door was rolled shut with a bang, and the minibus started. Behind her she could hear the hum of the electric motors as the lift was raised and slotted into place at the back of the minibus.

It would have been so easy to surrender to this total defeat, to the fear and the torrent of self-reproach—to hope for a long period of unconsciousness and a quick end to it all—but she couldn't. She fought her nausea with a series of deep breaths, scared of choking on her own vomit if she gave in, while those of her senses that were still working explored the inside of the minibus.

There was a man close to her. Probably on the rear seat to the left, facing backward to the platform and the rails to which wheelchairs could be attached and from which frail patients could be monitored. Garlic on the man's breath. Tiny sounds from clothes against clothes, clothes against the vinyl seat covering, boots against the floor. In front of the man there had to be two unoccupied double seats and then the driver's seat.

Where were L'Artista and the other ambulance driver? Not inside the bus. She felt sure of that. Desperately she flicked through her last visual impressions before she was dragged into the vehicle and found a long, dark blue European car with tinted windows parked roughly fifty meters away.

"Giulio," she muttered, slowly turning onto her back.

"Shut up," said the man in front of her without sounding especially angry.

His voice gave her some idea of his location. Very close.

"Are you awake?" she asked, and got a whack across her forehead with the rubber blackjack. Garlic breath close up. The man had leaned forward.

She could hear Forlani breathe. Her hands were numb and thick, and she wondered how long she had before they became completely useless. Her belly was exposed to her midriff, and she knew that the man on the backseat had a clear view of her stomach, her hip bones, and her white panties. The tip of the rubber blackjack slid slowly across her skin from her midriff, left around her belly button, and down to the zip of the low-cut jeans.

Sabrina knew that she had a very nice stomach.

Now.

Or never?

Now.

"Giulio?"

She turned her head again toward the paralyzed physicist.

"Shut your mouth," the man said. This time clearly excited by her skin, his omnipotence, or her disobedience.

Garlic breath and a squeaking from the seat as the man's weight shifted from his backside to the soles of his feet. He was now leaning forward.

While contemplating a suitable punishment, she assumed.

Sabrina pulled her knees up to her face, and the man began to warn her. She kicked out, and the soles of her boots hit something heavy and rubbery, which prompted a satisfactory outburst. She pulled her legs up again and snatched the Colt from her ankle holster with both hands. The barrel nearly slipped from her numb fingers, and she bit her lower lip until it bled in concentration. With her left thumb she released the safety catch and proceeded to fire three shots diagonally across and up.

There was a quick and surprised exhalation of breath, and her abductor crashed down on top of her as the minibus suddenly accelerated. She wiggled free from under the man, who was still moving. She got to her knees and nearly fell when the minibus turned left. She pushed against the floor and rested her forearms on the back of the seat in front of her. She didn't waste time trying to remove the hood but aimed at where she thought the back and neck of the driver ought to be.

One shot.

And one left in the cylinder.

The driver never made a sound, but the minibus went out of control and collided a second later with something immovable and solid.

Sabrina was thrown forward into the back of the seat in front of her so violently that her neck cracked and she nearly did a forward somersault. The bus keeled very slowly onto its off-side wheels and balanced for a moment at an incline of forty-five degrees before it crashed onto its side with the screeching sound of metal mixed with the short, crisp cracking of breaking windows. Shards of glass rained down over Sabrina and drummed against the floor.

Something in her chest must have been dislocated or broken because every time she tried breathing, she felt a stabbing pain. She lay still, curled up, and waited for the glass shower to subside. Finally she managed to ease her thumbs up under the cord of the hood, loosen it, and pull it back. She let it dangle from the soaked hair at the back of her neck and found she was looking straight into the face of the man with the rubber blackjack. His head lay at an unnatural angle to his neck. He might still be alive because his pupils were contracted, and she thought she could see an artery pulse under the skin on his neck. She had hit his left shoulder and the left side of his chest. She had no idea where the third shot had ended up, but she was content with the first two. She noticed a large automatic pistol in his shoulder holster. She dropped the Colt, which skidded along the sloping floor, and took the man's pistol.

"Waste not, want not," she muttered to herself, and crawled across Forlani's limp figure, which lay wedged against the side door. Through the minibus's missing side windows she could see blue sky. She pushed off with her boots against a seat leg and eventually managed to wriggle through a narrow window. She ignored the broken glass in the window frame, which was trying its best to prevent her escape.

"Stop! Stop, God damn you!"

In disbelief Urs Savelli leaned forward and put his hand on Claudio's shoulder. The young man hit the brakes, and the large Audi skidded to a halt with its disc brakes squealing in the middle of the road, fifty meters from the now wrecked minibus. The fake ambulance man next to the driver was thrown forward against his seat belt and swore loudly.

Until then everything had gone seamlessly. As planned, L'Artista had paralyzed Giulio Forlani and had then—as was her habit—made herself scarce. Presumably she was now driving home in her Berlingo. Perhaps she was listening to music in the car, planning what to buy for tonight's dinner—what did he know? Her part of the mission was over.

The intolerable little assistant public prosecutor had been dragged into the minibus and rendered harmless and . . . now this: for no known reason the bus had veered out of control, scaled a high curb, and just about avoided a tree but then had driven across the pavement and crashed into the outpatient building. And turned over on its side. They had heard shots fired.

Jesus, Joseph, Mary, and the donkey . . . !

The windows of the outpatient building filled with faces.

They heard sirens.

The three men sat absolutely still as they silently watched the small, disheveled, and bloody figure squirming her way through a broken window in the minibus. She was like an insatiable, unstoppable alien who had just consumed the crew of a spacecraft and was looking for fresh prey. She swung her legs up from under her and for a moment sat quietly on the bodywork. Then she turned her head slowly like a robot to locate them: her face was as white as chalk where it wasn't red. There was no expression in that face, but her eyes were wide open and all-seeing. She slid down the bodywork, landing heavily on her feet, and started limping toward them. In the middle of the road. Shedding glass splinters with every laborious step as if she were wearing cracked ice armor.

And though it looked as heavy as original sin, she raised the black automatic pistol to eye level. She started shooting as she walked.

The Audi's windscreen turned milky white around a star-shaped hole, and an invisible hand tore off an ear from the ambulance man.

The man screamed and the Audi rocked when the next two shots went through the hood and into the engine. Savelli let himself slide down to a lying position.

"I think we should leave the area now, Claudio," he said quietly, and pulled a face as the stuffing of the passenger seat was blasted away right above his head. "And if you can hit that stupid bitch in the process, I really would appreciate it."

The Audi leaped forward with a roar, and Savelli raised himself onto his elbow and looked out the side window. He saw Sabrina D'Avalos get back on her feet after rolling across the pavement. The tiny fury looked straight at him with a strangely determined expression in her cloudy gray eyes. Mesmerized, he kept watching her, now through the rear window. He had seen that promise before: in the eyes of her father, General Agostino D'Avalos. Then the terrible woman lifted her pistol again, and Urs Savelli slipped back onto the floor.

CHAPTER 44

Ospedale Maggiore, Niguarda Ca' Granda, Milan

She heard his voice outside the curtain but felt nothing. She was totally spent. The doctor injected a little more local anesthetic into her back and clucked like a worried hen.

The emergency room doctor kept finding more glass fragments in her back and neck. They fell with irregular clinks into a steel tray held by the nurse.

Primo Alba pulled the curtain aside and raised his eyebrows in comic surprise. Sabrina lifted the white ambulance blanket up to her shoulders even though Primo Alba had seen it all before. In another life.

She didn't look at him but at her hair, which lay in a thick, dark brown nest under her dangling, bloodstained feet. It had taken twelve stitches to close up the wound at the back of her neck. The nurse had offered to shave off only the hair around the cut, but Sabrina couldn't see herself with a bald spot at the back of her head.

"Take it all," she had said, and now her scalp felt naked, alien, and cool. The nurse, who was young and pretty—well, she would be, wouldn't she?—had operated the electric shaver with a kind of gleeful pleasure.

Sabrina couldn't possibly face Primo. She looked like a train wreck. Her hands were still swollen, and the cable ties had left angry red furrows around her wrists.

Primo Alba said nothing, but she was aware that he was smiling at the pretty, healthy, and undamaged nurse, whose body instinctively assumed a different and possibly more flattering stance. Perhaps she pulled back her shoulders a little, pushed her breasts forward and her hips out; the bowl with Sabrina's blood and pieces of glass was held up as if it were an offer of refreshing grapes to a travel-weary pilgrim.

Cazzo . . . Stop it now!

"You have a nicely . . . shaped head," he said to Sabrina, who slumped a little.

"Giulio . . . ? How is he?" she asked.

Alba's tanned hand swung back into her field of vision, and the tweed sleeve was pushed back with the other hand so that he could consult his wristwatch.

"He's awake, and in five minutes they'll take him up to the roof," he said. "From where he'll travel by helicopter to Aviano. The same place the widow and her son were taken. After that . . ."

"Yes?"

"The mandarins have met in Rome, Sabrina. One must presume they'll find a permanent solution to Dr. Forlani's problems."

"It never worked," she said, and felt tears forcing their way up under her eyelids as the doctor eased a particularly obstinate glass splinter out of her back. She gasped. "Ouch! It never worked . . . the invention. It couldn't . . ." Even though she felt dehydrated, she seemed to have an excess of sweat, because it kept running down her face. "It couldn't handle crossing datelines."

His hands disappeared into his trouser pockets. His face appeared not to reveal any kind of promise or interest, because the nurse turned her attention back to the doctor.

"Yes, I've heard that," he said. "They may not have gotten it right yet, but I sense that they still believe the technology has huge potential. Hopefully the good doctor Forlani will end up somewhere in the United States where he can carry on his work."

"Until they find him again."

He cleared his throat, and she finally looked at him. Just a glance. His face was paler than she remembered. There were more fine wrinkles and deeper laughter lines in his real-life face than she recalled. She tightened the blanket around her.

"That's where we come in, Sabrina," he said so quietly that a less attentive audience might easily have missed it. "We may have an opening. Promising but something of a long shot."

"We do?"

"Yes."

He started talking to the doctor as if she weren't there or as if she were an injured pet someone had brought in—an object obviously prized, at least to some extent.

"Has she lost a lot of blood?" he asked.

"Some. Not much."

"Any broken bones?"

"Strange as it may seem, Dottoressa D'Avalos escaped with only superficial cuts and bruises and then all this glass. It's actually a miracle considering her . . . efforts," the doctor said. "We won't get all the glass out today. We'll have to remove it over time. The glass doesn't show up on X-rays. The deepest bits will eventually work their way out to the surface and . . . present symptoms. Then we'll take them."

Or they'll work their way in, she thought.

There was a rasping sound as the doctor started tearing strips of surgical tape off a roll.

The compresses felt dry and cool against her skin.

"I'll wait outside," Primo Alba said.

"You do that," she mumbled.

She spotted her shoulder bag, which some kind and eternally blessed soul had rescued from the crashed minibus and placed inside the curtain.

"All done," the doctor said, and she let herself slide down onto the vinyl floor, then nearly fell over because she had no strength or control of her hips, ankles, or knees.

The nurse supported her. She smelled of some fleeting citrus perfume that Sabrina might have chosen for herself.

"Signorina? Will you be all right?"

Anxiously she looked into her eyes.

"My bag, *per favore.*"

"Of course."

She seemed to communicate something nonverbal to the doctor, who left.

"Here, signorina."

The nurse placed Sabrina's shapeless shoulder bag on the stretcher, and Sabrina let the blanket fall around her feet. She was naked beneath it.

"A bath?" the nurse suggested.

Sabrina looked herself up and down. She looked like a hunting trophy flayed by an amateur.

"No, I'm fine, thanks. Later. Doesn't matter."

The young woman smiled gravely and helped Sabrina find the last clean white T-shirt, a clean pair of panties, socks, and dark trousers from her pantsuit.

Sabrina struggled to get into the clothes. Everything hurt, and she had to move deliberately and carefully like someone underwater. The nurse was a credit to her profession, she really was, and Sabrina was able to forgive her the small flirtatious pantomime in front of Primo Alba. She had never been able to feel ownership of any living creature with the exception of Ismael and Ziggy, and she wasn't going to start now, certainly not for Alba, whom she would quite happily see swallowed up in the bottomless crevasse of a glacier.

She spotted him at the end of the gray hospital corridor. His figure was blurred from the backlighting from a large window behind him. He was speaking quietly into his cell, and she was about to dismiss her first impression of him as a carefree yuppie. He was a serious man, she thought, and his smiles were as rare as solar eclipses—when he was on duty. Which he probably always was. She walked as stiffly as if she had just gotten off a horse. Her clothes were uncomfortable and dry against her body, and new sore spots were constantly trying to draw attention to themselves.

Primo Alba ended the call when he noticed her and put the cell in his jacket pocket. With the light behind him, his face was black and unreadable.

He took her bag and slung it over his shoulder.

"An opening?" she asked.

"Or the chance of one," he replied, nodding.

"A chance of an opening? That sounds great. An opening to whom or what?"

"The woman. L'Artista. It was she and a little girl, possibly her daughter, who attacked Massimiliano Di Luca. A farmer watched the whole thing but didn't connect the incident to anything criminal until he heard about it on the radio."

"A little girl?"

He shrugged his shoulders.

"A little girl, a boy with long hair, a dwarf in a dress, what difference does it make, Sabrina?"

"None."

"Incidentally, you were right about the homing pigeons," he said. "Your boss Federico Renda is ecstatic. He sends his regards. A carpentry business is connected to Don Francesco Terrasino's estate by a particularly well-constructed and well-equipped tunnel. The carpenter is a well-known breeder of pigeons. That's the opening."

"Why didn't you tell me your name?"

"What we need are a couple of stoats or polecats. Do some damage. Make it look like an accident. The pigeons, I mean. Meanwhile we abduct a couple of them."

"Who is Nestore Raspallo?"

He started walking.

She hobbled after him.

"Are you with the GIS? You've been working for them the whole time, haven't you? You knew that Forlani was alive."

The tears started burning behind her eyelids, and she had to swallow several times.

"We think that L'Artista lives on a line north-northeast from Naples. We fit a couple of the carpenter's pigeons with a small GPS sender and follow them in a helicopter. At least that's the plan."

"Are you married?"

He groaned with exasperation.

She was like the journalist who insisted on asking about the divorce while the actor wanted only to promote his latest movie.

"Are you? What I'm saying is, right now is there a Signora Alba somewhere pining for you, darning your socks, ironing your shirts, cooking dinner for your children . . ."

"Jesus Christ, Sabrina! Do you think for once you could just be—"

"Professional? That's just what I was being. I killed two men, Primo."

He nodded.

"And what you did was clever and brave. Definitely. I'm in the GIS. I travel two hundred days a year. I'm not married, and I have no children. The closest I've come to having a family is my divorced sister, her two fairly intolerable daughters, and a cat who sleeps on my windowsill when it rains and I'm at home to open the window. I haven't even given it a name."

Sabrina stopped and stared miserably at the floor. Two hospital porters pushed a stretcher past them in the corridor. A sheet had been pulled over its contents.

"You knew that he was alive," she said. "He told me you were with him on the plane to the United States."

"I didn't know that he was still alive. I knew that he had survived the attack; that much is true. I knew that he went to Gloucester and got a job on a trawler. And then he disappeared."

"Disappeared?"

Primo Alba nodded wearily.

"We had a . . . system. Coded messages delivered with junk mail. Telephone numbers he could call if everything was all right and numbers he had to call if he thought someone was after him. He did neither. We sent people over there to look for him. In vain. We presumed that Savelli had found him."

"But why didn't you tell me?"

"Because I'm not allowed to, Sabrina! I work in intelligence, and I follow my orders—on the whole. When the bodies of Lucia and Salvatore were discovered and you started your . . . investigation, everyone was rather rattled. Because of . . . your father, whom many people regarded as a saint . . . Forlani disappearing. Mistakes had been made. Both during the attack on Nanometric and—" Alba looked at the floor. "—later, the general. It was unforgivable that we couldn't take better care of him. That *I* didn't. I spoke to him three hours before he was killed. I should have been there."

"Did Renda know that Forlani was alive?"

"No."

Sabrina nodded. She believed him, and there was a strange comfort in knowing that her boss had been just as ignorant as she had been.

"She's dangerous," she said. "L'Artista."

"I'm perfectly aware of that. Do you want to come along? Are you up for it?"

"I want to, but I don't think you understand just how dangerous she is. Have you seen her? And by the way, where were you an hour ago?"

He looked straight ahead.

"We were here. In the wrong place. We presumed that you and Forlani would leave the hospital by the main entrance."

"So we were bait? That's why you didn't answer your phone. You wanted it to look natural."

At least he had the decency to blush a little. One hand opened in a kind of gesture, and the other wiggled his wristwatch free from the sleeve of his jacket.

"We don't have very much time, Sabrina. I'm sorry."

"So am I."

CHAPTER 45

Three hours and ten minutes to dawn, and she was totally in the dark. She didn't know where they were, who the other people in the helicopter were, what they were doing, or what—if anything—was expected of her. She had spent five hours sitting still, trapped inside this metal cocoon, and she hated it. The matte black transport helicopter had picked her and Primo Alba up from the landing pad on the roof of the hospital. Alba had closed the sliding door after them, and the helicopter had taken off immediately. The few instrument lights in the cockpit had struggled fruitlessly against the darkness inside the body of the helicopter. At the first lurch, Sabrina had fallen into a canvas seat that she thought was vacant and that triggered an outburst and a hard smack to her backside that sent her deeper into the cabin to an empty seat. A hand had passed her a padded headset that she had put on, but still the engine noise was indescribable. It was like sitting inside a metal barrel while a group of eager blacksmiths worked on it with pneumatic drills. All the bones in her skull vibrated out of sync, and her teeth refused to stop clattering. She knew that this type of helicopter sometimes flew for hours without stopping during troop transports and rescue missions, and she couldn't imagine how people coped. After five minutes she was on the verge of a breakdown. Surely the pilots must be lobotomized before beginning active duty.

When her eyes had acclimatized to the darkness, she could make out half a dozen shapeless figures on the rough canvas seats. They didn't look particularly bothered by the infernal noise even though Sabrina couldn't see much of their faces. They all wore black helmets and ski masks. Even the area around their eyes had been painted dark gray with camouflage sticks. They stared right ahead, unmoving. They were experts at waiting.

There really wasn't much to look at, and apart from a few brief exchanges between the pilots and an occasional update from a military flight leader, none of those on board had spoken a word for the first couple of hours.

Then the miracle happened: she fell asleep.

She woke up when the helicopter landed at Camp Darby outside Vicenza. Primo Alba pulled her to her feet and helped her across the dark apron to a low, anonymous building.

In a drab changing room he watched while she put on the regulation black fighter suit, helmet, yellow shooting goggles, throat microphone, a Motorola communications unit and earpiece, a bulletproof vest, and boots one size too big. He strapped a plastic holster that contained a Beretta 9-mm pistol with laser sights to her right side.

"Do you know how to use this?" he asked, and she checked the magazine and nodded.

"How about you?"

Primo Alba was dressed in civilian clothing: a dark gray tweed jacket, a dark blue shirt, jeans, and black running shoes.

"This is fine," he said.

"Shouldn't you at least be wearing a bulletproof vest?"

"The Lord preserveth the simple," he said. "Besides, I'm the leader of this operation, and my apparent contempt for death inspires my team . . . and they can see who I am."

He winked merrily at her with one bright gray eye.

"Now you look ready and very dangerous," he declared.

*   *   *

Around five thirty in the morning the helicopter landed in an anonymous field outside Cremona, the engines were switched off, and everyone straightened out and stretched his or her limbs as far as the seat belts and extensive equipment allowed.

Someone eventually opened the loading bay, and Sabrina savored the fresh air. After a few minutes of silence the first brave cicadas resumed their nighttime concert. Sabrina looked up at the cockpit. A tall figure momentarily blocked the instrument lights before kneeling down and starting a hushed conversation with the pilots. Primo Alba, no doubt. The figure rose and resumed his seat at the front of the cabin.

She recognized the voice in her earpiece.

"Status update, ladies and gentlemen. Those of you who wish to are free to remove your helmets and masks."

There was a murmur of approval, and they all removed their helmets and balaclavas. Sabrina could smell a feminine shampoo close by. The person to her left ran a hand through short hair, and Sabrina could see that the profile was definitely a woman's. She also had a couple of rings in one nostril. The woman half turned in her seat and offered Sabrina a piece of chewing gum, then smiled with very white teeth in her camouflage-painted face.

Alba resumed his briefing.

"Exactly five minutes ago our friend Agent X in Naples released a couple of ferrets in Signor M's pigeon loft, and within a few seconds the animals bit the necks off practically all of Signor M's prize-winning homing pigeons with the exception of a few that Agent X had earlier evacuated from the central loft, the one which we believe houses the pigeons that consider L'Artista's den their actual home. They've been fitted with tiny GPS transmitters and will be released in a moment. We hope . . ."

Primo Alba held a rhetorical pause.

"Correction: we *very much* hope that the pigeons will lead us to L'Artista and not some hapless pigeon fancier who just happens to share Signor M's passion for breeding pigeons. In which case this innocent bystander will get the shock of his life and we, ladies and gentlemen, will have a hell of a lot of explaining to do. A well-fed homing pigeon in good shape can cover between 90 and 120 kilometers in an hour. At least. There is an AWACS aircraft in the air above Naples. It will follow the pigeon and give us its coordinates. We have every reason to believe that L'Artista's pigeon loft is equipped with some sort of alarm that will alert her to the arrival of a new pigeon. This means we have a very short time span from the arrival of the pigeon to the raid. We have a window, but only a very narrow one, before she disappears or arms herself. Besides, we don't know if she lives in a penthouse apartment in Turin or on a houseboat on the River Po. We've a lot of work to do, and everything . . . everything will be improvised."

Primo Alba fell silent without warning. He didn't ask if anyone had any questions, she noticed. Either it wasn't the done thing— a breach of professional etiquette—or the others had heard the word "improvised" and that rendered everything else irrelevant.

Chapter 46

Brescia

The young woman turned over in bed and found her wristwatch on the bedside table: 6:30 a.m. Not even dawn yet. She drank a mouthful of water from the glass next to the bedside lamp and wondered whether to ignore the alarm from the pigeon loft. She still ached all over from the collision with Di Luca's Bentley. Her left knee was swollen and discolored; she would have to have it checked out later today. She always went to the same private clinic.

No bird had ever arrived this early before, nor had she ever been given assignments in such quick succession. She swung her feet out onto the stone floor, got up, and found her dressing gown behind the door. She looked at her husband's dark, curly head on the pillow and smiled. Unlike her, he had been blessed with the gift of deep sleep.

She hobbled down the long passage that separated the bedrooms from the utility room, kitchen, and bathrooms. The first room on her right belonged to her daughter, Abrielle. The old stone walls retained so much of the daytime heat that the nights were always too hot. Their daughter had kicked off her comforter and was lying in her dark blue pajamas with stars, planets, and moons on them.

The woman pulled the comforter over the girl. Without waking, she turned over, found a cool corner of the comforter, and put it under her cheek.

The window was open, and Hector the cat was outside.

She stood for a moment with her arms folded across her chest and looked out the window. The bedroom was east-facing, and she could see the start of the pale gray dawn behind the spruces. She checked the time again. Two roebucks usually foraged at the bottom of a fallow field around this time.

But the field was deserted. And the animals had taken all sounds with them.

There were no birds singing, no cicadas. There were no head-lights from passing cars or trucks on Viale Sant Eufemia a couple of hundred meters from the cider house. The first shift workers should be on their way to work now; the first trucks should be arriving with deliveries for the supermarkets.

Signora Malvestre, who lived in a small stone cottage a hundred meters to the south behind a row of old apple trees, usually was up by now, light visible in her kitchen windows. She was the matron at a nursing home in Brescia and rode her bicycle there every morn-ing. Her house was dark, and the heart in the young woman's chest started to pound.

No noises, no light or animals. Nothing. As if the world around them were holding its breath.

She spun around and ran down the passage and into the liv-ing room. She had forgotten her injured knee and wrist. When she was a circus artist she invariably would have some sort of injury but would perform nevertheless. She had learned to ignore pain. She found the key on top of the gun cabinet, dropped it, and nearly screamed in frustration while she wasted precious seconds looking for it. She opened the cabinet and found a small Taurus 7.65-mm automatic pistol, put it in the pocket of her dressing gown, and snatched a Remington pump-action shot-gun from its brackets. She broke a nail when she ripped open a box of shotgun cartridges, tore the rest of the paper off the box with her teeth, and pumped cartridges into the chamber of the shotgun.

The weight of the Remington instilled some calm, and she got her breathing under control. She glided through the low, dark room with the shotgun ready at her shoulder. She waited ten endless seconds at the back door before she went outside on the wet flagstones between the house and her husband's studio. It was just at the time when the dew fell, and she felt moisture on her face. The sky was growing lighter with incredible speed and revealed trees, fields, and fences while she wanted only to turn back the clock to the darkness and the night so that she could get Abrielle and her husband to a place of safety. Far away from here.

She knelt down by the first corner and let the barrel of the shotgun swing in a wide arc around the corner before she followed. Hector was standing a few meters away with a mouse. He sat down on his hind legs, let the mouse escape into the tall grass, and pricked his ears as he watched her.

From the pigeon loft she could hear a sleepy cooing, as always when a new pigeon had arrived. She assumed it must be a kind of greeting. There were small piles of food and wood shavings in the tall grass, and they felt spongy against her bare feet. She rested the shotgun against the wooden wall of the pigeon loft and checked the little photocell in front of the landing board where a homing pigeon would break the light beam.

She had fed the pigeons before she went to bed. There had been three, but now she could make out four silhouettes behind the netting. She lifted the catch, opened the mesh door, and extended her hands into the pigeon loft. She made reassuring noises as the birds cooed anxiously, pressing themselves against the perch. She had always been good with animals. She let her fingertips glide over the neck of each bird, and when she got to the second one, she found a small metal cylinder attached to its left leg.

Something was wrong. Something was very, very wrong. The cylinder was too long, it felt different from the usual metal containers that Signor Marchese tied to the legs of the pigeons—and he always attached them to the right leg. Always. Signor Marchese was methodical in everything he did for Don Francesco Terrasino. And there was something else in the darkness of the pigeon loft that didn't belong: a small LED light casting regular green flashes across the claws of the pigeon.

She closed the hatch, turned to the fields, and spotted the first one.

Between the old apple trees. Very slowly, one of the trunks changed shape and became two outlines. The man emerging from the shadow of the tree ran through the long wet grass, in between the trees, and up toward the house.

And out of range of her guns.

She heard Radu cry out from inside the house. Her beloved roared like an animal. The scream was cut short by a noise like an ax hitting a watermelon, and the young woman ran silently around the corner, in through the back door, and onward through the living room, though she knew full well they were making Radu scream so that she would come running. She raised the shotgun to her shoulder, rounded the corner to the long passage, and shot at the shapeless forms that filled it. There were three of them, but she wasn't sure that she had hit anyone as they vanished like ghosts.

"Radu!"

His bloody lion's head and upper body lay in the passage. He was naked. He must have dragged himself out of the bed and across the floor when they came. She dropped to her knees a short distance from his face and rested her left shoulder against the whitewashed wall. Her beloved stared at her, and his mouth tried to shape a word . . . a warning. Someone dragged him quickly back into the bedroom by his feet. His hand grabbed the door frame, but the intruders were too strong, and his fingers straightened out and released. He was so far away, so very far. She hit one of the shadows with her next shot. The figure buckled in midstride and collapsed at the far end of the passage. She reloaded and fired two quick shots into the dark to keep others out of the passage. She got to her feet and was less than two meters from the bedroom when her husband—fully upright, which he hadn't been for eight years—slowly staggered into her field of view with a red cloud on his temple. Someone had hauled him to his feet and shot him through the head.

A few pellets had ricocheted off Sabrina's helmet, but the woman with the chewing gum had taken a full load from L'Artista and was lying a few paces from Sabrina's feet. The woman looked up at her, her jaws still moving. The ceramic vest had absorbed the impact of most of the pellets, but in the morning light Sabrina noted that the right sleeve of her uniform had been ripped open, and she could see white and black flesh and blood. The woman's partner bent down and dragged her out into the utility room while Sabrina knelt by the door frame and risked a quick glance into the passage.

The petite figure moved with incredible speed. She had stood up and was heading for the bedroom when her husband fell through the doorway with red mist coming from his head. The mist hit the white plaster opposite. The woman continued in a forward somersault and straightened up right before the doorway to the bedroom, and Sabrina instinctively released two pistol shots at the fleeing figure. L'Artista did not appear to notice the bullets that skimmed the hair above her scalp and sprayed plaster and brickwork on her head and shoulders. She continued to shoot at the invisible executioners in the bedroom. A roar could be heard on the inside, and the woman was on her way in like a fluid, vengeful fury when instinct made her glance over her shoulder.

Slowly L'Artista rose to her feet, the shotgun hanging from her right hand. Sabrina could have ended it all there and then. She had a clear shot, and L'Artista wasn't moving. Sabrina thought about her father, about Lucia and Salvatore Forlani . . . about Massimiliano Di Luca and Alberto in their eternal prison . . . about all the people she didn't know or hadn't heard of whom this creature had killed, but she saw only a mother whose daughter was currently dangling from Primo Alba's right hand, floating and silent in her pajama top, which had been pulled halfway up her naked chest and gathered at the back of her neck in the man's fist. A large gray pistol was pressed against the back of the girl's head, and Primo Alba's handsome face was motionless.

"Drop your gun, Anamarie Panevic," he ordered her.

The shotgun clattered against the flagstones.

Behind Sabrina the wounded woman got back on her feet. The screaming from the bedroom had ceased. A man stepped out into the passage with his machine pistol raised. He walked up to L'Artista and kicked her legs from underneath her, rolled her onto her stomach, and bound her hands with a plastic tie. He bent down and removed a small automatic pistol from her dressing gown. The woman turned her head and looked up at Sabrina. Without pleading for mercy. Nothing.

The last two men from the unit entered from the living room and took the daughter from Primo Alba. The girl started to scream and kick.

Sabrina could see the girl's screams etched in L'Artista's face. It grew smaller and paler. Primo Alba pulled her to her feet. He wasn't looking at anyone; his eyes were dark sockets, his face carved in stone.

The woman looked at her dead husband and her struggling daughter, and her gaze was indescribable.

Alba pushed L'Artista in front of him, and she seemed incredibly tiny and vulnerable. He opened the door to the girl's bedroom and pushed the woman inside. Sabrina had turned to the soldier with the chewing gum when two pistol shots rang out from inside the bedroom.

Primo Alba came back out into the passage and slowly and deliberately returned his pistol to the holster above his left hip. He took out a cell phone, turned away, and started speaking in a low voice.

Sabrina tried to walk toward him, but someone prevented her. She tore herself loose and had almost reached him when more people arrived, twisted her arms behind her back, and put her on the floor. In a pool of the cripple's blood.

Primo Alba marched briskly down the passage while he continued to speak on his cell, oblivious to the people behind him. And to Sabrina D'Avalos's curses, threats, and obscenities.

CHAPTER 47

Qualiano, Naples—Don Francesco Terrasino's Estate

There was a polite knocking on the door, but Don Francesco Terrasino already had heard the nurse's heels against the flagstones in the passage.

His fork lingered indecisively over a plate of ham and eggs, but he was no longer hungry. He was losing his appetite more by the day.

He had slept badly. A night filled with forebodings, faces, bodies, and troublesome memories. He didn't have the energy to get up and open the door to the nurse as he usually did. The sun was high in the sky, but the house was quiet. Guards and workers respected Don Francesco's morning hours that were spent in meditation and contemplation of that day's duties.

"Enter."

He coughed drily and dabbed his watering eyes with the starched napkin that the housekeeper placed alongside his plate and cutlery every morning.

He was looking deep into the black pupil of the espresso cup when the footsteps stopped in front of the table.

"*La signora?*" he asked without looking up.

"The same, Don Francesco," said a new voice. "Probably much the same as Massimiliano Di Luca, I presume."

Don Francesco Terrasino didn't move.

Of course. After a night filled with all those faces. It had to be. It hadn't been a nightmare but a premonition.

He looked up with a small smile. With his light brown hair and his clear gray eyes the young man looked like a prince. He also appeared to be unarmed, but Don Francesco didn't get his hopes up. This was the end.

The tall, lean figure balanced on the soles of his feet like an athlete. His arms were gathered in front of his body, resting, but Don Francesco knew his type, even if he didn't know the man himself: the GIS.

"My sons?" he asked.

"Gone."

"How did you get in?"

"The tunnel. L'Artista is dead."

"You killed Anamarie Panevic," Don Francesco Terrasino said. "What a shame. She had a rare gift."

"Undoubtedly, but born a couple of centuries too late. She belonged to the court of the Medicis."

The young man nodded, and Don Francesco closed his eyes. He heard nothing, but the young man was fast . . . terribly fast. A hard hand was placed over his mouth and chin, and Don Francesco Terrasino felt the knife enter below his rib and the explosion in his heart when the knife reached it.

"This is for Federico Renda and Agostino D'Avalos, *figlio di puttana*," the man whispered into Don Francesco's ear, almost as if he were praying, as he slit open the old man's white shirt and then his abdomen from his sternum to his belt buckle.

CHAPTER 48

Castellarano—Fourteen Days Later

The performance might not be remembered for its intense acting or its crystal-clear singing, but no one could say a word against the girls' makeup or hair. They were perfect. What the girls lacked in terms of talent during the school production of *The Mikado*, they made up for with commitment. There were long, extended rounds of applause when a gong struck by a pretty kimono-clad Japanese lady signaled the interval.

It was a strange setting, Sabrina thought, looking up at the tall Gothic arches over her head, at the ascetic portraits of saints and founding fathers who seemed to squirm uncomfortably at the colorful and happy tableau on the makeshift stage at the back of the nave. She smiled politely to the fragrant fur-clad woman on the arm of her husband in a dinner jacket as they tried to make their way down the central aisle. She pulled in her feet and knees and ignored the woman's look.

It was inevitable that she would attract a certain amount of attention.

Giulio Forlani and Antonia Moretti had insisted that she come to the performance. Sabrina rose and tried to make herself as small and inconspicuous as possible. With her shaven head, downcast eyes, bruises, and numerous fresh cuts to the face and scalp, she looked like an earthquake survivor whom a humanitarian organization had hastily fed, dressed, and flown into a charity event.

There was ecstatic conversation everywhere, the smell of expensive perfume, long glittering evening gowns, sparkling laughter, and expensive jewelry. After all, the girls—the majority of them—belonged to some of Europe's most privileged families.

She found a shaded niche, quickly emptied the first glass of white wine, and snatched another one from the silver tray of a passing waitress.

Forlani towered over everyone. He actually looked quite good in a dinner jacket, Sabrina thought. He was standing by a table covered with damask, canapés, and crystal and had turned his head slightly so that his good ear could pick up the words of Antonia Moretti, whose slim hands were folded around the stem of a wineglass. She looked happy, Sabrina thought.

She looked like a woman with a plan for the future.

Near the couple Sabrina spotted Gianni, Antonia Moretti's son. His hair was as thick and black as a troll's, and he was mesmerized by the girls who were bustling around the stage or had found their parents at the tables. He appeared to be looking for one girl in particular. A couple of times he had looked in Sabrina's direction with an expression so close to jaw-dropping hero worship that Sabrina had to look away.

It was the last thing she needed: a teenager who idolized her.

There were a few serious men and women who looked neither at the stage nor at the girls. All wore white earpieces, had their arms folded across their chests, and kept their faces alert. Without expression they scanned the audience, their surroundings, and the area around Giulio Forlani.

Urs Savelli was still at large.

The bodyguards' work would be complete tomorrow when Giulio Forlani, Antonia, and Gianni Moretti boarded a U.S. military plane to be flown to an undisclosed location on the U.S. east coast. Both the Secret Service, whose constitutional task was to prevent forgers from attacking the U.S. dollar, and Professor Mai Luán from MIT had pleaded and begged Doctor Forlani to come to the States and continue his work. A house, a car, a new identity, plenty of research funding . . . a pony for the boy . . . they could have whatever they wanted. For Gianni Moretti, one of the best schools in the world, and for *la signora* . . . well, there were plenty of undertakers in the United States. Unless she preferred living clients.

The physicist looked up, spotted Sabrina in the shadows, and went over to her. The crowd of gesticulating and chattering theatergoers parted in front of the giant. There was something about this scarred, somber man that was far too inappropriate and conspicuously serious for the occasion.

He reached Sabrina, and she smiled at him. She found it surprisingly easy to smile at Giulio Forlani but hard with everyone else.

"Are you enjoying it so far?" he asked her gravely.

"If I'm to be honest, it would have been kinder to put it out of its misery," she said.

He smiled.

"You look good without a beard," she said.

Forlani stroked his new smooth face. He was unrecognizable. He had also had a haircut. He actually looked distinguished in that graying, professorial way. Sabrina looked past him and spotted the gray eyes of Antonia Moretti. She studied the back of the physicist with an expression of concern and ownership that boded well.

"You're going to the United States?"

"With Alberto. They're flying him to Massachusetts General Hospital. Apparently they have an expert in exotic poisons. Perhaps there's some hope."

"But not Massimiliano?"

"He's dying . . . the poison . . . the cancer. There was some talk about giving him chemotherapy, but his family said no. I think they made the right decision."

"Does he still sing?"

Forlani studied the floor.

"It appears he has an inexhaustible repertoire."

"Perhaps it's a form of self-preservation," she said.

"Perhaps."

They looked at each other.

"Thank you," he said at last.

"For what?"

"All of it, really. Lucia and Salva . . . you were right. It did mean something . . . more than I can say, everything . . . To know. That they had been found."

Sabrina had attended the simple cremation of the remains of Lucia and Salvatore Forlani at the cemetery in Chiaravalle. Giulio Forlani's brother Bruno and his parents had been there. There had been a heavy mix of emotions around the grave, as one would expect, and Sabrina had kept her distance, as had Dr. Raimondo Sapienza, the forensic scientist from Rome, who looked extremely uncomfortable in his tight-fitting dark suit.

"*Di niente*, Giulio."

She held out her hand.

"Have a safe trip."

He took her hand.

"You're not leaving, are you?" he said. "You'll miss the second act."

"I'm still recovering, Giulio. My doctors say I mustn't get overexcited."

"Then you had better go."

"*Arrivederci.*"

"Take good care of yourself, Sabrina D'Avalos."

She waved over her shoulder without turning around, and she held back her tears until she reached the evening air. These days she couldn't stop crying.

CHAPTER 49

Palazzo di Giustizia, Naples

She had tried as discreetly as possible to slip back into her old life. Before the container. She managed fairly well at home, though she spent most of the time lying on the bed, smoking cigarettes, and staring at the ceiling or reading the first five pages of a book before putting it down. Sometimes she would sit in front of the mirror studying her new hair, trying to get it to grow faster by sheer willpower.

At work they treated her as if she needed handling with great care to avoid a sudden, disastrous meltdown. The other young assistant public prosecutors, her peers, looked at her differently, spoke to her differently, avoided her as far as possible and, when they couldn't, spoke in hushed voices with guarded smiles. Any excitement must be avoided at all costs, she understood. Her old cases had been delegated to her colleagues, and new ones had yet to materialize, possibly because no one really knew at which level she should work. Officially, she was still an assistant public prosecutor but one who had been allocated a brand-new Mercedes C350 saloon—bullet- and fireproof—and three drivers who took turns taking her around and always treated her with the utmost courtesy.

She was sure it was a precaution that would be withdrawn once they no longer believed there was any threat to her personal safety.

She had seen Federico Renda only once since Brescia. He had been very busy but also quietly congratulatory and impeccably polite. She'd had a million questions before she went into his office but hadn't been able to remember a single one of them when he paused in his congratulations and gave her an encouraging look with his unswervingly sad eyes. The photo of L'Artista that had always hung behind his desk chair was gone. In its place hung an architect's drawing of the new Palace of Justice, which was being built on the other side of the piazza.

They would have to think of a less formal event soon, he said. A little gathering. A private celebration. There were some people in Rome who would very much like to meet her. She stared at him in horror, and he waited a moment and then commented a little tartly on her lack of enthusiasm. She had a career to think of, he reminded her. If she wanted it.

Sabrina asked for new cases, and Federico Renda suddenly became busy with some papers.

They would just have to wait and see, he said without looking up. She was still seeing the trauma therapist. There was no need to rush things. Run risks. He suggested a vacation.

She pointed out that she wasn't suffering from shell shock, and Federico Renda smiled softly and looked at his watch. Renda's telephone rang, and she suspected him of arranging for one of his secretaries to call no later than five minutes after the arrival of young D'Avalos. He started muttering something about an urgent conference, plane tickets, and so on, life went on . . . That was the bottom line, wasn't it? You could only do your best.

She sighed and stood up, interrupting his grandfatherly platitudes.

Her desk was empty. She had sharpened all her pencils and arranged her notebooks at right angles to the edge of the desk.

She thought briefly about He Who Must Not Be Named, who had vanished into thin air. She had packed Primo Alba and all his being into a steel box, locked the box into a ship's chest, and dropped it into the Mariana Trench. Or into an active volcano—depending

on her mood. She was in no doubt that it was Alba who had killed Don Francesco in his own home even though no one knew for sure and Federico Renda had clammed up like an oyster. And Alba had shot L'Artista as if she were a mad dog. No one had wanted awkward court cases, celebrity lawyers, remorseful *pentiti*, endless negotiations, media hype, and the politicians getting involved, for God's sake! They hadn't wanted legal niceties mixed up in this case. The GIS and Federico Renda had sent an unequivocal message to Francesco Terrasino's heirs.

Sitting alone on the wide backseat of the Mercedes was luxurious but lonely, and Sabrina missed her old Opel, which was being examined by the army's explosives experts somewhere in Milan.

She asked the driver to stop outside the bookshop in Via Dei Mille and wandered around the shop for half an hour before she found what she was looking for: an illustrated atlas with thick pages that could do lots of exciting things: make a cardboard map open up and change into a globe, a starry sky that you could rotate, and funny holograms of animals typical of each continent. She intended to study it with Ismael. Approach the subject of Africa in a gentle and informative way. Perhaps the boy would like it, perhaps he wouldn't. It was impossible to predict. The only rule seemed to be that anything she herself had been desperate to get her hands on as a child—a remote-control car, a steam engine, an electric racing circuit—never found favor with Ismael and was passed on to the other children at the orphanage at the speed of lightning, whereas he would be mesmerized with gratitude for ridiculous cheap trinkets such as a small whistle, a carved figure, or a soft toy dog.

She would like to travel with him. A week somewhere warm. A week in a place where there was water—even though he hated the sea—possibly with some palm trees. The management of the orphanage and the child psychiatrist had their doubts about her project. A huge responsibility, Sabrina, they said. Very big. Perhaps it was more about her needs than Ismael's. She objected. Surely they couldn't know until she tried it. The way things were now, Ismael

never saw anything. When he was too old for the orphanage, where would he go? Another institution filled with strangers?

They had avoided her gaze. They wanted to wait and see. Perhaps a week away was a little . . . extreme. They suggested a day trip instead.

For security reasons, her driver informed the bodyguards' central office of the address of the orphanage and their arrival time. When they arrived, he got out first and checked the area before he gave the all clear to Sabrina. She hurried across the pavement with the carrier bag in her hand. She nodded to the student behind the hatch at the entrance and walked up slowly to the first floor. She stopped by a window on the darkened stairs and looked down into the courtyard. The light was on in the sports hall across the courtyard, and the corridors lay silent. Some company had donated a digital projector and a box of DVDs to the orphanage, and now every Tuesday evening was movie night. She stood on tiptoe and could see the top of the screen suspended from the wall bars at the back of the hall. She saw a close-up of Harry Potter's scarred forehead and intense eyes behind his spectacles. The young wizard would appear to be in the middle of yet another showdown with Lord Voldemort.

She walked down the corridor to Ismael's room. The boy never attended the screenings. The few lightbulbs in the ceiling that had not yet been smashed gave the linoleum floor a dull shine, and the shadows at the far end of the corridor were as black as ink. There was no light under Ismael's door.

"Ismael?"

His room was empty and the bed neatly made, as always. She smiled at the sight of the postcard from Milan. The cathedral. It had been stuck to the wall with Scotch tape. Ruler straight, like all her other postcards, in a row above his bed.

She put the bag from the bookshop on his bed and walked back along the corridor. She heard a noise from the bathroom at the far end of the corridor and turned around.

The large bathroom was cool and quiet. There were a dozen cubicles with toilets, but all the doors were missing and the light wasn't working. The switch merely gave a small, impotent click when she pressed it. A little light from the streetlights across the road fell diagonally through the windows and down onto the gray tiled floor. She turned on the tap and drank some cold water from the palm of her hand.

Sabrina straightened up when she heard the faint, regular clicks. Like a forgotten metronome in a music room. It took several long seconds before she identified the sound.

"If you hear that stick—like a chisel against a gravestone—you must run as fast as you can and don't ever look back. Will you promise me that?" Federico Renda had said. And there was nothing she would rather do. But there was nowhere to run. So she stood completely still while her mind raced and shut her eyes, which opened instinctively when she heard his whisper.

"Dottoressa Sabrina D'Avalos."

He was very close. The voice flowed from the shadows right behind her. A pleasant voice, the consonants well formed and clear, the Albanian accent barely noticeable.

She didn't move. The man's position also appeared to be stationary. Perhaps he was standing in the doorway. Perhaps. She had a panic button on a string around her neck connected to a receiver in her bodyguard's pocket but knew she would never get to press it.

"I find myself . . . for the first time since I was thirteen years old, incidentally . . . unemployed, Dottoressa D'Avalos. Fortunately I have numerous interests to keep myself busy. I lack for nothing. Nothing but a certain conclusion . . . You understand. I have nothing against you personally. Of course not. But there has to be a certain . . ."

Sabrina spun around, and her hand found the handle of the Walther. Since Brescia she had acquired the habit of having a bullet in the chamber. The weapon was ready to discharge once she pushed the safety catch forward with her thumb. Most people assumed that you waited politely while they finished speaking before taking the next step. Perhaps Savelli was one of them.

She had cocked the weapon when her arm grew numb and dead. Savelli had swung the makila in a large arc through the air while she was still thinking about drawing the pistol, and its lead-capped tip had hit her right upper arm just below the shoulder joint with full force.

He was a dancing, fleeting shadow. Free from sound or smell. He was very close to her, and she found herself lying on the floor without knowing how it had happened. The Walther skidded across the tiles and ended up at the far end of the toilets. She could see it in the distance. It winked wistfully at her, but it might as well have been on the moon.

She turned over on her side, her jacket fell open, and she studied the toes of Urs Savelli's shiny shoes in front of her face.

"I think we were interrupted, signorina," he said. "You really mustn't exert yourself."

She rolled over and tried to kick his legs out from under him or at least destabilize him. Her arm was heavy and leaden and agonizingly painful. The makila. A long thin blade emerged from the stick while he avoided her kicking feet effortlessly.

The blade swiftly and smoothly penetrated the right side of her chest, and her body froze in shock. She couldn't get her next breath. It was impossible. She tried sitting up before the darkness took her, but she needed the use of her right arm. She ended up on her left side and could now see his pale face above her.

Savelli smiled, and the blade of the makila sank into her again . . . more slowly this time . . . probing almost . . . into her chest cavity, now on the left side. A stream of bubbling blood was forced through her nose and mouth.

She thought that Savelli said something to her about giving in to it. Letting death take her. Like a warm bath.

Her chest heaved in wild spasms. It fought for her even though she had given up, and she managed to inhale a little bit of air. She felt drowsy. Warm. She, too, had started to smile when she noticed

Ismael. The boy was coming out of a cubicle, the last in the row. His shorts hung around his ankles, and he shuffled across the tiles, put down his comic, and picked up the Walther. He walked toward them with her gun in his hands. His sandals flip-flopped softly against the floor. Ismael's face was grave and introspective. He didn't look at her, and he didn't look at Savelli.

She lifted her head and saw a frown and a bemused smile spread across Urs Savelli's handsome middle-aged face. He held the bloody stick in both hands.

Now quite close to them, Ismael lifted the pistol and fired twice in quick succession.

Sabrina didn't see where the shots landed, but she heard a surprised deep sigh and a few seconds later a bump as Savelli sat down. The stick crashed down onto the tiles.

She got onto her elbow and looked at Savelli's face. There was a neat black hole in his neck, and his white shirt was already soaked in blood above his heart. He smiled apologetically at her.

Ismael carefully placed the pistol on the floor and looked at Sabrina.

"Bang, bang," he said quietly.

She thought she might have nodded. She couldn't agree more.

He walked back to his cubicle and picked up the comic on his way back before she had time to tell him that he was the best and cleverest and bravest boy in the whole world. He disappeared into the cubicle, and Sabrina wearily turned her head toward the voices and faces in the doorway.

She would like to have told them something about Savelli and Ismael, but she had no air for words. Her white shirt was red to her belt, and she could feel her throat filling up. She rested her cheek against the cool tiles.

Epilogue

It had been impressed on the staff in the intensive care unit that they mustn't speak to the man, that they should simply go about their work as if he weren't there.

He had been at the woman's bedside constantly. While she was in surgery for six hours—where the surgeons had given up on her several times but had carried on out of pure defiance, six hours in which her blood pressure disappeared and swearing anesthetists pumped plasma expanders and universal donor blood into all the small woman's accessible veins until her pulse line had tentatively reappeared on the monitors, only to disappear soon afterward and trigger shrill alarms that nearly drove everyone insane. He had sat like a sphinx by the side of her bed in the intensive care unit while they kept the seriously injured assistant public prosecutor in an artificial coma and a ventilator took care of her breathing. He barely moved. Didn't look at or speak to anyone.

Late in the afternoon on the second day, they had taken the assistant public prosecutor off the ventilator, and she had woken up a couple of hours later.

There were concerns that she might have suffered permanent brain damage from oxygen starvation.

When she was stable, she was moved to an ordinary side ward.

As the sun was setting behind the hospital's tallest buildings and the light in the ward was deep and golden, the department's most experienced nurse came to change the patient's drip. She discovered that Dottoressa D'Avalos had opened her eyes and was looking at her. For the first time the nurse observed the assistant public prosecutor's remarkable slanted smoky eyes that seemed unnaturally big in her white face. She put a hand on the bed rail and smiled at the patient. The water in the chest drainage canister bubbled steadily. Tomorrow, both her lungs probably would have unfolded completely and the canister could be removed. There were still the drains in the abdominal cavity, but here they had to take it one step at a time. When the patient had first arrived at the hospital, the admitting doctor had been about to declare her dead on arrival. Her lungs had collapsed, she had lost a lot of blood, and she had injuries from stab wounds to her chest, diaphragm, and liver. Yet a more experienced doctor had decided to start resuscitation. Just in case—and because His Excellency *il procuratore generale* Federico Renda was deluging the hospital with telephone calls.

The assistant public prosecutor had one foot in the grave and the other on a banana peel, as the doctor put it. Renda ordered him to get both of her feet back on firm ground again or find himself another profession in a different town.

Sabrina D'Avalos turned her head and looked at the young man on the chair.

She summoned all her breath.

"Go, Primo. Get out," she said in loud and clear voice.

The nurse was shocked.

The young man looked at Sabrina and shook his head.

As a precaution, the nurse left the door ajar when she left the side ward.

There was silence for a long time. Then agitated voices could be heard, and the nurse had put her hand on the door handle when something stopped her. It didn't sound to her as if the patient had lost the ability to string together a meaningful sentence; on the contrary, she was remarkably articulate. The nurse made a mental note to cancel the neurologist.

When she returned half an hour later on a made-up visit, the young man was pale and smiling.

Steffen Jacobsen is a Danish orthopedic surgeon and consultant. *When the Dead Awaken* is his third novel. He was inspired to write it by his travels around Italy and by the writer and journalist Roberto Saviano's *Gomorrah*, a nonfiction book about the Camorra.